The Assassin Chip

A Medical Device that Kills

James E. Mosimann

Brightview Press
Gainesville, Virginia

For my daughter Kateri,
and for Kateri Tekakwitha
for whom she is named.

Contents

Prologue

Late morning in Tel Aviv, and the sun cast short shadows on the sidewalk. Ari Riebman was afoot and tired. At thirty, he had slowed down. The Krav Maga refresher session had exhausted him. He waited for the light to change.

At the bus stop across the street, a group of Jewish children chattered happily while their teacher watched.

A young girl stood next to the group. She was no older than fourteen. Her hair and neck were covered by a tight scarf. She was obese and unsmiling.

Ari felt sorry for her. *Poor kid, alone and overweight.*

Down the street the bus approached. The girl's eyes glazed as she opened her jacket.

Her eyes! And she's not fat! That's a vest and her hand is reaching for ... My God!

A woman came running behind him. She screamed.

"Fatimah! Don't!"

Ari struggled for his Beretta. He too shouted.

"No!"

Too late! The girl's eyes fixed skywards as she grasped the detonator. Her lips moved.

"Allahu ak..."

The remaining syllables were lost in the explosion.

The blast flattened Ari backwards. His ear drum burst. His head hit the curb.

Mercifully, he did not see the bloody mayhem as small bodies crumpled amid torn fragments of flying flesh. Nor did he hear the subsequent moans and plaintive cries for help. He was unaware of the wails of the woman dying behind him, or that his ear oozed blood.

He awoke. A face leaned close to his.

"Sir, are you all right?

He stared at the speaker's lips. They moved, but he heard no sound.

1

"Sir, are you all right? … Can you hear me?"

Ari's head ached. He shut his eyes. *If only I had been quicker?* He passed out.

The man found Ari's wallet. He spoke to his companion.

"He's with the Mossad. Help me get him on the gurney."

They wheeled him to the ambulance.

***

******

Chapter 1
Monday, October 9

To Aileen, Harry Roberts, her co-worker at Mandley Test Services, had it all. He was a brilliant Ph. D. bioengineer, a hands-on electro physiologist, and a first-rate computernik. He drove a Mercedes. Moreover, he was tall and trim with natural good looks.

Jane Peterson, the receptionist at MTS, referred to him as "Handsome Harry." From her, this appellation carried extra significance. Jane had a striking figure, bright blond hair, albeit with dark roots, and was selective where men were concerned.

Aileen Harris was a budding electro physiologist herself, and an attractive natural blonde. And she was smart. A year ago she had enrolled in a doctoral program, but the divorce had quashed that, along with a good portion of her self-confidence.

Tonight she was worried. Something was wrong with Harry. He wasn't his usual self. Harry was a "neat" freak who cleared his desk every evening like clockwork. You could count on it. But tonight, there were papers everywhere, some crumpled, some intact. The surface of his desk was a mess.

Harry had run the experiment on Patient 68 (Mrs. Hartman) that afternoon, and Dr. Thibault wanted the graphs on his desk by 8:00 am tomorrow. Aileen's boss was not the forgiving type.

She stood by Harry's desk and muttered to herself.

"Damn, Harry, where are those printouts?"

Aileen thumbed through his papers. *Maybe under that pile?*

"What the hell are you doing at my desk?"

Harry stood in the doorway. His frown was not forgiving.

"Damn it, Harry, where are the data for Patient 68. I want to get home tonight."

"And you will! Get away from my desk. Now!"

Aileen started to back away, but spied the sheet she needed.

"Harry, here it is, right here. It's Patient 68."

Harry moved fast. He snatched the paper, wrenching it from her and twisting her about.

Aileen rubbed her shoulder.

"Harry, what's wrong with you?"

"Sorry, did I hurt you?"

But his eyes were cold and in no way appeared "sorry," plus her shoulder ached.

"What's with you, Harry? I need those sheets for Dr. Thibault."

Harry crumpled Patient 68's papers into a ball, and made a perfect three-pointer into the waste basket. He turned back to the desktop and fumbled through several piles of notes.

"Those were the wrong sheets. That was a practice run. These are the ones you want."

The papers too were labeled "Patient 68."

He handed the sheets to Aileen. His face was florid. His free hand was clenched.

"Take them. Now get out of here."

As she turned to leave she saw Harry's reflection in the glass panel of the door.

His eyes burned with hate! Or was it fear?

***

Back at her computer, Aileen studied the printouts. At the top was the file she needed. She prepared the data for display. *This is going to take a while.*

After numerous adjustments to the graph, her eyes began to glaze over. She looked at the clock. 7:00 pm. *Oh no. Late again!* She punched a number and heard a small voice.

"Mommy?"

"Yes, it's me honey. I'm late. Ask Granny if you can eat with her. I can pick you up about 9:00. See if that's all right with Granny ."

Small footsteps left the phone. Moments later, another voice came on the line.

4

"Aileen, where are you? You should be here. Mary Catherine is starved."

"I know Mom. But Dr. Thibault needs something for tomorrow morning. Can you feed her? I can pick her up at nine if that's OK with you."

"All right, but try to leave soon. You've been working too hard. We'll see you at 9:00."

Aileen hung up. Her mind returned to Harry. She heard his door shut.

Footsteps passed her door. Then the double doors to the suite clapped shut.

Harry was gone.

She turned back to her computer and clicked to finish Patient 68's graph. She had it!

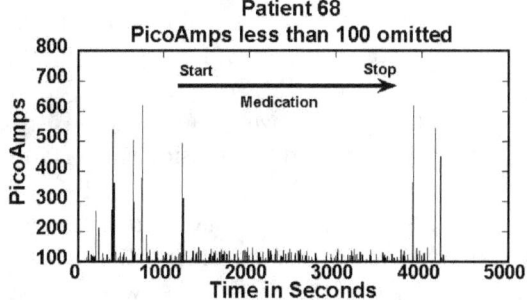

The graph was fine. The arrow on the graph indicated when the medication was applied. Soon after the medication started, the high spikes disappeared. The neuron stopped firing. All the spikes were low. Then when the medication stopped, high spikes indicated that the neuron started firing again.

"This is perfect. Just what Dr. Thibault wants! Harry what's your problem?"

***

Aileen was about to shut down the computer, when she stopped. *That's odd! I never noticed that before!*

Harry's file for Patient 68 had been saved at 5:30 pm, but Mrs. Hartman had left the suite at 3:00 pm. Aileen had seen her leave just as Jane took Dr. Thibault his three-o'clock coffee.

Aileen shrugged. *Maybe I just never paid attention to the times? Still that's a big difference.*

Aileen's employer, Mandley Test Services (MTS), was a subsidiary of Mandley Bionics. MTS was conducting tests for the parent company's latest PMA, a "Pre Market Approval Application," for the Food and Drug Administration.

Mandley had developed a wireless computer implant to monitor neuronal activity in muscle fibers, and to control the activity by computing doses to apply in real time. The computer chip implant and the medical device to apply the medicine were proprietary and more than state of the art.

For MTS' tests, the wireless chip sent the patient data directly to an Excel spreadsheet on Harry's computer. That was normal. But why would the file arrive so late?

Curious, Aileen examined Mr. Peter's file. He was Patient 27, and Aileen herself had run that session since Harry had been absent that day. She remembered that they had finished before 4:00 pm. (For once, she had picked up Mary Catherine early.)

Aileen looked at the computer screen. Sure enough, Patient 27's file had been saved at 3:45 pm, just when the session had finished.

Harry had mentioned a "practice" run. But the protocol did not allow for "practice" runs. Moreover, Mrs. Hartman had been long gone by 5:30 pm when Harry had saved the file.

Aileen had been in Harry's office at 6:30. The file had been saved only an hour earlier.

She thought of the wadded sheets Harry had thrown away. *Damn it! Something is wrong!*

***

Aileen looked at her watch. It was time to pick up Mary Catherine. She packed up, switched off her computer, turned off the lights in her office, and locked the door.

She put the graph for Patient 68 in Dr. Thibault's box and headed out.

Her path took her by Harry's door. Curiosity overcame her desire to be on time.

She tried the handle. It was locked.

The cleaning crew will come by soon, and Harry's trash will be gone. I've got to get that paper before they do!

She took out a credit card and pushed it through the door crack.

The spring lock did not budge.

She slipped it in again. This time the catch sprung.

She was in!

Aileen left the lights off. In the shadows, Harry's desk appeared in its normal state. The top was devoid of papers or ornament of any sort.

The waste basket, however, overflowed with discarded papers. She sifted through the contents. Most were torn fragments, not wadded. Her hand scraped the bottom and felt a ball of paper, the "practice" print out for Patient 68.

She switched on the desk lamp.

The numbers were not the same as those she had just graphed!

Now Aileen was really curious. She turned on Harry's computer.

The machine booted slowly. At last, it was ready.

She searched for recently deleted files.

There! She had it!

The "practice" file had different numbers. It had been deleted at 3:15 pm.

That made sense. Harry had deleted the data shortly after Mrs. Hartman's departure.

She recovered the deleted file. It was not written-over.

OK Aileen, let's get this done.

Aileen graphed the real "practice" data to compare with the one she had left for Dr. Thibault.

Both graphs appeared.

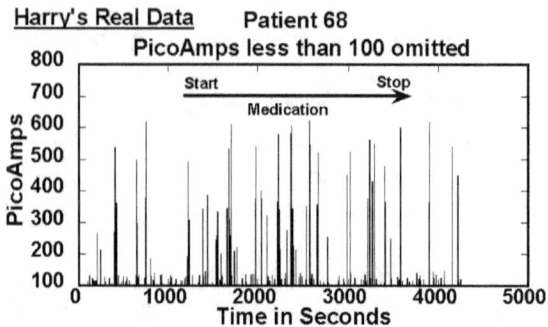

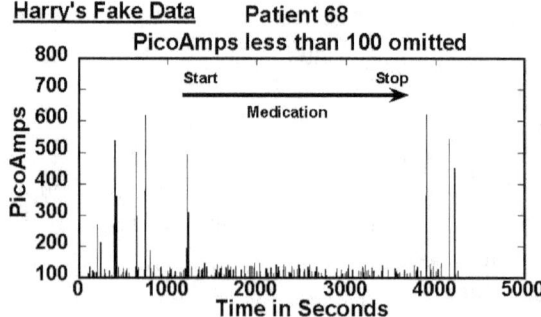

Aileen gagged.

In the real experiment there were high spikes throughout the period of medication, but in the faked experiment Harry had eliminated those numerous high spikes.

Mandley's treatment had not helped Mrs. Hartman at all. If anything, nerve firings and muscle fiber contractions were more severe with the medication than without. The abundant spikes during the period of medication meant that the treatment may have made her worse!

With this result, the FDA would not approve Mandley's application! The treatment was a bust!

And Harry had deliberately given Aileen the fake data to graph!

She was about to send both graphs to her own computer when she heard footsteps. She snapped off the lamp and froze.

The footsteps stopped at the door!

Harry was back!

***

Aileen stuffed the wad with the real data in her bra, and shut down the computer.

The screen still shone bright blue. She watched "Windows is Shutting Down," on the screen. *Hurry up. Hurry!* At last the screen went dark.

She knelt behind the desk. The door opened. She heard humming, *Harry!*

Before he stepped in, she heard a voice from the hallway.

"Harry, the graph looks great. You did a good fix on Mrs. Hartman's data!"

"Dr. Thibault, I did the best I could. I'm glad you're satisfied."

"You did great. But why did you call me? What's so important? It's 9:00 o'clock."

Aileen winced. She was late to pick up Mary Catherine.

"Aileen was in my office this evening. She was looking for Hartman's data. Why would she snoop?"

"I told her to get me Hartman's graphs right away. I must have made her nervous."

"Maybe so, but I don't like it. She's spying. She must suspect something."

"Come on Harry, Aileen's not the brightest bulb on the block. What could she suspect? Everything's going to be fine. Aileen won't be any trouble."

"Maybe you're right. Her office is dark. By now she is home with the kid."

Dr. Thibault's voice rose.

"Wait a minute Harry, doesn't Aileen drive a Toyota? It's her car that's still down in the lot. I saw it when I parked. She's still here!"

Harry slammed his fist against the wall.

"That bitch! I knew it. But where is she?"

***

Aileen could not see Harry or Dr. Thibault, but Harry's door slammed. Footsteps resounded down the hall way.

She exhaled. The gravity of what she had heard sank in. The treatment had failed! Mrs. Hartman was not helped! Harry had falsified the data and Dr. Thibault knew it!

They would be back. *How can I get away? Think, Aileen. Think!* Outside the door, all was quiet. She crept from behind Harry's desk. She eased Harry's door open and peered out.

No one was in the hallway, but her office door was ajar and the light was on. They were there. Aileen headed the other way. She reached the end of the corridor. The door was posted.

Emergency Exit, Alarm will sound.

This was a real emergency. She grabbed the handle.

"Aileen, stop! Come back here!"

It was Dr. Thibault.

Aileen hesitated. She heard running. Harry!

She pulled the handle and pushed the door open to duck through. The alarm rang out.

"Brannggg! ... Brannggg! ... Brannggg! ... Brannggg!"

Then Harry caught her. He grabbed her arm and yanked her back into the corridor.

"You little bitch! Where are you going? Who are you?"

His first blow spun her head to the side. The second numbed her arm and shoulder. She struggled to focus. Her blouse ripped as Harry reached in her bra. The wadded data sheet!

"Brannggg! ... Brannggg! ... Brannggg! ... Brannggg!"

Harry forced the lever back. The alarm stopped. He pushed the wad into Aileen's face.

"You stole this, you bitch! What else did you take?"

He slapped her, backhanded.

She tried to turn, but he held her and punched her hard. Her head drooped. He drew back his fist for a final blow.

***

"Harry, stop it! What are you doing? Stop!"

Dr. Thibault came puffing. He saw the exposed bra.

Aileen shook her head and leaned against the wall. Through swollen eyes she focused on the doctor. She tried to talk through puffed lips, but Harry broke in.

"She stole Mrs. Hartman's file. She knows about us. The bitch is a spy and a thief."

"Let her go, Harry, and give me that paper. I'll destroy it. Without it she can't prove a thing. She's got nothing!"

Dr. Thibault turned to Aileen.

"Ms. Harris, you broke into a company office and stole company documents. You're no longer wanted here. You're fired!"

He grimaced.

"And Ms. Harris, if you cause any trouble, any trouble at all, I will press charges! Don't forget that you have another mouth to feed besides your own!"

Harry glared.

"Forget her Harry. We've got the records. Look at her. She's a slut coming on to you like she did! She must use drugs. If she complains, I'll see that she loses custody of that daughter."

Aileen gasped. Dr. Thibault continued, as if to himself.

"Her word against ours! Who would believe her?"

He turned back to Aileen.

"Ms. Harris, you are no longer with MTS. Leave! And do not take anything. Jane will box your things tomorrow."

Harry stared as Aileen stumbled down the hall. He gritted his teeth.

Thibault is soft. This bitch knows too much. I have to fix this myself!

***

Aileen drove to her mother's house with one eye swollen shut.

At the sight of her daughter's battered face and torn clothing, Mrs. Harris forgot her lecture about being late.

"Honey, what happened to you? Who did this?"

"Mom, can it wait? I can't talk right now. Where's Mary Catherine?"

"It was late so I put her to bed. But you? What happened?"

"Mom, they fired me."

"Fired you? How could they do that?"

"Believe me, they can and they did."

"But you …"

"Mom I told you I can't talk now. Let me be. OK?"

"I'll get you something to eat."

"No, I can't eat. Look, something's terribly wrong at work, and I found out about it. That's all I can tell you. I need to think."

"Fine, but you'll sleep here tonight. I'll warm some food for you, just in case."

Aileen did not argue. She went up the stairs. Mary Catherine was asleep. Her breathing was regular. Aileen sat by the bed and shivered. *At least Harry doesn't know where my mother lives.*

That thought was short-lived. For the first time since her divorce, Aileen regretted going back to her maiden name.

Harry could easily find her mother's house!

***

At his apartment, a wide-awake Harry Roberts clicked on the Internet. Aileen's maiden name was "Harris" and she always left her daughter with her mother during working hours.

Apart from Aileen, there were only six local listings for "Harris." He printed off the addresses and shut down the computer. Tomorrow, he would locate the mother's house where Aileen left her child during the day.

***

******

Chapter 2
Tuesday, October 10

The coffee shop of the Burris Building in Bethesda, Maryland, was small but classy. This morning there were only two customers. One was a middle-aged man, Wayne Johnson. The other was a stunning red head, Jeannine Ryan. Both were with StatFind, a small statistical/computing firm in nearby Rockville.

Wayne was the owner of StatFind and Jeannine, a Ph. D. statistician, was head of the Statistical Evaluations Section in the Survey Unit. (The section was a fancy appellation for herself and a part-time undergrad intern.)

Today, at Wayne's insistence, Jeannine wore a tan business suit instead of her preferred jeans and sweater. She crossed her legs uncomfortably. Wayne fidgeted with his tie.

Jeannine smiled. *At least he's suffering too.*

"Wayne, when's the last time you wore a tie? And where did you get that monstrosity?"

Wayne was too nervous for banter. This meeting was important and he was edgy. He tilted his cup and drained it.

"Drink your coffee, Jeannine, the meeting is in ten minutes."

"Easy Wayne, my watch says fifteen minutes, and yours is fast."

She pushed the red hair off her forehead, and looked at her notes.

"OK, you say the analyses will be "signal processing." What's happening?"

"We'll find out more upstairs. Our meeting is with Dr. Thibault of Mandley Test Services. MTS is a subsidiary of Mandley Bionics, the really big boys."

"Boys?"

Wayne winced. *Oh. Oh. Did it again.* He reloaded.

"Anyway, Mandley Bionics is considering us for a contract bigger than anything StatFind could imagine. First we have a small contract with their subsidiary, and that's why we're here today. If we do a good job for MTS, we're a lock for the main contract with Mandley Bionics."

Wayne took a breath. Jeannine intervened.

"OK, but what about today?"

"Mandley has developed a wireless chip implant with microelectrodes, state of the art, that not only monitors muscle fiber activity, but provides electronic feedback to alter or stop the fiber's neuron from firing. Also, they have developed a bedside unit to receive transmissions from the chip and administer medicine only as needed by IV. One idea is to achieve local control of neurotransmitter secretion, and things like that. They want to miniaturize the administration device too. Among many possible uses, think of Parkinson's or Lou Gehrig's disease."

Wayne finally took a breath, but only for a second.

"Anyway, today we're to be briefed on a chip implant that can monitor the firing of very small groups of -- or even individual -- fibers, as well as a new biotech product that they say can locally deactivate the firing."

Wayne's conversations usually consisted of single sentences between substantial periods of silence. The vision of untold millions in the coffers of StatFind had altered his speech pattern.

At the risk of another lengthy discourse she asked.

"OK, OK. But what do you expect of me? Why am I here?"

"MTS has conducted experiments with both the implant and the proprietary compound on 60 patients. They've monitored and controlled single or small groups of fibers. It's the first step. They have prepared a PMA, a Pre Market Approval Application, for the FDA so that Mandley can market the implant chip. MTS has done its own statistical analyses but wants a review by StatFind, that is by you, to rebut reasons the FDA might use to reject the PMA."

Jeannine peered into her coffee. *OK, good enough, I got it.* She took a final sip.

"We'd better go now, Wayne. It's time?"

Wayne jumped to his feet.

"Why did you let me talk so long!"

He dashed for the elevator.

***

The MTS suite was a cut above StatFind's offices.

First, it was really "above." The suite was on the fifth floor, in contrast to StatFind's ground-level rental.

Second, whereas StatFind's illumination was strictly fluorescent and little outside light penetrated its cubicles, the reception area at MTS was bright with natural light. A wide window provided a panoramic view of Bethesda's Wisconsin Avenue as far north as the fenced grounds of the National Library of Medicine.

Wayne strode straight to the blonde receptionist. Her nameplate said "Jane Peterson." She was sorting papers into stacks on the polished surface of her desk.

Ms. Peterson looked up. Wayne spoke.

"Mr. Johnson and Dr. Ryan to see Dr. Thibault."

"Mr. Johnson. Please have a seat. I'll tell Dr. Thibault you're here."

Wayne stood in anticipation, but Ms. Peterson finished sorting the remaining papers. Finally she punched the intercom.

"Dr. Thibault, Mr. Johnson and ..."

She paused and assessed Jeannine's status. Jane Peterson knew that Dr. Thibault did not like to treat women as professionals. She broke his rules. With no change in tone she continued.

"and a *Dr.* Ryan are here to see you."

Jeannine had passed muster. Ms. Peterson gathered her papers and stepped out of the office.

Wayne sat down. Jeannine went to the picture window and stared out.

She stepped back to Wayne.

"It's past time. Why do they make us wait?"

"Come on Jeannine. This is the way it works. MTS is big. StatFind is not. We have to be on time. They don't. Their time

15

is important. Ours isn't. It's all a game. Don't let it get you. This is the way it is. You'll get used to it."

Jeannine had experienced priggish professors in her graduate studies and she had never gotten used to them. She doubted she would get used to self-important entrepreneurs.

She wanted to snap at Wayne, but could not. *Shut up Jeannine, he hired you when you had to leave grad school, and he paid you enough to go back and finish the Ph. D. Be grateful. Don't dump on him!*

She sat down and tugged at her skirt. A pleasant remark was needed.

"Look, Wayne, I was out of line when I said your tie was a 'monstrosity.' It's actually kind of attractive. I'm just not used to suits. Don't mind me. I'll adjust."

Wayne looked at her, unsure how to respond. He did not have to. A male voice broke his thoughts.

"Mr. Johnson, I'm Dr. Roberts, I'm a bioengineer here with MTS. I'll take you to Dr. Thibault."

Dr. Roberts turned to Jeannine. One look convinced him that less formality was desirable.

"First names are easier for me. I'm Harry, and you are?"

Wayne broke in.

"Dr. Ryan's name is Jeannine."

Harry turned back to him.

"And your name is Wayne, right."

Harry smiled at Jeannine and beckoned.

"OK Jeannine, Wayne, we'd better go. We don't want to keep Dr. Thibault waiting."

Jeannine grimaced. *Horrors? Dr. Thibault might have to wait?*

For Wayne's sake she held her tongue.

***

Dr. Thibault was all warmth. He jumped up from behind his desk and crossed the room before Wayne and Jeannine had broken the threshold.

"It's good to meet you. Wayne Johnson, right? And Jeannine Ryan? I'm Dr. Thibault, and you've already met Harry Roberts."

The doctor grabbed Wayne's hand in a crushing grip. Then he turned to Jeannine. With her he was gentler. Even so, after a vigorous shake, she rubbed her fingers to recirculate the blood.

"Wayne, Jeannine, we're glad StatFind agreed to help us. Welcome aboard! We've heard nothing but good things about your work. This is great! But, let me show you our facilities before we discuss the project. Harry will explain the more technical stuff."

Always the analyst, Jeannine deduced, correctly, that Dr. Thibault's use of first names was not for familiarity, like Harry's.

The M.D. in Thibault simply could not yield the title "Doctor" to a Ph.D.!

***

The tour started with Dr. Thibault gesticulating grandly at sophisticated electronic equipment. Jeannine followed attentively in spite of his pomposity.

Dr. Thibault reminded her of the physician researcher who had wrecked Jeannine's doctoral studies at Fairland University. Wayne Johnson had rescued her with the position at StatFind. She had finished her Ph.D. at another school.

When finally, Thibault pointed to an oscilloscope with a flickering wave form, Jeannine broke in. She turned away from Thibault and towards Harry.

"Dr. Roberts, for your Fourier transforms what sort of window do you usually use?

Harry recognized her aim. He liked this red head.

"Jeannine, we use multiple electrodes, so our signals are never, well almost never, of comparable strength. We don't have much use for rectangular windows. We like Hamming's."

He went on with more jargon. For more than a minute their discussion continued while excluding an impatient Thibault.

Finally, Thibault interrupted.

"Ms. Ryan, we need to show you the data you'll be examining for us."

Harry spoke.

"Dr. Thibault is right. Jeannine, let's go to the conference room. I have a PowerPoint presentation that will save us time. Wayne and Dr. Thibault can discuss the contract."

He took Jeannine's elbow to guide her.

She did not draw away.

***

It was late afternoon by the time Wayne and Jeannine left Mandley Test Services. Both MTS and Harry Roberts had moved fast. In response, StatFind had promised a quick review of the PMA.

Jeannine cradled the bulky PMA in both arms.

"Jeannine, are you sure you can give them our critique in two days."

"I don't see why not. The analyses are right up my alley. Harry Roberts is sharp. He was very clear. I'm sure there won't be major problems."

"It's not much time."

"Relax. They want it fast. They'll get it fast."

She continued.

"They're a few things on the physiological side I need to study, but the stats and time series are my thing. And we have the software at StatFind. Tonight I'm going to tank up on coffee. By tomorrow morning, I'll know for sure."

Wayne was satisfied.

"How can I help?"

Jeannine paused.

"I'll know more tomorrow, but you'll have to run some programs and edit the critique."

Jeannine lapsed into silence. Her thoughts were not on the "all nighter" ahead, but on Harry Roberts. *Harry is really intelligent and he isn't bad looking. He certainly knows his signal processing. Maybe we … ?*

Her thoughts became words.

"You know, Harry's pretty smart."

Wayne hesitated. He had never interfered in Jeannine's personal life, but he did not like Harry Roberts. He blurted.

"You know Jeannine, I don't trust that guy!"

"You mean Dr. Thibault?"

"Not Thibault. It's Roberts that worries me. I think you should be careful around him."

This was new terrain. She was not ready to be Wayne's daughter.

"Damn it, Wayne, mind your own business! Harry's intelligent. Is he too smart for you?"

Wayne was not intimidated. His years of statistical computing included everything that Harry called "Signal Processing." Wayne knew the subject well, but by another name, "Time Series Analysis." He pushed on.

"Jeannine, I just want you to be careful. Don't get involved with that guy. There's something about him."

"You're right! There is something about him. And I like it. How about driving and leaving me alone?"

The traffic light went yellow. Wayne hit the brakes hard. Jeannine jerked forwards.

For the rest of the trip she stared straight ahead.

***

Back at MTS, Dr. Thibault looked up from his desk.

"Harry, can we trust this Ryan woman?"

"She knows her stuff, but she only has the faked data. The real data are wiped. With the data she has, she will have to reach our conclusions. She is just what we need, an objective third party that will support our PMA."

Dr. Thibault frowned.

"Now, about Aileen Harris, I want you to forget her. I've handled that situation. She doesn't want trouble. All she wants is to be left alone. So leave her be! Clear? There's more at stake than you can imagine."

Harry frowned in turn.

"OK, OK. Have it your way!"

Thibault waved his hand in dismissal.

***

Once in his office, Harry pulled up the address for "Harris" that he had found this morning. It was Aileen's mother's address. He knew Aileen's daughter spent the day with her grandmother. He frowned. *The brat will help me shut Aileen's mouth!*

If Thibault wouldn't act, he would!

***

Late that night, Jane Peterson awoke to the insistent ring of her phone. She lifted her head off the pillow and fumbled for the noisy instrument. She recognized the caller, Fareed Hamza, head of security for Mandley Bionics.

"Fareed, it's late. What do you want?"

"Do not question me. I am your husband."

"Naam, Yes, but why at this hour?"

"I just listened to the tapes of Thibault's calls. He thinks he has silenced Harris. He called her mother and gave her money. Thibault thinks he can handle Harris without us. Also he's worried about Harry Roberts. He called a private investigator to watch him."

"Thibault is an ass."

"True, but he is useful, and Roberts *is* unpredictable. Watch him. Keep us out of it if you can, and keep me informed about Harris and Thibault."

He hung up without waiting for a response.

Jane pulled the covers up to her chin. *Thibault, you are a fool and Fareed you need to learn Western manners!*

Her head sank into the pillow and her eyes closed.

***

******

Chapter 3
Thursday, October 12

Twenty seven years ago a baby girl was born in Montréal, Québec. Jeanne-Anan Audet had her mother's black hair, but her blue eyes were from her father. Still her dark-eyed mother must have given her one blue gene, recessively hidden in those brown pupils.

Jeanne-Anan's father was a Québecer who had met her mother in Beirut and converted to Islam to marry her. He brought her to Montréal, but when her mother, a good Shiite from the Bekaa Valley, refused to abort Jeanne as he demanded, he promptly abandoned them before the baby was born.

When, in elementary school, Jeanne was told the circumstances of her birth, she erased all thoughts of that "sperm-supplier," from her consciousness. She would never call that man, "father." No way! Pas possible! He did not exist. Her mother loved her. That sufficed.

Nonetheless Jeanne hated the headscarf her mother made her wear at elementary school in Montréal. Still, it was a small price to pay for the love her mother lavished on her. As for the kids who teased her, Jeanne learned to fend for herself. Most kids teased her only once. Her response to their jibes was decidedly not peaceful and often inflicted pain.

She was a shy spindly fifteen-year old when Moustafa moved next to her mother. He was a radical member of Shia Islam. He quickly realized the deficiencies in Jeanne's education and personally undertook her religious formation.

Under his tutelage she learned that Muslims are the true monotheists, while the inferior Québec Catholics were polytheists who skillfully hid that pagan belief under a Trinitarian cloak. She learned to disdain "infidels," and to detest those who call God "Father," as if Allah, the almighty, would take a wife or "beget" a son. The little she knew of her own father convinced her that God could never be one.

After two years of Moustafa's instruction, she adopted her Arabic name, "Anan" and embraced a young Arab girl, Fatimah, as her hero. Fatimah had achieved momentary fame by blowing herself and ten Israeli children into bloody particles of flesh at a bus stop in Tel Aviv.

Anan told her mother that she idolized Fatimah, and that she wanted to be like her. That statement produced only a shoulder shrug. But when she added a request that she be allowed to accompany Moustafa to Lebanon on his next trip, her mother took immediate action. Moustafa was locked out, and Anan locked up, until the erstwhile mentor had boarded his overseas flight.

Thenceforth her mother took charge. As a Muslim immigrant, she knew the difference between her own impoverished education and that available to her daughter. Jeanne-Anan was no longer allowed to attend school on a casual basis. There were no more missed classes such as those that made time for Moustafa's indoctrination. Every night her mother, tired as she was from work, sat with her daughter to see that she completed her assignments.

Anan worked hard to please her mother. She studied, and kept on studying. In fact at nineteen, a desirably-fleshed young woman, she received a scholarship to McGill, Montreal's premier English-speaking university. She studied Political Science and graduated Cum Laude.

By now an accomplished tri-lingual (Arabic, French and English) she accepted a clerical job with the Canadian Embassy in Washington, DC. There she dyed her hair blond, met an American named Peterson, married, and became a U.S citizen herself.

A short time later, after a quick divorce, she was hired by Fareed Hamza, an acquaintance of Moustafa, to a security position with Mandley Bionics under her new name, Jane Peterson.

After a year at Mandley's Delaware facility she was assigned her present position in Dr. Thibault's office at Mandley Test Services.

***

Dr. Thibault strode confidently through the foyer of the massive Parklawn Building in Rockville, Maryland. At his side, Jane Peterson pulled a wheeled carry-on behind her. Thibault had chosen the striking receptionist to help him deliver the PMA for Mandley's "Parkinson" chip to the Food and Drug Administration's Parklawn offices.

The pair paused to wait at a bank of elevators.

Dr. Thibault became expansive.

"Jane, after we drop this off, let's celebrate with lunch and a couple of drinks. This is a big day for us. This PMA is a cinch for approval. Harry Roberts prepared a super application, and Ryan and StatFind did a thorough critique for us."

He eyed Jane's trim figure appreciatively as he continued.

"You deserve to relax. What do you say?"

"You told me to finish the payment of StatFind's invoice, remember?"

He grinned.

"That can wait. They won't mind. You can do that tomorrow. We'll have lunch. Afterwards you can take the rest of the day off."

Jane looked away. She did not consume alcohol, and certainly would not do so with Thibault. Fortunately, the elevator arrived before she could answer. She pushed in among the other riders.

Thibault squeezed in after her.

***

At noon, Jeannine Ryan was still in her bed. She had worked all night Tuesday and most of Wednesday to repeat Harry Robert's analyses for Mandley's PMA.

Harry impressed her. His perceptive reasoning was supported by sound statistical analyses. She had told him as

23

much when she transmitted her report to MTS yesterday evening. She knew he had been pleased by her comments.

Jeannine rolled over and squinted at the alarm clock. Earlier, she had silenced that noise-box with a firm whack of her fist.

Still exhausted, she shut her eyes. *Forget it Jeannine. No way you're going to StatFind today! Go back to sleep.*

Her head fell back on the pillow.

***

Meanwhile, at her school in Bethesda, Mary Catherine's Pre-K was over at noon.

Across the street, Harry Roberts waited. He stood next to a lamppost and looked down. He did not want to be noticed.

An elderly lady appeared. Harry recognized Aileen's mother. He knew her, but he had never seen the little blonde girl who ran to her. That child must be Aileen's daughter.

The little girl stood next to Mrs. Harris. They waited for the cars to stop while the crossing guard walked to the middle of the street and held up her hand. At her signal, Mrs. Harris spoke.

"Hold on, Mary Catherine. Let's go."

That did it! This was Aileen's daughter.

Mary Catherine held tightly to her grandmother. Together they crossed to the public parking lot. There they got into a car and drove away.

Harry smiled. He now had what he needed.

His Mercedes was parked around the corner. He walked that way.

***

That evening, Jane Peterson opened the door to her apartment and sighed. She had survived Thibault's advances. She had spilled her drinks into an adjacent potted plant and frustrated the plans of that old lecher.

Tired, she sank into her chair just as her phone rang. It was Fareed.

"What is Thibault doing?"

"He took me to lunch. He wants to seduce me. How long do I have to put up with that idiot? He's an old fool."

24

"You did not drink?"

"You know we do not take alcohol."

"I know Anan does not drink, but what of Jane?"

"You insult me. Jane does not drink."

"Good. Now tell me what is happening with Harris, and Roberts."

"Harris is quiet and Roberts has been busy with the PMA."

"All right. We'll stay out of if we can, but keep seeing Roberts. I need to know what he knows about us. That man is a time bomb. Do whatever you must to keep him talking."

"Fareed, are you sure you want me to do that?"

"Listen. Deception is permitted for Allah's purposes. Do you not know of the taqiyya?"

"Of course."

"Then follow my wishes."

He added.

"We have had a true success. Watch the TV news. Our plan is underway."

He hung up.

Jane picked up the TV remote and clicked onto the news channel. Minutes later a bulletin flashed on the screen.

Breaking news from Beirut
Kevork Abassian, a prominent Christian Leader died suddenly today in a meeting with representatives of Hezbollah to negotiate limits on Hezbollah's police and administrative functions in southern Lebanon. Abassian, who had a prior heart condition, suffered an attack during the meeting and could not be resuscitated. He was pronounced dead upon arrival at a Beirut hospital. He was 54 years old.
With Abassian's death, the future of the negotiations is uncertain.
In local sports, the Washington Redskins announced
...

Jane smiled in triumph at Fareed's success.

She turned off the TV, and went to her dresser to study her blond tresses. She liked the color, but she knew that sometime in the future her hair would assume its natural black sheen.

With each victory, that day grew closer.

Jane went to the bathroom and ran warm water in the shower. She slipped out of her clothes revealing a firm body. She was in excellent shape. She stepped under the stimulating spray and fingered the plastic cap that protected her hair's false color. As to her false name, "Jane," someday, hopefully, she would be "Anan" again.

But I am "Anan."

She relaxed and rubbed the water from her eyes. They, at least, were truly blue. *Black hair and blue eyes? Anan, you're a misfit. You'll never fit in.*

She closed her eyes and thought of Harry Roberts with guilty feelings. Getting Harry in bed had brought her pleasure! She shrugged. *But I must obey Fareed.*

Deception for Allah's purposes was permissible, and Fareed knew when deception was necessary.

She stepped out of the shower, donned a bathrobe and covered her hair. She laid down her prayer mat and prepared to pray.

***

******

Chapter 4
Monday, October 16

In Rockville, StatFind was in a joyous tumult. Wayne Johnson, wrapped his arms around Mona Larson, the "motherly" secretary, and danced a jig! At least he tried. No matter, they kept their feet hopping.

Next to them the usually stoic financial officer, Bill Hamm, bent over with laughter, spilling coffee in the process. So what! He kept laughing.

The clamor brought Jeannine to the door. Bill flashed his broadest smile. Jeannine was desirable, even in her casual outfit of dark jeans topped by a sloppy gray sweatshirt. She was a definite "Ten."

"Jeannine! Come on in and give me a hug! We got the Mandley Bionics contract. This is big! Your critique for MTS impressed them."

Jeannine stood silent. Bill persisted.

"How about that hug?"

"Try somebody else, Bill!"

She turned to Wayne.

"So MTS liked the report?"

Wayne's feet stopped hopping. Mona, released, collapsed breathless into her chair.

"Like it. They loved it. And their FDA-contact told Harry Roberts, unofficially, that it was one of the best applications for Pre Market Approval he had seen."

Two more employees arrived to celebrate. Wayne turned to them.

"Mandley Bionics wants us to oversee the statistical analyses for their upcoming clinical trial. We owe Jeannine for that!"

More staff crowded into the office. Bill Hamm stood close to Jeannine. He put his arm around her.

"Damn it, Bill, back off!"

Wayne heard her retort.

"Jeannine, Bill's a good financial officer. He doesn't mean anything."

"OK, then tell him to stop bothering me!"

Wayne pleaded with his eyes. Jeannine softened, and turned to Bill.

"Look Bill, there's still work to do. We need to know how FDA/CDRH functions, and we need to know who to talk to there. In particular, to know how 'OSB' functions and who will be monitoring the PMA. Bone up on those organizations for me. We will be interacting with them."

"FDA/CDRH and OSB, is that English?"

Jeannine turned to leave. She could see long hours ahead. She spoke over her shoulder.

"It's just 'Governmentalese.' Check them out. You need to know who we're working with."

She left. Wayne turned to new arrivals.

"Listen up folks. This is big! We've never had a contract near this size. We've had to expand to handle this, and I'll need all of you to give it your best effort. This is great news for all of us!"

***

Back in his own office, Bill Hamm googled "OSB" and "CDRH," and read the search results on the screen.

The Office of Surveillance and Biometrics (OSB) is the office of FDA's Center for Devices and Radiological Health (CDRH) that is responsible for the statistical review of marketing applications and postmarket surveillance.

When he saw the words "statistical review," Bill smiled. *Wayne will need Jeannine more than ever. Great!* Then he frowned. *But she doesn't like me.*

Bill was not used to outright rejection. He was tall and well-built, and while no one would say that he was handsome, he certainly was not ugly. His features were regular, if a bit rough, and a small scar on his left cheek was more intriguing than disfiguring.

Further, he was in good physical condition. At StatFind he sat behind a desk, but he exercised regularly and his previous occupation had been an active one.

He sat frustrated before the computer screen. *Damn, she really doesn't like me.*

***

Wayne was excited. For the new contract, StatFind had doubled its space. He took Jeannine's elbow and guided her across the hall.

"OK girl, this is your new office. No more cubicle! You have windows, a door you can shut, high speed internet, the works. You've earned it."

For once, Jeannine stood speechless. Even the term "girl" failed to trigger a response.

"But …"

"No 'buts.' It's yours."

"Yes, but what's that pile of paper on *my* new desk?"

"Oh that. Harry Roberts sent you some more stuff from MTS, and I got some job applications off our web site for you to look at. And Bill Hamm had some papers for you to sign about your raise. Good luck."

Wayne was gone before Jeannine could collect her thoughts. She leaned over the new desk. Attached to the MTS pile was a note from Harry Roberts.

> *Jeannine,*
>
> *Thanks for your great critique. How about dinner tomorrow night?*
> *Fondly, Harry*

She smiled, but a knock on the door interrupted her musing. Bill Hamm stood in the doorway.

"A door even! Nice. Real Nice! You're coming up in the world!"

"What do you want Bill?"

29

"Nothing. Wayne told me you had new digs. I thought I'd check them out."

"OK, you've checked, now let me work."

He turned to leave, but the phone rang. He paused and listened.

"Harry! I got your note. Sure, I'd like to have dinner tomorrow. Where? That sounds good. OK! See you then."

Bill spoke through the door.

"Jeannine, was that the Harry Roberts at MTS?"

"None of your business!"

"If that was him, stay away. I know that guy. He's no good!"

Jeannine's face reddened.

"Go!"

Bill went.

Jeannine shuffled papers mindlessly. *Wayne, Hamm is a jerk. I can't work with him. Keep him away from me. And yes, Harry's smarter, and he's fun too!*

***

Jeannine studied the job applicants, but the buzz of the phone broke her concentration. *OK, a door doesn't stop all interruptions.*

She picked up. It was Mona, Wayne's secretary.

"Jeannine, there's an 'Aileen Harris' on the line. She saw our web site. She's a whiz with computers and wants to work in the Rockville area. Wayne wants you to talk to her. She impressed him."

"All right. Put her on."

"Dr. Ryan, my name is Aileen Harris. I saw the position notice on StatFind's website and Wayne Johnson said I should talk to you. I'm interested in your position."

Aileen explained her qualifications. Jeannine liked what she heard.

"Aileen what statistical software have you used?"

"I've used SAS, including time series and repeated measures procedures."

Jeannine was sold.

"That's good, Aileen! Where are you working now?"

"I'm not."

"Where was your last position?"

Aileen paused.

"I'd rather not say. It didn't work out."

Jeannine was concerned, but she liked Aileen's credentials.

"OK, I can accept that. I've had problems like that myself."

Aileen exhaled in relief. *I'm over that hurdle, Thank God! Maybe I can get through this.* She thought of her daughter. *OK, honey, we're going to make it!*

"Dr. Ryan, err Jeannine, I really need this job. If you want me I can start right away."

"We can arrange that."

"Wonderful! Thank you very much! I won't let you down."

Aileen's enthusiasm further impressed Jeannine. She wanted a willing worker.

"I'll talk to Bill Hamm. He handles the paper work. You can start tomorrow as a temp while we make permanent arrangements. We have a ton of work to do for our new contract with MTS."

The line fell silent.

"Aileen? Are you there?"

The reply was a whisper.

"I'm here. Err ...Is that 'MTS,' as in 'Mandley Test Services.'"

"That's the one. Dr. Thibault's group. Is that a problem?"

The reply was whispered.

"Thanks for your time."

The line went dead.

***

Alone in her mother's house, Aileen stared at the phone.

She was numb.

It was a week since her discharge from MTS and that fearful beating at Harry's hands. She touched her cheek gingerly. Most of the swelling was gone. She had stayed with her mother

31

since that disastrous evening. Each day her mother had driven Mary Catherine to school.

Today she had searched the internet for jobs. Finding StatFind had generated a fresh hope!

But that hope was gone. Harry and MTS unwittingly had seen to that.

She buried her face in her hands.

***

The door opened. Aileen jumped up.

"Who is it? Who's there?"

Small steps sounded in the hallway, her mother and Mary Catherine.

"Honey we're back. I brought Chinese for us and a burger and fries for Mary Catherine."

Small arms threw themselves around Aileen's neck and squeezed hard.

"Mommy, look what Granny bought me!"

Mary Catherine stepped back and held out a stuffed bear, white with a red sash.

"That's nice honey. Did you thank Granny and give her a big hug?"

Mary Catherine nodded.

Aileen had to smile. At least her daughter was happy.

***

Her mother called from the kitchen.

"Aileen, tell Mary Catherine to wash up. We'll eat in here. Oh, there's a letter for you on the hall table with the mail."

Aileen kissed her daughter.

"Go wash your hands for Mommy. Granny has your food in the kitchen."

She stepped into the hall to check the mail. One item was a yellow envelope. It was addressed to Aileen Harris care of her mother, Bernadette.

Aileen's stomach sank. *Who knows I'm here?* She stared at the envelope. There was no return address, and the address was printed in block letters. She tore it open.

There was no letter, only a photograph.

Aileen gasped.

The photo showed her daughter with Aileen's mother as they crossed the street from school.

A black "X" was inked over Mary Catherine's face.

***

Aileen stared, shaking, at the wall. She knew the photo was from Harry. *You bastard! Stay away from my daughter!*

Aileen could tolerate threats to herself, but not to Mary Catherine. Her divorce had proved that she would fight for her daughter.

Damn you Harry. Who do you think you are? Leave my daughter alone!

Up to now, Aileen had not decided to blow the whistle on Dr. Thibault and Harry. Her mother had repeatedly cautioned her not to.

Harry's threat changed that! To do nothing would mean living with fear.

You bastard! I will not let you hurt her!

***

******

Chapter 5
Tuesday, October 17

Harry Roberts was pleased with his choice of restaurant and seating. The dimly lit corner table was partially shielded from other diners by the pointed leaves of a potted fig tree.

The light from the table's lone candle sparkled erratically off the twin glasses of Cabernet Sauvignon. The reflected red rays highlighted Jeannine's auburn hair, while under her sparkling eyes shadows emphasized her striking cheeks.

Harry had entertained at this table before, including Jane, the MTS receptionist, but Jeannine was far and away the most appealing prize to occupy this seat.

"Jeannine, you look great, and your comments on my analyses were the most perceptive I've received. You are really special."

Harry smiled. He knew that the candlelight emphasized the ruggedness of his features. This table had worked its charm more than once.

"I'm glad you came."

"Harry, it's a real treat."

Jeannine sipped her wine. It was more than a year since her last romantic outing. *He's smart, and he's certainly good looking. Maybe? Why not?* She looked into his eyes. They were difficult to read. *Anyway, he's a good mathematician! Maybe this can work.*

He took her hand and spoke with confidence.

"You know, we should get to know each other, I mean tonight."

That thought was interrupted by the arrival of the waiter. He placed an exquisitely presented dish before Jeannine.

"Un tournedos pour Madame …"

He turned to Harry with a second steak.

"Et aussi un pour Monsieur."

The waiter hovered over them.

"You desire more wine?"

Harry nodded affirmatively while Jeannine mustered her sparse French.

"Non, Merçi."

She eyed the tournedos. A rich sauce Béarnaise covered the tender meat. A fork alone sufficed to separate the first morsel from the body of the steak.

She chewed slowly to savor the flavor. She sipped the Cabernet Sauvignon, a perfect complement to her entrée.

"Harry, this is delicious. You chose well. And this wine fits."

"Thanks. It's local, from a vineyard in Virginia."

Harry looked away. *She likes the food, but she only took one glass of wine. I'll get her an after-dinner brandy. She's worth working on!*

Jeannine had her own thoughts. *Maybe he is the one.* But both Wayne and that jerk Hamm don't trust this guy. *Still, what do they know?*

She took a sip of wine. *OK, I like him, but I need to know him better.*

"Harry, I had an odd call today about a job at StatFind."

"Odd? In what way?"

"It was a woman. Her name was Aileen Harris. She was really interested in working for us, but then I mentioned MTS and she hung up. Do you know her?"

Harry bit his lip. *That little bitch.* He recovered.

"Yes I know her."

"So what's with her and MTS."

Harry's silence was prolonged. Finally he spoke.

"She's no good. She used to work for us, but Dr. Thibault had to let her go. I agreed with him."

"Anything particular I should know about her?"

"Not really. What did she say?"

"Nothing really. When I mentioned MTS she hung up. That's all."

"Nothing else?"

"No that's it."

"You're sure?"

"I told you! Of course I'm sure."

"Look, she's a nut. She makes up stories. That's why Dr. Thibault had to let her go. She's not stable."

The thought of Aileen telling her story to Wayne Johnson or Jeannine caused Harry to cut short his plans for the evening.

"Jeannine, would you like some desert, a crème brulée or something?"

"No, I'm fine. But if you want some?"

Harry shook his head. He sat erect.

"Damn, I forgot. I have to prepare a report for Dr. Thibault. He needs it in the morning. I better go back to the lab."

Harry signaled for the check.

As they left the restaurant, Harry spoke.

"You have your car, don't you? Or I could give you a ride."

Jeannine frowned. *I've been dumped!*

"No thanks, Harry, I'll take my car."

"Look, I'm sorry. I'll call you tomorrow."

There was no embrace. Harry turned away and headed for his Mercedes.

She watched as he drove away.

***

Rob Wilson, ex-FBI, was a private investigator. He watched Harry leave Jeannine and drive off in the Mercedes. Rob started his Ford Crown Vic and pulled discretely behind Harry.

Harry turned right at the first light. Rob did likewise and punched a number. His boss, Frank Hardy, answered.

"Yes?"

"Roberts dumped the red head, and he's headed into Bethesda on Wisconsin. Shall I follow him?"

"What the hell am I paying you for?"

"OK, OK. I'm on it."

"Good. You've got the Harris address?"

"Yes."

"All right. If he goes anywhere near there let me know right away. Clear?"

"Sure."

A light rain fell as Harry's Mercedes turned into a quiet neighborhood. Rob turned on his wipers. An increasing wind rustled the branches of the trees that stretched over the street.

***

The Harris house was dark.

Inside, Aileen lay awake, staring upwards. Outside, the street light shone through wind-tossed branches to cast undulating shadows on the ceiling above her. The unpredictable patterns seemed to presage her unknown future.

Suddenly a car broke the silence of the neighborhood. She sat bolt upright. She heard the repeated click-clack of the motor and knew the engine was a diesel.

To Aileen there was only one car with such an engine, Harry's Mercedes.

She slipped to the window and peered out. Across the street, partially illuminated by the street light, a Mercedes had parked. Inside, she could see the silhouette of a man.

Harry!

Trembling, Aileen stayed by the window in the dark bedroom. Minutes passed as she kept her vigil. Then suddenly Harry pulled from the curb and drove away. She watched until his tail lights disappeared.

Shaken, Aileen stepped to her daughter's bed. Carefully, she laid herself down next to Mary Catherine and put her arm around her. Finally, soothed by her daughter's regular breathing, she fell asleep.

***

At his home in Bethesda, Dr. Thibault answered his phone.

"Hello."

"You were right about Roberts. Wilson tracked him to the mother's house."

"What did he do?"

"He parked across the street. He sat there a while. Then he drove off"

"Who's in the house?"

"They're all there, the Harris woman, the daughter and the grandmother."

"Damn! I warned Roberts to stay away from Harris. He's going to screw me over piddling fake data. Aileen is scared. She is not talking. Damn Harry!"

"So what will we do about Harris?"

"I'll call you tomorrow. We may have to use your plan."

***

Harry Roberts parked the Mercedes in his condo parking. *That damned photo should have settled it. Damn you Harris!*

And she had ruined his night with Jeannine. He threw himself on the empty bed.

Tomorrow he would increase the pressure on Aileen Harris.

***

At his home, Dr. Thibault sniffed his brandy. He tilted the glass and sipped. It went down smoothly.

Harry was a real problem. He would not calm down.

Damn, Aileen would be under control if not for Harry. Frank Hardy was right. It would be better for Aileen to disappear, maybe have an accident, far away. Then Harry could relax. He still needed Harry, for a while anyway!

Thibault made his decision. Tomorrow he would tell Frank to implement his plan.

That decided, the doctor tilted his Lazy Boy backwards. His head fell sideways and he dozed.

***

******

Chapter 6
Wednesday, October 18

At her mother's house, Aileen watched her daughter eat breakfast with an enthusiasm shown only for Granny's "cooking," a bowl of Fruit Loops, Mary Catherine's favorite.

"Mom, Mary Catherine can't stay here anymore. Can she go with you when you visit Aunt Agatha. She could miss a few of weeks of Pre-kindergarten without a problem."

Bernadette Harris nodded.

"That's a good idea. You'll be free for job interviews. I'll tell the teacher she'll be gone when I drop her off today. We can leave after school. I can handle a four hour drive."

Aileen relaxed. Mary Catherine would be far from Harry.

***

After a final farewell hug from Mary Catherine, Aileen watched Granny take her daughter for a final day at school. Now she was free to solve the "Harry" problem.

Harry's "visit" last night had strengthened her resolve. She punched the same number she had called the day before. A pleasant voice answered.

"StatFind."

"Dr. Jeannine Ryan, please."

Jeannine answered her buzzer. Aileen spoke.

"Dr. Ryan, I spoke to you yesterday."

"Right, Ms. Harris. I remember. You hung up."

"I'm sorry, but I need to talk to you."

"Ms. Harris, I already spoke to Dr. Roberts about you."

"Did he tell you he hit me?"

"Ms. Harris, if you are calling about our position, I don't think it would work."

"But …"

"And I'm very busy at the moment."

Aileen spoke rapidly.

"Please wait. It's something else. It's not about the job. It's important."

Jeannine sighed.

"Go ahead."

"The data you reviewed for MTS are fake, at least some of them! You should be aware."

"Please Ms. Harris, I don't have time for this."

"Please listen. I know that Patient 68's record is falsified. I saw the correct data."

"Do you have them?"

"No. Harry, ... Dr. Roberts, took them."

"Goodbye Ms. Harris."

"Please wait. And Dr. Thibault knows too."

"Of course, but you have no proof."

"I did, but I don't know. They took it. I was beaten up. You can ask my mother."

"She saw them beat you up?"

"Not exactly."

"Goodbye."

Aileen volunteered a final fact.

"But I do know that Patient 27's data are good. I recorded them myself."

"Goodbye Ms. Harris. You should try and get help. And don't call back."

This time Jeannine hung up.

***

Jeannine immediately called Mandley Test Services.

"May I speak to Dr. Roberts please. This is Dr. Ryan from StatFind."

Jane Peterson remembered "Doctor" Ryan. Despite Jane's reputation as that "Blonde" she welcomed the intrusion of a professional woman into Dr. Thibault's domain.

"Dr. Ryan, he's not here. Would you like to speak to Dr. Thibault."

Jeannine noted her warmth.

"Well yes, that would be good. Thank you."

Dr. Thibault came on the line.

"Ms. Ryan, how can I help?"

"Dr. Thibault, Harry told me you fired Aileen Harris. You should know that she's making trouble. She called me. She says you faked data. I told her she should get help."

"How did she take that?"

"She did not listen. I think you should know what she's saying."

Dr. Thibault broke his own rule about titles and Ph. D.'s.

"Dr. Ryan, thanks very much for your concern. Aileen hasn't been the same since her divorce. Her imagination has gone wild. It was a shame we had to let her go."

He added.

Did she say anything else?"

"She said Harry beat her up."

"Good grief! She had a bad fall in the parking lot. That's all. It's worse than I thought. She does need help. But I'm not sure what I can do."

He paused. He was damned sure what he would do. *If Harry finds out he'll go ballistic. Harris will have to disappear. Aileen you should have kept your mouth shut!*

"Dr. Ryan, thank you very much."

"You'll tell Harry?"

"Of course, and thanks again."

***

At StatFind, Jeannine looked up to see Bill Hamm at her door.

"Were you talking to Harry Roberts?

"No. ... I mean not Harry, to Dr. Thibault.

She caught herself.

"Damn it Bill why do you want to know? Why are you hanging around my office?"

"To give you your promotion papers. They're all signed. You should see the money in the next check."

Bill added.

"Aileen Harris called me too. I'm tempted to believe her story. There's something about her that rings true. I warned you about Roberts."

"She hates Harry as you do! You're jealous. Why can't you leave Harry alone?"

Bill's cheeks flushed red.

"Don't ask me. Ask my sister, and Harry too!"

He started to leave.

"And enjoy your damn raise!"

Jeannine never had seen Bill so agitated.

***

Bernadette Harris drove north on her way to Johnstown, Pennsylvania. Mary Catherine was asleep in her car seat. Just past Hagerstown, Maryland, her cell phone buzzed.

"Yes?"

"Mrs. Harris, do you know who this is?"

She recognized Dr. Thibault's voice.

"Yes, of course. You are …"

"Please don't mention my name. Did you get the money I sent you."

"Yes, and I'm most grateful. Your help means a lot to us."

"You know I want the best for Aileen, but don't tell her. She wouldn't understand."

"Of course not. I did as you said. I want to thank you for protecting Aileen from that Roberts monster. I know she's scared."

"What has she shared with you?"

"Nothing, really, but I can tell she's scared of Harry. When I saw what he did to her."

"Mrs. Harris, I'm afraid Harry is more dangerous than ever."

"Good God!"

"And that's why I'm calling. I've arranged for a Private Agency to take Aileen away for a few days to keep her safe. No one, not even I, will know where at first. Most importantly, Harry won't know!"

Thibault continued.

"There'll be a private investigator with her at all times. She'll be safe until I can neutralize Harry."

"How will I convince her to go."

"I don't know, but you'd better. Did you know Harry was at your house last night?"

Bernadette Harris gasped. Thibault continued.

"Don't mention me. Tell her that StatFind believes her, and thinks she needs protection for a few days. Tell her you saw Harry at the house. Tell her anything. If you love your daughter make sure she listens! I'll send more money to you. I'm on your side."

The doctor paused.

"Someone will pick her up in two hours."

He hung up.

Bernadette Harris was troubled.

Dr. Thibault was helpful, and a real gentleman. She appreciated his concern, but how to convince Aileen to leave?

Fifteen minutes later, she had her argument prepared.

She would convince her daughter. She steered with one hand and speed-dialed Aileen with the other.

She talked rapidly. By the time she passed Hancock and crossed into Pennsylvania, Aileen had said "yes."

***

From his office at MTS, Dr. Thibault called Frank Hardy. Each knew enough about the other's dealings to ensure mutual silence.

"Frank, is your man really dumb enough to fall for this."

"His name is Rob Wilson. He trusts me. I told him that the whole protection bit is a farce. He doesn't think there's any danger for the girl. The clincher is that he has a dog that he dotes on. I'll use that fact for us."

He continued.

"Hell, it's "locals" down there that will do the damage. They've never heard of you or me. My contact will fix everything. Don't worry. All Rob Wilson will know is that he blew the assignment. That's all."

"But …"

"Forget the 'but.' We've been through a lot worse. Now get me my cash. I have to get this started."

***

******

Chapter 7
Wednesday, October 18

Jeannine arrived early for lunch. She picked a corner booth. Harry had suggested a Cajun Restaurant and she had agreed. She liked the New Orleans decor on the walls. The French-language posters reminded Jeannine of her best friend from Canada, Monique Martin (née Laurier.)

Monique was an immunologist from Montréal, and she and Jeannine had grown close under the duress of exposing fraudulent data in breast cancer research. Both had lost their university positions as a result. Later, Monique, with Jeannine's approval, had married Jeannine's former boyfriend, John Martin. The couple taught biology at a small college in Pennsylvania. Their daughter, now four, was named "Jeannine."

Harry's arrival snapped Jeannine out of her reverie. She smiled and said.

"You look sharp today. What going on at MTS?"

"Nothing much. Pretty boring actually. How about StatFind?"

"I like my new office. It's bright, and thanks to you and the MTS contract, I now have a door. I can actually shut it and work. Today I reviewed some old math, 'Lighthill's generalized functions.' I still like his approach."

Harry's response was real.

"Me too. I like the rigorous approach to Dirac's delta."

This discussion went on for several minutes until the waiter came for their order. When he departed, Jeannine leaned forward.

"Did Dr. Thibault tell you about the Harris woman?"

Harry was taken aback.

"No. What do you mean?"

Jeannine recounted Aileen's accusations and her talk with Dr. Thibault.

Harry's face went ashen. His mind raced. *OK, Thibault's a bastard. I know that, but why didn't he tell me?* His thoughts slowed. *Calm down! Make sure this girl is on your side.*

He took Jeannine's hand.

"You know I really like you. It's time for us to know each other better. How about tonight? Drinks at my place?"

Jeannine started to respond, but felt the vibration of her cell phone. She looked at the number.

"Harry, this is an old friend. Out of town. I have to take it."

"A guy?"

"Monique is a funny name for a guy."

"All right then, but how about tonight?"

"The answer is 'Yes.'"

Harry grinned.

"OK, I'm back to work. See you then."

He took the check and left.

Jeannine spoke into her phone.

"Monique! How are you? And Jeannie? And John?"

***

An upset Jeannine returned to her office at StatFind. The conversation with Monique had started pleasantly. Jeannine had described Harry and the recent successes at StatFind.

But then she had mentioned Aileen's accusations of data falsification.

Jeannine had been ill prepared for Monique's response.

Jeannine! I can't believe this is you! Have you forgotten how Fairland University hounded us when we told them Mike was faking data! You lost your fellowship! I lost my Postdoc!

You don't want to believe Aileen. You are afraid she is right and that you would lose this guy Roberts, and lose that darn office door and window or whatever, and that plush contract and all that money.

Your head is the sand! You're afraid to check her story!

Maybe Harry is your 'Mr. Right,' but you have to check! You'll never be happy otherwise!"

By now, Jeannine had a serious headache. Monique was right.

She called Harry. He wasn't there. At the beep she left a message.

"Harry, it's Jeannine. I'm not well. I need a rain check for tonight. I'm Sorry. Thanks for the lunch. Maybe tomorrow night."

Please let Aileen be a nut and Harry be for real, please.

Numbly she sat and stared at her desk.

Dark clouds covered the sun. Little light came through the window.

She did not turn on the lights.

She put her head in her hands.

Harry I want to trust you! I do! But Monique is right. I'm supposed to be objective! I've got to check Aileen's story. No matter if she is crazy.

She prided herself on intellectual objectivity. She had her ideals.

Now the office was dark.

She turned on the desk lamp to dial Aileen's number.

"Rring ... Rring ... Rring ... Rring ... Rring ..."

There was no answer and no beep to receive a message.

Jeannine brewed a pot of coffee. That "perk" was an added benefit of the new office. She sipped it black and prepared for an all-night session.

Aileen had said that the data for Patient 68 were "bad." But she had mentioned another patient. *OK Jeannine, concentrate! Yes. It was Patient 27!* Aileen said that she had recorded the data for Patient 27. She claimed those data were "good."

If the data were honestly represented, then the MTS conclusions followed, and the PMA merited approval.

But if the data were falsified, a *forensic* approach was needed. For example, did the "questioned" data of Harry's

Patient 68 differ somehow from the "unquestioned" data of Aileen's Patient 27?

When she had checked the PMA for MTS, Jeannine had copied some of the files from the report onto a CD. She inserted the disk and brought up the graph for Patient 68 on the screen.

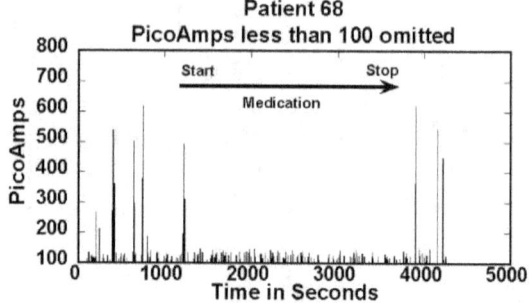

Patient 68

Nothing appeared out of the ordinary. Mandley Bionic's treatment worked. Major contractions of the muscle fiber (high spikes in PicoAmps) did not occur during the period of medication and the nerve-firing was controlled.

She turned to the next graph for patient 27, data collected by Aileen Harris.

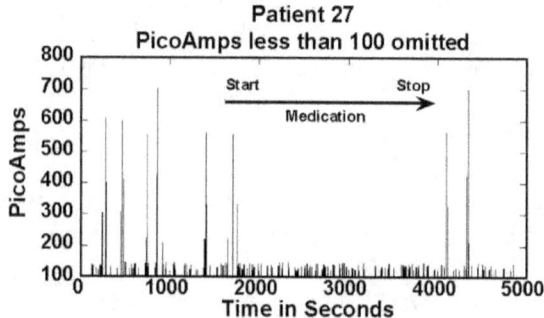

Patient 27

Patient 27 repeated the pattern of Patient 68. As before, high spikes did not occur while medication was given. For both patients, the contractions were controlled. The treatment worked!

Next, Jeannine listed the raw data for Harry's Patient 68. There were tons of numbers, far too many to read and absorb.

Harry's Data for Patient 68											
Sec	Amp	Sec	Amp	Sec	Amp	Sec	Amp	Sec	Amp	Sec	Amp
102	114	752	619	1435	130	2112	129	2721	115	3544	129
116	135	754	148	1486	110	2115	119	2726	106	3560	119
150	123	802	188	1533	115	2130	116	2767	127	3562	122
168	117	814	130	1540	126	2160	133	2776	110	3577	114
186	115	832	119	1553	126	2189	109	2887	119	3581	109
196	117	844	140	1554	142	2190	113	2894	131	3598	117
202	269	914	132	1555	133	2215	138	2942	124	3647	125
240	213	920	129	1574	118	2218	142	2954	113	3675	113
246	105	924	135	1587	129	2227	113	2983	113	3711	115
288	128	930	111	1596	128	2235	116	3020	130	3758	139
290	126	936	104	1604	135	2241	135	3024	120	3774	121
294	114	1016	114	1630	109	2257	122	3026	142	3788	124
338	123	1022	132	1649	123	2296	124	3069	125	3796	134
364	108	1028	126	1655	133	2303	142	3136	122	3802	118
392	272	1040	128	1677	139	2319	135	3164	120	3834	122
402	538	1072	107	1683	123	2363	119	3166	119	3890	364
420	361	1074	102	1690	116	2371	118	3178	138	3896	620
440	133	1084	121	1693	109	2381	115	3187	133	3898	203
442	131	1134	117	1697	126	2395	138	3196	118	3900	134
476	112	1152	111	1706	134	2420	125	3211	141	3938	145
494	117	1154	116	1737	126	2454	128	3213	110	3948	126
500	131	1174	125	1742	121	2468	141	3231	123	3972	136
526	115	1198	129	1765	136	2472	141	3245	126	4012	106
532	122	1212	195	1826	125	2484	131	3265	108	4026	127
538	129	1220	493	1862	137	2531	120	3285	133	4064	148
562	116	1232	309	1870	113	2533	128	3308	122	4152	543
638	134	1270	134	1922	136	2565	120	3311	105	4214	450
644	501	1332	112	1938	138	2571	134	3360	107	4220	112
654	196	1338	124	1952	138	2584	124	3392	113	4248	122
656	298	1346	134	1973	133	2595	139	3397	122	4252	122
666	126	1377	125	1977	147	2617	121	3403	139	---	---
670	133	1392	130	2034	147	2653	121	3406	119	---	---
740	126	1412	146	2043	120	2667	135	3465	108	---	---
744	379	1434	135	2097	129	2690	118	3469	126	---	---

The printout listed the Time (in Seconds) at which a Peak occurred along with the height of the Peak (in PicoAmps.) A narrow column to the left of the Seconds-Column was "Black" if medication was being administered. A glance at the table sufficed to show that she needed the computer for her analyses.

Jeannine plunged ahead. She clicked and brought up the data for Aileen's patient 27.

Again there were too many numbers to analyze by eye.

Aileen Harris' Data for Patient 27											
Sec	Amp	Sec	Amp	Sec	Amp	Sec	Amp	Sec	Amp	Sec	Amp
116	140	854	426	1642	224	2406	121	3106	140	4042	142
132	137	862	701	1702	555	2416	121	3118	121	4070	133
164	128	916	208	1750	332	2434	127	3164	145	4072	120
190	124	930	142	1760	136	2468	133	3170	126	4092	220
212	137	948	126	1768	143	2500	128	3298	138	4094	563
218	136	962	146	1772	132	2508	137	3306	135	4116	328
236	304	1042	142	1786	144	2532	144	3360	127	4176	125
276	608	1050	145	1802	127	2534	137	3374	133	4198	131
278	401	1052	126	1812	125	2544	121	3412	131	4242	125
328	136	1058	135	1826	140	2560	132	3446	128	4300	140
330	133	1068	121	1832	139	2566	138	3452	129	4314	129
332	133	1164	127	1868	126	2584	133	3454	144	4324	422
392	126	1166	136	1888	144	2624	121	3510	131	4338	703
408	126	1172	143	1890	125	2632	144	3588	140	4346	210
448	307	1188	138	1916	140	2646	143	3612	141	4380	142
462	601	1224	123	1926	125	2702	123	3622	133	4444	123
480	409	1228	123	1930	141	2704	130	3634	137	4446	133
498	145	1238	139	1940	121	2718	140	3642	122	4454	131
502	143	1292	121	1942	132	2736	134	3648	137	4456	146
544	126	1308	125	1948	132	2762	136	3676	141	4502	143
568	140	1312	125	1988	144	2796	121	3682	129	4516	127
570	125	1338	130	1992	127	2822	142	3688	133	4538	139
594	127	1376	130	2018	144	2830	141	3712	144	4580	126
604	141	1388	220	2088	136	2836	139	3732	125	4602	138
614	144	1398	560	2132	139	2896	143	3756	133	4648	128
648	128	1404	333	2142	132	2900	128	3776	131	4744	131
728	143	1450	136	2196	145	2930	144	3784	138	4818	121
742	222	1524	125	2212	137	2936	146	3838	146	4820	123
746	556	1526	131	2222	145	2952	145	3880	136	4852	143
748	320	1530	129	2248	128	2970	133	3882	139	4858	137
754	132	1572	144	2256	145	2998	123	3888	140	---	---
762	144	1592	135	2324	145	3032	131	3892	134	---	---
840	130	1618	146	2328	132	3046	129	3956	125	---	---
850	144	1638	140	2396	132	3068	125	3964	129	---	---

This printout, too, listed the Time (in Seconds) at which a Peak occurred along with the height of the Peak (in PicoAmps.) Again, a narrow column was "Black" if medication was being given and otherwise blank.

The phone interrupted Jeannine's thoughts. The call was from Monique.

"Jeannine, je suis désolée et, …, I mean I'm sorry."

Monique was agitated. Her native French broke into her normally perfect English.

"I shouldn't have talked to you that way, jamais! And I'm glad you found someone like Harry, et j'espère, ..., I mean, I hope that ..."

"Monique, stop. You did the right thing. It hurt, but don't back off. You were right. It's hard, but I have to find the truth. I'm checking Aileen's story now. Thanks for calling me out. I'll call you back."

She put the phone down and returned to the sheets of numbers.

The phone rang once more. She looked at the calling number.

It was Harry. He had gotten her message.

She stared at the instrument.

What if Aileen Harris is right and Harry beat her? Harry, did you do that?

Immediately she regretted her doubts.

Damn, I'm betraying his trust. Why should I believe Aileen Harris? She's bitter. Besides, I like him, and he's smart.

While she processed these thoughts, the ringing stopped.

Harry had given up.

She turned back to the data. She had to write new computer programs to do her analyses. She groaned and typed rapidly on the keyboard.

***

In South Carolina, Rob Wilson sighed. What a waste! He had driven the Harris woman for eight hours from Rockville to Myrtle Beach just to babysit. No one cared about her and what she supposedly knew.

Still the pay was good and the condo first rate, and he had stocked the fridge with Coors.

But now he had to return home. His dog, Andy, was missing. He had to find him. It was an all-night drive. It meant deserting the girl, but she did not need him. She was safe, asleep, in the condo. He'd be back tomorrow. He took the elevator to the parking.

A full moon illuminated the motionless cars. His Crown Victoria glistened dimly in the moonlight. He touched the hood and felt the moist film of salt spray. On the beach the moon highlighted white lines of foam that rippled towards the beach to crash on the blanched sand.

Rob hesitated. He had to leave. No one knew or cared that Aileen was in Myrtle Beach. He looked up. All the windows of the condos were dark.

The Vic's motor rumbled smoothly. That reassured him. He'd be back. He would find his dog, and he'd be back. He drove north towards Highway 9 that leads to I-95 North.

***

On the fourth floor of Aileen's condo, a cigarette glowed from a dark north-facing window. The smoker's eyes followed the taillights of Rob's Crown Victoria as they dimmed in the distant darkness. Deft fingers smashed the cigarette into a cup. (There were no ashtrays, the room was non-smoking.) The watcher punched his cell phone."

"Frank, your guy left, just like you said. Harris is alone."

"Good, Tom. Do it!

Tom doused his cigarette. It was 11:00 pm. There was plenty of time. That idiot Wilson would not be back before noon tomorrow. He lay on top of the bed cover and dozed.

***

******

Chapter 8
Thursday, October 19

In Bethesda, Maryland, Rob Wilson was relieved. His dog, Andy, was safe. This morning, the neighbor to whom the dog had been entrusted had answered his doorbell and found Andy tied there with a friendly note from some good Samaritan.

Apart from excessive thirst, Andy was fine.

Rob's cell phone vibrated. Frank Hardy, the boss, was on the line.

"Where are you?"

"I'm in Bethesda."

Frank feigned surprise.

"What the hell are you doing there? Where's the Harris woman?"

"Frank, she's safe, in Myrtle Beach."

Frank smiled to himself. *This is working fine.* He continued his charade.

"Damn it Wilson, you're supposed to watch her!"

"But …"

"Get the hell back there. You'd better pray that she's OK. Call when you're back. Go!"

The line went dead.

***

Frank Hardy called MTS and spoke to Thibault.

"Rob took the bait like we thought. He left Harris alone at Myrtle Beach. I just sent him back there."

"You're sure no one can connect me to this?"

"Damn it, I'm sure. Don't worry."

Frank hung up.

Jane Peterson, who had listened, hung up too. *Thibault, you old fool. This had better work.*

She called Fareed to report the developments.

***

At Myrtle Beach, South Carolina, the ocean sunrise was spectacular. To the East the horizon shone pale blue and green. There were just enough clouds, in thinly scattered layers, to reflect the golden sheen of a sun not yet visible. Away from the horizon a gray darkness ruled.

The sun emerged as a half circle that radiated yellow over the horizon. It shone on the glass windows of the condo. A bright beam pierced the cracked curtains of the dark room. The rays crossed Aileen's eyes and highlighted her loose blonde hair. She stirred, but only to bury her face in the pillow.

Mom, you were right. Harry is dangerous, but I'm safe here. And Mary Catherine is at Aunt Agatha's with you. She's alright.

Her thoughts ceased and she slept.

When she woke up the sun was above the horizon.

Bored, she stepped out onto the fifth floor balcony. A stiff breeze fluttered the discordant wind chimes that hung there. Chilled, she clutched her arms together and tightened her hood, her head completely shielded from the wind.

She looked down, not expecting to see anyone this early on the cold beach. But a family with two small children, well-wrapped, romped on the sand. No one was in the uninviting water. She wondered what Mary Catherine was doing. *Relax Aileen. She's safe at Aunt Agatha's.*

The male parent wore a hooded sweatshirt. He approached her building and skillfully fingered the strings of a black kite that was shaped and toothed like a shark. The ugly kite undulated towards her.

For an instant her eyes met those of the kite-flyer below. Hastily she averted her gaze. *What's the matter with me? Why did I do that?* Then the kite jerked away, seized by a sudden gust.

Aileen stepped back from the rail, and huddled in her chair. She wrapped a towel about her legs and pulled her hood even tighter about her face. She wanted to forget everything, kites, MTS, StatFind and most particularly, Harry.

She shut her eyes. In spite of the chill wind she dozed.

***

Bill Hamm normally arrived at StatFind at 7:00 am. Today was no exception. But today someone was already there.

Jeannine was asleep at her desk, red hair flopped over folded arms resting on piles of papers.

She lifted her head.

"Bill, what are you doing here?"

"I was about to ask you the same thing?"

She moaned. Bill rested his Starbucks cup on her desk.

"You look like you need some coffee. I'll split mine with you."

He poured half his coffee into her empty cup. She picked it up and took a swallow. Her eyes cleared.

"Thanks, Bill. That helps."

"But why were you here all night?"

"I was looking at some of Mandley's data to see if they were fake, but I didn't get anywhere. My ideas didn't pan out."

She shoved a graph at him.

"Look at this graph of Maryland Lottery numbers. The bars are all about the same height. That means that the digits 0, 1, 2, 3, up to 9 occur with the same frequency."

"So the lottery looks honest."

"Right! That's the way it should be in a fair lottery. Otherwise, if some digits occurred more than others, you could bet on numbers with those digits, and win more than lose."

"I got it. The bars on the graph are about the same height. Over time, all the digits from 0 to 9 occurred equally often. That means the Maryland lottery is fair. But what does this have to do with fake data?"

Jeannine swallowed the last of her coffee and handed him a table with numbers.

Repeated Experiment Results			
	Control	Drug A	Drug B
Sept. 4	23,286	85,074	64,132
Sept. 11	23,460	85,419	64,473

"Bill, this table shows the effects of two drugs plus a Control. You can see that Drug A gave better results (higher numbers) than Drug B and both were better than the Control. The experiment was performed twice, on September 4, and again on September 11. The leftmost digits on September 4 (23, 85 and 64) are the same as on September 11. The leftmost digits are repeated. They have scientific meaning."

She took a breath as Bill chimed in.

"So the information is in the two initial digits. The magnitudes 23,000, 85,000 and 64,000 are the same on both dates, so the initial digits (23, 85, and 64) are the same in both. But what about the rightmost digits?"

"The last two (rightmost) digits do not repeat and don't have much experimental information. They are like random."

Her auburn hair flopped on her forehead. She flipped it back, blue eyes scintillating in the light of the lamp.

Bill grinned, but she was all business.

"Stick with me, Bill."

She shoved a paper in front of him. On it was a graph showing the occurrence of the rightmost two digits."

"Look at this graph."

He refocused as she continued.

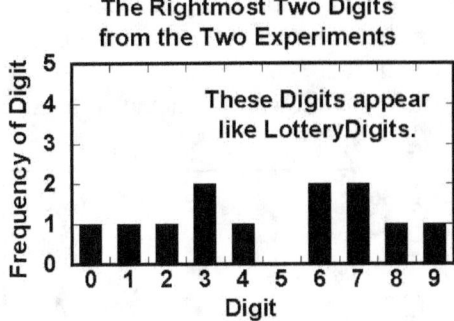

The Rightmost Two Digits from the Two Experiments

"These are the two rightmost digits from both experiments, twelve in all. They don't repeat and they don't mean anything."

"I see they are spread out, like lottery digits and may be random. Where are you going with this?"

"If someone makes up fake data, they make sure that the leftmost (meaningful) digits show what they want them to. Those digits are repeatable. If the cheater tacks on rightmost digits to show that the results vary like real biological data, he or she may unconsciously have favorite digits like 1, 2, 3, or 7. If so, then these digits occur too often and the rightmost digits won't be random."

"Why does this matter?"

"We have a 'He-Said-She-Said' situation. Harry claims that the data for both Patients 27 and 68 are real. Aileen says her Patient 27 data are real, but claims that Harry's data for Patient 68 are fake."

Jeannine sipped her coffee and pushed on.

"The data for Harry's Patient 68 are questioned. Those for Aileen's Patient 27 are not. If Patient 68 has favored rightmost digits, while Patient 27's are lottery-like, then Aileen's accusation would be supported, and merit investigation. But if the digits behaved the same for both patients, and in particular like lottery digits, then Harry would be supported, and Aileen's claim would have less support."

She emptied the cup and sighed.
"But the lottery-digit approach didn't help. I'm stuck."
Bill was ready to leave, but tried one last question.
"How are you stuck?"
She pushed a graph towards him and groaned.

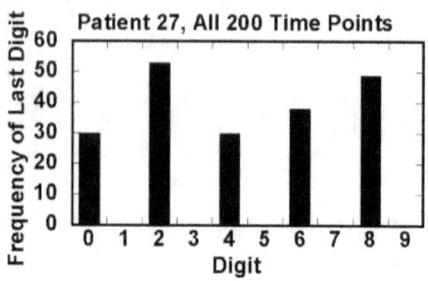

"Look for yourself. This shows the last digit for the Times (in Seconds) for Patient 27. There's not a single odd last digit. All of them are either 0, 2, 4, 6, or 8. No way these are lottery digits. What's going on?"

The question was rhetorical. She did not expect an answer, least of all from Bill.

But he surprised her.
"Jeannine, maybe I can help!"
She gaped and stared.

***

Jeannine continued to stare at Bill. She was never patient with him, but now with no sleep she was exasperated.

"How do you think you can help, Bill?"

"It's a detail I learned in accounting class called 'banker's rounding.' When a number ends exactly in 5, bankers don't want to always round up, or to always round down, so they round to the nearest 'even' number."

He added.

"So 10.5 is rounded down to 10, which is even, and not up to 11, which is odd."

Jeannine saw where he was going. *Maybe he has something.* She jumped in.

"And 11.5 is rounded up to the even number 12, and not down to the odd number 11."

"Right, so the rounded numbers *end* with *even* digits. If the digit *before* the 5 is random, like a lottery digit, then you'll round *up* half the time and *down* the other half. Bankers use this technique to avoid an up or down bias."

"I see that, but for all the 'times' to be even, they all would have to end in 5 *before* rounding. That's not possible here.

Bill shrugged and turned to leave.

Jeannine picked up Mandley's documentation for the chip and thumbed through it.

"Wait, Bill, don't go. Damn it, you're right. It *is* banker's rounding!"

She grabbed his sleeve.

"For a nerve-firing that occurs somewhere between 100 and 101 seconds, the MTS chip guesses the 'time' of the spike as the *midpoint*, that is, 100.5. The chip can only record the times (100, 101 and 100.5) as whole numbers, so the number, 100.5, is rounded so it can be stored. And the times are always one second apart, so the midpoint is always at half a second. It always ends in 0.5."

She continued.

"And it says here that Mandley's chip follows the standard for rounding used by the American National Standards Institute and the Institute of Electrical and Electronic Engineers (ANSII/IEEE Std 854/1987) for integers. That standard is 'banker's' rounding!"

She jumped up.

"All the spike times must be even!"

She threw her arms around him and hugged. Then she waved her arms.

"All the midpoints end in '.5' so when they are banker-rounded an *even* whole number is stored in the chip's memory."

An even bigger hug.

"Bill, you're a genius. The last digits have to be even!"

At that she kissed him on the cheek and drew back.

"Thanks, Bill. I'm not stuck anymore. Now I can prove that Harry's data are OK."

She pushed him out the door and headed for the lady's room.

***

At the condo in Myrtle Beach, Aileen awoke and opened her eyes. The towel had blown from her legs and landed pressed against the railing. She shivered and looked down. The family had left the beach, but they had abandoned the toothed kite. It twisted, flopped, and flapped on the sand, just as a real shark, beached, might thrash about.

She glanced at her watch. It was almost noon. That damn dog! Why am I here? If a lost pet was enough to take Rob away, there couldn't be much danger. Could there?

She stepped in from the balcony, and closed the sliding doors behind her. The condo's décor was exquisite. She flopped into an oversized chair and flipped the hood backwards. Her blonde hair fell free.

The huge TV beckoned, but she resisted. Her laptop was on the table, but she did not want to work. She strapped it into its case. She could not stop thinking. Mrs. Hartman's data were faked while Mr. Peters' data were not. Without successful results for Mrs. Hartman, MTS would not get FDA approval.

Dr. Thibault knew that too.

She thought of the graphs she had produced using Harry's fake data. Jeannine Ryan only had Mrs. Hartman's fake data. And Jeannine believed Harry. There was no hope there.

Yet her mother had said StatFind wanted Aileen protected for a few days. That made no sense at all!

A loud knock on the door of the condo broke into Aileen's musings. *Harry? No. Calm down Aileen? No one knows you're here. Oh! Maybe Rob is back?*

She peered through the peephole. The man wore a hooded sweatshirt. His face was in the shadows. *Who?*

The man mumbled.

"… to fix the toilet …"

Rob's instructions had been clear. *Don't open the door for anyone!*

"Not now. Come back later."

The hooded figure withdrew. Aileen strained to see sideways through the peephole.

She did not hear the slight grating of the sliding doors to the balcony as they opened, nor the soft steps behind her in the hallway.

She felt a heavy hand on her shoulder. She turned to see dark eyes under a dark hood. There was a whiff of chloroform and then all went black.

***

******

Chapter 9
Thursday, October 19

Somewhere in the Carolinas, Aileen's head throbbed. She was no longer in the Myrtle Beach condo, but in a shack with gray planks for walls and no windows. The boards were loosely spaced and she could see through the vertical cracks that the sun was low in the west.

She shivered and sat up.

Where am I? What am I doing here?

She stepped outside. The soil was sandy. A few gray boards lay nearby. She lifted one. A lone black beetle, disturbed, scurried away.

She looked about. The shack was on a small islet surrounded on three sides by a somber swamp whose black water was crowded with cypress and gum trees with swollen bases. Elsewhere there was the open water of a lake whose distant shore was marked by a border of pines and mixed hardwoods. Without a boat, she was trapped.

Whoever had brought her here had left no food or water.

Aileen spotted a worn wooden box nailed to the trunk of a large cypress tree. *Maybe cans are stored there?* Several yards of dark swamp water stretched between her and the tree. She could not judge the depth.

Splash!

She looked sideways to see circular ripples spreading from a point where an object had hit the water. A snout topped by two round orbs broke the surface. Only a frog!

She stepped into the water. Blackened leaves and bubbles swirled to the surface as submerged dead branches cracked and snapped under foot. The water was above her knees before she felt firm bottom. Her right shoe was sucked by the muck, but she eased it free by crimping her foot. She reached the base of the cypress. Now the water only reached her ankles. She balanced herself with one foot on a protruding cypress knee and peered in. The box was empty. *Damn!*

The sound of an outboard motor broke the silence of the swamp. A boat was approaching.

***

At StatFind, Jeannine was exhausted. It was late afternoon and the data for patients 27 and 68 were finally ready for plotting.

OK, Ms. Delusional Aileen Harris, this will settle your wild accusations against Harry!

She made graphs of the terminal digits of the "Time Values" for Patients 27 and 68, four graphs in all.

Aileen claimed Patient 68's data had been faked by Harry, but that Patient 27's data were fine. According to Harry, both patients had good data.

The phone on her desk buzzed. It was Mona Larson.

"Jeannine, It's Dr. Roberts. He wants to know if dinner is on for tonight."

"Mona, tell him I've got a splitting headache. The answer is no, not tonight. If he wants lunch tomorrow, the answer is 'maybe.'"

"Jeannine, why don't you tell him yourself."

"Please, Mona, do that for me, OK?"

"All right honey, if that's what you want."

"Thanks, Mona."

Jeannine turned back to the unquestioned data of Patient 27. She looked at the graph for the last digits from the control times.

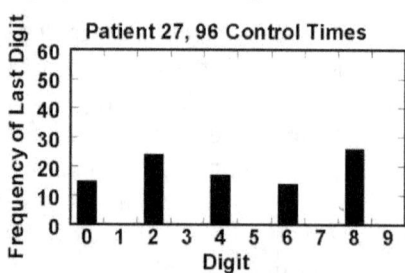

All the digits were even, none were odd.

No last digit could be odd thanks to the banker's rounding forced by the MTS chip. Next Jeannine brought up the graph for the times while the treatment was administered.

As before, there were only even digits.

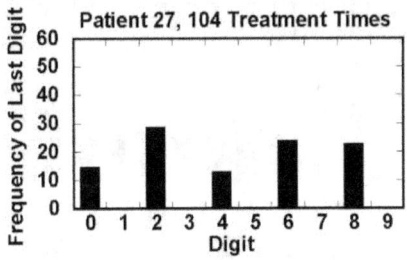

All control and treatment times for Patient 27 ended in even digits. The data were consistent with the chip's rounding.

OK, Jeannine, so far so good.

Now to scuttle Aileen's wrongful accusation against Harry!

She worked fast. She wanted to get this over with.

The graph for Patient 68's control times appeared on the screen.

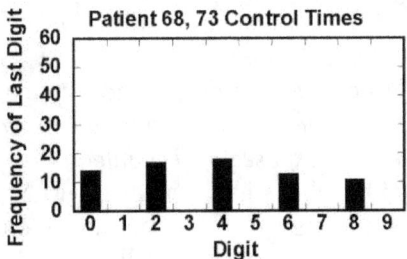

Jeannine smiled. All the control times for Harry's Patient 68 ended in even digits, as required by the chip.

Everything was OK.

Take that, Ms. Harris!

All that remained was to check the last digits for the treatment times of Patient 68. Confident now, she leaned over the keyboard.

She tapped the "Enter" key.

There!
She leaned back as the graph came onto the display.
Oh no! No!

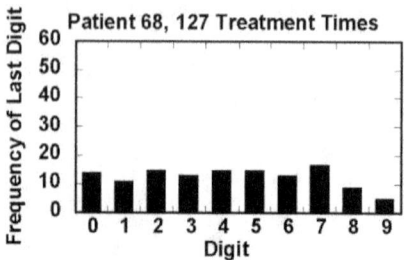

She slumped forward and bit her lip. Many of the treatment times ended in *odd* digits. No way could they be from the experiment. All times from the chip had to be *even*.

Aileen was right. The values for Patient 68 had been faked.

Harry was a cheat!

Frozen, she gaped at the telltale graph.

Could Harry explain this? Impossible! Maybe he did assault Aileen? She's right on the data. Maybe she's right about the beating? And what about the contract with Mandley Bionics for its clinical trial?

Jeannine leaned over her desk, head hanging, hands shaking. *Poor Wayne! Mandley Bionics would dump StatFind when the PMA with MTS was exposed as fraudulent!*

The buzz of the phone interrupted her. Mona again.

"Dr. Roberts wants to know about lunch tomorrow. He can pick you up at noon? What shall I tell him?"

Jeannine set her lips.

"Tell him it's on. I'll be waiting by the door."

Mona exhaled. She was no longer in the middle. She switched back to Harry.

Jeannine left her notes and graphs on the desk.

OK, Harry, I'll hear your side tomorrow, before I talk to Wayne!

With no sleep last night, and what she had found about Harry, she needed to crash.

***

It was late afternoon when Rob returned to the condo in Myrtle Beach. His worst fear was realized. No Aileen!

Her purse was in her bedroom, untouched. The furniture in the living area was not disturbed, but her laptop was gone. The front door lock was intact, but the catch of the sliding door on the balcony was broken.

The balcony was on the fifth floor. As Rob stepped out, wind-chimes jangled lightly in the slight breeze. A Ring-billed Gull floated by, wings motionless, relaxed in the updraft. The afternoon sun was warm and the ocean calm, its white caps small and widely spaced. Below, on the strand, a mother with two small children, lightly clad, ran to and fro, leaning occasionally to pick up shells.

Rob returned his attention to the balcony. He checked the metal railing and found two deep scratches on the black metallic paint. He leaned over. The scratches faced a balcony one floor below. It was offset to the side and had a privacy barrier that shielded any occupants from view. From there it would have been easy for someone not afraid of heights to hook Aileen's railing with a rope and climb up.

"Damn."

He reentered the condo and sat on the wicker couch. He knew he should call his boss, but to what purpose. He would be fired, finished once and for all, and someone else would be dispatched to Myrtle Beach.

And he wouldn't call the police either. Aileen wasn't missing 48 hours yet, but the truth was that he wanted to find her himself and save his job. He needed to look around before calling anyone. He needed to think!

"Brring-ring, brring-ring."

Rob jumped at the ring of his cell phone. He looked. As expected it was the boss. Rob did not answer.

***

Rob's next thought was to check the parking lot. It was off-season for the beach. When he had left the night before, there had been only three other vehicles. The minivan with the palmetto-tree plates was from South Carolina, as was an old Ford Escort that had a "Maid Service" logo on the door. Finally, the red Ford pickup with an extended cab had a North Carolina plate.

This afternoon, only the minivan remained along with his Crown Vic. His guess was that the minivan belonged to the family he had seen upon his arrival with Aileen.

He next checked the condo directly below Aileen's. He knocked loudly. No answer. He knocked again. Still no answer. Rob was ex-FBI and still possessed certain skills. The door's deadbolt was not thrown, and its spring lock yielded easily to his manipulation.

The odor of stale cigarettes filled the unit. In the bedroom, butts were pressed into a kitchen cup. There were no sheets. No one had planned to stay.

Out the window he saw his Crown Vic parked below. From a second window facing north, the highway was visible for more than a mile. His departure had been monitored from here, by someone who was more than a casual smoker.

Rob went down the hall to the living area. The balcony doors were unlatched. He peered around the balcony's privacy wall. There was firm footing for anyone to hook Aileen's railing, and climb up. This condo had been used to watch him, and to snatch Aileen.

***

Rob headed for the beach. He rolled up his pants and strolled barefoot onto a weathered walkway through dunes capped by sea oats. A steady breeze pushed the tufted stems downwards. Near the beach, sand drifted over the rough planks and soothed his bare feet.

Rob was still on the wooden walkway when the young mother with her two children came up from the strand. They stopped to wash their feet under a gray spigot. The little boy was first. As soon as his feet glistened free of sand, he splashed his sister in the face.

"Tommy, stop that! Let her wash too."

Tommy's reply was to splash again, harder.

Rob arrived.

"Tommy, listen to your mother."

The mother, whose name was Mary, eyed Rob warily. She was uncertain how to respond, but Tommy knew. He stopped splashing his sister.

Rob spoke.

"I'm sorry. I didn't mean to interfere. I'm Rob Wilson, on the fifth floor, I can't find my friend. She has blonde hair. Her name is Aileen. Maybe you saw her?"

Mary dried her daughter's feet. She was not sure about this stranger.

"My *husband, Tom,* and I were on the beach this morning, and there was someone on your balcony. She had a hood on. Tom said she was blonde. He was flying a kite."

"Was she there after lunch? Please, it's important."

"I don't think so."

"Maybe your husband saw her."

Mary looked into Rob's eyes. She decided to trust him.

"My husband travels. He's working in North Carolina this week. He left at lunchtime. He wouldn't have seen anything. He left before the kids' naps."

"So the F150 with the extra cab was his truck, the one with the North Carolina plates?"

"That's it, the red one. It's his company's. They're based in Manteo."

"I'm sorry to push, but beside your minivan, were any other cars around?

By this time Tommy was pulling at his sister's hair. Mary grabbed him firmly.

"There was an old blue pickup with rope and junk in the back. It had North Carolina plates too. Some workmen. I met one of them on the elevator. He said he was a plumber. I didn't talk to him. He was spooky."

"Spooky?"

But now Mary was desperate. Tommy tugged at her with all his strength."

"Sorry, I've got to go. I really hope you find your friend."

She was gone before Rob could react.

***

As Mary Dean returned to her condo, her thoughts were of what Rob had told her.

She grabbed Tommy by the wrist, marched him to his room and shut the door. Then she carried Annie, the recipient of Tommy's splashes, to her room.

Now she could think.

Rob Wilson disturbed her. Rather, what Rob had told her about "Aileen" disturbed her.

Was Tom, her husband, up to his old tricks? He had focused on Aileen's balcony from the moment they had hit the beach. And he had flown the kite near her balcony on purpose. Why?

He had referred to Aileen as "that blond," but her hair had been completely covered by that hood. How could he know she was blond? The girl on the balcony, if she was Aileen, had been asleep most of the time. Her hair never had been exposed.

Moreover, Mary had spied Tom talking to that spooky "plumber." Tom and the plumber had exchanged something. What was that about?

Am I imagining all this? Maybe this Aileen, or whoever, is not really missing? Tom promised me he would change. Why should I believe that guy Rob?

But she did believe Rob, and her worries would not go away. She could not rest.

She turned on the TV softly so as to not wake the children. She knew Tom was involved in Aileen's disappearance?

Tom, now what have you done? God help me!

***

The small outboard sputtered to a stop near Aileen's shack. The flat-bottomed aluminum boat scraped the shallow vegetation until firmer soil held it fast. There were two men in the boat. The white-haired man spoke first.

"Damn, Jack. Why did you stop me this afternoon. We could be done with her."

Jack, clad in a checkered flannel shirt, jeans and folded-down hip boots, shrugged and stepped onto land. He pulled the boat a few feet drier.

"You're too old pops. That's a fine looking woman we left here. She's not going nowhere with water moccasins and gators in that swamp. Another day won't matter."

Pops snorted, but Jack kept on.

"I figure she needs company, and it ain't rape when she asks for it."

"Damn it to hell, Jack. Leave her alone. I'll make her disappear, and we'll be done. You screw her and you might screw us all."

"Hell Pops. Look at that old shack. She's looking at us now right through the cracks in the shack. She's saying to herself, 'who's that handsome guy with the flannel shirt, and who's that ugly old man with the white hair?'"

Jack grinned.

"That's you Pops. She's got you pegged now. You got nothing to lose. You may as well have fun after me."

In response, Pops glanced sideways at the cabin and frowned.

"That shack is awful quiet. Nothing's moving over there."

At Pops' words, Jack stopped grinning. He dashed to the shack and pulled at the half-slung door. The remaining hinge sprang loose. The door fell outwards and grazed his thigh. Jack did not notice. He stared.

"Pops, she's gone!"

***

Pops reached for his shotgun, a 12-gauge, and scanned the islet.

At the edge of the swamp he found a water-filled footprint. He rubbed white whiskers.

"Over here Jack. She went into the swamp. Hell, she's not going nowhere."

Pops studied the black waters in which cypress and gum trees stood somber and silent.

The silence was broken by two loud splashes.

"Pops, over there. That's her!"

"Jack, you spooked two frogs from the bank. Don't you know frogs yet."

The sun was gone, and shadows obscured the water's surface. Pops pulled a flashlight from his jeans and shone it in the direction of the splashes. Sure enough, two pairs of bulbous eyes reflected brightly in the beam.

"There, you see, Jack, plain old green frogs."

Pops pointed his beam at a tall cypress. A gray box was attached to the trunk.

"Hey Jack, that old wood duck nest box is still there."

"Pops, she must be near here."

Pops knelt down.

"Look, Jack. That cypress knee is scraped. She went that way. But it's getting dark. She's stuck in the swamp tonight, maybe forever. We can't do anything in the dark. Let's go."

Pops winked at the younger man. With a wave of his hand, he signaled Jack to go the boat, start the motor, and put away from land.

For his part, Pops squatted silently at the edge of the dark swamp and listened.

***

Aileen huddled knee-deep behind the cypress trunk. The thought of that animal, Jack, made her shudder. He was worse than Harry!

She shivered, but determined not to move until the sound of the motor disappeared. Sure enough, the staccato putt-putt of the small outboard faded away. She rubbed her legs to stand up.

Pops heard the movement. He rubbed the butt of the shotgun and waited. His finger felt for the trigger. He pointed the 12-gauge at the cypress trunk.

***

Quietly, Jack paddled the flat-bottomed boat back towards the islet. He could barely make out the outline of the old shack in the dim moonlight. He could not see Pops. The boat rocked gently in the open water. The gentle slap-slap of the water on the bottom of the boat lulled his senses. His eyes started to close.

"Brroom!"

The shotgun blast reverberated over the lake. Jack jumped up. The boat rocked. Startled Night Herons took wing. Their rustling and flapping produced an eerie murmur.

The boat stabilized. Jack cried out.

"Pops, what was that? Was it her!"

"Over here! I thought something moved behind the tree. It must have been one of those Night Herons. I'm losing my touch."

Pops stood and approached the bank. He waved his light.

"Hell! Let's go. Get over here and pick me up. It's got way too dark. We'll come back tomorrow. That girl ain't going nowhere in that muck."

***

Aileen was soaked to the thighs. She waited until the sound of the motor disappeared. She had to get dry, but the islet was not safe. Whoever they were, they would be back.

She turned and waded deeper into the dark swamp. In a triangle formed by three large trees she found elevated ground. She removed her jeans, wringing them out as best she could. Her sweatshirt was mostly dry. She leaned against a gum tree and wrapped her knees in her arms. She shut her eyes. *Mary Catherine, Honey, I love you.*

She shivered in the shadows.

***

******

Chapter 10
Friday, October 20

At last the rays of the morning sun penetrated to the floor of the swamp forest. Aileen started up suddenly. The sun's warmth, though filtered by dense branches of cypress and gum trees, still encouraged her.

She stood up. Branches snapped behind her. She turned in time to glimpse a large brown form with a waving white tail disappear among the low-growing leaves and branches. It was a deer, a White-tail, startled by the sudden motion.

Aileen was no ecologist, but she knew that deer preferred dry ground over the swamp water. She marked the direction in which the deer had disappeared. There, low brushy vegetation signaled that enough light reached the ground to sustain growth.

A wide stretch of water separated her from the point where the deer had disappeared.

OK, Aileen how to cross this?

She looked back from where she had come. There, protruding branches and sticks, along with emergent cypress knees indicated relatively shallow water, up to her knees at most. In contrast, to reach where the deer had been she would have to cross water whose surface was smooth and uninterrupted by protrusions. That water was deep.

The sun was higher and the air warmer. Aileen picked up her jeans. They were nearly dry. She rolled them up and lifted them above her head. Carefully she entered the black water. Despite her caution, she immediately found herself thigh deep.

She was about to give up and retreat, when a familiar sound echoed through the swamp.

"Putt-putt-putt. Putt-putt-putt."

That sound convinced her. Jack's outboard was returning as promised. She set her lips and pushed forward.

The water reached her thighs, but no higher.

The putt-putt was louder. She held her jeans above her head and stepped forward. She slipped deeper. The water lapped her waist. With one hand she desperately tugged her sweatshirt above her breasts and held her jeans high with the other. *It's too deep!* She hesitated.

The putt-putt of the motor stopped. Jack and Pops were back!

Through the trees she heard shouting. She could not distinguish the words.

From the opposite bank, a sinuous something slid into the water. A stout-bodied brown form undulated towards her. She froze. She had never seen a water moccasin, but this must be one. Behind her she heard splashes and sloshing steps.

"Come on Jack. She went this away!"

The voice was Pops'.

Aileen, waist deep, poked the rolled-up jeans at the snake in front of her. To her relief, it swung wide and headed for the knoll she had left.

Pops' voice was louder now.

"Damn it, Jack, that's a gator over there. Come this way. Follow me. She can't be far."

Aileen struggled the remaining distance. She sank to her shoulders. Still, she held the jeans high and dry. Would the next step be over her head? She stepped right and stumbled forward. Her feet felt bottom. No deeper!

She pushed forward again. Success, a step up! She stood only thigh deep.

Two final steps and she reached the dry bank. Exhausted, she slid behind and under vine-covered bushes by a small evergreen, a holly tree.

The sharp holly leaves and thorny green-stemmed vines mercilessly scratched bare legs and thighs as she pressed her body against the ground.

Just in time!

Across the way stood Pops, staring, shotgun in hand.

***

Pops examined the ground where Aileen had spent the night.

"Over here, Jack. She was here for sure."

He scanned the bushes across the way. Aileen pushed closer to the ground.

Pops lifted the gun to his shoulder and fired.

"Brroom!"

The leaves and branches above and to the right of Aileen cracked and rattled as the shot scattered and bit through the holly branches. She pressed further down despite the thorns and sharp-tipped leaves that pressed back.

She heard Jack.

"Why'd you do that Pops?"

"Shut up Jack."

Pops lifted the gun to his shoulder and fired again.

"Brroom!"

This time the shot rattled the branches on the ground to Aileen's left. A mini cloud of brittle leaves, dirt and twigs peppered her side. Still none of the buckshot struck her. She stifled a yell

"Pops! What are you shooting at?"

"Jack, don't you see where we are. This here's that big gator hole. I ain't crossing it, so I blew away the bushes. If she's over there, she'd hollered or jumped. Those were buck shot loads."

Aileen shuddered at those words. Jack responded.

"But Pops, she's a city girl, she don't know about gators. She might have crossed."

Pops laughed.

"Maybe she don't know gators, but I do. I lost my hound, Jerry, to a big gator in this hole two years ago. If you want to go across Jack, go ahead. I'm staying here. Besides, look there, by your foot."

At the edge of the knoll, a sluggish brownish coil unwound itself and opened a fanged white mouth that gaped at Jack. He jumped back.

"Pops, a cotton mouth. Shoot it!"

"Leave it alone. I ain't wasting no more shells this trip. Stomp it if you want."

Jack backed away further. His boots were going nowhere near that snake!

Pops took one more look across the "gator hole" and shrugged.

"I'm going back. She may be alive now, but she'll never get out of this swamp. She's done for. Our job's done. Are you coming?"

Jack took another look at the cotton mouth still coiled defensively only a few feet away. The snake's scales, wet from its swim, shone brightly. The snake did not budge. Jack decided to retreat.

"Pops wait. I'm coming!"

Sloshing steps splashed in the direction of the shack. Aileen listened until the sounds ceased. She held her breath and remained motionless. Only when she heard the putt-putt-putt of the outboard, did she breathe freely.

***

The sound of the outboard was no longer audible, but Aileen waited. Exhausted, she lay on her back. Above her the blue sky shone through the stark branches.

Jack and Pops no longer trailed her, but she was soaked and weak, and her scratched and bleeding legs itched unbearably. She stretched them in front of her to rub them dry as best she could.

She stood up, pulled her jeans on, and wrung out her sweatshirt. It was damp and clammy against her skin.

She bent over to catch her breath. A fortunate move. From her low vantage, she saw that the brush was separated as if repeatedly worn aside by passing bodies. The white-tail must have gone that way.

Aileen had discovered her first deer trail. It followed a ridge pressed in on either side by dark swamp waters. She took heart. Surely the deer knew its way out of the swamp!

She stumbled along shielding her face from stiff branches and thorny Smilax.

Hang on Mary Catherine, Mommy's coming home!

***

Aileen forged ahead as dark swamp water seeped onto the trail. The ground was soft, and brown water oozed into the impressions left by her steps.

She could no longer see clearly. She stumbled on.

"Squish, squish, squish."

The sounds were her own footsteps. Ahead the trail disappeared beneath deep waters where large bald cypress and tupelo gum trees allowed only scattered cones of twilight to reach the dark still surface.

There was no movement, only silence. The humid air was heavy and oppressive.

This was a dead end.

There was no more trail.

Mary Cath .... Aileen slumped to the ground.

***

In Rockville, Jeannine took her seat and clicked the seat belt. Last week she had been suitably impressed by the luxurious interior of Harry's E-Class Mercedes. Today however, the elegant leather seats and walnut burl panels had no appeal.

Harry drove with eyes fixed straight ahead. He doubted Jeannine's reason for her earlier cancellation, and was disturbed by her delay in accepting lunch today. He did not like being "put off" by any woman, including Jeannine. But he kept silence. He needed information before revealing his irritation.

Jeannine sensed his discomfort. She spoke.

"Harry, why did you do it? What happened? What reason could you have for doing this?"

"Doing what? What are you talking about?"

"I think you know. Don't lie to me. I trusted you. I mean Mrs. Hartman!"

"Mrs. Who?"

"Mrs. Hartman, Patient 68. You know what you did."

If only Harry would freely confide in her, he might have a plausible reason for his actions.

"What do you say I did?"

He's not going to tell me anything.

"I say you faked the data for Mrs. Hartman. I say the data you gave Aileen Harris were fabricated. You made up the record for the time Mrs. Hartman was on medication."

Harry winced. *How does she know I faked the medication data but not the control data?*

"Did Aileen tell you that?"

"She said the data for Mrs. Hartman were fake."

Harry contrived a smile.

"And you believe her instead of me? Is that all I mean to you?"

It was Jeannine's turn to wince. *Jeannine, you've been really stupid about this guy!*

"Aileen can jump in the lake. It's not about her. I know you faked the data and I can prove it! Damn it Harry, I liked you!"

Harry blanched. *How can she be sure?*

"And I like you. And you can still like me."

"Then tell me why you did it! Maybe you had a reason?"

That gave Harry hope. Maybe he could lie his way out of this.

"Look, the restaurant's just ahead. Let's eat, and I'll tell you everything. Briefly, it's not me. It's Dr. Thibault. He's the one."

Jeannine gamely clung to the hope that Harry somehow was OK.

He parked. In silence, they went into the restaurant.

***

The meal matched the mood. The wine was acidic, the tortellini was cold and the waiter was brusque.

Jeannine sat stonily as Harry tried to exonerate himself and implicate Thibault.

Harry was puzzled. Mrs. Hartman's real data had been destroyed. Lacking those, Aileen could not prove that he had faked data. *But even Aileen didn't know that only the medication data were faked. How did Jeannine know that?*

Jeannine gave up.

"Harry, you're not telling the truth. I'm leaving."

"No, wait. Please."

She rose. Harry caught his breath.

"What does Wayne say about this? Or Bill Hamm?"

"I haven't told them yet. Dumb me, I wanted to give you a chance to explain. I thought I owed you that much. But I don't like being lied to! I was a fool. We're done here!"

She spun from the table leaving Harry to pay the bill.

***

Harry pulled out his cell phone.

His first call was to Dr. Thibault at MTS.

His second call was to Wayne Johnson at StatFind.

"Wayne, it's Harry Roberts with MTS. I want to alert you. Dr. Thibault is upset. He has a problem with Jeannine. He says Mandley must trust its contractors and that trust must be reciprocated. He says Dr. Ryan does not want to honor that trust."

Harry paused.

"This is serious. I think Dr. Thibault is going to tell Mandley Bionics not to finalize the contract with StatFind. He wants you to you call him right away. You'd better do that."

On the receiving end, a stunned Wayne listened in amazement.

***

Dr. Thibault swiveled his chair to the side. Damn Harry. What a screw up. And how was that Ryan woman sure about the fake data? She did not believe Aileen before. What changed her mind?

He swiveled forwards and slammed his desk.

This is bad! Ryan will go straight to the FDA, whether or not Wayne fires her.

Jane Peterson was at lunch so calls were routed to Thibault's desk. He saw the light blink on Line 1. *It's Wayne at StatFind. He'll have to wait.* He pushed "hold."

Dr. Thibault picked up an open line.

"Frank, we've got an emergency here. Listen carefully ... Right. ... Yes, she took a cab. ... No, Harry told me. ... He's still at the restaurant. ... You can still catch her. ... Right. ... I don't give a damn how. ... Ryan is more dangerous than Aileen Harris. ... Get on it!"

With that conversation over, Dr. Thibault loosened his collar and composed himself. The light on Line 1 was steady. Wayne Johnson was still on hold.

Dr. Thibault picked up.

"Wayne! Thanks for calling. Listen, we need to talk about the contract."

***

In the swamp in Carolina, an exhausted Aileen lay half conscious as the muscles of her calves contracted, quivered, and ceased movement.

She was in her jeans lying on the beach, looking up at the condo. Mary Catherine was with her! No honey, you can't go in the water. It's too cold.

Then Mary Catherine was gone! Oh no! Who's that over there? It's Harry! Go away!

She shut her eyes. When she opened them she was alone on the sand. She looked at her feet. Water swept over them, a wave. Oh no! I'm all wet! Why didn't I move away?

She awoke. There was no beach.

She was surrounded by swamp. Water had oozed over the trail and she was wet.

OK, Aileen, what now?

She shook her head clear and stood on shaky knees. She regrouped.

OK, the deer trail led this way, and I don't think the deer crossed that water ahead. If not here, where? It must have found another way.

Right or not, she retraced her steps. She saw the impression of twin hooves in the soft earth. They pointed outwards from one side of the trail. There the water's surface was broken by emergent twigs and branches. It was not deep.

She stepped out. Bubbles rose from under dead leaves, but her foot met firm resistance at ankle depth. She waded on, balancing on dead branches that cracked and split under her weight. Still ankle deep. She sloshed on. At last, she stepped out onto a dry knoll.

There in the soft earth, was another familiar split-hoof print. With renewed confidence she pressed ahead.

***

In Rockville, Jeannine stepped out of the cab. She had to talk to Wayne right away. Wayne needed to know. *Damn it Harry. I thought I liked you. Jeannine, you are a dunce. You sure can pick them.* She tipped the driver.

A gentleman stood by the building's entrance. He blocked her path.

"Dr. Ryan?"

"Yes."

"A Dr. Monique Martin asked me to reach you. There's been an accident."

"What? Who?"

"It's little Jeannie. She's at the hospital. I've got the number on my cell. My phone's in my car over there. Monique wants you to call right away."

Jeannine looked. The car had Virginia plates.

She did not think. She followed the stranger.

He opened the back door. She leaned in.

***

85

******

Chapter 11
Friday, October 20

At StatFind, Bill Hamm had never seen Wayne so distraught.

"Wayne, what's the matter? What's wrong?"

Wayne stared at the wall. He could not face Bill.

"It's the Manley contract."

"That's settled. I talked to their finance guy yesterday."

"Well that was yesterday. Today they've got a problem. I mean we've got a problem."

"Well?"

"They won't work with Jeannine. They want us to get rid of her."

"You can't do that."

"I know, but it's Jeannine or the Bionics contract. Hell we've just leased all that new space. We'll go bust."

"I don't get it, Wayne. Did they say why?"

"Something about Jeannine not trusting Dr. Thibault, and not trusting Harry, or the experiments in the PMA. They've had it."

"That's a switch. Yesterday they loved her!"

"Well not today they don't."

Bill Hamm sat down.

"What are you going to do?"

"What can I do. We expanded for that contract. We need it to survive."

Bill slammed his fist on the desk.

"You've got to hear Jeannine's side! I talked to her. She thought their data might be faked."

He stared at Wayne.

"You've got to talk to her. She deserves that much."

Wayne blanched.

"I want to, Bill, but where is she? She was supposed to be back two hours ago!"

***

In North Carolina, the two pickup trucks were an incongruous pair. The recently-washed red F150 outshone the battered blue Ranger.

Both were parked on the edge of a dirt road whose sandy shoulder was dry and firm. There was no danger of getting stuck, but the sharp drop through weeds and brush to the dark waters of the Alligator River posed a distinct hazard.

The occupant of the F150 stepped out first. His face flushed.

"Pops, what the hell do you mean, 'you don't know where she is?'"

"Mr. Smith, she's in the swamp. She's going nowhere. She's done for."

"Mr. Smith" was not placated.

"Get the hell back there and finish the job. You want your money? Then go back and bring me a damned photo of the body. Damn you. Can't you do anything right?"

Pops shrugged.

"OK. But about my money?"

"You'll get yours when I get mine. Get me the damn photo. The boss needs proof."

Pops started to reply but thought better of it. He mounted the cab of the blue ranger and left, its rear end rattling.

The F150 was pointed in the opposite direction, towards North Carolina Highway 64. "Mr. Smith" (Tom Dean) stood by the door and punched his phone. At the beep, he left a message.

"Mary, I'm still in Manteo, I'll try to get back to Myrtle Beach in a couple of days. I'll call you tomorrow."

A lie, he was not in Manteo!

His next call was to Frank Hardy. Another beep, another message.

"Frank, we have a problem. I may fix it myself. Call me back."

Tom reached into his camouflage pants and produced a 9 mm Beretta "Storm" pistol. He hefted it. Satisfied, he slipped it back. A glance behind him confirmed that his pump-action Browning "Stalker" 12 gauge shotgun was in the rack.

He was ready for what he had to do.

He wheeled the F150 about and headed after Pops.

***

The swamp trail was dry underfoot, but Aileen, on shaking knees, was unaware of that detail. Mechanically, she stumbled along. All sense of direction was gone. Only the thought of her daughter pushed her onwards.

She slipped on a pine cone. Smooth pine needles matted the trail. *Have to see Mary Catherine.* Dullness set in. *Move leg. OK, Move other leg. Move leg again, I'm coming, ... Move leg, Move other!*

Somehow she kept on.

Finally, her muscles refused all commands to contract. Her steps stopped altogether. *Mary Cather... .* All went black and she collapsed. Her body pitched forward onto the dry sandy earth.

She did not hear the wind-rustled Loblolly pines that shaded the trail. Nor did she see through a border of those same pines, the russet field of broom grass that shone in the afternoon sun.

She did not know it, but she was out of the swamp!

***

In Myrtle Beach, the late afternoon sun warmed the condo. Mary Dean listened to her husband's message. From the bedroom she could hear little Tommy stirring. Naptime was over. She had time for one call. She reached her husband.

"Tom, where are you?"

"Didn't you get my message?"

"Yes, but where are you now?"

"In the truck, not far from the Alligator River. What's up?"

"There was a man here today. His name is Wilson. He's looking for the girl that was on the fifth floor. You said she was a blonde."

"So?"

"Well, tell me how you knew her."

"Mary, we've been through this. I'm not messing around. There's no cause to be jealous."

89

"Tom, that girl's missing. What do you know about it."

"Nothing. I told you."

"Then what were you doing talking to that 'plumber' in the blue Ranger."

"Mary, now you're imagining things. What blue Ranger? When?"

"I saw you through the blinds. You didn't know I was awake."

"OK, so I gave some guy directions. So what! Mary, I've got to go. I'm busy."

"No Tom. You handed him something. You knew him."

"Mary, I don't have time for this."

"Click."

Mary stood staring at the phone.

***

Tom Dean grimaced. He was glad to end his wife's call. He had caught up with Pops.

He slowed down. He did not want Pops to spot him. He kept his distance from the truck.

Tom felt for the Beretta in his pocket. He was mad. Pops had let him down.

Maybe Aileen was dead, and maybe not, but Pops was sloppy. Aileen may have seen Pops' face. If she was still alive, she might be able to identify Pops. But there was no way Aileen could know about Tom. Only Pops could ID "Mr. Smith," or maybe that dumb ass nephew of his? No, the nephew had never seen "Mr. Smith." Pops was the only link between Aileen and Tom.

All right Pops, maybe she's dead and maybe not? Either way, you are my problem now.

The narrow road was lined on both sides by tall pines. Ahead, Pops' blue pickup turned onto a fire lane, a two-rut road that disappeared in the shadows of the woods.

Tom slowed and took the same turn off.

***

90

Pops wasn't stupid. The moment he saw the F150 in the rear mirror, he had guessed "Mr. Smith's" intentions. *Wants all that money for himself does he? Nobody stiffs Pops. I wasn't born yesterday.*

In only minutes, he had made his decision to take the old fire lane towards Alligator Swamp.

Now his pickup rattled and vibrated on the scalloped ruts raising a trail of cloudy dust behind it. His destination was an old live oak that marked the shack of a former share-cropper.

He turned off the road to park behind the roofless ruin. An adjacent growth of blackberry bushes concealed the Ranger.

The dust had just settled on the roadway when the shiny F150 drove past the oak tree.

Pops held his shotgun and crouched behind the oak. His ambush was ready. The road dead-ended in the swamp and Mr. Smith would have to come back this way. Pops would blast him through the driver's window. *Mr. Smith, I'm not so easy to kill.*

The late afternoon sun threw shadows sidewise from the branches of the old oak tree. The only sounds were faint swishes of wind through the surrounding trees.

Pops waited.

***

Seconds after passing the large oak, Tom Dean realized that he had missed his prey. The blue ranger was not in sight, and the ruts in the road ahead were filled with brown swamp water. Ahead was only swamp. Pops must have turned off, and the only place for that was by the dilapidated shack he had just passed.

Tom stopped.

Pops must have spotted him.

There were two possibilities. Either Pops had fled after Tom had passed and was gone, or Pops was waiting to ambush Tom on his return.

Looking ahead, the loblolly pines gave way to a mixture of hardwoods and vine-covered thickets. Further along, brown swamp water covered the roadway making it impassable.

Looking back towards the old shack, the pines thinned to reveal a large area of broom grass, a one-time cotton field used by the share-cropper.

Tom laughed. *Nice try, Pops, you swamp devil, but not good enough!*

Shotgun in hand, Tom maneuvered around the edge of the field and approached the gray shack from the rear. He pushed through spiny blackberry stems that pulled and tore at his camouflage pants.

There was the blue Ranger, and there, hunched behind the oak tree, was Pops!

***

Tom pumped the shotgun and raised it to his shoulder.

At the scratchy sound of the pump action, Pops turned. He was licked. He threw his double-barreled on the ground and grinned.

"OK, Mr. Smith. You got me. You win. I wasn't going to do anything. I was just waiting for you to leave. That's all."

Pops held his hands apart in a gesture of openness.

"You old bastard. You were going to shoot me."

"No. No, you got it wrong. I was scared that's all. I thought you were after me."

It was Tom's turn to smile. *You're right, I was.* His finger squeezed tightly on the trigger.

Pops sensed the taughtness of that finger.

"Wait. Wait. We can still find the girl. There's only one way out of that swamp without drowning, or feeding a gator. That way is right up ahead. If she made it out, she'll be around here."

"Pops you're a liar."

"No look. Come with me. We'll check. The trail's just ahead. Follow me."

Tom Dean motioned Pops away from the oak. He drew his Beretta from his pocket and thumbed the safety off. With his free hand, he broke open Pops shotgun and shook the shells from the double barrel. He tossed the empty weapon into the tall grass.

He waved the Berretta at Pops and retrieved his own shotgun.

"OK, Old Man. You've got one last chance. Either we find her, or you're done."

He motioned Pops down the road ahead of him.

***

Aileen's swollen left eye was half closed and both face and arms were scratched and bleeding. Her legs ached and her right arm was numb. She struggled to think. *Where?* Then she remembered. *The swamp? Where's the water? What?*

Through hazy eyes she saw two men coming towards her. *Oh no! Not again! Help!* She gathered her strength and dragged herself, half-rolling, behind a thick tangle of blackberry bushes. She peered through the thorny stems.

She knew the first man immediately. *It's Pops. Did he see me?* She flattened her bruised body down against the brambles.

Pops shuffled by, unseeing.

She did not know the second man. He had a handgun in one hand and cradled a shotgun in the other elbow. *Maybe he's the police?* One glance at those expressionless eyes told her "no."

She knew those eyes. *The kite flyer at the beach!* Horrified, she saw the man casually point his handgun.

"Pops, look back here!"

Pops turned. Aileen could not look. She shut her eyes

"Crack! Crack!"

Aileen opened her eyes to see Pops on the ground, chest heaving.

The man collected two empty casings from the roadway. He studied Pops. Two crows high in a Loblolly Pine, cawed and chattered disturbed warnings.

Pops tried to lift his head. His eyes roved wildly from left to right and back.

"Crack!"

93

Pops' chest flattened, flexed upwards, and fell still. The crows overhead fled their perch. Their caws reverberated through the still pines.

The shooter picked up the last casing.

Suddenly, he turned. His eyes probed the tangle of blackberry bushes.

Aileen shuddered.

My God! He's looking for me!

***

Tom Dean took a step towards the blackberry brambles when his cell phone vibrated. He stopped.

Frank Hardy spoke.

"I got your message. What's the problem?"

"Nothing now. Our man screwed up. I fixed it."

"Good, because I've got another delivery for you."

Tom snarled.

"Forget it."

"I'll pay you double, in advance."

"You haven't paid me for the first one yet."

"That too! My man will have it all for you. Meet him tomorrow, at our spot 'Under the Bridge.'"

"Why 'Under the Bridge!' That's stupid."

"Just do it. He'll have your money. All of it. And don't bother me with details. I don't know anything and I don't want to know. Just be there!"

Frank hung up.

***

******

Chapter 12
Saturday, October 21

It was a typical beach scenario. After several days of fun, Mary Dean had laundry to wash; sandy towels, sandy shorts, sandy jeans and sandy pullovers. She stepped onto the balcony to shake the pullovers free of sand.

As she shook Tom's, a piece of paper fell and landed at her feet.

On the paper was a name plus a phone number.

She started the washer. Tommy and Annie were still asleep and all was quiet. The only sound was the muted rumble-rumble of the wash.

The quiet was interrupted by a loud knock.

Outside stood Rob Wilson. His hair was awry and he needed a shave.

"Mrs. Dean, can I speak to you?"

"The children are sleeping."

"I won't be long."

"What do you want?"

"It's the blue pickup. The one that was here. They bought gas at the BP station down the road. I got their plate number."

"So?"

"So, I am hoping you can help me. Didn't you say your husband's company was based in Dare County, in Manteo, and that the red F150 was the company's?"

Mary emptied the washer. She stuffed the load in the dryer.

"That's right."

"Well the blue pickup is registered to a Dare County address. Is there a chance your husband knew the driver?"

Mary turned from the washer and faced Rob. She studied his eyes. He appeared sincere.

"He said he didn't."

"You mean you asked him! When did you do that?"

"After I talked to you. I didn't tell you, but I saw him talking to someone by the blue truck. I wanted to ask him first."

Mary took over.

"Now, I have a question for you. This girl Aileen is a blonde right?"

Rob nodded.

"Is she pretty?"

"Very! She's like, you know, a 'Ten.'"

Mary fell silent. *Damn you Tom, I won't go through this again. You promised me!* She had one more question.

"Is Aileen's name 'Harris.'"

"Yes."

Tom, how could you? To hell with it. Mary literally threw the paper at Rob.

"I found this in my husband's pullover."

Rob saw the name "Harris," on the paper.

Worse, he knew the phone number written next to that name. *Damn!*

It belonged to his boss, Frank Hardy!

***

Rob Wilson had been a crackerjack FBI field agent. He had started young and retired young, after his twenty years. At the time of Rob's retirement, friends outside of law enforcement told him that he should trust people, that his FBI experience and training had hardened him against his fellow human beings.

Rob made a conscious effort to be more "gullible," particularly where his boss, Frank Hardy, was concerned. Frank had dealt with the same "dirt bag" types as Rob, but had a higher opinion of human nature than Rob. At least he seemed to.

Trusting Frank had been easy. Rob simply did not care. Being a private investigator was boring, but Rob needed the money.

First, Aileen's disappearance had made Rob doubt Frank's judgment. Now, the phone number on Dean's paper shocked him. Frank was a rat. He had used Rob.

And Mary Dean's "dirt bag" of a husband was no better! Rob looked at Mary. She was attractive, and evidently honest, but Tom?

Some guys have all the luck and don't appreciate what they have!

Mary was unaware of his thoughts.

"Mrs. Dean, is there ... ? Is there anything I can do?"

She made her decision and acted.

"There might be. I need to talk to my husband. I have to go to Manteo. If you want to come along, I could use the company. The children will stay with a friend."

She turned away and called.

"Tommy, wake up. Mommy has to go somewhere. You and Annie are going to have fun at 'Miss Betsy's' house. You'll sleep with her tonight."

A quick trip to the dryer, and pajamas and jeans were stuffed into an overnight bag. By the time little Annie, rubbing her eyes, emerged from her room, Mary had fixed her makeup.

***

From North Myrtle Beach to Manteo was a solid six hour drive. It would be late afternoon before their arrival.

Mary agreed to let Rob drive his car. She sat in the passenger seat.

The Crown Vic rolled smoothly north. Rob knew that his Maryland concealed weapon permit was not valid in North Carolina. Still, he kept the revolver in his jacket.

Mary's thoughts were only of Tom.

They drove in silence.

***

At Pop's house, Jack strode to the kitchen window and looked out. *Pops, where are you?*

Pops had not come home last night.

He wasn't on the lake. The flat-bottomed aluminum boat sat marooned on the trailer near the driveway. And the blue Ranger was gone. Only Jack's car remained, parked next to the shell of an old Ford Maverick and the rusted John Deere.

Jack glared at the phone, but that instrument was not intimidated, it stayed silent. *Pops, why don't you call?*

Yesterday, Pops had gone to collect their money from "Mr. Smith." Pops had taken the beat-up blue ranger, and the old double barreled 12 gauge. Jack didn't know "Mr. Smith," but he knew that fancy red truck of his.

Maybe Pops had taken the money and gone drinking. *Out all night, where's my share?*

He took his coffee and stared out the window. *Where are you Pops?*

***

Tom Dean awoke sexually spent, but refreshed. This was Manteo. He could relax in his apartment. Back home in Dillon, South Carolina, there were always the kids, and Mary's nagging. Here there were no kids, no wife, and no nagging. *Tom, why don't you spend more time with us? We're your family! Shut up, Mary!*

Mary had insisted on the vacation at Myrtle Beach. He had agreed, but only because Frank had arranged for Aileen and that dumb ass Rob to be there.

The plan was for Aileen to disappear. Single girls at Myrtle Beach were there for a good time. They weren't "missing," they were "hopping about," having fun somewhere else.

And no one would connect a "missing" girl from Myrtle Beach with far-away sleepy Manteo.

Lise's voice broke into his thoughts. She was a slim blond, not much over eighteen, still featuring her summer tan.

"Tommy, I have to go to work now. Should I come by tonight?"

"Not tonight. I have to call my wife soon and take care of some business. Are all your things out the bathroom?"

Lise stopped at the bedroom door.

"Yes, sure. But what are you afraid of? She's in South Carolina isn't she."

"Don't smart-mouth me. Go!"

Lise left.

Tom smiled at his cleverness. Pops' body would never be found!

He shaved and dressed. He had to pick up Frank's second delivery, "Under the Bridge."

***

Elsewhere, Jeannine awoke to a throbbing head. She had lost all track of time. She was in a van with bare walls and no windows.

The van's tires clapped rhythmically on the concrete slabs of the roadway. The speed, plus the concrete surface, told her she was on an interstate.

Jeannine's ankles and wrists were wrapped with duct tape. A strip over her mouth ensured her silence.

She twisted and pulled at the tape about her wrists.

***

Rob Wilson and Mary Dean reached the Manteo dealership at closing. A blonde girl behind the counter looked up as they came through the door.

Mary spoke.

"I'm looking for Mr. Dean, my husband. Do you know what motel he's staying in?"

Lise raised her eyebrows. *So you're the wife. What did he ever see in you?*

"You mean Tommy? He's on the road today."

"Yes, but when will he be back? Where is he staying?"

"Why don't you call his cell phone?"

"I did. He's not answering. Do you know where he is, when he'll be back?"

Lise recalled "Tommy" saying that he had to call his wife today. *You liar! Who did you call?* Her suspicions made her more scornful.

"I doubt he'll be back tonight, he would have told me."

At that, Mary turned her eyes to Rob in appeal. He simmered with anger.

"Just give us the address."

"His apartment is at 64 Turtle Street."

She stared at Mary.

"He doesn't stay at a motel anymore. He's had the apartment for two months."

Lise smirked.

"It's fixed up real neat."

Mary went ashen. She stepped away. Rob turned red. He cracked his knuckles.

"Just tell us how to get there!"

He took the directions as Mary fled outside.

***

Back in the car, Rob spoke first.

"Mrs. Dean, I'm sorry. That little …"

"No. It's OK. I know my Tom. That girl isn't to blame. She'll find out about him soon enough."

"What can I do?"

"Just take me to the apartment. I'll wait for him there."

"I'll wait with you."

"Mr. Wilson, I don't think that would be wise. Tom has a terrible temper."

Rob felt the revolver in his jacket pocket. Tom was a dirt bag. He knew his type.

Lady, there is no way I am leaving you alone with that scum.

***

******

Chapter 13
Saturday, October 21

Following Lise's directions, Rob Wilson and Mary Dean located Tom's apartment.

It was the left side of a duplex, the only building on an unpaved lane dubbed "Turtle Street."

The landscaping for the duplex consisted of a lone palmetto tree and several crepe myrtles. Additionally, nature provided several tall pines that coated the sandy soil with slick pine needles penetrated in spots by tufts of wiry grass. Beyond the pines, the waters of Croatan Sound shimmered in the evening sun.

Rob knocked. There was no answer.

"Mary, do you want to get in?"

"I don't have a key."

The dead bolt on the door was thrown, but a ground-level window was not fully latched. Moments later Rob was inside. He opened the door from the inside.

Mary stood in the living area. *My husband lives here?* Her eyes took in the wall-mounted TV, numerous home-theater speakers, and large leather sofa. The furnishings were luxurious. *Tom, where does this money come from?*

In the bedroom, she saw a mirror on the ceiling above the bed. *Tom, how could you?*

Then she spotted the laptop on the chair in the corner. She waved and called out.

"Rob, come in here. Look!"

A tag hung from the handle of the laptop's case. On it a name was printed.

"AILEEN HARRIS."

***

Tom Dean stopped his F150 under the overpass for I-95 and waited, his motor running.

He lit a cigarette and listened to the rumbling of 18-wheelers overhead, going south.

Tom was angry.

Frank's meeting place made no sense. This exit had no reentry to I-95. There was no gas or food within several miles and the nearest town was ten miles away.

Tom preferred busy meeting places.

He puffed nervously.

The delivery was late.

If Frank had not doubled the money, Tom would not be here.

A lone car left the interstate, but it went west, away from Tom.

He lit another cigarette.

***

Jeannine had been in back of the van for hours, when the vehicle slowed and turned off the interstate.

It came to a stop.

Moments later she heard voices.

"Sir, do you have a problem? Do you need help?"

"No, Officer. No problem, I was tired and thought I'd better pull off the highway."

"Who was waiting in the red pickup that drove off when he saw me? Why were you meeting him?"

"I got no idea, Officer. I don't know any red truck."

"Sir, do you mind if I look in the back?"

"I'm sorry Officer, but I do mind. I have a delivery scheduled."

The state trooper frowned.

"Driver's license and registration, please."

A long silence followed.

Evidently the officer was at his computer, checking.

During the wait, Jeannine had her first success. She freed both wrists from the encircling mass of tape and jerked the tape from her mouth.

But before she could shout, the driver's door slammed and the van lurched forward.

The patrolman had not found cause to detain them.

They were en route again.

***

Tom Dean was furious. Frank had picked a stupid meeting place. The appearance of the North Carolina State trooper proved that.

At the sight of the police car, Tom had hit the accelerator and left, leaving the man in the van to deal with the cop.

No one could connect Tom to the van, except Frank. The package was lucky. Meanwhile, he was still not paid for the Harris job, much less the new one.

Ahead on the right was a billboard. He pulled off behind it and cut the engine. In the twilight, he was scarcely visible from the roadway. *The van was headed this way. If that cop lets it go, I can still take delivery.*

***

The van rolled along. The twists, turns and bumps told Jeannine the road was no interstate.

With her hands free, Jeannine pulled hard at the sticky gray tape that was wrapped about her ankles, anchoring them to a metal bracket on the floor.

She licked her finger. *Blood. The edge is sharp.*

With renewed energy, she pushed and pulled the tape against the cutting edge. Finally, it parted from the bracket.

Her legs were still bound, but she could move about.

She half rolled, half crawled to the back of the van. With both hands she grabbed the catch and pushed upwards, hard. The roll-up back released.

She lifted it up as far as she could.

Through the dusk and shadows, low bushes marked a shoulder that sloped away from the roadbed.

The van slowed for a turn. *OK, Jeannine, this is your chance. Now!*

She rolled out the van into the darkness.

***

The van drove past the bill board. The cop was gone. Tom Dean chuckled.

He followed it as it turned onto an unpaved road. It was dark now with no moonlight. Tom blinked his headlights. Immediately his cell phone vibrated.

"This is 'City Dog.' Who are you?"

Tom had the answer.

"This is 'Swamp Man.'"

Frank's choice of contact names was as dumb as his choice of meeting place, but at least the disposable phones worked.

The van stopped. Tom pulled in front, blocking it. He stepped out of his pickup.

"Where's the package?"

"She's in the back."

"Don't screw with me. The back's open. Where is she?"

The driver hurried to the rear. The panel was partly rolled up. He searched the interior with his flashlight.

"Hell! She's gone!"

"So that's why the cop didn't keep you. The back was open. He could see there was no girl. What is Frank's game?"

"Wait. Wait. No game. It was shut. She was here. That cop had no cause and he didn't have a warrant."

"You lie."

The driver flashed his light onto a floor bracket.

"Look. See the duct tape. She was here. She cut herself loose and jumped out."

"So you say. Are you sure the money's in the envelope?"

"It's there. All of it. Check it yourself."

Tom opened the envelope.

***

Tom's eyes darkened. He lifted his Berretta.

The driver drew back. *My God! He's going to kill me.*

"You've got the money. Let me … ."

"Crack. Crack."

The van's driver pitched backwards and collapsed.

Tom nudged the body with his foot. He emptied the wallet, wiped it and threw it beside the body. Then he picked up the flashlight and collected the spent shells.

The van's motor was running. Tom let it run and returned to his truck.

"Frank, our partnership is dissolved."

***

Mary Dean was afraid. The scorn of Lise, and the discovery of Aileen's computer had confirmed her worst fears. *My God, Tom! What have you done? Who are you, really?*

She turned to Rob.

"Mr. Wilson, I have to leave. I can't stay here any longer."

It was dark now. Rob secured the window, and motioned Mary to the door. He left the computer untouched.

Across Roanoke Sound they found the Nags Head Inn.

Rob took the room adjacent to Mary's. He had blown the assignment to protect Aileen. At least he could protect Mary from her husband.

And this might take days. He called his neighbor in Bethesda.

"Sue, could you take Andy to the kennel at the vet's for me. I know you're busy and I'm not sure when I'll be back. And thanks a lot for taking care of him."

With his dog no longer a worry, he went to bed, his revolver by the bedside.

In a few minutes, he was snoring.

Next door, Mary sobbed into her pillow.

***

Jack was frustrated. After three beers, he still was not calm. *Pops, where the hell are you.* He took a fourth Bud out the fridge.

He leaned back and propped his feet up. Midway through the Bud, his head fell on his shoulder. *Tomorrow, Pops. I'll find you. Tomorrow, I'll ... .*

***

105

*****

Chapter 14
Monday, October 23

Jeannine rolled over. A crisp white sheet brushed her cheek. *Where am I?* A smiling face leaned over her.

"You're awake. Good. How does this feel?"

Jeannine felt a moist cloth pass lightly over her forehead. She tried to sit up. A firm hand held her back.

"Take a few seconds. There's no hurry."

"Where am I?"

"You're in Elizabeth City, in the hospital. I'm Barb, the morning nurse. Here let me fix that bed for you."

Barb raised the back of the bed. Jeannine sat up. She felt her shoulder. It was sore.

"How did I get here?"

"First things first. Do you know your name?"

"Ryan, Jeannine Ryan."

"Do you feel you can talk? Are you up to a visitor?"

"I think so."

"Jeannine. There's a policeman outside. He's been waiting for you to wake up?"

"Wake up? How long have I been here?"

"Since yesterday, Sunday afternoon. The state police found you unconscious on the side of the road. You were in shock when you got here. They examined you and gave you something to sleep. You're OK, except for some bruises and that lump on your head."

Nurse Barb lowered her voice.

"They say you weren't raped. There's no sign of any sexual assault."

She stepped towards the door.

"I'm not supposed to talk to you. I'll get Dr. Jones. If he says it's OK, then I'll let the police talk to you."

Jeannine shut her eyes. Her head fell back on the pillow.

***

The detective showed Jeannine his badge. She spoke quickly.

"I'm Jeannine Ryan. I live in Rockville, Maryland, and I need to let my boss know where I am."

"Ms. Ryan, just tell me what you remember."

"Last Friday, I was going back to work after lunch. There was a sedan parked outside my work. A man got out and said that a friend's daughter had an accident."

"What happened then?"

"I got in the car and someone put a rag over my face. I blacked out."

"When I came to, I was in the back of a van. No windows. It was moving. I was tied with duct tape, but I managed to get my hands free."

She rubbed her wrists.

"We were going fast, like on a throughway. We got off and stopped. A policeman talked to the driver. My feet were taped. I got them free by rubbing against a bracket."

She slowed. The detective caught up with his notes.

"You never saw the driver?"

"Never. I got loose and rolled up the door. The van slowed around a curve. It was dark. I jumped off into the bushes."

She caught her breath.

"The next thing I remember is waking up here, in this room."

The detective pondered. Jeannine could not resolve the killing of the van's driver. She had been found unconscious a mile from the death scene with her feet still tangled with tape. It all checked.

She was not involved in the murder.

The weapon was missing. Someone else had been there. *The red truck the patrolman had seen? And why had she been abducted. And by whom?*

"Ms. Ryan, could you identify the man who spoke to you about your friend's 'accident?'"

"Maybe. He wore glasses, was six feet or over, and was trim."

"Ms. Ryan, thank you. Would it help if I called your office for you?"

"No. I'll call them myself. But, didn't you find my wallet or anything."

"Nothing. You were a 'Jane Doe.'"

Nurse Barb entered.

"Time's up! That's all for now, officer. Ms. Ryan has to rest."

Barb lowered the back of Jeannine's bed to nearly level.

Minutes later, Jeannine was asleep.

***

Aileen awoke to a bright sun that managed to penetrate a grimy window pane but could not disperse the shadows on the walls of a drab room. She was in bed, fully-clothed in her sweatshirt and mud-stained jeans. Her knotted hair clung to a gray pillow. The bed sheets were twisted and dirty.

She ached all over and her mouth was dry.

A man appeared in the doorway. He was shirtless, lean and muscular. He had a tattoo on his right shoulder and upper arm. She could not decipher the pattern. He hefted a heavy skillet in his left hand. She smelled bacon.

He waved the skillet in her direction.

"Gal, are you hungry?"

She knew that voice. *My God! It's Jack!*

Jack leaned over her.

"Don't worry. I won't hurt you. Not if you're good."

Aileen froze.

"Damn it, get up. You've got to eat."

Jack pushed her into a chair next to a bowl of steamy white grits with a square of molten butter on top.

"Here eat. Ma always gave me grits when I was sick."

Aileen took a spoonful of the semi-fluid. Two more spoonfuls followed quickly.

Jack shoved a cup of black coffee under her nose.

"Drink."

She swallowed, put down the cup and spoke.

"Water?"

Jack went to the sink and filled a glass. She gulped it down. She turned back to the grits. They slipped down easily and warmed her inside.

Jack poured more coffee for her.

"I'm not going to hurt you unless you run. Do you understand?"

She nodded "Yes."

He pointed out the window.

"You see that blue truck? That's Pops' truck. I found you by it. Where is he?"

Aileen lost hope. *Tell him the truth. What difference does it make?*

"He's dead."

Jack grabbed her throat. Her eyes rolled back. All went black.

***

Aileen awoke on the kitchen floor with a pillow under her head. Her throat burned from whiskey that trickled from the corner of her mouth.

Jack pulled her to a sitting position.

"Wake up, gal. I'm sorry. I didn't mean it. How do you know Pops is dead?"

"He was shot."

"You're lying. He could take care of himself."

"I saw it. I was hiding in the bushes."

Jack smashed his fist into his hand.

"Who did it? Do you know him?"

"No. He had a red pickup, a Ford."

Jack froze. *"Mr. Smith," you bastard!* His voice softened.

"Pops was like my Pa, only better than my real Pa."

He fell silent. When Jack spoke next, it was with admiration.

"How did you get out of that swamp?"

Aileen shivered and stared at the floor.

***

The morning mist over the Croatan Sound was lifting. From the Crown Vic, Rob and Mary watched Tom's building.

All day yesterday they had kept the same vigil, without any sign of Tom.

Mary watched Rob scan the entrance with his binoculars. He put the glasses down. His eyes had a hint of sadness, but gentleness too.

After the encounter with Lise, Rob had been kind. That touched her. She trusted him.

She wondered. *What did I do wrong Tom?* That thought was short-lived. *No, Tom you are the cheat. My God, Tom, you have a family. What about me, and Tommy and Annie?*

Rob pointed to Tom's door. She took the binoculars and focused.

An envelope was taped to it. It had not been there last night.

Rob left the car and ran to the door. Returning, he handed the envelope to Mary. It was addressed to "Mrs. Dean," in a man's handwriting.

She ripped open the flap and read.

Mary,

Lise told me you'd been snooping around. I know you were in my apartment. I don't blame you, but you should have trusted me. Now you've screwed things up real good. Lise says there was a guy with you. From what she said, he sounds like that dope Rob Wilson. Mary, you can do better than that. But thanks for sleeping with him. It'll make the divorce easier. I want my son Tommy. You can keep Annie.

By the way, Betsy called me. She was looking for you. I told her I'd pick up Tommy. She's meeting me near Morehead City.

By the time you get this, Tommy will be with me. Call her to see where you can pick up Annie.

Tom

Mary called Betsy right away.

"Rring, …Rring, … Rring, … Rring, … Rring, …"
The message came on.
"Hi this is Betsy. Please leave me a message. Thanks."
Mary was frantic.
"Betsy, if you get this, call me right away. Please! Please!"
Mary's lips quivered and her shoulders shook.
For the first time, Rob touched Mary. He put his arm around her.
She sobbed.

***
******

Chapter 15
Monday, October 23

It was mid-morning at StatFind and Mona Larson manned the phones. She recognized the caller right away.

"Jeannine! Where are you? We've been worried."

"It's a long story. I need to speak to Wayne."

"Wayne's not here. He's at Mandley Bionics all day. Let me give you Bill Hamm. But, are you all right?"

"I'm fine Mona, thanks. I'd better talk to Bill."

Bill Hamm was at his desk.

"Jeannine! Where are you?"

"I'm in North Carolina, Bill, in the hospital."

"The hospital? Are you all right? What happened?"

Bill listened as Jeannine recounted all the events she could recall, starting with last Friday and ending with her interview with the detective.

Bill was speechless. *Kidnapped? Homicide? What's going on?*

Jeannine added.

"And the FBI is coming this afternoon. We crossed state lines."

Bill found his voice.

"But are you OK?"

"I'm fine. The hospital says they'll release me tomorrow, and the local police are letting me leave North Carolina."

She spoke rapidly.

"Bill, Harry Roberts is to blame. He faked the data for the PMA, and after I cornered him, someone grabs me, and ... These people are killers! I've got to warn Wayne about the fake data. We can't work on this contract."

"Jeannine, I've got some bad news. I'm really sorry."

"What?"

"Wayne took you off the Mandley project. Harry Roberts is assigned to StatFind to do the work. He has your office. He and Dr. Thibault came in this weekend and collected all their papers and data from your files. Then they wiped your hard drive, and reloaded the computer with their software. Harry's in there working right now!"

Jeannine was stunned. Bill continued.

"I'm really sorry. I tried to stop them, but there was nothing I could do."

Jeannine remained silent.

"Thibault threatened Wayne. He said MTS could not work with you. He said he would kill the contract. We were overcommitted. It would have been the end of StatFind."

Still silence.

"I fought for you. At least you can still work here. You have your old cubicle back."

No response.

"Jeannine, are you there?"

More silence.

"Jeannine? Jeannine?"

"I'm here. Good bye!"

"Click."

***

After she hung up, Jeannine shook uncontrollably. Nurse Barb appeared.

"What's wrong? What's the matter?"

"I've been unconscious in a van, trussed up like a pig. I've cut myself loose, jumped off a van into the dark, and escaped from a killer."

Jeannine stared at the wall.

"I'm pissed at my boss, I mean my ex boss. I've lost my job and been replaced by a guy whom I used to like, but who turns out to be a cheat, a liar, and maybe even a murderer."

She looked at Barb.

"And I'm stuck in this damned hospital for another day and night."

"Honey, I hear you, but you need some rest."

She handed two tablets to Jeannine along with a glass of water.

"Here, take these. I guarantee you a good nap. I'll see that nobody bothers you."

Barb continued.

"And I'll hold lunch for you. I picked the menu for you, chopped steak, mashed potatoes and gravy. The rest of the food today is crap."

She fidgeted with the bed controls, and straightened Jeannine's pillow. By the time she was done, Jeannine's eyes were half closed.

Barb closed the blinds and left.

***

The blue pickup rattled over the washboard surface of the old fire lane. The worn shock absorbers could not stop the seats from bouncing up and down.

Thorny branches scratched at the side of the pickup, but Jack never braked. He drove with abandon. In the passenger seat, Aileen stared straight ahead.

Jack stopped the pickup by the Live Oak near the old shack.

"Where did he shoot Pops?"

Aileen pointed. Jack nodded.

"All right. Now show me where the bastard threw Pops' gun?"

She pointed at a stand of tall grass.

Jack gave her a "Don't move" stare. He kicked at the tufts of wiry grass.

Suddenly, he reached down. He lifted the shotgun. It was Pops' favorite, double barreled, broken open and empty of shells.

Jack peered through the barrels. They were clear of debris. He took two cartridges from his pocket, inserted them and snapped the barrels shut.

He pointed the gun at Aileen.

She ducked. Jack chuckled.

"All right, gal. Your story checks so far. Now where is Pops?"

Aileen pointed down the road, towards the swamp. Jack glared.

"Speak up, damn it! I'm trying to be good."

"I don't know. The red truck was over there. I was afraid to move. I was under the bushes over there. He dragged the body that way."

She pointed once more in the direction of the swamp.

Jack cradled the shotgun in his right arm. He signaled Aileen with his left.

"All right, walk in front of me. Get going."

To Aileen, it was déjà vu.

Except this time Aileen was in front of Jack, as Pops had been in front his killer.

***

Rob was hungry. He pulled into the McDonald's drive-through and ordered a Big Mac Combo meal. Mary sat next to him. She did not eat. She stared at her phone.

The chimes signaled an incoming call. Mary put the phone on speaker. It was Betsy.

"Mary?"

"Betsy, where are you. Where's Tommy?"

"We're all in Myrtle Beach."

"You're not in North Carolina?"

"No. I'm in Myrtle Beach. I guessed something was wrong when you left the kids with me. When Tom called, I knew for sure. He was weird, agitated. He told me to bring Tommy to him at Morehead City. I said I would, just to get rid of him."

Betsy continued.

"I would never do that without checking with you first."

Mary let out a long breath.

"Thank God! Betsy, Tom is dangerous. I don't know all he's done, but it's bad. What time did you say you'd meet him at Morehead?

"About four hours ago."

Mary gasped.

"Betsy, you've got to get the kids out of your condo, right away. Please, Tom could be on the way there now."

"Are you serious?"

"Deadly serious. He's leaving me and he wants Tommy, and he's done other things too. He's dangerous."

"Mary, I'm sorry. Just a minute. Someone's at the door."

Mary yelled.

"Betsy, don't go. It might be Tom!"

There were muffled sounds. She heard her son's voice.

"Daddy, No! ... No!"

The connection was broken.

She redialed immediately.

"Rring, ...Rring, ... Rring, ... Rring, ... Rring, ..."

The recording switched on.

"Hi this is Betsy. Please leave me a message. Thanks."

"Beep."

***

In minutes they were at the Manteo dealership where Tom worked. Mary stayed in the car. Rob rushed in.

"Where's Lise?"

A stranger stood behind the counter.

"She's off today."

"Is Tom Dean coming in today?"

"He's off too. They take Monday off together."

"Do you know where they are?"

The man raised his eyebrows.

"How the hell would I know? And who the hell are you?"

Rob ignored him and left.

In the car he spoke outright.

"Lise is with him."

He added.

"It'll make it easier to find him."

Mary nodded. She slumped in the seat.

***

Rob thought fast. The likelihood was that Tom would come back to the Manteo area. It was unlikely that he would take Tommy to Dillon. Mary found her voice.

"We have to go to Myrtle Beach."

"I think he'll bring Tommy back here."

"But what about Betsy? And Annie?"

Rob nodded.

"You're right. Try and call again."

Mary redialed.

"Mary, is that you?"

Betsy's words were punctuated by tears.

"Mary I'm sorry. ... They took Tommy. ... I couldn't stop him. ... There was a girl with him. ... I'm so sorry."

A pause.

"Tom threw my cell phone off the balcony. I just found it. I was calling you when it rang. I'm so sorry."

Mary grew calm. She had to regain her son.

"Betsy, which way did he head?"

"They went north. They could be headed for Dillon, or maybe back to Manteo."

"Betsy, let me talk to Annie."

Mary reassured her daughter. Then she turned to Rob.

"I think he's coming back to Manteo. I think we'd better stay."

She flushed and quickly added.

"I mean I'd better stay."

Rob nodded. *Mary, I'm sticking with you, no matter what happens.*

He started the engine.

***

Aileen's feet were soaked. The edges of the roadway were under water that seeped into the ruts and coalesced in pools. *My God, he's making me go into the swamp. I can't do this again.* She turned and faced Jack.

"Do what you want, but I'm not going any further."

Jack lifted the shotgun in her direction.

"You're going to help me find Pops."

"No. I have no idea where your uncle's body is, but he's dead. He was shot three times before he was dragged away."

Jack studied Aileen's eyes. *Hell, this girl's got spunk, and she made it out of the swamp by herself.* He lowered the shotgun.

"All right, come back here."

She did not move.

"Come over here, gal. Damn it. Don't be scared."

Listlessly she dragged herself to where he stood. Jack pointed back where they had come.

"See those bushes, see the branches and grass mashed down and that mud. That's where Pops was dragged."

They retraced their steps. The depressed vegetation ended in a smooth path of mud that disappeared under black swamp water. Aileen knew the water was deep. There were no protruding twigs or branches. Across the smooth water stood cypress and gum trees with swollen trunks.

Jack's brow furrowed.

"I thought you were trying to con me, to lead me away from it, but I reckon not. That's a big hole. A real big gator used to be in there. From that muddy slide, I'd say he still is."

He paused.

"If that gator's still around, the only way we'll find Pops is to slit that big scaly belly wide open and look inside."

Aileen choked. Jack smiled.

"I guess you been telling the truth. Get in the truck. We're going home."

Home? Aileen shuddered. *God, help me.*

***

The bathroom in Pop's house had a single window. Aileen watched as Jack hammered in two large nails to secure it.

He tossed a denim shirt and overalls on the straight-backed chair.

"All right, gal clean yourself up. You can use Pops' clothes. He won't be needing them. I'll fix us some supper. No use trying to run. I'm right here."

Aileen looked at the four-legged bath tub, and then through the open door to the stove where Jack stood, stirring a pot.

She slammed the door, and braced the back of the chair under the door knob. It held. She went to the lone window. Jack had nailed it tight. There was no hope there.

She gave up. *Why not get clean?* She ran warm water in the tub. Her thoughts drifted to her daughter. *Mary Catherine, Mommy is in trouble. She needs help, bad! You listen good to Granny and you'll be safe. I love you.*

She sat in the water and soaked. She tried to relax in the warm suds, but her mind raced and her muscles stayed tight and tense. *My God, what's happening? Who wants me dead? Harry? Dr. Thibault?*

Jack's voice pierced the thin walls.

"OK, gal. Times up. Come on out and let me see you."

***

Rob pulled the Crown Vic into the Shell station. Mary manned the pump while he went into the office.

"Can you tell me how to get to this address?"

The clerk looked.

"That's over on the mainland, near the Alligator River Refuge. You take highway 64. After you cross the Alligator River, stop and ask somebody. They'll point you to the right spot."

Rob returned to the car. Mary finished filling the tank.

"Mrs. Dean, I don't think your husband will come back to the apartment. At least not right away. He knows we were there."

"But where else can we look?"

"I got Lise's address too. She lives with her parents. He won't go there."

"Then that's that. What can we do?"

"Remember the blue pickup. I got the plate from the BP station in Myrtle Beach. I have the address. Your husband doesn't know we have it. There's a chance he'll go there."

"Rob, Tom's a good marksman. He practices all the time. What if you find him?"

Rob thought back to his active days with the FBI. He was well-versed in handguns, rifle and shotgun. Still, he had not practiced much since leaving.

He set his lips.

"Mary, we're going to get Tommy back. Don't worry. Leave your husband to me."

They drove across the Croatan Sound on Route 64 and headed for the Alligator River.

***

******

Chapter 16
Monday, October 23

In the kitchen of Pop's house, Jack stood shirtless. He flexed his arms for his "guest" to admire. The tattoo running down his shoulder was a fanged snake twined about a skull and cross bones.

Aileen concealed her breasts in Pops' over-size shirt and overalls. Her hair was still knotted, but clean and no longer muddy. She had it in a bun.

Abruptly, Jack reached across the table and pulled the bun apart, so that long blonde strands hung damp and loose over the denim shoulder straps. He frowned.

"Aren't you done eating yet? Hurry up."

Jack picked up his dish and put in the sink.

"You're wasting time. Get done. We got to get to know each other,"

Aileen shuddered. Her only hope was to keep Jack talking. She picked at her plate.

"Jack, how did Pops help you when your dad wouldn't?"

Jack opened two bottles of beer. He set one before her.

"Here, drink up. My Pa was a real bastard. Pops, he tried to …"

Aileen dawdled over her bottle.

Jack rambled on.

***

Four bottles, dribbling amber liquid, lay askew on Jack's side of the table. He hefted a fifth to his mouth. Two gulps and half the beer was gone. He wiped his lips.

"All right gal, come here."

He reached across the table and grabbed the straps of Aileen's overalls. A twist of his hand, and one strap fell loose. He pulled her across the table. Dishes and bottles flew as she thrashed and kicked.

The table tipped over. He held her down on the floor. He reeked of stale beer.

"Come on. Be a good gal and I'll be nice. I know you want me."

She tried to twist away, but he held her tightly. He tore the last strap loose and reached through her shirt. She bit his arm. He ignored her and pulled at the overalls.

"Stop!"

He laughed.

Jack was strong. He dragged her towards the bedroom. Her heels scraped the floor. He slapped her and seized her hair. He jerked her up.

"Get up. Now!"

He did not wait. He threw her on the bed.

She shut her eyes and lay motionless. *God, help me.*

Jack turned back to the kitchen.

"That's better, much better. Wait here, I need another beer."

He laughed.

"Don't go anywhere. I'll be right back."

***

Aileen heard a loud banging on the door.

Jack burst into the bedroom. He wadded a napkin into her mouth and used a shirt to tie it securely. At the same time he yelled.

"Hold your damn horses. I'm coming."

The banging continued. He secured Aileen's wrists and ankles with electric cord and yelled louder.

"Hold your damn horses. I'm on the way."

He left. Aileen heard the door open.

***

A man stood outside the entrance. He had a Fish and Wildlife Service patch on his sleeve.

Jack caught his breath.

"What the hell do you want, Scot. I'm busy."

"Shut up, Jack. Let me in."

Jack blocked the entrance.

124

"Nope, I said I'm busy damn it."

"All right, Jack. Have it your way. Where's Pops?"

"Why do you want to know?"

"Because I've been hearing shotguns from across the lake, and today I found a Red Wolf carcass along this road."

"So?"

"So you know damn good and well they're protected. The Park Service didn't spend all that money introducing these wolves here so you and Pops could take target practice. Where is Pops?"

"He's not here. And he never shot no wolf anyway. Maybe he thought it was a stray dog like we've got hanging around here."

"Which is it, Jack. Did he shoot a 'dog' or didn't he. And that's Pops truck parked here. He's home. Let me in."

Jack started to panic. *Not in the bedroom, No! I got to get rid of this guy.*

"Pops isn't here, damn it. You're not coming in."

"All right, Jack, but I'll be back with a warrant. Everybody knows Pops, and everybody knows he hates wolves."

"Wait. I'll help you. I'll go with you and see that dumb varmint you say is so important. Maybe I'll figure out who shot your damned 'wolf.' Hell, I'm a good citizen."

Jack cast a glance back at the bedroom door. *The bitch is quiet, good.* He turned back to Scot.

Scot frowned.

"You're stalling Jack, but I'll go along. You want to prove somebody else did the shooting? OK. Get Pops' truck and follow me. Let's go before it gets dark."

Aileen heard the door slam.

***

Rob kept his attention on the road, eyes fixed straight ahead, as they crossed the expanse of the Alligator River where it met the Albemarle Sound.

Quietly, Mary Dean studied his features. They reassured her.

She was a good Southern Baptist. At least she thought she was, but her current thoughts made her wonder. *Mary, what are you thinking. You hardly know this guy. And you're still married for better or worse. OK, worse.*

Curiosity overcame her. She glanced sideways at Rob.

"Rob, when you find the blue truck, you hope to find Aileen too, right?"

Rob nodded assent.

"Excuse me. I know I shouldn't ask, but are Aileen and you, you know, a couple? I mean you really like her, don't you? You said she was a 'Ten.'"

Rob swerved to avoid a fallen branch.

Mary blushed.

"I'm sorry. I didn't mean to pry into your personal life."

Rob slowed the car. He turned towards Mary. His eyes searched hers.

"Mary, I barely know Aileen."

Mary exhaled.

"But …"

Rob resumed the speed limit.

"I never met her before this job. I was with her on the trip down from Maryland, but we didn't talk much. I don't know her at all. What I do know is that I blew my assignment. I was supposed to guard her, and I screwed up. I screwed up bad."

Mary touched his arm.

"Don't beat yourself up. I'm grateful for all you've done for me. You've been great. I know I've been a real bother to you."

Rob swallowed.

"Mary, I … ."

He hit the brakes. The sign indicated a road ahead on the left. He changed the subject.

"This is where we turn."

They left the highway. The road was paved, but narrow and deserted.

Ahead of them on both sides were pine forests with occasional fields. They saw no houses.

Rob continued to drive. Mary kept silent.

***

It was dusk when Rob turned into the sandy driveway of the old house. A flat-bottomed aluminum boat sat on its trailer in the high grass nearby. There was one functional car parked between the wreck of an old Ford Maverick and a rusted tractor.

Rob stepped out of the Crown Vic as overhead, Fish Crows flew towards a communal roost in tall hardwoods to the east.

He studied the layout. *Damn it. This is the address, but no blue truck, and no red pickup either.* He pulled the screen door open for Mary.

"I'm sorry, but Tom's not here, at least his truck isn't."

Mary kept up hope.

"It's a long way from South Carolina. He might still come."

She tried the handle of the main door. It opened.

The kitchen was a shambles. Beer bottles, dishes and broken glass were scattered about. One chair was overturned, and another lay on its side with two legs broken.

The table top was slanted sideways. On the floor was a deposit of dishes and scraps like the debris from an avalanche.

The air reeked of stale beer.

Mary turned to Rob.

"We don't belong here. Maybe we'd better go."

Rob hesitated. There had been a struggle here. Litter was pushed aside as if something had been dragged to the bedroom.

Mary was adamant.

"Rob, I don't like this place. We'd better go."

Rob turned towards her. *There's no blue truck. Maybe I'm at the wrong address? Maybe that house a mile back is the one?*

Mary was already outside.

He followed.

Inside, their voices had drifted into Aileen's consciousness. She awoke briefly, but could barely breathe.

She cried out.

Help. Help.

But Jack's gag choked her and no sounds passed her lips. She passed out.

***

Jack drove home fast. He was angry.

Pops had shot that damned wolf. Pops always did as he pleased and Pops hated those Fish and Wildlife guys telling him what to do.

Jack agreed with Pops. Wolves were supposed to be gone. They didn't belong. Why the hell bring them back now?

Scot had told him that the fine for killing one stinking varmint was $3,000. *Screw you, Scot, and your damn laws too. Screw that Code 16 or 1531 or whatever you always blabber about.*

He switched targets. *Damn you Pops, Scot blames me for that stinking wolf. Why did you do it Pops? I don't have any money. Thanks for the inheritance.*

***

Jack accelerated. "His" blonde was on the bed, waiting. He licked his lips. *Gal, you'll love it. You'll need me. You'll beg to stay with me.*

She would learn. Tomorrow she'll start cooking, after she cleans the mess she made in the kitchen. *Look at me, Pops, I was right. You wanted to waste her. You got too old. You forgot.*

Jack was full of his thoughts. He turned into the driveway, but the way was blocked by a blue Ford Crown Victoria with two individuals seated in front. Perhaps it was the deceptive light of dusk, or perhaps it was all that beer, but in the shadows he was sure there were three antennas sticking up from the rear of that Ford.

It was the classic unmarked police car!

Damn! Dumb-ass cops! Kidnapping!? Not me. I'm out of here!

He slammed into reverse, backed onto the road, and raced away.

***

Rob saw the blue pickup back away. He thought to pursue, but stopped. He turned to Mary.

"That was the pickup, the blue Ranger. This is the right house. It must be!"

He thought of the wrecked kitchen. *My God, the bedroom. That path through the litter. Some thing was dragged there. Or someone!*

He raced for the house and burst through the bedroom door.

Aileen's face was blue. He removed the gag.

She retched.

"Miss. Harris, Aileen, I'm sorry, real Sorry. I shouldn't have left you. You're safe now. You're going to be OK."

Her eyes opened and seemed to recognize Rob.

She fell backwards onto the bed.

***

******

Chapter 17
Tuesday, October 24

In Elizabeth City, Nurse Barb wheeled Jeannine through the lobby of the hospital. Jeannine was not leaving quietly. She twisted her head and confronted her "driver."

"Look at those people. They think I'm an invalid. I can walk as well as you can. Let me out of this wheel chair."

"Sorry, Hon, it's hospital rules. As soon as I get you outside, you can dance, jump or break your neck if you want, but until then, you ride."

Jeannine leaned her head forward and shut her eyes in resignation. *Calm down girl, Barb's been good to you.* She twisted and looked back.

"Seriously, Barb, thanks for everything. I've been a real grouch."

"Hon, with what you've been through, you've got a right to be mad. I wish I could have helped. Come back and say hello sometime."

Jeannine smiled.

"Not soon, I hope. No hard feelings, but this is a hospital."

Barb pushed the wheelchair across the threshold onto the sidewalk. She leaned over and flipped the foot supports to the side. Jeannine jumped up.

Barb squeezed her big time.

"OK, Hon, you're free. I hope things go better for you."

Jeannine squeezed back.

"Thanks Barb."

The nurse headed back through the entrance as Jeannine started towards the taxi stand.

A tall man, his back to her, blocked the way.

He turned.

Jeannine frowned.

"Bill Hamm! What are you doing here?"

Bill smiled.

"I thought maybe you could use some company. My car's over there."

"But?"

"No 'buts.' Here. Give me that bag."

Jeannine was too surprised to resist. She handed him the plastic bag of hospital "take-homes."

Bill talked as he drove.

"When I got your call, I knew I had to do something. I told Mona I'd be gone for a few days. I drove down last night. I'm really sorry about everything."

"What did Wayne say?"

"He doesn't know where you are. He was at Mandley Bionics all day. I couldn't reach him after you called. I left a message on his desk that you're OK."

She spit out the reply.

"That's it? I'm supposed to be OK?"

"You know what I mean. Wayne's a mess and StatFind is screwed up by the Mandley deal."

"You seem to be surviving."

"Me? I guess so. But I had to get away for a couple of days. I can't stand your Harry Roberts. I want to punch him out. I had to leave. You're here, so here I am."

He added.

"Besides, Harry took over your office. He thinks he's a king or something."

"Bill, the numbers we talked about on Friday, after you left, I proved that Harry is a fraud. He faked the data. Aileen Harris was right and I can prove it."

She paused.

"I mean I could have proved it before they took my notes and wiped my hard drive."

She continued.

"Harry's worse than a fraud. I had lunch with him after I saw you. I told him I knew he was cheating. He kept lying to me so I got up and left. He knew I was on my way back to the office to tell Wayne the data were fake."

She ground her teeth.

"A man stopped me outside our building. They chloroformed me. When I woke up, I was tied up in a van. I got loose and jumped. Next thing I know I'm in the hospital in Elizabeth City, and the police tell me that the van driver is dead, murdered."

Her shoulders shook.

"I'm sure that's what they planned for me. Harry's a murderer."

Bill whistled.

"It makes sense. You would disappear, and Mandley would have clear sailing with the FDA. Meanwhile, Harry could clean up any evidence you left behind."

Jeannine added.

"But without a copy of their proposal and my computer and notes, I can't prove a damn thing. They win."

They reached an intersection. The sign indicated "Nags Head" to the right and "Chesapeake City" to the left. Bill stopped and pulled off the road.

For the second time in as many meetings with Jeannine, he said.

"You know, maybe I can help!"

***

Jeannine suppressed her retort. Bill had helped the last time with banker's rounding. Maybe he could help again. She waited.

Bill spoke slowly.

"Last Friday when I saw you in your office, the desk was piled with notes, papers and data CD's. You had worked all night."

Jeannine nodded. Bill went on.

"You talked about fake data, and digits. You even gave me a kiss when I told you about banker's rounding."

He touched his finger to his cheek.

"Get to the point, Bill."

"OK. Wayne told me that Thibault and Harry were coming over and that they wanted your computer locked up. No one was to go in your office. I asked myself, 'Why?'"

Jeannine brightened.

"Bill, please tell me that you did what I think you did."

"I used my key and slipped into your office. I grabbed some of your notes, graphs and CD's from the desk top. That was all I had time for before they arrived. They're in that box on the back seat. I brought my own laptop too."

Jeannine released her seat belt. She twisted to look in the box. She recognized the CD's she had made of the Mandley data. She hugged Bill and let her lips brush his.

"Bill, what can I say? Thank you. Thank you."

Bill wanted this mood to last.

***

Jeannine withdrew to her side of the car.

"Let's go, Bill. Why are we still stopped?"

Bill indicated the sign pointing to Nags Head.

"I need a few days off. I think you do to. My sister, Sarah, owns a place at Nags Head. It's on the front beach. I thought maybe we could spend a few days there and get rested up for the battle at StatFind."

Her eyes flashed.

"You think I'm going to sleep with you? Damn it Bill, I was just starting to think you were OK."

"That's not the idea. You need a friend and you've got one whether you like it or not. You're still in danger. If it was Harry that set up the kidnapping, you sure won't be safe at StatFind. No one knows I'm here and nobody knows about my sister's beach house."

He swallowed hard.

"Besides, I warned you about Harry. God knows I've got no reason to like that bastard."

He added.

"And you're not the first person I like that's fallen for his line. He's poison."

"Go on."

"If you agree, we'll stay at my sister's beach house. Sarah and her husband are married for five years now. They're doing great. They have a little girl, Betty, three years old."

"Why is that relevant?"

"Betty is not my sister's first child. There was a little boy. He was Harry's son."

"My sister was young, a sophomore in college. Harry had just gotten his Ph. D. and a fancy car. He told her they would get married. A few months later she was pregnant. Harry didn't like that. He beat her. He tried to force her to abort. She refused and he left. Afterwards, she had a boy and put him up for adoption. He would be eight now."

Jeannine listened.

"When Harry left, Sarah tried to kill herself. She almost succeeded. My Mom helped her a lot. Anyway Sarah pulled through and made a life for herself."

"I told Sarah I was coming to Elizabeth City to pick you up. When I told her about you and Harry, she mentioned the beach house. It's October and it's empty. She gave me the keys. She thought you should rest up. I think it's a good idea. We can figure out how to get Harry and straighten out StatFind."

He closed with.

"And no, I'm not trying to sleep with you, though I'd like to."

He looked ahead, as if talking to himself.

"That's something else Harry 'taught' me. The next time I sleep with a woman, it will be for keeps. And I'll damn well be there as long as she needs me, like my Mom for Sarah and me."

He paused and added.

"And she had better feel the same way I do!"

His eyes remained fixed on the windshield.

Jeannine thought of her own past, her shared bed with John Martin. *A false commitment. We're adults, we can each go our own way whenever one of us wants!* Luckily, she did not get pregnant. And John was no Harry. John was a good man. When they broke up he found his colleague and her friend, Monique. Now John and Monique were happily married. Their daughter was named "Jeannine."

"All right, Bill, you can turn right."

Bill started the engine and drove towards Nags Head.

***

Aileen sat in the back of Rob Wilson's Crown Victoria. She was fortunate. Aside from some nasty scratches and bruises, she was OK. Maybe Jack's hominy grits had worked.

A silent Mary Dean sat in the front while Rob headed for the FBI office in Elizabeth City.

Aileen used Rob's phone to call Aunt Agatha. At the sound of her daughter's voice she wept and laughed at once. She had despaired of ever hearing her daughter again.

Rob drove while she talked.

***

The Field Office of the FBI in North Carolina was located upstate, in Charlotte, but they maintained a Resident Agency in Elizabeth City. Bob, the agent on duty recognized Rob.

"Rob Wilson. What are you doing here? I heard you retired."

"You're right Bob, I'm private now. I'm here about an abduction. A girl named Aileen Harris. They snatched her in Myrtle Beach and brought her to Dare and Tyrell Counties. That must be your territory."

"Sure is. Where is Harris? Is she all right?"

"She's fine. She's in the car. I'll bring her in."

Aileen told her story to Bob, who scribbled lots of notes. Rob stood by, silent.

An hour later they were done. Aileen left.

Bob motioned to Rob to stay.

"Rob, someone in your agency has to be involved. These guys were waiting for Harris at Myrtle Beach, in the same condo. How else would they know where she was."

"I think my boss Frank Hardy was involved. Tom Dean had his phone number. You should check him out."

Rob rose to leave. Bob spoke.

"Will do, but before you leave there's something else."

Rob turned back. Bob continued.

"We had another abduction. The victim was from Rockville too. Her name is Jeannine Ryan. A late-model red pickup truck may be involved. Any ideas?

Rob sat down.

***

Outside, Mary Dean and Aileen waited in Rob's car.

"Mary, Rob's taking a long time with that FBI guy. There's a McDonald's over there. You want something?"

Mary nodded and they crossed the street.

The restaurant featured a play area that featured high-climbing tubes and twisted slides. A small boy was taking off his shoes so he could climb in the colorful tubes. Mary pointed.

"That boy is my Tommy's age."

"Your husband wouldn't hurt Tommy, would he?"

"I don't know. A few days ago I would have said 'No,' but the man who shot Pops sounds a lot like my Tom. I thought he loved Tommy, but then I thought he loved me."

"Maybe the shooter wasn't Tom."

"A red F150? And your laptop in his apartment? It was Tom and he's got Tommy."

Aileen reached across the table.

"Rob says we'll find Tommy. Don't give up. He found me."

"I want to believe you. At least your Mary Catherine is safe."

Mary studied Aileen. In spite of her ordeal, Aileen was definitely pretty. Her bruises and scratches gave her an added intrigue, like cosmetically placed birthmarks. And Aileen was smart, an electro-something scientist. Rob had to be interested in Aileen.

Yells from the high slide snapped her out of her musing. The boy Tommy's age slid out of the exit tube and toppled laughing at his mother's feet.

Mary cringed. *Tom, if you dare to hurt my boy, I'll …*

But then Rob arrived at their booth.

"There's more news. Let's get back to the car."

***

They left Elizabeth City for Manteo. This time Aileen was in the passenger seat. Mary sat in back. Rob spoke over his shoulder.

"Mary, I'm sorry, I don't know how to say this, but Tom might be involved in another abduction, and another murder."

"What do you mean?"

"The FBI office here has two abduction cases. Last Friday a woman was abducted in Maryland, in Rockville. They brought her to North Carolina. Aileen's not the only one."

"You said 'murder.' She was murdered?"

"No. She's OK. She was tied up in a van. The driver of the van was shot."

"And Tom is involved?"

"It appears a red pickup, an F150, met the van, or at least tried to."

"Wasn't his truck in Manteo?"

"Not near his apartment. You and I watched it all day Saturday."

Mary fell silent. Aileen broke in.

"Rob, you said 'Rockville.' What was her name."

"Jeannine Ryan, she worked for a company called StatFind."

"That's Dr. Ryan! She's the one I told about Harry's fake data. Your boss is in Rockville. Call him. He can check on Harry and MTS."

"No, I can't trust my boss."

He turned his head.

"Mary, that paper you found in Tom's shirt had Aileen's name and a number. That was my boss's phone number. He and Tom are working together. They set me up."

Aileen broke in. She touched Rob's arm.

"Rob, Dr. Thibault, my old boss, called my mother. He told her that Harry was dangerous and I should go away for a while. Thibault told my mother not to tell me about him but she did. It was Thibault who fixed it for me to go with you."

Rob looked at Aileen.

"That means …"

"Right. Dr. Thibault and your boss Frank Hardy are in this together!"

Mary watched as Aileen's hand lingered on Rob's arm.

***

The blue Toyota was on I-95, south of the North Carolina border. An enormous sign, a man with a neon sombrero, marked a sprawling motel complex, "South of the Border."

Lise spoke.

"Can't we stop? I'm tired."

Tom Dean kept driving.

"Tommy, I'm tired. Your kid wears me out. I never counted on a kid."

"Shut up and let him sleep. You sleep too."

The Toyota crossed into North Carolina.

***

Dr. Thibault relaxed. It had been a long day, but a successful one. He had "neutralized" Aileen Harris, and Ryan, and Harry was at StatFind to clean up the fake data mess.

The phone broke into this reverie. He picked up.

"Thibault, what have you done? Ryan and Harris are alive. They've gone to the FBI!"

Thibault steadied himself on his desk. His throat constricted.

"Thibault, you will take a vacation. We can not be connected to you, or you to the new chip."

"But?"

"Shut up. You will be contacted."

Thibault mixed a martini. One gulp and it was gone. His hands shook. He called Frank Hardy. The message machine answered. He spoke rapidly.

"Frank, the packages weren't delivered. The FBI knows. I'm leaving town. You should too. Don't ask why. Just do it."

***

It was afternoon in Lebanon. Waseem Hamza called his brother at Mandley Security in Delaware.

"Fareed, Anan called. She said there is a problem at MTS."

"Anan is right. It is two women. The doctor at MTS tried to remove them and failed. My men are handling the situation."

"See that they do. And this Doctor Thibault?"

"Soon he will not be a problem."

"Keep me informed."

***

******

Chapter 18
Wednesday, October 25

Late autumn on the Outer Banks is that in-between season when the mottled heads of the Laughing Gulls, no longer resplendent in breeding black, witness to summer's departure, while early migrants from Canada, like Scaup and Ring-necked Ducks, warn of winter's arrival.

The morning sun was particularly bright. Over night, the mild waters of the Gulf Stream had overridden the cold Labrador Current to produce a warm turbulent surf. The tide was low, and the strand was wide. A steady offshore breeze blew the beach free of insects and flattened the fruited heads of the sea oats low over the dunes.

From the deck of the beach house Jeannine watched the dark silhouettes of migrant ducks as they bobbed on the reflective waters beyond the breakers. Ever the statistician, she struggled to count their number, but their sporadic diving frustrated her efforts. She gave up and looked down the beach. In the distance a man was jogging in sweatshirt and shorts. She smiled. It was Bill Hamm.

This was their first morning at the beach. True to his word, Bill had paid little attention to her. Once he had settled Jeannine in her room, Bill had disappeared into his own bedroom. After that the only evidence of his presence was the sound of the television coming through the wall.

Her sleep had been long and deep.

This morning, when the bright sun crossed her eyes, she had awakened to an empty house. A note on the table said simply that the fridge was full and Bill was gone for a run on the beach.

Also on the table was that box he had filled with her MTS notes and graphs.

She turned to the stove. Soon crisp bacon strips were degreasing on paper towels while onions and potatoes sizzled in the pan. Toast was down in the toaster, and eggs fried slowly in the other skillet. The aroma of Colombian coffee mixed with the scent of onions and bacon showed this was not a continental breakfast.

Bill appeared at the door on the deck.

"Wash the sand off your feet, Bill. Your sister's carpets are clean."

Bill complied. He stepped in.

"I thought you were the croissant and cheese type. This looks like a man's breakfast."

"Be quiet, and eat. I was raised in West Virginia."

"What does your dad do?"

"He was a physicist, at Morgantown, but we lived in a little town south of there. He died a while back. My mother remarried, and before you ask, my stepfather's a jerk. He thinks he's my age."

She shook the auburn hair off her forehead.

"Enough of that. I don't talk much about it. Where are you from?"

"Cumberland, Maryland. My folks are dead, a car accident. Sarah and I are the only ones left except for an uncle in Ohio."

He dug into the heaped plate.

"You got any more? This is good."

Jeannine spooned potatoes and onions onto his dish and added bacon strips on top.

"I can make more eggs too."

Bill looked up. This was not the Jeannine he was used to.

"Thanks, no. This is great."

He dug in again.

Jeannine went outside and reclined in the sun. She sipped her coffee, and stared out over the ocean. The ducks were gone, but a pale gull with a dark ring on its bill lit on the deck rail. She tossed a morsel of bread high in the air. The bird took wing, snatched the bread, set its wings motionless and drifted away with the wind.

Jeannine closed her eyes. Thoughts of MTS, Harry, duct tape, and StatFind likewise drifted away as the healing air of the Outer Banks filled her lungs.

***

The run on the beach had given Bill Hamm an appetite. He stepped to the stove. The iron frying pan still held fragments of potatoes and onions. These he scraped into his mouth. He patted his stomach.

His cell phone vibrated.

"Yes?"

"Mr. Hamm this is Aileen Harris. Mona, at StatFind, gave me your number."

"I remember you."

"Is Dr. Ryan with you?"

Bill was silent. Aileen continued.

"I know Dr. Ryan was abducted. I know she escaped and was in the hospital in Elizabeth City, and I know that a man met her when she was discharged. I assume that man was you."

"What do you want?"

"I have to see Dr. Ryan. It's about the PMA for MTS and Harry Roberts. It's urgent. I was abducted too, and I know by whom."

"Ms. Harris, Aileen, I'm not telling anyone where we are. Not even you."

Aileen fell silent. Bill could hear her breathe.

"All right, Aileen, where are you now?"

"I'm in Kitty Hawk, driving towards Nags Head."

"OK, listen. There's a Catholic chapel, a frame building, at Whalebone Junction, across from the Kentucky Fried Chicken. Ask anybody, they'll tell you where it is. I'll meet you there in thirty minutes. How will I know you?"

"Our car is a blue Crown Victoria Ford. They'll be three of us. But how will I know you?"

"Don't worry. A Ford Crown Vic! I'll find you."

Bill broke the connection.

***

In a gray Audi, the listener put down his headset. It was attached to an electronic box on the back seat.

"I told you Hamm's cell phone was the answer."

"Yes, but he was smart. He didn't give us the address."

"He's a yokel. He can't be that smart. We'll find him at Whalebone junction. We can be there in twenty minutes. She's in Rob Wilson's blue Crown Vic. It'll be easy."

The gray Audi headed for Whalebone Junction.

***

Bill looked at Jeannine. She was on the deck, sleeping.

The beach house was elevated on posts so that the second story was actually the first. Bill's car was parked under the house, out of sight of the road. He slipped out the front door and down wooden steps to his car. He drove fast. He had to arrive at Whalebone Junction before the others.

***

No one was in sight when Rob's blue Crown Victoria arrived at Whalebone Junction, Rob spotted the sign in front of the white wooden building. It was a Catholic chapel.

He turned into the sandy parking lot behind the frame structure.

Immediately his cell phone buzzed. He heard three words.

"Under the Oleander."

Then the connection was broken.

"'Under the Oleander!' What does that mean?"

Mary Dean pointed at the back of the chapel.

"'Oleander' is a bush for landscaping. That's one over there by the door."

Rob stepped out of the car. Under the Oleander, half concealed, was a brown envelope. He tore it open. Inside was a message.

If you got a call "Under the Oleander," someone is following you.

Get to a landline phone.

Call the number below.

Rob pulled out of the lot and headed north.

A gray Audi pulled out from the KFC lot and followed.

***

Bill Hamm waited by the pay phone, a relic from other times. Finally it rang. The voice was Rob Wilson's.

"What now, Bill?"

"Did you see the gray Audi that followed you?"

"Yes. They're right across the street from us. There are two guys."

"They must have monitored my cell phone, or maybe yours. Anyway, here's what you do."

Bill gave Rob detailed instructions.

"... Then you U-turn and stop. They'll pretend they're not following and drive by. The road narrows after that for more than a mile with sand on both sides. They won't be able to turn around without getting stuck."

Bill hung up. Rob walked back to the Crown Vic.

***

It was afternoon when Rob's car finally arrived at the beach house. Bill waved it into a space underneath so that neither car was visible from the road.

They mounted the steps to the house.

Bill stood at the top of the steps. Rob held out his hand.

"I'm Rob Wilson. What's with all the drama?"

Bill responded.

"You tell me. After what happened to Jeannine, I don't trust anybody. And I specially don't trust cell phones. After Aileen called I went to Whalebone Junction and planted that envelope. Then I waited down the road. A gray Audi pulled into the KFC lot. When nobody got out, I guessed they were waiting for you."

Bill continued.

"When you pulled out in the Crown Vic, they followed, so I guessed right. You're sure you ditched them."

"No problem. That was a good trick. What's your background."

145

Bill smiled.

"I'm an accountant, but before that I was CIA."

"That explains that. I'm retired FBI, but I don't feel retired now. We've got two dead. What's happening?

"I don't know, but it's big. It's more than one cheating scientist."

"You mean Roberts?"

"Right. He's not big enough or smart enough to plan two abductions, and track us down here. And he doesn't have the guts for murder.

Bill paused.

"Rob, Mandley Bionics, Thibault and whoever, are desperate to hide what they're doing. Whatever it is, it's big, and Jeannine and Aileen are threats."

They entered the house. Jeannine, Aileen and Mary were engaged in serious conversation.

Jeannine knew one thing, her "vacation" was over.

***

The beach house was the scene of loud and, at times, frantic discussions, but by evening, all five individuals were in agreement.

Rob refused to leave Mary Dean alone until there was news about Tom's whereabouts. Thus Rob and Mary would leave immediately for Myrtle Beach to pick up Annie. Then they would drive to the Deans' home in Dillon and, depending on news about Tom, would either stay in Dillon or meet Bill, Jeannine and Aileen somewhere to be decided.

Rob was to buy a prepaid phone on the way to Myrtle Beach. Bill had just purchased one, and Rob had the number.

Neither Rob's nor Bill's old cell phones were to be used again. Rob would discard both of them somewhere en route to Myrtle Beach.

Rob was not to contact Frank Hardy in any way. Jeannine and Bill wanted Aileen to stay with them, a move favored also by Mary. Rob agreed to leave Aileen, but only after much persuasion.

Aileen and Jeannine were to study what material Bill had salvaged from Jeannine's desk with a view to convincing the FDA that Mandley's PMA was fraudulent. No one was to contact StatFind or Mandley. In the event it was necessary to call Bethesda, Bill would do the calling.

***

Rob and Mary Dean said goodbye to the others.

As Bill went to the door. Rob whispered.

"Do you have a gun, Bill?"

"My sister keeps a .22 rifle here."

"Load it and keep it by your bed tonight. And check the window locks. Hopefully, tomorrow we'll know more what we're up against."

Bill nodded.

Rob went to the car. Mary was in the front seat.

He did not turn on the headlights until he was away from the house.

***

They were at a "Comfort" Inn near Highway I-95, but there was no comfort for Lise. She was terrified.

The room had two double beds. "Little" Tommy was finally asleep in one of them. Tom Dean lay on the other.

"Lise, get over here. I'm waiting."

Lise stared at herself in the full length mirror. Her youthful body still had some tan, and her svelte form was firm and doubtless as desirable as ever. This was a ritual. She would emerge from the bathroom, and thrill to see Tom's eyes devour her.

But tonight was different. For the past few days the gleam that signaled his desire for her was gone. There was no hint of romance in his fathomless, empty eyes.

She studied her body in the mirror. She had not changed. He had.

The "teen" in her nineteen years asserted itself. *Mom, I wish I was home. God I'm scared. I'm sorry. Help.*

Tom's voice reached through the door.

"Lise, hurry up. Get out here."

She shivered.

On the other bed, little Tommy likewise shook with fear. He kept his eyes shut, tight.

***

In the gray Audi at Nags Head, the phone was on speaker. Hazim, the driver, listened as Fareed Hamza spoke.

"You lost both Wilson and Hamm! How could you do that? This is important. Do you forget the meeting is in two weeks"

"Fareed, we underestimated Hamm. He acts like a pro. We can still get him and Ryan."

"When? After the FDA blows our cover? Hazim, you must stop them now."

"We will not fail. Hamm is somewhere near Whalebone Junction. They are not many people at the beach now. We're checking houses with cars or with lights at night."

***

Aileen was asleep in her bedroom.

The only illumination was the flood of moonlight through the sliding doors to the deck. Bill set the "Charley" bar to jam them shut.

Jeannine watched.

"What's the rifle for, Bill?"

"Those guys, whoever they are, are busting their guts to find us, namely, you."

"Is the .22 loaded?"

"Yes there was a box of ammo in the dresser drawer."

"Do you know guns?"

"I do, but this is a kid's weapon."

Bill put the rifle down. Jeannine turned towards him.

"Bill, I'm sorry I've been a jerk, and here you risk yourself to help me."

The moonlight enhanced her attractiveness. Bill remembered his promise. He straightened up to leave. She touched his arm.

"Bill, thanks for everything."

***

Rob drove south in silence. Numerous signs on his right announced that "Pedro" welcomed visitors to the motel complex "South of the Border" for the night. He was near the South Carolina border.

In the passenger seat Mary Dean slept fitfully.

She was back at Myrtle Beach. Her husband held Tommy by the ankles over a balcony. My God, No! Stop! He turned and stared. His eyes were black. Behind him stood Lise, smirking. Mary looked back at her husband. His hands were empty. He looked over the railing and smiled. She screamed.

Rob shook her shoulder.

"Mary, are you all right?"

"No, I'm not. Not at all."

They drove into South Carolina.

***

******

Chapter 19
Thursday, October 26

At the beach house, Aileen watched as Jeannine opened Bill's laptop.

Bill put down the phone.

"We can't get Aileen's computer, you'll have to use mine."

Jeannine looked up.

"Because?"

"Because the Manteo police won't release it. They're holding it as evidence against Tom Dean in the slaying of Pops. That was in Tyrrell County, not Dare, so the Columbia Sheriff may need it to establish motive. The FBI wants it too, as evidence for Aileen's kidnapping. The bottom line is that we have to work without it."

Aileen stood up and stretched.

"Bill, what about Tom Dean?"

"Manteo is watching his apartment. Everybody, Manteo, Tyrrell County, and the FBI want to find him. The only uncertainty remaining is to tie him to Jeannine's kidnapping. The FBI's betting on it. And the murder of the van's driver was in Pasquotank County. They want to find him too. Everybody wants to talk to Mr. Dean."

Aileen mused.

"That should keep him from bothering us for a while."

Bill shrugged.

"I hope so."

Jeannine broke in.

"Aileen, you and I need to get to work. We have to tell the FDA about Harry. I need to load the CD's that Bill rescued onto his laptop."

She handed a pile of papers to Aileen.

"Sort through these for me. They're notes from MTS. You should recognize most of them."

Aileen buried herself in the documents while Jeannine copied the first CD-ROM onto Bill's hard drive.

***

The sun was still high. Cumulus clouds filled the sky. Their reflection on the computer display obscured Jeannine's numbers. She yawned and adjusted the blinds so that the numbers were legible. She turned to Aileen.

"You had 60 patients in this study, right?"

Aileen kept sorting papers. She did not look up.

"That's right."

"Then how come Mrs. Hartman has number 68?"

"We had about 100 applicants for the study, and we numbered all of them. Only 60 people qualified. Mrs. Hartman was applicant 68, that's all."

"I get that. Another question. That Tuesday when you found Mrs. Hartman's data were faked, you said Harry seemed different. Hair messed up, desk cluttered and things like that."

"That's right. He acted different."

"Had that happened before?"

"If it did, I never noticed."

"That's what worries me. Suppose Harry never faked data before Mrs. Hartman's. He could tell the FDA, that it was only one mistake. That one case doesn't really matter, that the study is valid without her."

Jeannine handed a sheet of numbers to Aileen.

Mandley's 60 Patients	Success	Failure	Total
Real Treatment (Active Implant)	31	7	38
Dummy Treatment (Placebo, Inactive Implant)	6	16	22

"Look at these results for all 60 patients. All 60 received a chip implant, but for 22 of them, the chip was a "dummy." And

31 of 38 patients with the real chip were a success, while only 6 of 22 patients with the dummy chip were. These results look good for Mandley even if we discount Mrs. Hartman. If Harry's cheating was a one time aberration, The FDA could still approve the PMA."

Aileen protested.

"But you showed that Mrs. Hartman's data weren't 'banker's rounded' and couldn't be real. Why not look at the rounding for the other patients?"

Jeannine slammed her fist into her hand.

"Because Harry and Thibault took my computer. Bill was able to salvage only the data for Patients 27 and 68. I copied those to a CD. The other data were on my hard drive. They're gone. There's no way to know if the times ended in even digits or not."

"What about the other CD's? Don't they have that data."

"No. All they have is scheduling, when different patients were tested. Things like that."

Aileen slumped into her chair.

Bill Hamm appeared.

"How's it going?"

They stared. He got the point.

"Look, let's take a break for lunch. I'll make some sandwiches."

They ate in silence.

***

The fluffy cumulus clouds had morphed into towering gray formations that darkened the sun. At sea, jagged streaks of lightning jabbed at the ocean's surface.

Jeannine pulled the blinds wide.

A plastic chair flew against the rail of the deck, while a towel blown away, landed in a tangle of sea oats whose brown heads were bent low.

The glass doors were splattered with large droplets.

The storm came ashore as furious gusts sprayed the glass with waves of water that flowed downwards in coalescing sheets.

Jeannine backed away from the window and went back to the computer. A spread sheet was on the screen.

Bill looked over her shoulder.

"Jeannine, I see those patient numbers, but what's this column of letters."

Jeannine looked. The column was one character in width. Each entry was either a "J" or an "H," except for a single "A." She called out.

"Aileen, what do these letters mean?"

"The letter says who recorded the data. The 'A' for Patient 27 means I ran that session."

"So the 'H' stands for 'Harry?'"

"Right, and the 'J' for 'Joan.'"

"Joan?"

"Yes, Dr. Joan Garreau. She was the electro physiologist before Harry. Thibault fired her. He said she didn't know what she was doing. Thibault hired Harry to replace her."

"You mean Harry didn't do all the recordings?"

"That's right, Joan did some too."

Bill broke in.

"What's this column with 'S's and 'F's?"

"That says whether the experiment was a success or failure."

Outside the storm raged.

A determined Jeannine stayed at the computer.

She clicked fast, compiling numbers.

Finally she turned back to Bill and Aileen.

"Look at this, guys. These are the results Harry obtained by himself."

Aileen came and stood with Bill. Both studied the screen as Jeannine continued.

"Harry is a whiz at getting "good" results. He recorded the data for 44 of the 60 patients. He got a whopping 28 successes out of 31 patients for the real treatment and only 2 successes out of 13 patients for the dummy treatment."

Harry's 44 Patients	Success	Failure	Total
Real Treatment (Active Implant)	28	3	31
Dummy Treatment (Placebo, Inactive Implant)	2	11	13

"Now look at Joan's experiments. She ran 15 experiments. We can add in Aileen's single experiment with Mr. Peters. That gives us 16 experiments not done by Harry."

Jeannine frowned.

"Look at what Joan and Aileen got. They have only 3 successes out of 7 for the real treatment, and 4 out of 9 for the dummy treatment. The real treatment has no effect!"

Joan's and Aileen's 16 Patients	Success	Failure	Total
Real Treatment (Active Implant)	3	4	7
Dummy Treatment (Placebo, Inactive Implant)	4	5	9

Jeannine added.

"Technically, the 'Odds Ratio' for Harry's table is a whopping 51.3, but is only 0.9 for Joan's. That's even less than 1. He faked enough data to bring the Odds Ratio for the combined table with 60 patients up to 11.8."

Bill interrupted.

"Jeannine, that's jargon."

"Right, and we should look at the natural logarithms anyway, but I don't want to explain it now."

Bill was happy for that.

"OK, so summarize what you have proved."

Jeannine smiled.

"This is what we have. First we prove definitely that Mrs. Hartman's data are fake. They are not banker-rounded. Harry recorded them, so Harry faked them. Further, we have Aileen's independent testimony that not only are Hartman's data faked, but her real data showed the treatment was a failure. Mrs. Hartman's case is clear. We know that for her, Harry faked 'Success' where there was none."

She continued.

"Next, we have a whopping discrepancy between Joan's results (including Aileen's) versus Harry's. According to him the treatment was an overwhelming success, but we already know that he faked success in *at least one case.*"

She went on.

"Finally, Joan Garreau is a Ph. D. like Harry. She's competent, and she found no effect of the treatment in 15 patients, whether or not we include Aileen's patient, Mr. Peters."

Jeannine closed her argument.

"The only evidence for success is Harry's, and we can prove he's a cheat. Joan's evidence shows the treatment does not work. The preponderance of the evidence indicates massive fraud by Harry and MTS."

Aileen was silent. Bill too was lost in thought.

Jeannine stood and went to the window.

Over the ocean the dark clouds were dispersing. The sun pierced through them in broad glowing swaths that gave promise, somewhere, of a rainbow. Jeannine's hair glowed in the muted light. Her blue eyes shone with conviction.

Bill was smitten. He could not look away.

Aileen glanced from Jeannine to Bill and back before speaking.

"Jeannine, you've nailed it. No way the FDA can approve the PMA now."

Bill shook his thoughts back to Mandley Test Services and Harry.

"The whole scenario makes sense. Thibault wants this chip on the market, Joan Garreau's early tests are completely negative so he fires her and hires Harry. Harry cheats and "makes" the experiment succeed. Now Thibault can get the FDA's approval. But along comes Aileen and exposes Harry."

He added.

"Here's what I'm wondering. "Mandley Bionics is huge. What could be so important about this particular chip or drug that Thibault would risk the company's reputation with a fraudulent study?"

A dark cloud cut off the sun and shadowed the room. He lowered his voice.

"And kidnapping and murder too?"

***

In Myrtle Beach, Betsy was waiting outside her condo when Rob and Mary arrived. Mary jumped from the car and grabbed her daughter. Betsy spoke.

"Mary, I'm so sorry …"

"Betsy, thank God you're OK. Tom's gone bad. I'm just glad he didn't hurt you."

"But Tommy?"

"You did what you could. I know that. As for Tommy, I've got to believe that Tom would never hurt him. I have to believe that."

After several tearful minutes, Rob spoke.

"Mary, we have to get Annie to your mother by tonight.

"What about my van? I can't leave it here."

"Betsy can keep the van for you. I'm not letting you out of my sight."

Mary was exhausted.

"Rob, what would I do without…?"

Holding Amy, she opened the door of the Crown Vic.

The rain started as they left Myrtle Beach. It came hard, and all at once. Sheets of water lashed the windshield and obscured the road ahead while the slashing wipers repeatedly tried to clear a fan-shaped opening to peer through. In a minute the roadway had accumulated a layer of water. Oncoming cars sprayed fountains to the right and left as they approached.

Rob drove slowly.

They headed back towards Dillon. Only the "whup-whup" of the wipers broke the silence.

***

It was not raining in Nags Head when the two men entered the convenience store. Both were "overdressed" for the beach. They made no pretense of being vacationers.

It was off-season. No one else was in the store.

The first man handed two photographs to the clerk.

"Have you seen either of these two women?"

The clerk examined the photos.

"Pretty nice."

The man was not amused.

"Have you seen them?"

"Nope."

The man showed Bill Hamm's photo to the clerk.

"How about this guy?"

"Are you police or something?"

The man nodded, but offered no identification. The clerk handed the photos back.

"I've seen him. He was here yesterday, came in and bought some milk, eggs, bread, stuff like that. He hasn't been back."

"You know where he's staying?"

"No. He drove south when he left. Most likely near Whalebone Junction, I guess. Rodanthe's too far and anyway they have their own store down there. He could have gone to Manteo, but they have their own stores too, and they're bigger than this one."

"Thank you."

Moments later, the clerk looked out the window. A gray Audi pulled out of the lot and headed south.

***

Wayne Johnson missed Bill Hamm. StatFind needed him.

He missed Jeannine even more. He wanted to explain to her that Mandley had given him no choice. Still, he knew she would not listen.

Mona appeared at his door.

"Sir, on your call to Dr. Thibault at MTS, I couldn't reach him."

"Mona, please try again."

"It's no use. Jane Peterson says he's been reassigned in Mandley Bionics. She doesn't know where. This just happened this morning, and she's got no way to contact him."

"No way? That's weird. What about our contract?"

"She says not to worry. She'll call you when his replacement arrives."

"That's a screwed up way to run a company? All right. Where's Harry Roberts?"

"He's here, in his office."

Wayne jumped up. He had to see Harry. What the hell is going on?

***

Frank Hardy knew that Thibault was a coward, but the doctor was not stupid.

Those guys at Mandley were dangerous.

Besides, that maniac Tom Dean was out of control.

He decided to heed Thibault's warning.

Suitcase in hand, Frank stepped from his office and locked the door.

His agency now was officially defunct.

***

Lise was stir crazy. Another day cramped up in this damned motel with the kid.

Next to her Tom lay snoring. What's he worried about? *It's his kid, isn't it. That's no crime. He's not done anything. Let me out of here.*

In the other bed little Tommy gave a soft cry.

Lise rolled over. *Shut up kid.* She hid her face in the pillow, but sleep would not come. She tried to count the 18-wheelers as they rumbled by on the highway. Nothing worked.

She turned on the TV, but left the sound off to not disturb Tom.

A news channel reported a new wave of rocket attacks in northern Israel. The strip at the base of the screen stated that Hezbollah was responsible.

She switched channels, but dropped the remote when she read the news strip at the bottom of the television. The police had a suspect in the disappearance of Horace "Pops" Simons.

Then a man's face filled the screen. Tom!

Lise switched off the set and sat shivering before the dark screen.

***

******

Chapter 20
Friday, October 27

Bill Hamm awakened to one of those bright October days on the Banks that the natives never advertise, for fear of attracting anew a swarm of tourists to despoil their "private" pleasures of the Fall.

Along the beach, a four inch "cliff" of undercut sand marked the high water line of yesterday's storm. Scattered broken shells, sea weed and algae lay clumped and drying along the shore, but not for long. The relentless lapping waves of the incoming tide steadily rearranged and erased the storm's litter.

Bill sat on the deck intrigued by the irresistible forces at work on the strand below.

Inside, Aileen and Jeannine huddled together over a mass of papers, graphs, and spreadsheet printouts. Periodically, one of them would type furiously on Bill's computer.

Bill smiled. He was glad that these two scientists were on his side. He would not want to be opposed by them.

***

In Dillon the morning air was cool, but the sun was bright. On the street, storm-broken twigs and branches lay amid myriads of pine needles. Rob Wilson guided the car carefully through the debris. He pulled into a driveway bordered by pines.

Mary Dean's mother waved from the doorway. Mary and Rob walked up to the porch. Annie was asleep in the car.

"Mother, this is Rob Wilson."

Mrs. Morton ignored Rob. She spoke to her daughter.

"Mary, what's this about you and Tom? Where is he? And where's Tommy?"

Rose Morton had never liked her daughter's husband. His moods scared her. He was no gentleman.

"Mother, don't you watch TV? The police are looking for Tom. They think he killed a man. Tom's got Tommy. I'm looking for him. Mr. Wilson is helping me."

Mrs. Morton glanced at Rob and turned back.

"Mary, no matter what Tom has done, you are a married woman. Don't forget that."

"Mother!"

"All right. You know where I stand. Tom was at your house Tuesday morning."

"Did you see Tommy?"

"I didn't see him, and I didn't see Tom either. I saw his truck. It was parked behind the old smoke shack in back. I saw the girl. She was parked in front of your house."

Rob broke in.

"Mrs. Morton, did you see what kind of car she had?"

Mrs. Morton spoke to Mary.

"The car was a blue Toyota with North Carolina plates. A fender was dented. Who was that girl?"

Rob had seen a blue Toyota with a dented fender outside the office in Manteo. He moved in front of Mary.

"Mrs. Morton, your son-in-law is having an affair. The girl's name is Lise. She works for Tom's company. Your daughter just found out."

"Mary, I'm sorry."

"It's all right mother. I don't care about Tom. I want to find Tommy."

Rob spoke again.

"Please Mrs. Morton, is there anything else you remember?"

Finally, Mrs. Morton looked at Rob.

"Mr. Wilson, Tom's mother and father died before he married Mary. His father had an estranged sister, Carla. She did not come to his funeral. She married a 'Cooper.' She lived in North Carolina, Robeson County, near Pembroke. Maybe she still does. He might go there."

"Thank you Mrs. Morton. That may help."

Mary embraced her mother.

"Thanks, mother. Pray for Tommy, please. I'll call you."
In the car, Annie was still asleep. Rob turned to Mary.
"It would be better if Annie could stay with your mother."
Mary nodded. She carried her daughter into the house.
Rob waited in the car.

***

Tom Dean was on the move. He left I-95 and headed east.
Lise turned towards him. Tom frowned.
"What now?"
"The kid's hungry. I am too."
"All right. All right. Just wait."
Ahead on the right was a Hardee's fast food restaurant. They pulled off.
"Tommy, you stay in the car and be quiet. Miss Lise and I are going in. Don't cry. Stay put."
At the entrance, Lise turned right. She spoke over her shoulder.
"I'm going to the bathroom."
"Hurry it up."
She went in.

***

Lise wept into the restroom sink. *He's going to kill me. Maybe I can get away? God help me.*
An elderly woman came in and Lise pretended to wash her face. When the woman left, Lise studied her image in the mirror. Her hair was tangled and her eyes were swollen red. *Tom won't like that.* She straightened her hair.
She steeled herself to face him and opened the door.
Tom was not there.
She looked out the window. Her car was gone!

***

Rob and Mary were on I-95 entering North Carolina. His new cell phone vibrated.
"Rob Wilson, here."
It was Bob, the FBI agent in Elizabeth City.
"Rob, they just found the girl, Lise."

163

"Where?"

"Robeson County, at a Hardee's near Pembroke. Dean ditched her. For once he did something right. She's alive and well."

"What about the boy, Tommy?"

Mary leaned in and strained to hear.

"Dean still has him."

Rob shook his head at Mary. She slumped in her seat.

"And the Toyota?"

"Dean has it, but by now he may have stolen something else. I'm checking reports now."

"Bob, thanks. Thanks a lot."

Rob headed for Pembroke.

***

In Nags Head, Aileen and Jeannine had been at the computer all day.

Bill Hamm rose from the table. His cup was empty, he rose to get a refill. He stopped by the window.

The row of houses on the front beach curved slightly leaving a gap between two homes about six houses away. Through that space the road behind them was visible. A car had stopped there.

Bill lifted his binoculars.

It was the gray Audi.

"Box up that data girls. We have to leave. Now!"

He grabbed the .22 from the table.

"They'll be here any minute. Let's go."

Jeannine and Aileen stuffed the papers and graphs into the box. Aileen grabbed the laptop. Jeannine hoisted the box. They scrambled down the wooden stairway. Bill locked up. He came down and tossed the car keys to Jeannine.

"Here, you drive."

Bill climbed in the back holding the rifle.

Jeannine accelerated onto the road.

***

******

Chapter 21
Friday, October 27

It was afternoon by the time Rob and Mary located Carla Cooper's house on a dirt lane, not far from Pembroke. It was a white frame two-story building with a porch on two sides. The ground-level doors and windows had boards nailed across them. In the back was a detached frame garage, presumably white at one time, but now weathered gray. The front yard had a summer's growth of waist-high weeds, most of them no longer green, but with dried "pods" atop stiff brown stems.

The weeds were undisturbed. It was evident that no one had approached the house from the front. Equally undisturbed was the sandy driveway. Weeds and grass thrived amid the pine needles in the shallow ruts. No car had been there either.

They drove by slowly. Rob looked at Mary.

"He's not here."

She nodded and shut her eyes. Her shoulders shook uncontrollably as she tried to contain her tears.

With one hand on the wheel, Rob leaned across the seat and touched her arm.

"Mary, Tom did the right thing by Lise. He let her go. He'll do the same for Tommy. He's his son. Tommy will be OK."

"Rob, Tom is possessive. He will not share Tommy."

Before Rob could reply, he caught a movement in the rear view mirror.

Down the road a car approached, its wheels churning a dusty cloud in its wake.

It was dark colored. It could be blue.

He looked again. It *was* blue. Rob thought quickly. Their primary goal was to get Tommy back. Catching Tom was secondary, Tommy's safety came first. Rob increased his speed.

"Rob, what are you doing? Stop. That could be Tom, and Tommy could be in that car. Go back."

Rob kept driving.

"Mary, if that is Tom, he's headed for that old house. If we stop he'd be afraid to. He'd keep going or turn back."

Ahead was a sharp bend in the road. Just past it, Rob pulled his car onto the shoulder.

"If it's not Tom, that car should pass us in a few seconds."

Rob reached under the seat and checked his revolver. Then he checked his watch. They waited.

***

No car passed. Mary looked at Rob.

"It was Tom, who else would stop at the old Cooper house."

Rob turned the car around.

He drove slowly past the white frame building without pausing. The high weeds in the front yard still were undisturbed, but the overgrown drive displayed two lines of tire-mashed weeds that disappeared around the back of the house. No car was visible from the road.

Rob continued past until they were out of sight.

"He's there. You stay here. I'm going back on foot."

"I'm coming with you."

"Mary you should stay here."

"No. Tommy is there. I'm coming."

She followed him.

They made their way through the pines to the rear of the old garage. An open space of brown wiry grass separated the garage from the rear of the house.

Rob crouched and looked around the corner. The rear door was ajar. Two boards had sealed the opening. One now hung loosely from the frame. Another, with upward-protruding nails, lay on the ground. Parked not far from the door was a blue Toyota.

No sound came from the house.

***

In Nags Head, Jeannine drove. Aileen sat in front and Bill in the back. Through the rear window, Bill saw that the gray Audi had stopped several houses away.

Jeannine continued to the south. A few minutes later, they passed the Kentucky Fried Chicken on the right. The Catholic Chapel was on the left. Bill signaled Jeannine to turn north onto Route 158.

They drove in silence. Bill kept looking back. There was no sign of the Audi. He laid the .22 on the seat beside him.

Ahead on the left loomed a huge hill of sand.

Bill spoke.

"That's Jockey's Ridge ahead. That's where Nags Head gets its name."

"Bill, there's a road on the right, parallel to the beach. Do you want me to take it?"

"No. Stay left on 158. It's quicker than the beach road. We want off the island."

They passed Conch Street. Hardly a block long, it connected their highway to the beach road.

A few seconds later, Bill looked back.

A car had turned from Conch Street onto Route 158.

It was the gray Audi.

***

At the old Cooper house, Tom Dean peered through the slits in the boarded window. Something had moved near the garage. He waited. Sure enough, a man's head appeared around the corner at the back. *Police? Not likely. Nobody knows this place!*

He strained to see. *Who? Wait, Mary's mother knew the Coopers. It's Mary. And that must be that FBI guy. Frank's dope who loved his dog.*

The head appeared again. This time Tom recognized him. *It is Wilson. Mary must be with him.*

He turned to his son.

"Don't move. Wait there and be quiet."

Tommy shrank into the corner. He had found that the only way to win dad's approval was to shut up and sit still.

Tom climbed the stairs to the second floor. The window was not boarded up. He cracked the shutters and called out.

"You out back. Stay where you are. If Mary wants Tommy she can come in alone. You stay put."

He waited.

Mary's head appeared from behind the garage. She walked slowly towards the door.

Tom held his Beretta ready. He went down the stairs.

Mary stood at the door.

Tom Dean smiled.

Mary ignored him.

"Tommy, come here. Come to mommy."

Tommy looked to his father. At Tom Dean's nod, he ran to his mother. Mary scooped him up. She turned to her husband.

"Tom, what have you done?"

Tom Dean peered through the crack between the boards.

"Where's your friend, Mary?"

She noted the gun in his hand.

"I made him promise not to move. We did just as you said. Tom, what has happened to you."

"OK, call him in here."

"No. I can't do that."

Tom turned towards her. His eyes were blank. He pointed the gun at her. She shuddered. He spoke.

"Call him."

"No."

His eyes darkened. Mary had never seen that expression before. Tom held the gun to Tommy's head.

"Call him!"

Tommy whimpered. Mary sobbed.

"He's your son! Please!

"I said call him! Tell him it's OK to come in!"

Mary grabbed Tommy and went to the door. She squeezed him tight.

"Rob, come on in. It's, it's … OK."

***

Tom Dean waved Mary to the lone chair by the table. She sat down numbly, clutching Tommy. Tom went to the door. An empty-handed Rob Wilson stepped into the open. Tom smiled.

"Good. Wilson, get your gun out, slow, and toss it to me. Real careful."

Rob tossed his revolver down.

Tom's mouth widened to a grin, but his eyes were blanks.

"Stay where you are."

Tom called over his shoulder.

"Mary, come out here. I want you to see this. Leave Tommy inside."

Mary came, but Tommy clung to her. She stooped to put him down.

Tom's eyes stayed on Rob.

"Mister, nobody screws my wife, least of all a dumb dog lover like you."

He lifted his Beretta.

***

To Mary, the next few seconds were multiplied into minutes. In the first second, still bent from putting her son down, she looked up and saw that Tom's arm and gun were pointed downwards.

She watched as Tom extended his arm from his body. She gasped as the deadly gun reached horizontal. Next she saw the board with nails that lay at her feet.

She felt two hands grasp the board and lift it.

As if in a dream she realized that the hands were her own.

The gun jerked upwards, as if it had been fired. In the same instant she felt the board rip across Tom's arm. A red line traced the passage of a nail through torn flesh.

Tom's eyes turned on her. He struck her, hard. She heard Tommy's scream.

Sounds of a scuffle filtered through her barely conscious brain. Mary rolled over to shield her son.

By the time she could focus, there was no more struggle. Tom had run for the Toyota and opened the door.

Rob, lifted his revolver and aimed.

"No. Rob, No. Not you. Don't shoot him. ... Not you."

Rob looked her way. When he looked back, Tom was in the car. It pulled away, fast.

Tom was gone.

Mary threw her arms around Rob.

"He's my husband, at least he was. I couldn't live with you being the one to kill him. I couldn't. Not you. Somebody else has to do that."

"Mary, if it wasn't for you I'd be dead. You did a brave thing."

"It wasn't brave. I didn't know what I was doing. Besides, if it weren't for me and Tommy, you wouldn't have been exposed. I should never have called you to come out. It was selfish, but he was going to kill Tommy, his own son!"

"Your voice cracked. I knew something was wrong."

"Rob, you gave yourself up for us. I'll never forget that."

Tommy pulled at her leg. She hugged him.

"Tommy, this is your 'Uncle Rob,' you're going to know him real well."

They hiked back to the car.

***

Dusk was falling as Jeannine drove across the long bridge to the mainland. In the back seat, Bill Hamm clutched the rifle. The gray Audi was no longer in sight. It had followed them up to the bridge and then, unexpectedly, stopped.

Bill was not relieved.

Route 158 lay on a narrow peninsula with the Currituck Sound to the East, and a branch of the Albemarle Sound to the West. There was only one way to go.

Somewhere along Route 158, someone was waiting. They were trapped.

***

******

Chapter 22
Saturday, October 28

The sun rose over the Currituck Sound and silhouetted a row of tall pines on the distant shore of Corolla. The morning mist dissipated to reveal calm waters that reflected yellow and green, the colors caught by the scattered clouds from the rising sun.

The natural beauty of the scene was lost on the occupants of the black Mercedes. The driver, Abed, talked into the phone. His partner, Brendan, sipped coffee and listened.

"They did not pass us. We have been here since you called. They have stopped somewhere, maybe Jarvisburg, there is an old motel there. Drive the Audi across the bridge to the mainland and start north. We will start south. They are still between us. They cannot escape."

Abed hung up and turned to his partner, Brendan.

"Keep that AK47 out of sight, put it on the floor."

***

Bill Hamm stood on a dilapidated wooden dock that stretched into the marshland of a section of the Albemarle Sound. He was on the phone.

"Rob, where are you?"

"I'm back in North Carolina. I drove all night. I'm with your friend, Hammond, in Old Trap. He's getting the boat ready for me."

"Is Mary with you?

"No. I left her and Tommy in Dillon with her mother, but what about you? Are Aileen and Jeannine OK?"

"They almost got us last night. At Nags Head, an Audi followed us and a black Mercedes was waiting at Grandy. We spotted the Mercedes and turned back to Jarvisburg. We're, stuck between two sets of Mandley's thugs. Tell Hammond we're south of Fisher Landing, he'll know. And come quick."

"OK, Bill, I'm on the way. Hammond says it will take two hours."

Bill hung up and turned to Jeannine.

"You and Aileen get your stuff together. Wait here. I'll ditch the car and come back."

"Bill, the dock's dry. There's no water, just muck."

"It's still tidal here, the water will come in."

"And then?"

"Then we'll see. Here, you hold the rifle. I'll be back as soon as I can."

***

The women deposited their duffel bags on the gray boards. The weathered dock stretched across the marsh and ended in shallow water insufficient to float the small dinghy stranded on the mud flat. Ripples swirled around the end of the craft as the water inched landwards.

Jeannine and Aileen shivered in the chill morning air. Their night had been sleepless. They stared numbly at the incoming waters. A Great Blue Heron waited nearby, beak poised over an incoming rivulet, waiting for a tide-borne meal.

The sun rose higher. Now water lapped the poles of the dock. Jeannine, Aileen and the Blue Heron waited.

***

The sign said "Jarvisburg." Abed stopped the black Mercedes at a roadside stand where a woman was loading packages into the back of a pickup.

Brendan leaned out the window.

"Excuse me, I'm looking for friend. He has a white Accord. My sister and her friend might be with him. My sister has red hair. Her friend's a blonde. Have you seen them?"

"There was a guy with a white car this morning. He took that road over there, by that row of pines. It goes to Fisher Landing."

"Thank you."

Abed called the gray Audi.

172

"Hazim, I have them. Jarvisburg! Turn left on Fisher Landing Road. Get up here!"

Abed turned onto Fisher Landing Road. To the left were empty bare fields, ahead in the distance a grove of trees offered the first possibility for concealment for his prey.

***

Bill Hamm parked his Accord behind the shed. It was the best he could do. A sharp eye would spot it, but at least it was partly concealed. He locked the car and pushed his way through a stand of milkweed whose airborne seeds wafted skywards behind him.

After several minutes he regained the road. The sun was warmer now. High overhead, a lone vulture circled. Bill glanced at his watch. He must hurry.

No cars were on the road. He jogged on the sandy shoulder.

***

The Mercedes drove slowly. The road went through flat fields, very flat.

A brief glare momentarily blinded Abed.

"Brendan, look over there. That reflection by the shed. It's a windshield. It could be Hamm."

They reached the shed, but the Accord was empty. Abed looked about. The only trees were to the west.

"It has to be Hamm's car. There's no place to hide. They're at the Sound. Let's go. We can't wait for Hazim."

They drove toward Fisher Landing.

***

The sun's rays dispelled the October chill. At the end of the dock, the dinghy was afloat in a foot of water, its rope stretched taut by the incoming tide.

Bill Hamm appeared running. The heron flew away.

"Quick! Into the dinghy. They're coming!"

He ran to the end of the dock. Jeannine and Aileen jumped into the boat. He tossed the duffels to them.

"Careful. Watch your balance. Here's the rifle."

He seized the oars and stepped in. He handed one to Jeannine.

"Push off on that side. I'll take this one."

With their weight, the stern of the boat scraped the mud as they pushed. Finally they floated free in the channel, but the incoming current pushed them creekwards, away from the open sound.

Bill stroked the oars with all his strength. He pulled hard for the open water.

***

Their little boat rounded a promontory. A second dock, bordered by trees came into view. On it were two men. One held a weapon.

Successive splashes approached the side of the boat.

"Splat, splat, splat. ... Splat, splat. ... Splat, splat, splat!"

Bill shouted.

"Automatic fire. Keep down. Keep down."

He arched his back and pulled hard on the oars. The dinghy responded.

"Splat, splat, splat. ... Splat, splat. ... Splat, splat, splat!"

One side of the boat was sprayed with water. Bill kept pulling.

"Splat, splat, splat. ... Splat, splat."

These last splashes fell short of the boat.

Bill pulled hard on the oars. They rounded a bend in the shore. The dock was no longer visible.

They did not see the angry gestures of the men on the dock.

***

Aileen slumped backwards. A red stain spread through her blonde hair. Jeannine held her and tried to stanch the flow of blood.

"Bill, she's hit."

Bill looked shorewards. There were no more docks. Only pines bordered the extensive flats of marsh.

"A stray must have ricocheted off the water and hit her. Do what you can for her. Those guys will watch the shore. We have to head out."

He pulled away. There was nowhere to go except the open water.

A light rain began to fall and the waves grew larger. The little boat tipped precariously.

***

On the shore, a gray Audi pulled up behind the Mercedes. Hazim got out.

"Abed, where are they?"

"They're out on the sound. We hit the Harris girl. She may be done for."

He added.

"It's a trashy little row boat. They can't make it anywhere. They've got to come back. They can't handle the open water in a 12 foot boat. It's rough out there."

"I don't see them."

"They're beyond that bend with the pine trees."

"What should we do?"

"Abed pointed. We must finish this. We'll patrol the shore. You cruise Route 158 in case they get by us. Don't go far. They will be afoot. Hamm's car is useless. I shot out the tires, the windshield too.

The men in the Audi drove away.

***

The little boat pitched and yawed as the wind increased. Jeannine held Aileen tightly. At least the wound looked superficial. The bleeding had stopped.

"Bill, we need help. It's too rough. We're too far from shore."

Bill strained to keep the bow of the rowboat facing the oncoming waves. The bow lifted and slapped downwards with each passing crest. He looked at his feet. They were wet.

"We're taking water. Hang on. If you know any prayers, say them now."

"Bill, we have to go back."

"Not with those guys on shore. We stay out here."

The wind died, and the waves lessened. The boat was still.

Bill looked back at Aileen. Her breathing was regular.

He shut his eyes and prayed. He heard a motor, and looked up.

A boat was approaching, fast.

***

Bill squinted as the boat drew near. He laughed.

"It's OK Jeannine. It's Rob. He has my friend's boat."

The old classic Chris-Craft Commander idled near them. Jeannine recognized Rob's voice.

"Bill, row over here. I can't get closer. The wash will swamp you."

"Rob, Aileen's hurt. Grab this line. I'll hand her up."

They left the dinghy awash and transferred to the 41 foot craft. It wasn't land, but it was a lot more secure than the fragile row boat.

Bill and Jeannine took Aileen below and laid her on a bunk.

Above, Rob gunned the twin engines and headed across the sound to the North River.

***

In Delaware, Fareed Hamza, head of security at Mandley Bionics, spoke into his phone.

"Abed, you cannot be sure that they drowned."

"Fareed, the water was rough. Their boat was small."

"And you say Brendan hit the Harris girl?"

"He hit her. I know that. I saw her drop."

"All right, but we must make sure they are dead. If Hamm did make it across the Sound, he will either head south to Manteo and Columbia, or north to Elizabeth City. My suspicion is Elizabeth City. You will go there."

Fareed paused.

"Have Hazim check the Outer Banks Hospital on Nags Head and Manteo and Columbia. If they are alive, Harris will be treated somewhere."

The Mercedes headed north on 158. The gray Audi headed south to Nags Head.

***

Rob's blue Crown Victoria was waiting dockside. Rob helped a pale Aileen into the back seat. She managed a wan smile. He turned to Bill.

"What now?"

"Hammond will pick up his boat here. Jeannine and I will rent a car in Elizabeth City. You drop us there, then you and Aileen head for Aunt Agatha's. Get her wound checked on the way."

"You'll have to use your credit card for the rental car. They'll know that."

"There's no choice. We'll lose ourselves in Norfolk."

Jeannine sat in back and held Aileen.

The drive to Elizabeth City was not long. Rob found the car rental and dropped Jeannine and Bill there.

Aileen stayed with Rob. Her headache had lightened, the throbbing was gone, and her hair no longer was marked with blood. She moved to the front seat next to him.

"Aileen, you look better. Thank God that bullet was a stray." She touched his arm.

"Rob, you've been super. Thanks. But will Mary and Tommy be OK in Dillon without you?"

"I hope so. They're at her mother's. The police are watching the house. Dean should leave them alone. He knows the police are looking for him."

"She's lucky you were there for her. Me too."

She closed her eyes and leaned on his shoulder.

***

After renting a Camry in Elizabeth City, Jeannine and Bill took route 17, North. Jeannine drove. Keeping her eyes on the road, she spoke.

"Bill, I'm sorry I didn't treat you right you at StatFind."

"Forget it. I don't want pity."

"That's good, because you'll get none from me."

177

They laughed. Bill grew serious.

"We need to hide. We'll get a motel in Norfolk. It's a big city."

Jeannine's brow furrowed.

"Bill, those guys on the shore, why didn't you shoot back at them?"

"A popgun against an AK47? No thanks. We had to get away fast."

"But have you ever killed anyone, I mean shot to kill?"

Bill stared straight ahead. He spoke slowly.

"Jeannine, I would not answer that for just anyone."

He looked sideways.

"The answer is 'Yes.'"

"I hope you don't have to shoot anybody because of me."

"Me too."

They drove in silence.

***

******

Chapter 23
Monday, October 30

Monday morning at StatFind. A listless Mona took the call. She perked up when she recognized Bill Hamm.

"Bill, where are you?"

"Mona, I'd rather not say right now. May I speak to Wayne?"

"He's not in yet. Shall I have him call you?"

"He won't know how to reach me. I'll call back.

"Do you know how I can reach Jeannine?"

"Why do you want her?"

"I want to tell her about Dr. Roberts."

"What about Harry?"

"Last Friday was his last day with us. He cleaned out his, I mean Jeannine's, office and left. Saturday night he had an accident."

"What?"

Mona liked attention. She was in no hurry.

"He totaled his Mercedes on the Baltimore Washington Parkway. He was alone."

She hesitated.

"He was driving fast. He hit a tree. The Police say he'd been drinking."

One final pause.

"Bill, Harry's dead!"

***

Dr. Thibault sat at the bare desk. He was in exile, in Building 10 of Mandley Bionics' secure facility on the DelMarVa Peninsula in rural Delaware.

A male voice spoke through the intercom.

"Dr. Thibault, Jane Peterson is on the phone."

Dr. Thibault was pleasantly surprised. He missed Jane's trim figure.

"What is it Jane?"

"Dr. Thibault, Bernadette Harris, Aileen's mother has called several times. She's been informed that you are reassigned overseas, and that you are not available."

"That's good, Jane. I may go to Lebanon, so it could be true. How is Dr. Roberts?"

"Harry is dead. He had too much to drink and totaled his Mercedes on the Parkway."

"No! What about the PMA?"

"He finished the PMA at StatFind. I'm just glad he did not know about chip *A100*."

Dr, Thibault inhaled sharply. If Jane knew about *A100*, then she was linked to Fareed Hamza and his group. *The bitch was spying on me!* He spoke.

"Jane, how do you know about *A100*. Did Fareed send you to MTS to spy on me?"

"Do not criticize Fareed. We only do what we have to do. By the way, Frank Hardy has disappeared. Did you warn him?"

"Certainly not! I have no idea where he is."

"And you never should have talked to Aileen's mother. Now she's a problem to fix."

"Jane, have Harris or Ryan contacted the FDA?"

"No. We'll know as soon as they do. It won't matter. Even if our man can't bury their complaint, the last PMA will be approved soon, maybe tomorrow. I have to go now."

"Jane, I appreciate your calling." *You spying bitch.*

In another room, a listener replayed the tape of the conversation. He laughed. *Thibault was an idiot to not know about Jane.* He initialed and dated the tape for Fareed Hamza.

***

The luxury hotel was in downtown Norfolk. Jeannine and Bill took rooms on the eighth floor, overlooking the Chesapeake Bay.

Jeannine stared out the window at the white sails that dotted the waters. The Bay was calm. Her thoughts were not.

Someone at Mandley had ordered her and Aileen eliminated because they had discovered Harry's fake data. Now Harry was dead.

What was Mandley trying to hide?

She opened Bill's laptop. The FDA's website for Medical Devices listed summaries of the PMA's for older versions of Mandley's chip, approved some years earlier. The summaries contained tables and graphs, but no original data files. Raw data (and their digits) were not available.

Bill appeared at the door.

"What are you doing?"

"I'm on the FDA's Medical Devices Section website, looking at a graph from a past PMA for a Mandley chip. The FDA lets applicants use prior experience to justify new modifications. It's like a Bayesian approach."

"Bayesian?"

"Never mind. To test if the new modified chip is an improvement over the old chip, Mandley counts the number of 'spikes' for each patient before and after the implant."

"Do I need these details?"

"Just listen. Mandley subtracts a patient's count *after* from its count *before* and calls it an 'Improvement Score.' If the count *after* is the same as *before*, the score is 'zero.' If the count *after* is higher, the patient got worse and the score is 'minus.' If the count *after* is lower, the patient improved and the score is 'plus.'"

"So?"

"So Mandley arranges the patients in order by their scores and plots each score against the per cent of patients with that score or less."

"Why do they do that?"

"To see what per cent of the patients improved."

Bill's brow furrowed.

"I don't get it."

"You will. You told me about banker's rounding, remember. This isn't any harder."

She smiled and brought a graph up on the screen.

"Mandley studied 260 patients, 110 had the old chip, and 150 had a new modified one. They presented this graph in their PMA for the new chip.

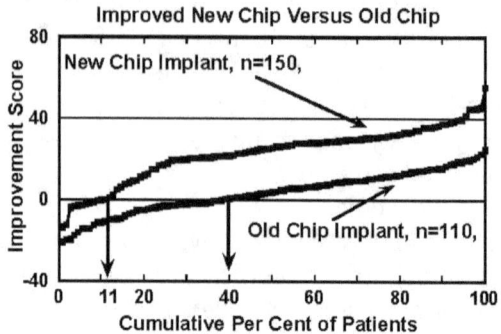

"The vertical axis on the graph gives the Improvement Score. The horizontal axis shows the percent of patients with that score or less."

"What are the two curves?"

"The bottom curve is for the old chip and its 110 patients. The arrow from zero on this curve points down to 40, so forty per cent of the patients have scores zero or below (no improvement). That means that 60 per cent have scores above zero. Those patients did improve."

"OK, so 60% of the patients got better."

"Right, at least somewhat. Now look at the top curve. It's for 150 patients for the new chip. That arrow from zero points down to 11, so eleven per cent of the scores are below zero. That means 89 per cent improved."

"So the improvement rate for the new chip is 89 per cent compared with the 60 per cent rate for the old chip.

"That's right, the improvement rate is much higher. That's why the FDA approved Mandley's new chip for marketing."

Bill rolled his eyes. Jeannine touched his arm.

"Stick with me, Bill. There's another graph that makes it clearer. Mandley also provided the FDA with a detail from the first graph. It shows only that part where the new-chip patients showed no improvement."

She tapped on the keyboard. Another graph appeared on the screen.

"Bill, this shows the worst eleven per cent of patients for each group."

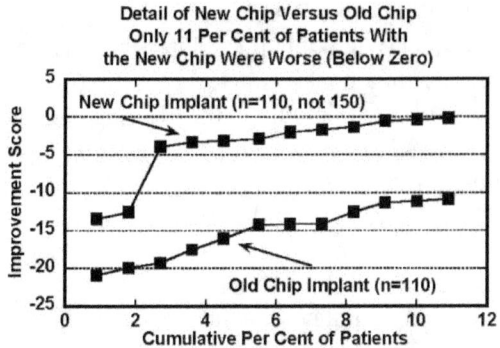

**Detail of New Chip Versus Old Chip
Only 11 Per Cent of Patients With
the New Chip Were Worse (Below Zero)**

Bill looked.

"There are twelve points each, so twelve new-chip patients got worse with scores of zero or less, and twelve old-chip patients have scores minus ten or less."

Bill's brow furrowed. He shook his head.

"Jeannine, to get a percent, you divide by the number of patients, right?"

"Right, and then multiply by 100."

"Then something is wrong. This graph tells me that twelve divided by the number of new-chip patients gives the same per cent (eleven) as when I divide twelve by the number of old-chippers. That would mean that the number of patients is the same in the two groups!"

"Damn it Bill, you always do this! The numbers are not the same in each group. This graph can't be right!"

She studied the graph for a moment.

"Look, the points for the new chip are directly above those for the old. Both groups add only, 0.9 per cent per person. That means both groups have 110 patients, because 1/110 works to 0.9 per cent while 1/150 works to 0.7 per cent."

"Does it matter, 110 or 150?"

"You bet! The FDA thought the old sample of 110 was low. They instructed Mandley to get 150 patients for the new-chip. Mandley faked the new per cents."

"But why didn't the FDA catch this?"

"The FDA was looking for scientific consistency not fake data. Probably they concentrated on the first graph with all the patients. There the plotted points overlap and you can't see individual points."

Jeannine grabbed his arm.

"What can I say. You and I are looking for fake data. Even so, if Mandley had not included the detailed graph in the PMA, we wouldn't have caught it either."

"But how did Mandley fake the new sample?"

"I don't know. Maybe they took a spread sheet column of old chip data and made up new values without changing the length of the column. But no matter how they did it, the new per cents are fake."

"Could this just be a slip of division, like having 150 patients, but dividing by 110? That would be a simple error, not faking."

"No. Look at the first graph, it stops at 100. If there were 150 patients and you divided by 110, the top percent would be 136, way over 100."

She grimaced.

"Mandley faked having 150 patients to satisfy the FDA."

"So they cheated. And Harry wasn't with Mandley when this PMA was submitted."

"Right. Let me think a minute."

Jeannine stopped and took a deep breath. She sat and surfed through several screens on the web site. Moments later she looked up.

"Damn! Here are two more PMA's where Mandley Bionics did the same thing. The per cents in their graphs are impossible, and Harry wasn't with Mandley then either."

Bill frowned.

"So Mandley has a pattern of presenting fraudulent data to the FDA, and they are scared enough of you and Aileen to risk killing you to keep you silent. Whatever their reasons, they can't tolerate an investigation."

He frowned again.

"What the hell have we gotten into?"

***

It was late afternoon and Rob was tired. Aileen was asleep in the passenger seat.

The traffic on the Pennsylvania Turnpike was slow and heavy with eighteen wheelers.

Finally, Rob reached the Bedford exit. He pulled up to the booth and paid the toll.

He was hungry, but drove by the fast food restaurants without stopping. He headed west on State Highway 56. They were only an hour away from Aileen's Aunt Agatha and Mary Catherine. Food would have to wait.

Rob looked at his passenger. Her breathing was regular.

Aileen was definitely attractive. The bandage on her head could not hide that.

He found himself studying her.

Aileen was prettier than Mary Dean, and doubtless smarter, but?

Aileen's eyes were shut, but she was aware of his scrutiny. She smiled to herself.

Ahead, the road rose steeply. The curves became intense and the ascent steepened. Rob concentrated on the climb.

Aileen's thoughts turned back to Mary Catherine.

***

******

Chapter 24
Monday, October 30

Aunt Agatha's fieldstone house was located at the base of a steep hillside covered with hardwoods. The branches were mostly bare. The lawn in front was littered with leaves variously tinted red, yellow and brown. Only the Norway Maple by the road retained some green foliage.

The Pennsylvania air was cold. The sun had disappeared behind a mountain ridge to the west when Rob pulled into the driveway. Aileen leapt from the car, clutching her arms to her body for warmth.

Bernadette Harris appeared in the doorway.

"Aileen, what happened? Not again!"

She pointed to the white bandage on her daughter's forehead.

"Mom, where's Mary Catherine?"

"She's upstairs asleep. It's nap time"

Aileen dashed up the stairs. Halfway up she turned.

"Mom, meet Rob Wilson. He's a friend whose been helping me."

She disappeared upstairs. Rob stood in the doorway.

"How are you Mr. Wilson? Thanks for bringing my daughter here. What happened to her?"

"Mrs. Harris, I'd rather she told you. Can I come in?"

"Of course. But you're cold. You need a coat."

"We should have stopped to buy warm clothes, but Aileen wouldn't let me. She had to see Mary Catherine."

Mrs. Harris smiled.

"Come in and sit down. If I guess right, Aileen wouldn't let you stop to eat either. I'll fix you something."

"I'd like that."

Squeals of delight echoed down the stairs and into the parlor. Obviously Mary Catherine was awake.

***

They sat in the parlor. Rob balanced a plate of chips with a ham and cheese sandwich. His right hand held a cold bottle of Budweiser.

Mary Catherine sat on Aileen's lap. Bernadette Harris sat opposite and listened to her daughter's account with mounting concern. She turned to Rob.

"I don't know what to say. You're telling me that Dr. Thibault was behind Aileen's disappearance. But I believed him. He seemed so kind."

"Mrs. Harris, He and my boss arranged her kidnapping. Your daughter is fortunate to be alive."

Aileen smiled at Rob.

"Mom, if it weren't for Rob, I wouldn't be here."

"Mr. Wilson, I'm truly grateful to you for my daughter. Is there anything I can do?"

Rob lifted his bottle.

"This Bud is a great start, but seriously, when is the last time you spoke with Dr. Thibault?"

"I called last Friday. The secretary told me he was reassigned to some "Bionics" company and that he was unavailable. She didn't know how to reach him."

"Did you tell her where you were, where this house is?"

"No, Aileen told me not to tell anyone about my sister Agatha."

"But you tried to reach Dr. Thibault at MTS."

"Right."

"And you called them from this number?"

Rob indicated the phone in the hallway, visible through the open double doors.

"Yes, of course."

Aileen stood up.

"Rob, 'Caller ID.' They know where we are!"

***

To the front of Agatha's house, a grassy slope descended to a rippling stream bordered by alders and other woody plants.

Elsewhere trees surrounded the property. The nearest neighbor was a mile down the road.

The sun was below the ridge to the west when the gray Audi drove by the fieldstone house. The driver of the Audi spoke.

"Hazim! That's Wilson's Crown Victoria in the driveway. We'll bag the woman and her mother at the same time. We have them."

"But we had the woman in North Carolina, too, remember?"

"That is why we are going in now."

***

As Aileen spoke, Rob spotted the gray Audi as it passed slowly.

"Mrs. Harris who else is in the house?"

"No one, Agatha won't be back until tomorrow afternoon."

"Does Agatha have any guns?"

"She's a widow, but her husband had a shotgun. I think I can find it."

"Any shells, a box, anywhere?"

"I can check."

Mrs. Harris left the room. Rob turned to Aileen.

"Is that door to the basement?"

"No basement. My uncle dug out a cellar. That's it."

"Aileen, we can't run. You take Mary Catherine to the cellar. Get behind anything you can. Hide. I'll send your mother after you. No, wait!"

Mrs. Harris appeared holding a shotgun, a box of shells, and a .22 caliber revolver."

Rob hefted the shotgun, broke it open and looked down the barrel. It was clear. He checked the label on the box.

"Good. Buckshot loads for a 12 gauge. We have a chance."

He handed the revolver to Aileen.

"Just cock it like this, point and shoot. Don't hesitate. Think of Mary Catherine."

Mary Catherine clung to her mother's leg. She liked the excitement.

Dusk was falling. They did not turn on the lights.

Rob pushed Aileen towards the cellar door.

"Take the bulb out of the socket, so they can't turn on the lights, and hide behind something big. Is the furnace down there?"

"It's an old iron one."

"Good. Get behind that. Can you see the top of the stairs from there?

"I think so."

"OK, practice aiming at the door. If anyone gets by me he'll come through the doorway. Shoot quick. Don't hesitate. Stay low until I call you."

He turned to Mary Catherine.

"Honey, you're going to have to be very quiet for mommy. Do you understand?"

Mrs. Harris took Mary Catherine into the cellar. Aileen stopped.

"Rob, wait!"

She planted a firm kiss on his lips.

"Thanks for everything, … and be careful."

She followed the others. Rob shut the door behind them.

***

Rob stood in the dark parlor. *OK, Rob, what now?*

His own .38 was in the pocket of his jacket. He picked up the shotgun. It was an old double barreled weapon with two triggers. Two shots and then reload. Slow, but with buck-shot loads, it would inspire caution in an aggressor.

Rob formed his plan. The foundation of the old house was field stone, and the cellar had been dug after. The cellar was safe from outside fire. The front wall on the first floor was faced with stone, thick enough to withstand automatic fire. Only the windows were vulnerable, particularly the picture window in the parlor.

The second floor was different. Any advantage its height offered was offset by thin walls covered anew with aluminum siding. He would not venture up there.

Rob was sure there were only two men in the Audi. The assault would probably involve one man approaching from the rear, while the second raked the front of the house with covering fire.

He was right about the covering fire.

"BrBrBrup, …, BrBrBrup, …, BrBrBrup, …, Brup."

The bursts of fire were followed by crashing glass and stone fragments that flew throughout the parlor and impacted the interior walls.

Rob crawled into the kitchen

"BrBrBrup, …, BrBrBrup, …, BrBrBrup, …, Brup."

More broken glass and splintered furniture in what had been the parlor.

"BrBrBrup, …, BrBrBrup, …, BrBrBrup."

The last of the lamps crashed to the floor. There was no more glass to crash and tinkle. The parlor was wasted.

In the kitchen, Rob eased beside the Frigidaire and waited. He pointed his shotgun at the rear door.

***

In the dim light, the handle of the kitchen door turned slowly. The door opened a crack and then pushed wide. No one appeared.

Rob waited.

"BrBrBrup, …, BrBrBrup, …, BrBrBrup, …, Brup."

The front parlor again reverberated with splattered splinters and bullets rattling whatever remained.

Rob was not distracted. A head appeared in the kitchen doorway. Then a body. The intruder eased in. Rob squeezed the trigger.

"Brroom! … BrBrBrup."

The intruder's weapon discharged into the ceiling as he fell backwards towards the yard. Rob ran to the door.

"Brroom!"

The second barrel discharged. The intruder disappeared into the trees.

Rob retreated back from the door.

Silence.

***

Rob leaned against the fridge and fumbled in his pocket for shells. He reloaded the shotgun and snapped it shut.

"Click."

That sound was nearly fatal. The kitchen came alive with nozzle flashes from the front hallway.

"BrBrBrup, ... BrBrBrBrup, ... BrBrBrup."

The kitchen table collapsed. Splinters flew. One stabbed Rob's shoulder. He pulled it out and rolled to the other side of the fridge. Without aim he squeezed the trigger.

"Brroom!"

The cloud of buckshot dismantled the table in the hall and rattled the banister on the stairs.

Rob lay still. He held the second barrel ready.

Again, silence.

***

In Norfolk, a weary Jeannine sealed the padded envelope. She handed it to Bill.

"There, the files on that CD will force the FDA to rescind the approval to market the Mandley chip. It proves that Mandley Test Services are a bunch of frauds."

"Did you include the part about banker's rounding?"

"Yes. And again, thanks Bill for salvaging my papers."

Jeannine threw her arms around Bill's neck and kissed him. Before he could react, she sat down.

"Bill, you think you like me?"

"You know I do."

"But you don't know me."

"I think I do."

Jeannine frowned.

Sit down, Bill. I want to tell you about me and John Martin."

"Jeannine, you don't have to do this."

"Yes I do. And you may not like me afterwards. Bill, I always say what I think, and I'm lousy at picking men."

Bill laughed.

"Don't laugh. Look at Harry! You and Wayne both tried to warn me about him. It's only fair after all you have done for me to let you know who I am."

"All right then, tell me about you and this John Martin."

"He was a Postdoc, an immunologist. We shared an apartment for six months. I thought I loved him. And I thought he loved me."

Bill listened as Jeannine recounted how she realized that she did not love John, and that he did not love her. She continued.

"I drove him away when he needed me most. The university accused him of faking data for breast cancer research. Mike, another Postdoc had done that, not John ... Anyway, John just left. He disappeared."

She hugged herself as if trying to keep warm.

"I was jealous of Monique Laurier, too. She was a postdoc in the same lab. I knew John and she were friends. I hadn't even met her."

"The truth is that John was a good guy. He was totally dedicated to research, but the university drove him out. Anyway he and Monique are married now."

"But you told me Monique is your best friend?"

"And she is. She and John named their daughter for me! When we finally met we hit it off. She's simple and honest, and a first-rate immunologist herself. Together, we tried to clear John's name. Her lab chief fired her, and killed my university fellowship. That's when I ended up at StatFind."

She went on. For the first time ever, she shared the wounds, frustrations and guilt from that difficult and confused time.

And she revealed her present loneliness, in contrast with John's and Monique's happy life together.

Bill listened. Her moist blue eyes entranced him. He was in awe that this intelligent and beautiful woman wanted to share her pain and insecurities. He was hooked. She stopped.

"Jeannine, ..."

"No! Don't say anything. Just sit here with me. Don't talk."

They sat in silence.

On the table, the brown envelope addressed to the OSB, CDRH, FDA, Parklawn Building, Rockville, Maryland, lay forgotten.

***

Rob lay on the kitchen floor, motionless. Someone moved in the hallway. The voice came from there.

"Wilson! Do you hear me?"

Rob gritted his teeth. He could not reveal his position.

"Wilson, this is not your fight. You can leave now. No one wants you. Where are the women?"

Rob waited.

"Be reasonable, Wilson. No one wants you. Just tell me where they are!"

Suddenly, the kitchen window shattered. Flashes filled the frame.

"BrBrBrup, ..., BrBrBrup, ..., BrBrBrup, ..., Brup."

Glass and splinters flew. The fridge was pierced in several spots. Rob rolled to the stove. One load remained in the shotgun. He pointed and pulled.

"Brroom!"

The blast of shot cut a swath through the window. Rob heard a heavy thud. Outside someone had fallen hard.

The shotgun was empty. Rob slid it across the room.

This time, the hallway was lit by flashes.

"BrBrBrup, ..., BrBrBrup, ..., BrBrBrup, ..., Brup."

The butt of the shotgun was shattered.

Rob drew his .38 from his pocket.

"Crack. Crack."

He shot blindly into the hallway.

Once again silence.

He waited.

***

Rob heard the front door close.

Then nothing.

He struggled to his feet. He felt pain in his leg and looked down. A splintered fragment from the door frame protruded from his left thigh. His pants were wet with blood.

He struggled through the hallway. A trail of blood led to the door. It was not his. He cracked the door and peered out. Two forms were visible in the Audi. The one on the passenger's side was slumped motionless, head against the dash.

The Audi roared away into the dusk.

Rob checked the back porch. There was blood there also. He had hit both invaders.

His head ached, and his eyes blurred. His pant leg now was soaked dark brown. He was tired. He could no longer stand. He twisted a dish towel tight around his leg and crawled to the cellar door.

Vaguely he recalled that Aileen was to shoot if opened. He pounded and called out.

"Aileen. Don't shoot. It's me. They're gone! Help!"

The ceiling rolled in front of his eyes and he passed out.

***

******

Chapter 25
Wednesday, November 1

The air was chill. Gray clouds hung over the medical complex in Windber, Pennsylvania. Aileen drove the Crown Vic along Somerset Street. She pulled to the curb in front of the hospital and waited for the nurse to wheel Rob Wilson outside.

The nurse helped Rob into the passenger seat.

"Rob, you look like hell."

"Thanks a lot. I'm OK. How's Mary Catherine? And your mother?"

"They're fine, but Aunt Agatha is in shock after seeing her house. We're at the Holiday Inn Express in Johnstown. Where do you want to go?

"Downtown Johnstown. The FBI has a Resident Agency on William Penn Avenue. They came to the hospital yesterday. They told me there were no gunshot wounds at hospitals in the area. But a neighbor saw an Audi with Delaware plates near Aunt Agatha's on Monday."

"Have you talked to Mary Dean?"

"This morning. She and the kids are fine. The police are watching the house."

Rob glanced sideways at his driver. Her blond hair was neatly done, and, for a change, she wore makeup. He frowned.

"I never should have left you alone at Myrtle Beach."

"That's history. You risked your life for us. I'm grateful."

"Rob, I've seen how Mary Dean looks at you. I want you to know that I think you're pretty special too."

Rob smiled.

Aileen relaxed. *Good, I've got a chance.*

She headed to Johnstown.

***

In Delaware, the jangling phone woke Dr. Thibault. He fumbled for the instrument and listened.

"Thibault, my men missed the Harris women. You must disappear. You'll be picked up in an hour. Be ready."

"But where?"

"To Montreal, Dorval airport. You'll get instructions there. Use the 'Cloutier' passport."

The line went dead.

Thibault zipped his bag shut and sat on the bed.

His hands shook. His heart pounded.

***

He was a minor clerk in the Mail Room in the FDA's Parklawn Building in Rockville, Maryland. He was anxious to advance.

All he had to do was set aside certain parcels addressed to the Office of Surveillance and Biometrics (OSB) and/or to the Center for Devices and Radiological Health (CDRH) for review by the boss. It was a simple task. Only items capable of holding a computer CD, a paper manuscript, or a flash drive needed review.

This morning, he already had set aside two items. Now it was coffee-time. He yawned and stretched, ready for his break.

Then he spotted the brown envelope. It was not large, but it was wide enough to contain a computer CD. He felt the envelope. His fingers met firm resistance.

Bingo! That's a CD.

He put the envelope along with the two previous selections on the boss's desk. Then he headed for the coffee machine.

***

Fareed Hamza, chief of security at Mandley's Delaware facility stared out the window.

In the parking lot below, a resident doctor and an aide lifted a wounded man from the gray Audi to a stretcher. At least the driver could walk, albeit with a limp.

Hazim and Raakin were two of his best men, beaten by a broken-down FBI retiree!

Thibault, Aileen's last link with Mandley Bionics, was on the way to Montreal. Without him or Roberts, Aileen Harris had nothing. It was time to concentrate on that uppity Ryan woman and her so-called "statistical" evidence.

Fareed needed some good news.

The light flashed on his secure phone. He listened.

"I've got the package. Hamm and Ryan mailed it."

"I'm sending a helicopter. I want to see what they have."

He smiled to himself. *Ryan will think her package got through to the FDA.*

He looked at his records. *Hamm checked out of the hotel in Norfolk on Tuesday morning. We just missed them. He hasn't been back to North Carolina for his car. I knew he wasn't that stupid. They're still laying low. I wonder ...?*

The secure line flashed again.

"Yes?"

"Hamm returned the Camry in Williamsburg. This time he rented an Accord, a blue one."

"When?"

"About three hours ago

"You have the plate number?

"Yes."

"Good work. Keep me posted."

He smiled to himself. He had seen pictures of Jeannine Ryan. *Williamsburg! Seems like Hamm is having a vacation with that bitch. I can't blame him.*

He chuckled. *Drink and be merry, for tomorrow you die!*

***

Bill Hamm drove. He was relieved. The FDA must have Jeannine's CD by now.

"Where are we, Bill?"

"We're in Maryland, on Highway 301. We just crossed the Potomac River at Dahlgren."

"That's southern Maryland, Bill. I thought we were going north to meet Rob."

"Maybe we will, but after what happened at Aunt Agatha's, we want you two separated. Mandley wants both you and Aileen. We don't want to make it easier for their goons."

199

Jeannine pushed the hair from her forehead and opened her eyes. Dry fields filled the landscape.

"Bill, when are we going to get our lives back?"

He looked into her eyes.

"I don't want mine back. I like the life I'm finding now."

Jeannine looked down.

"Stop it Bill. Give me my space."

"Don't worry. I told you I wouldn't touch you. The next time I'm with a woman it will be for keeps. Harry taught me that much."

"Harry?"

"Yes, Harry. … How he almost destroyed my little sister. He was a taker; take, possess and discard. That was his way. When my sister fell apart and tried to kill herself, I realized then that sex was not just for selfish satisfaction."

He lowered his voice.

"It's about giving and receiving. It's about giving one's self for the sake of the other person, and maybe even a third person, a baby. We are not animals."

"Don't you believe in evolution?"

"Sure. But that's not the point. We are not *just* animals. There's more. There's 'love.' That can't be measured in a lab."

"You don't believe in pleasure?"

He took his eyes off the road. Even in worn clothes, this woman was desirable. He damn well believed in pleasure.

"Sure, but that's not enough. It shouldn't be a contract, like 'You give me sex' and 'I give you money,' or even 'You give me pleasure' and 'I give you pleasure.' It's about persons, individuals. I give you myself, you give me yourself. 'I am yours and you are mine.' 'In sickness or in health,' like in the old movies."

"Damn it Bill, don't preach."

"Sorry. The kicker is that I want to be yours, exclusively yours, nobody else's. That's the 'I am yours' part. What do you say?"

Jeannine frowned. *This is heavy. This is a proposal!*

"Bill, I can't handle this. ..."

She was about to reply sharply, but stopped. *Jeannine, this guy is risking his life for you. Logic isn't everything. Don't be a jerk.*

"Bill, I like you. I'm grateful and I do trust you. The other night I shared things with you I've never talked about. Maybe that's 'love.' But for now, I can't be sure of anything."

She cleared her throat.

"When, or if, we're out of this mess who knows if we would even like each other?"

"Fair enough. But I wasn't trying to preach. I wanted you to know how I feel."

"I accept that. Now can we talk about something else?"

She leaned back in her seat. *He's hurt. I disappointed him.* She shut her eyes. He spoke.

"Jeannine?"

"What now?"

"In the mirror. A black Mercedes! Don't look back. They're following us."

***

Rob drove the Crown Vic as he and Aileen returned from the FBI office in Johnstown. She sat in the passenger seat.

She leaned towards him.

"Rob, when I came out of the basement and found you lying on the floor, I was scared. I was afraid you wouldn't live. All that blood. ... "

Rob shrugged.

"Not all that blood was mine. And my leg's pretty much OK now."

"But you could have been killed. You saved our lives!"

He studied her face. The gratitude was real. She was young. She could easily mistake that emotion for love. Suddenly he wanted to "comfort" Aileen. He reached for her, but Mary Dean's face flashed in front of him.

He drew back and focused studiously on the road ahead. He started to speak, but Aileen stopped him.

201

"It's OK, Rob. I get it."

Then she added almost mischievously.

"But I'm still here. OK?"

The rest of their trip back to the Holiday Inn Express was silent.

***

Dr. Thibault's Canadian passport stated that he was Jean Cloutier, a native of St. Jérôme, Québec. He handed it to the agent.

"Bienvenue au Québec, Monsieur. Vous êtes né a St. Jérôme?"

"Yes I was born in Saint Jerome."

"Ah, you speak English? Have you forgotten your French?"

"Non. Je parle encore."

"Bon! Have a good stay, Monsieur."

The immigration officer turned away.

"Next in line, please. Le prochain, s'il vous plaît."

Dr. Thibault entered the terminal and found his meeting place. The clock on the wall said 2:00 pm. For the first time on this trip "Monsieur Cloutier" relaxed.

He sat and waited.

***

******

Chapter 26
Wednesday, November 1

Bill Hamm studied the Mercedes in the rearview mirror. When he slowed, they slowed. When he speeded up, they speeded up. It was clear that they were content to follow without overtaking. He turned to Jeannine.

"They don't seem to want to catch us. Maybe they don't know we've spotted them."

"But what do we do?"

"We wait."

They drove by open fields, with little roadside cover and little traffic.

Finally, an eighteen-wheeler appeared ahead in the distance.

Bill set his lips.

"If I can catch up with that truck, I might be able to shake them."

He floored the accelerator.

Minutes later he passed the eighteen-wheeler, and cut in front of an irate trucker.

Luck was with Bill. The dry fields were replaced by woods on both sides of the highway. Ahead was a sharp curve.

"Hang on, Jeannine."

Just past the curve, he swung the Accord abruptly off the highway onto a dirt lane and stopped, sheltered from view by the woods.

The eighteen wheeler sounded its horn in anger but rolled by without slowing. Moments later the Mercedes, apparently unaware of the maneuver, drove by.

Bill caught his breath. He backed the car around and turned back on Highway 301.

"You're going back?"

"Right. We passed a road to Newton a mile back. By the time they realize we're not in front of them, we'll be on that road and way out of sight. At Newton, we can pick up Highway 6."

"Does that mean I can relax and take a nap?"

"Why not? We're OK at least until Newton. They'll probably wait for us at La Plata."

There was no reply. Jeannine's head was tilted back, her eyes closed.

***

Some minutes later the driver of the Mercedes snorted in disgust.

"Damn that Hamm."

His partner called to report.

"We lost Hamm south of La Plata. What do you want us to do. He's behind us somewhere. Ryan's still with him."

"So he's a smart bastard. Wait at La Plata until I call."

"We're a mile south of there."

"Good. Just wait. Hamm has no idea who he is dealing with."

***

Wayne Johnson stood by his window at StatFind. He was troubled.

First, StatFind's contract with Mandley was in shambles. No one had contacted him since the departure of Dr. Thibault. Jane Peterson's non-responsive answers to his frequent calls frustrated him. He wasn't sure what to do. Harry was dead and his desk vacant. Whoever was in charge at Mandley had not sent a replacement.

Second, and personally distressing, there was no news of Jeannine since the message Bill Hamm had left. *Is she OK? Where is she? I need to speak to her?*

Thibault had bullied him into reassigning Jeannine and taking on Harry. He should have stood up for her. He had to live with his cowardice, and it was not pleasant.

Wayne sighed and looked out the window.

A man was kneeling by his car, a late model Buick parked in the open-air lot by StatFind's building. The man was on the ground, reaching under the Buick's chassis.

Wayne headed to the door to accost him, but a buzz interrupted him.

Mona's voice came over the speaker.

"There's a Mrs. Landry wants to speak to you. She says she's Dr. Roberts sister."

"Mona, give me a minute. Someone outside is messing with my car."

He put the phone down and looked again, but the man had disappeared.

He turned back to the phone

"This is Wayne Johnson."

"Mr. Johnson? I'm Harry Robert's sister. I wanted to know if you got the parcel I sent you."

"It just arrived by FedEx. I was about to open it. What is it?"

"I'm not sure. It's odd. It's a DVD or a CD. Harry gave it to me Saturday morning, the day of the accident. It's like he knew something was going to happen to him. He said that I could trust you if something happened to him."

"Where are you now Mrs. Landry?"

"I'm at home. I have small children. I can't leave the house."

Wayne looked at the address. Pamela Landry lived in Clinton, Maryland.

"Mrs. Landry, I'll check on this right away. I'm sorry I won't be at the funeral tomorrow, and I'm sorry about your brother. He was truly brilliant."

There was no reaction to these condolences.

He added.

"Thanks very much for sending this. I'll be in touch."

A sigh was his only answer.

Mrs. Landry hung up.

***

Wayne immediately slipped Harry's CD into his computer.

On it were a number of files with names like *page1.txt*, *page2.txt*, etc.

Wayne looked further. Other files were presumably romantically named, like *ruth.txt*, *jane.txt*, and *never_been_kissed.txt*.

To Wayne's relief there was no file called *jeannine.txt*.

He arbitrarily chose *page9.txt* and opened it. A flood of numbers greeted him.

```
             Harry's File, page9.txt
104418135997  153856625592  045272374173  169307899534
182989968074  036838611891  059922894765  211011390085
091677313371  028262627667  231881938501  223928881437
152486417939  114219090491  020624169290  164073011799
020624169290  233308165160  095687694068  122989235661
210451600716  011413860699  232088336581  092809302344
169337113806  140331669337  156534038071  122989235661
177141066691  228226998601  007146329718  232088336581
072467843580  167417215020  042993163430  231881938501
140331669337  066416826014  129367731090  130209456483
153856625592  140331669337  211263076123  228226998601
177781160345  211263076123  228226998601  015922649436
129367731090  117465504657  057038046945  156832939056
059922894765  219671910910  156832939056  077469129362
029000331035  156534038071  201636118322  169337113806
140331669337  231593267173  245988073123  091677313371
028262627667  231881938501  223928881437  228226998601
167417215020  113307017805  101827560589  059922894765
114219090491  098602688005  015922649436  059922894765
020624169290  132630411414  226179758829  129496108422
062736431903  091677313371  156534038071  136223529614
195516905380  139529274134  114219090491  029000331035
122233366371  147481930781  127834276142  114219090491
064059644252  218839133179  248569862062  004767618473
221341948153  153137225609  095687694068  091677313371
064882838536  214960931912  010250398725  096336636166
```

"Damn it Harry. You encrypted this file."

He opened several more files, but found only numbers. *Everything is encrypted. What can I do with this? If only Jeannine were here?*

The phone buzzed again. It was Mona.

"It's Bill Hamm, sir."

Wayne picked up.

"Bill where are you, and where is Jeannine? Is she with you?"

"Wayne, before we talk, I'm sure they're listening."

"Listening? Who?"

"Whoever's been chasing us all over North Carolina and Virginia. They're connected to Mandley somehow. I just lost their last tail, a black Mercedes. But they'll find us again."

"Is Jeannine OK?"

"For now, yes. Wayne, we have some things you need to see. Do you remember where we ate after we played golf last Spring. I can be there in an hour."

"I remember, but it will take me more like two hours."

"We'll wait. Make sure nobody follows you."

Wayne fingered the CD from Harry.

"Bill, I've got something to show Jeannine too."

"All right, bring it along, but get here as soon as you can."

***

In a building nearby, the silent listener removed his earphones. *Damn it Hamm, you think you're clever, but we're not stupid.*

He looked at the screen in front of him. A flashing blip indicated the location of Wayne Johnson's car, stationary in the parking next to StatFind's building. *Nice try Hamm, but we tagged your friend's car.*

He speed-dialed the black Mercedes.

"Hamm is going to meet with Wayne Johnson. I've got Johnson's car tagged. Most likely he'll head towards Waldorf. Try to pick him up there. Best guess is Hamm and Ryan are somewhere near there. I'll track Johnson from here and keep you posted."

The Mercedes drove north, fast.

***

Wayne Johnson stood by the window and reflected. Harry was certainly capable of industrial espionage. He had been capable of anything. And Mandley Bionics had incredible electronic capabilities that surely included eavesdropping, tracking and surveillance.

He went to his computer and "burned" a fresh copy of Harry's CD. That he put into the company safe. Next he went to his computer where he found several harmless memos and reports of Harry's. These he "burned" onto a new CD which he stuffed into the FedEx mailer from Harry's sister.

Minutes later, he summoned Mona Larson to his office, and wrote out a set of instructions for her. She nodded her assent.

Then she wrote her own suggestions on the paper pad. He smiled in gratitude. Loyal Mona!

He left the office. *I hope I'm doing this right.* He opened the door to his Buick.

***

The man in the nearby building watched Wayne Johnson get into his car, pull from the lot onto the street, and head south.

He checked the flashing blip on the computer screen. The blip moved towards the south. Good. Everything is working.

He settled back in his seat.

The blip stopped.

Evidently Johnson had stopped at a 7-Eleven that was two blocks away.

The blip stayed motionless.

The watcher waited patiently.

Minutes later, the blip was on the move again, headed, south on the Beltway.

The watcher smiled.

***

Bill and Jeannine arrived at the rendezvous, a park near the Patuxent River. They rested at a picnic table under the shade of large Tulip Poplars.

"Bill, this is pretty isolated. How will Wayne find us here?"

"We ate lunch here last year after a charity golf tournament. He'll remember all right."

"Don't mention food. I'm hungry."

She stretched out on the picnic bench and shut her eyes.

***

Wayne left the beltway on route 50 headed towards Annapolis.

The watcher's response was immediate. He called the Mercedes.

208

"Damn. Forget Waldorf. Johnson just took route 50. Come north fast. Maybe you can intercept him at Bowie."

He settled back as the blip continued eastward.

***

Jeannine opened her eyes. It was past noon. The shadows of the trees now leaned east.

"Where is Wayne?"

"He will be here. Don't worry. It's a long way, and there's always traffic."

"OK, but I'm still hungry, get me those Doritos from the car."

Without thinking, Bill obeyed.

Jeannine smiled.

***

When the blip reached the town of Bowie it abruptly reversed direction.

"What the hell!"

The watcher called the Mercedes.

"Johnson turned around. He's coming back. Where the hell are you?"

"We're on route 50, just outside of Bowie."

"Head for the Beltway. He's doubled back."

The watcher was puzzled. The blip had not stopped since the 7-Eleven. Johnson could not have met Hamm and Ryan. Had he given up?

It appeared that he had. The blip turned north on the Beltway.

The watcher laughed. *Johnson wised up. The wimp wants no part of this deal.*

The blip continued north.

***

It was warm for early November and Bill Hamm was in a light sweater. He sat on the picnic table, head between his hands. Jeannine, tired of inaction, spied a trail through the woods to the river.

"Bill, I'm frustrated, I'm going for a walk."

"Wait."

"Why? Are you worried that Wayne won't come."

"I was sure he would, but now I don't know. He should have been here an hour ago."

"Could it be Beltway traffic?"

"I don't think so. I allowed for that. He should be here."

Bill's face was drawn. Jeannine was uneasy.

"What if he doesn't come?"

"Whether or not he does, we will need a safe place to stay. I'm running out of cash, and if I go to an ATM they'll track me for sure."

Jeannine looked at her watch.

"Do you think we should leave?"

"Give him another half hour. If he doesn't show by then we can go."

***

Bill sat on the picnic table while Jeannine paced. Minutes passed, but there was no sign of Wayne's Buick.

Jeannine stopped pacing.

"Bill, something has happened. Wayne's not coming. I think we should go."

Bill started to reply, but the sound of a motor interrupted him.

He looked up.

A strange car was approaching, fast.

***

Wayne Johnson turned into the parking lot by StatFind. He went straight to his office and picked up the phone. Jane Peterson answered.

"MTS."

"Jane, this is Wayne Johnson at StatFind."

She broke in before he could continue.

"Mr. Johnson, there is no news from Mandley about Dr. Thibault's replacement."

"That's not why I am calling. Dr. Robert's sister sent me a CD from Harry. I think it belongs to MTS. Could you send someone to pick it up?"

"From Harry? Just a second."

Jane's line went silent. Moments later she was back.

"Mr. Johnson, thank you. I'll send someone right over."

"Good. It doesn't seem important, but he worked for you, not us."

"Thanks again, Mr. Johnson."

Wayne hung up.

Only minutes later, Wayne stood by his office window. If he had doubted the efficiency of MTS since Dr. Thibault's departure, those doubts were dispelled as a black Mercedes stopped next to his Buick.

Two men, well-dressed, stepped from the Mercedes. Seconds later, they were at the door to his office.

"Mr. Johnson, Ms. Peterson said you had something to give us."

"Right. Here it is."

He handed the FedEx mailer with the innocuous CD to the men.

"Thank you sir. Is that all?"

"That's it. Oh, and please advise Ms. Peterson that I'm still waiting for Dr. Thibault's replacement."

"Yes Sir, and thanks again."

The two men left.

Wayne went to the window. He watched the men in the parking lot.

Neither man touched Wayne's Buick. They drove away in the Mercedes.

***

Bill stood empty-handed to face the strange car, a Saturn, that pulled up to him. The .22 rifle was on the back seat of the Accord some distance away.

The Saturn's windshield reflected the sun's rays directly at Bill. He shielded his eyes. He could not see the driver.

But he heard a familiar voice.

"Bill, Mr. Hamm, It's me."

"Mona?"

It was indeed the secretary. She stepped out of the car.

"Where's Jeannine?"

Jeannine stepped from behind the trunk of a Tulip Poplar.

"I'm here, Mona."

Mona grabbed her and hugged.

"We've been worried sick about you."

"I'm OK now, thanks to this guy."

Bill spoke.

"Mona, how did you find this place?"

"Wayne mapped it for me. He thought his car was bugged, so he sent me. He wants you to look at this CD from Harry's sister. Harry told her if he died to send it to StatFind, and he had the accident right after, that night. Spooky! I'm scared."

She added.

"Wayne looked at it. He says the files are encrypted."

The next half hour was spent briefing Mona about Mandley's FDA proposals, and the multiple instances of data fraud.

Bill finished. Mona spoke.

"I told Wayne you two can hide out at my cabin on the Bay. He thought that would be wise. You can stay as long as you want. And I brought you groceries. There's no one in the cabin now."

She caught her breath.

"And Wayne sent you this cash and this prepaid phone. He has the number. He'll call later."

Mona grabbed Jeannine.

"Wayne feels rotten about how he treated you. Try and forgive him. He's a good guy. He'll do anything to make things right."

"Thanks, Mona."

Moments later, the Saturn sped away.

***

Back in Johnstown, Rob and Aileen left Bernadette Harris, her granddaughter, and her sister Agatha at the Holiday Inn Express to drive to Monroeville, near Pittsburgh.

After driving for a half hour, Rob felt relief. No one had followed them.

He relaxed, and the Crown Vic rolled smoothly.

Aileen's hair was carefully groomed. Her head wound was no longer apparent.

"What do we do now, Rob?"

"We'll get a motel in Monroeville, and lay low. Bill will call us there."

"Where are Bill and Jeannine now?"

"He didn't say, but it's a safe spot, a vacation cabin somewhere on the Chesapeake Bay."

Aileen hesitated.

"Did you call Mary today?"

"I did."

Not the answer she had hoped for. Rob continued.

"Mary and the kids are fine. But I'm worried. The police think her husband is in South Carolina."

Aileen fell silent.

***

*****

Chapter 27
Wednesday, November 1

Mona's cabin stood atop a cliff on the shore of the Chesapeake Bay. At the base of the wave-washed cliff lay mounds of fallen earth, a somber reminder of storms that undercut the unstable heights. Gray branches and dead roots on the strand testified to the lethal effect of salt water on the exposed fallen vegetation.

The cabin itself was set safely back from the cliff, where intervening trees had been cut to give a view of the bay. Assorted hardwoods and pines along a mile-long access road concealed the existence of the dwelling from any traffic on the state highway. Mona's property adjoined land purchased by the Nature Conservancy for a future wildlife (and fossil) preserve. The nearest human neighbor was several miles away as the crow flies.

Bill Hamm parked the blue Accord between the woods and the house, hidden from both the road and the bay. He switched the motor off, and sat, silent. He stared straight ahead, collapsed in thought.

Jeannine let out a deep breath of relief. They were safe, at least for the moment. She turned towards him and regarded his features. His looks were not exceptional, but he had a "solid" face, and honest eyes. *Where would I be without this guy?* Unexpected emotion stirred within her.

She touched his arm.

"Bill, what are you thinking?"

"I'm thinking that you and I are alone and that I might have trouble keeping my promise to stay away from you."

She shook her head.

"But you will keep your promise, for two reasons. The first is that you promised me. The second is that I like you and I wouldn't resist you, but part of my 'like' is that I trust your promise."

Bill turned. *Did she say what I think she said?*

Jeannine smiled.

"Come on. Let's unload these groceries and clear the table for your laptop. We need to get organized so we can see what's on Harry's CD."

***

Some time later, the sun hung near the western horizon. Over the bay, dark brooding clouds formed low over surging waters. Gray shadows filled the space between clouds and rippling whitecaps. Rain!

The storm came ashore, fast.

Inside Mona's cabin, Jeannine stopped arranging cans and boxes and stepped to the window.

A gust sprayed the window pane, leaving hemispherical drops that clung to the glass only to loosen and slide downwards in wet elongate trails. Nearby, the top branches of Tulip Poplars rotated wildly in the wind. Yellowed leaves and broken twigs twisted loose and whirled downwards in disarray.

She shuddered. Bill moved beside her and circled her shoulder with his arm.

Jeannine looked up.

"Why do I feel secure when I'm with you?"

He was too pleased to reply. He squeezed her shoulders.

Outside, several Fish Crows, blown from their roost high above, struggled against the wind until abruptly, their leader gave up, set his wings passively, and was wafted away. The others, likewise set their wings and were driven in the same direction

Jeannine was pressed against Bill when a flying branch slammed the roof and rattled the glassware on the shelves.

She jumped. The mood was broken.

The kitchen table was covered with vacation paraphernalia; game boxes, playing cards, and a partly-completed picture puzzle. She looked up at Bill and smiled.

216

"Why don't you finish putting Mona's supplies away while I clear a space on the table for the laptop. We need to see what Harry found."

She pushed the games and puzzle to the side, settled the laptop on the open space, and inserted Harry's CD.

Clicking rapidly, she found a file named *page1.txt,* and opened it.

Numbers, too many to read, filled the screen.

Harry's File page1.txt

```
015922649436 244791290679 026606065308 081177020100 114219090491
098602688005 045272374173 137938617669 232088336581 133063718917
184388073144 015922649436 020624169290 029000331035 211217470108
169337113806 220116884001 029000331035 138542319960 132830309684
169337113806 136223529614 232088336581 056993045645 203987994478
193460589651 091677313371 119382425296 228226998601 091238069280
064882838536 136997993274 172816431820 028435443036 091677313371
155435549728 112869260982 147481930781 182989968074 072467843580
146075088581 221341948153 247521296449 136223529614 068213385980
064882838536 014130367205 098602688005 195516905380 139529274134
098602688005 129496108422 062736431903 098602688005 167417215020
091677313371 156534038071 107060911959 025647817949 122233366371
055731617662 109100271266 236370208461 084329400539 082965116675
129367731090 045272374173 086099349749 122562793806 002369310443
089306905260 114219090491 029000331035 122233366371 147481930781
072467843580 091677313371 156534038071 029000331035 015922649436
129367731090 138542319960 132830309684 169337113806 136223529614
195516905380 139529274134 098602688005 015922649436 129367731090
129496108422 062736431903 091677313371 042993163430 119382425296
146075088581 098602688005 169337113806 140331669337 156534038071
163842353800 211473740452 016203255841 203995479382 028262627667
027573665763 211011390085 091677313371 160685694105 211263076123
019376104384 239709459572 203987994478 195516905380 218839133179
247521296449 172283052225 064059644252 119382425296 228226998601
193460589651 091677313371 028262627667 098602688005 129496108422
062736431903 098112718220 127434415570 012391209599 098112718220
114219090491 228226998601 193460589651 180231626304 175988754793
153137225609 004128447573 122233366371 013737820022 232088336581
111706850802 029000331035 129496108422 062736431903 096336636166
```

Bill looked over Jeannine's shoulder.

"What's all this? I can't read all these numbers."

"Of course not and you shouldn't. The message is encrypted."

She touched his arm.

"Hang on Bill, we'll check this out."

She opened several files.

"Damn, these other files are encrypted too, just like Wayne said. Here's a file *n500000.txt.* It has a different kind of name. Maybe I can read it. "

She examined the file. There were far too many numbers for a single screen. She scrolled through them. They were arranged in increasing order.

Puzzled, she turned to Bill.

"This file is something else. These numbers do not represent an encryption. They're arranged in order."

She scrolled down to the end and printed the last three lines.

499819	499853	499879	499883
499897	499903	499927	499943
499957	499969	499973	499979

"Jeannine, what's this all about?"

"I don't know. Give me a second to think. Wait. I see something. All the last digits are odd."

She typed furiously. Moments later a graph appeared on the screen.

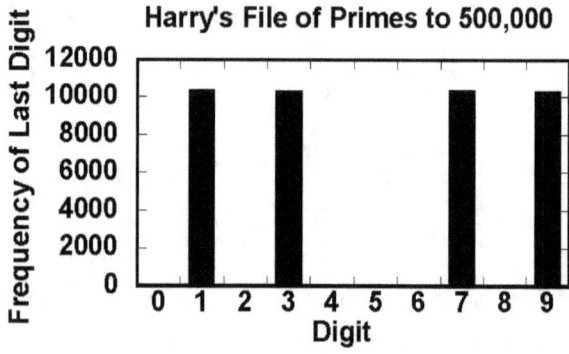

"Just as I thought. Harry generated a file of the prime numbers up to 500,000."

"Primes?"

"Yes, a number that is only divisible by itself or by 1."

"How can you be sure?"

"I'm not sure, but it looks like it. All the numbers end in digits 1, 3, 7, or 9. The only even prime number is 2, and above that no even number can be a prime, and there are no even last digits in the graph. Further, except for 5, itself, no prime can end in 5 because any number that does so is divisible by 5. A prime greater than 5 must end in 1, 3, 7, or 9, and that's what the graph shows.

She brought another graph up on the screen.

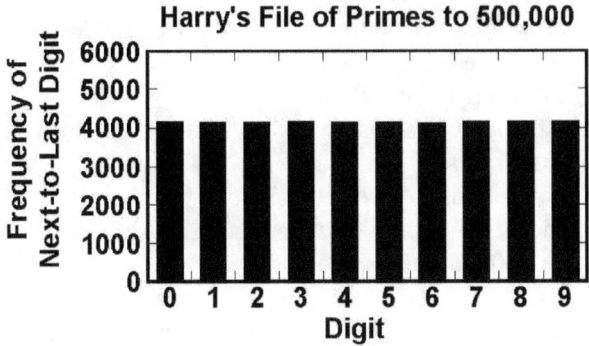

"That about clinches it. The next-to-last digit is uniform, like a lottery digit."

"But why would Harry give us a file of prime numbers?"

"Because he wants us to decrypt his notes. The primes are a clue. I'm betting that he encrypted his messages with a method called 'RSA' that uses the product of two primes in the process."

Bill looked out the window. Gray clouds still filled the horizon, but the wind had abated. The rain had diminished to a drizzle and the window was mostly clear of droplets.

He turned back to Jeannine.

"So?"

"So using RSA, Harry would have a "public" key, and a "private" key. Using his public key, anyone could encrypt a message to him, but only Harry could decrypt it, using his private key."

"Jeannine, you've lost me."

"Forget it. We need the private key. There are other clues somewhere. Harry wanted us to read these files."

Bill scanned the directory on the CD.

"What about this file, *ruth.txt*? Or here's another one, *never_been_kissed.txt*.

"Try the last one."

The file contained three sentences.

Never been kissed, but one year later?
Half a million less two?
Gallia est omnis divisa in partes tres,... .

Jeannine frowned.

"What's that say to you, Bill."

"The first line seems easy. 'Sweet sixteen and never been kissed' plus one. It's 17."

"That makes sense, 3 and 17 are two numbers commonly used in public keys. What about the second line?"

"Why not 500,000 minus two, 499,998."

"I don't think so because 499,998 is 'even.' It's not a prime. I think he means the two highest primes under 500,000. That's why he gave us that file of primes. In Harry's table, 499973 and 499979 are the two largest primes less than 500,000. Multiply them together and you get 249,976,000,567."

Jeannine took a deep breath.

"Most RSA users would choose much larger primes, like over 90 decimal places instead of six, but for those Harry would have needed a program language for extended precision integers. He was in a hurry. He chose primes with only six decimal places. Their product has only twelve places and he could program in 'C'; using 'large integers' or in PowerBasic using 'quad integers.' Harry had no time to install and learn another language that had extended precision capabilities."

Bill's eyes glazed over.

"Don't tell me I need to understand everything you said."

"You don't. I was just thinking aloud, but damn it, Harry *wanted* his notes to be decoded. That's why he left us all these clues."

Her cheeks flushed to a color akin to her hair. Bill smiled.

She ignored him and continued.

"If I'm right, Harry used an RSA encryption where the public key is 17, and the product of the two primes is 249,976,000,567."

"But you said we need the private key to decrypt his notes. What is it?"

"We don't have it yet, but Harry left us the prime factors, p = 499973 and q = 499979. That means I can calculate his private key. It will take me some time. I'll need to write code for the Chinese Remainder Theorem."

"The what?"

"Forget it. What about Harry's last clue."

"You mean *'Gallia est omnis divisa in partes tres,... .'* That's the first line of Caesar's 'Gallic Wars.'"

Jeannine laughed.

"That's it, Bill! That's the final clue. My Latin's non-existent, but I see what Harry's telling us. As an extra twist, he used the 'Caesar' cipher. It's a simple cipher that Caesar used in his campaigns. Each letter is replaced by the third letter after it."

She hunched over the computer.

"Bill, go take a walk. You might want to check the roof and walls for damage. I'll work here. It's going to take me a while to write code to calculate the private key so we can decrypt these notes."

***

Over an hour later, Bill returned from his survey of Mona's cabin and grounds. The roof of the cabin was intact, and only one nearby tree had fallen.

Jeannine was slumped over the keyboard, eyes closed. An empty coffee cup was near her elbow.

He touched her shoulder.

She yawned, shook her head, and tossed auburn hair off her forehead.

"Sorry. I must have dozed off."

She hit the spacebar and the screen saver disappeared.

"Anyway look at the display. I got the private key. It's 14704411801."

She clicked fast to decrypt Harry's code, 'page1.txt.' Moments later she was finished."

She hit "Enter."
A message appeared.
Bill stared at the gibberish.

wkledxow|lv|ghdolqj|zlwk|dq|ludqldq|frpsdqb|lq|
sdulv|wkdw|iurqwv|iru|whuurulvwv|pdqgohb|
elrqlfv|vhoov|fklsv|wr|wkh|frpsdqb||165|uxh|gh|
odsdld||lq|sdulv||wkhq|wkh|frpsdqb|vhoov|wkh|
fkls|wr|kdpdv|dqg|khceroodkvlsshg|wkurxjk|
pduvhlloo|zkdw|lv|wklv|fkls?|d100?||lw|lv|qrw|rxr
sdunlqvrq|fkls|

"What's all this?
Jeannine looked up.
"Sorry! That's the Caesar text. Wait, I'll shift the letters."
She tapped rapidly on the keyboard. Fresh lines appeared.

thibault|is|dealing|with|an|iranian|company|in|
paris|that|fronts|for|terrorists|mandley|
bionics|sells|chips|to|the|company||165|rue|de|
lapaix||in|paris||then|the|company|sells|the|
chip|to|hamas|and|hezbollahshipped|through|
marseille|what|is|this|chip?|a100?||it|is|not|our
parkinson|chip|

A sudden gust off the bay rattled the window. Wind peppered the pane with drops that slid down the glass until the quickening torrent coated the window with sliding films of water. A torn branch slammed against the wall and rattled the cans on the counter.

But Bill and Jeannine stood fixed before the silent computer.
Hamas? Hezbollah?
Terrorists!

***

At the airport in Montreal, Dr. Thibault looked at the large clock opposite. The big and little hands both pointed at the 4. He had waited for over two hours at the airport, and no contact had appeared. He shifted in his seat and fidgeted with his briefcase.

A young couple arrived two seats away. The woman was obviously flustered as the man threw her carry-on onto the seat and stalked away. He glared at Thibault as he passed. Dr. Thibault shrank back and lowered his eyes.

The young woman leaned towards Dr. Thibault, and touched his hand.

"Pardonnez-nous, monsieur. Mon mari n'est pas toujours si brusque."

Dr. Thibault returned her smile and accepted the apology for the husband. He leaned towards her, but she rose, took her bag, and strode in the direction that her husband had taken.

He looked down. A scrap of paper lay in his lap. He looked about. No one was nearby. He palmed the paper and headed for the Men's Room. There he read the words.

M. Cloutier.
14935 rue du Collège, Ville St-Laurent, trente minutes.

He had thirty minutes to reach that address.

***

Outside Dr. Thibault waited in the taxi line. His turn finally arrived, and he told the driver to head to Ville St-Laurent, a northern suburb of Montreal. Upon arrival, he paid his fare and waited alone before 14935 rue du Collège.

A small car pulled to the curb. The driver was the young woman from the airport. Her "husband" was in the rear seat. He gestured to Thibault to sit in the passenger seat.

No words were exchanged.

They left the city, and headed north to St. Jerome and the Laurentians.

***

Outside Mona's cabin, swirling branches were silhouetted in a flash of light that was followed by a thunderous crash. In the kitchen the lights blinked once, and then went off. In the dusk the screen of the laptop glowed like a beacon. It had shifted to battery power.

"Bill where are you? What's that scratching noise?"

"It's me. The drawer stuck. I'm looking for a flashlight."

Jeannine stared out the dark window. Forked streaks of light stabbed the bay. Distant thunder was followed by a nearby muffled roar and a thunderous crash.

Startled, she reached for Bill. He grasped her shoulders.

"Part of the cliff just gave way. The cabin's not near the edge. We're OK."

"Damn it Bill, why do I feel safe around you. It's crazy."

Jeannine leaned against him, but then the lights flickered and came back on. She pulled back and straightened her blouse. The laptop shifted back to full power.

"There are more files to decode. Let's see what *page9.txt* says."

She went back to the laptop and ran the RSA decryption program. Julius Caesar's text appeared.

l|xqghuhvwlpdwhg|wkledxow||l|dvn|derxw|
mhdqqlqh|dqg|kh|mxvw|julqv|wrr|edg|vkh|
irxqg|rxw|derxw|wkh|idnh|gdwd||gdpq|khu|
dqg|gdpq|wkledxow|wrr|zkdw|lv|wkdw|d100|fkls|
wkhb|vhoo|lq|sdulv?||l|zloo|ilqg|rxw|wrqljkw|

Bill waited while Jeannine brought up her shift program and hit "Enter."

i|underestimated|thibault||i|ask|about|
jeannine|and|he|just|grins|too|bad|she|
found|out|about|the|fake|data||damn|her|
and|damn|thibault|too|what|is|that|a100|chip|
they|sell|in|paris?||i|will|find|out|tonight|

Jeannine looked to Bill.

"Thibault was behind my abduction, not Harry. Harry was a jerk, and he was willing to cheat women and the FDA, but he was still an American. It cost him his life, but he left us his records."

"You make him sound like a damned patriot."

Jeannine pulled Bill down to her and kissed him full on the lips.

"Don't be jealous. He couldn't compare to you. He was a rat and I know what he did to your sister. But in the end he tried to do something good, and he died trying."

"You're right that he died, and he warned us, but it means we're up against international killers who will snuff us out thinking they are praising Allah."

Wind-borne rain rattled the window pane. A crackling roar of thunder rolled outwards across the bay as ominous clouds darkened the sky. Bill went to the window and looked out. Crashing branches signaled a strike as lightning lit the trees nearby. Inside, the lights blinked again but stayed on. He turned back to Jeannine.

"This changes everything. It's Jihadists that are chasing us, not ordinary thugs."

He continued.

"I've got to warn Rob."

"Are we safe in this cabin?"

"For now, yes. But they will find us. It's a matter of time."

She shuddered at his words. He frowned.

"I know these types from my CIA days. Damn, I thought I was done with that life. I need more than this .22 pea shooter."

He picked up the rifle.

"I'll keep this next to me tonight. You take the bedroom. I'll crash on the couch."

Outside, the wind diminished, but the rain stayed steady.

***

The sun dropped below the horizon. Thibault shifted uncomfortably in the passenger seat. His companions were silent.

They had driven well over an hour from Montreal, before leaving the main road. The car climbed from the alluvial soils of the St. Lawrence valley onto the granitic terrain of the Canadian Shield. Here for thousands of years continental glaciers had gouged and scooped the earth loose from bedrock, only to deposit the unsorted debris in moraines at melting edges to the south.

The glaciers were gone, their past presence was proved by scalloped gouges in the bedrock that filled with water to produce lakes in abundance.

Large and small, they dotted the poorly drained landscape. Some, stocked with trout, were a fisherman's dream. Others, mostly sterile, still offered clear and beautiful water surrounded by dark forests of spruce and fir. The only access to many of these waters was by unpaved gravel roads, often dead-ends.

It was on such a road that the young woman drove before the road gave out at the edge of a small lake.

The car stopped.

***

The driver turned to Dr. Thibault and broke her silence, in slow English and then in French.

"Here one walks. *D'içi on va à pied.*"

In the dusk, individual trees on the opposite shore were no longer distinguishable. Thibault hesitated, but the "husband" in the back seat tapped him firmly on the shoulder. They stepped out together. Ahead, the "wife" beckoned.

"Voici la piste. Venez vite. Come quick, trail is here."

Thibault clutched his bag and followed. The husband walked close behind. After a few minutes, the trail ended. Across the lake, a distant light indicated a house. They stood on a gravel shore devoid of plants showing that boats were launched here.

But there was no boat.

The young woman smiled but her eyes were dull.

She beckoned to her husband.

Thibault heard a sound behind him. He turned.

Too late.

Something hard and metallic slammed behind his ear. His skull crushed inwards and he fell face down into the water.

The woman quickly emptied Thibault's pockets. She spit on the body.

"Kafir!"

She turned to her companion.

"*Tu l'as bien descendu.*   You killed him good."

They returned down the trail to their car.

***

******

Chapter 28
Thursday, November 2

At the motel in Monroeville, Pennsylvania, an exhausted Rob slept on the sofa.

The phone rang. On the bed, Aileen moaned and pulled the covers over her face.

After repeated rings, Rob struggled off the couch and fumbled for his cell phone. His fingers felt it. Tired as he was, he recognized Bill Hamm's voice.

Rob mumbled.

"Damn it. It's three in the morning."

"We've got to get together."

The conversation continued in a cryptic fashion. No names, people or places were identified. All references were by allusion only. Finally, Rob was satisfied.

"Got it."

Bill Hamm hung up.

***

At Mona's cabin, Jeannine opened the bedroom door to the odor of fresh coffee.

Bill handed her a steaming cup.

"Thanks. Bill if you get married, would you do this for your wife?"

"If it's you, you bet!"

She laughed.

"OK, but it's a new day and we have work to do. I've got to decrypt the rest of Harry's files. I wish I could talk to Aileen. She knows the physiology and what the chip does."

"I've already been working. I'm meeting Rob and Aileen this afternoon in Baltimore so I can bring them here. And while I'm away I'll try to call the FDA to see what they think about the package we sent."

"Is that wise? Won't they track us?"

"I hope not. The cell-signal will bounce off a tower north of Baltimore. It should be OK."

"How long will you be gone?"

"I should be back tonight."

Jeannine touched his arm.

"Bill, be careful."

"You, too. I left the rifle in the corner for you. Don't go out, OK."

Before she could react, he pinned her arms and kissed her.

Seconds later he was gone.

***

The sun had risen when Thibault awoke. He was dying. The blow behind his ear had fractured the temporal bone of his skull sending sharp delicate fragments of the otic complex into his brain. The slightest twist of his head caused stabs of excruciating pain and momentary dark shadows that canceled his vision.

He had been conscious when he had fallen face forward into the reedy shallows of the lake. He had held his breath so that no bubbles revealed what life remained in him. Fortunately his assailants, seeing the bloody indentation in his skull and his face submerged in the water, had judged him dead. They had left just before he raised his head to gulp air. After that breath, still prone, he had pushed himself back from the water and promptly passed out.

The sun did not relieve the chill of the Canadian air. Thibault shivered. He had little time left.

Somehow he dragged himself along the trail to where the car had stopped last evening. As he feared, the couple had left nothing behind.

But Thibault, as a seasoned international traveler, wore on his belt a flat wallet that flipped inside his pants for concealment. He fumbled for it.

He blacked out. When he could see again, his hand was clutching the wallet. He took a breath and pushed at the smooth leather. The wallet was open, but his vision blurred again. He

230

felt the useless paper currency and flipped it aside. His fingers reached the folded envelope.

Now he felt his shirt pocket. His pen was still there. They had not taken it. They would pay for that oversight.

The pen came loose in his hand as he tried to write.

Thibault was not a believer, but as if in answer to an unspoken prayer his vision cleared suddenly. He could see.

Slowly, painfully he wrote. Done, he tried to add an address.

Blackness again, the most severe pain yet. His hand froze.

This time his "prayer" was conscious, albeit soundless, *Please!*

The envelope came into focus and he finished writing a name and a town.

But his head fell sideways. The broken bone fragments in the temporal lobe of the cerebrum penetrated farther, severing critical blood vessels and causing massive hemorrhaging.

Vaguely he wished he had fled the airport before his contacts arrived, but knew it would not have mattered. Those bastards knew how to track people. Screw them all. If only the letter? His head fell back and all thought ceased.

***

At Mona's cabin, the vacation paraphernalia, playing cards, and puzzles were put away. The kitchen table was crowded anew with papers. Jeannine hunched over the latest of Harry's files.

|thibault|at|the|delaware|center|today|
||specs|of|chip|a100|areon|his|computer||
cant|crack|his|damn|password|||jane|
peterson|is|a|snoop|more|than|me||she|
watched|me|allday||she|hates|thibault||
she|was|great|in|bed||whats|her|game?||is|
she|really|divorced?||who|is|she?|her|
montreal|name|jeanne|anan|audet||her|french|
better|than|thibaults||

Jeannine leaned back. So Jane Peterson is not who she seems. So what does that mean?

She was tired. The coffee cup was pushed dangerously close to the laptop's keyboard, but she did not notice.

The decryption task was tedious. Harry's RSA code was much longer than the short messages it encoded. She understood why people only use RSA to encrypt their keys and use a stream cipher for the actual messages.

She yawned and pushed "Enter." The next file appeared. She stiffened, alert.

|got|it||mandley|chip|a100|transmits|signal|
only|when|muscle|near|implant|is|moved||
remote|bomber|needs|no|cellphone|range|
20feet|||transmitter|dormant|and|no|signal|
to|detect|unless|specific|muscle|
movement|||i|still|need|to|get|past|
second|firewall|at|delaware|center|

She looked at her watch. Bill would not be back for hours. She needed Aileen's expertise in neurophysiology to evaluate Harry's notes.

If Harry was right, the Parkinson chip implants were prototypes for their chip *A100* to detonate explosives. No wonder they were willing to fake the medical efficacy of their "public" chip.

Up to now, Jeannine's only experience with terrorism was through TV and newspapers. But suicidal jihadists didn't need a remote detonator device. Why an *A100* chip and remote detonation? Explosives still had to be introduced to the site. And twenty feet away is no way safe?

Even to her amateur appraisal, Harry's last note raised more questions than answers. Did the chip have yet another use?

***

It was late afternoon when the call came on the secure line at MTS. Jane Peterson answered at the first ring. The caller was a woman.

"Yes."

"Ms. Peterson?"

"Speaking."

"C'est fait."

"Merçi."

She hung up the phone satisfied.

The message meant that Thibault was dead. With he and Harry both gone, Aileen and her mother were no longer prime targets. Jeannine Ryan, was now the number one concern.

She thought for a moment before calling the Chief of Security at the Delaware Center.

"Yes?"

"Johnson at StatFind is pressuring me. When do we get Thibault's replacement?"

"I'm holding up the clearances, but maybe this week."

"And what about me? How long must I stay here?"

"Until we get Hamm and Ryan. We intercepted their CD at the FDA. They know about the other fake studies for the *Parkinson chip*. We lost them in southern Maryland. What do you know?"

"I'm sure Wayne Johnson knows where they are."

"You could get him to talk."

Jane knew what he meant. She stretched out a shapely leg and regarded it critically.

"He's a bit old, but maybe?"

"Do it!"

That command was followed by a slammed click.

For the third time in ten minutes Jane was on the phone.

"Mr. Johnson, please. This is Jane Peterson at MTS."

Mona was elated.

"Ms. Peterson, I know he's waiting to hear from you. He's not in his office but I'll find him. Just a second."

Wayne came on the line, breathless.

"Jane, what's up? Has Thibault's replacement arrived?"

"Not yet. This week, I'm sure. But something important has come up and I need to talk to you, privately. Could we meet for dinner this evening? At l'Auberge Vert? It's really important."

Wayne was well aware of Ms. Peterson's charms, though he could have been her father. He thought of his wife and hesitated.

"Please, Wayne, I need your help."

The first name plus the plea for his help settled it. He would arrange it.

"What time?"

"Seven, I'll make the reservation. You know where it is."

"Yes."

"And Wayne?"

"Yes?"

"Thanks. Thanks a lot."

She hung up.

***

Bill Hamm returned the blue rental Accord in downtown Baltimore. He took a bus north towards the Homewood campus of The Johns Hopkins University. He had time before meeting Rob and Aileen. The Baltimore Art Museum was located adjacent to, and virtually on, the campus.

As an undergraduate, Bill had visited the museum daily at lunchtime. With frequent visits he could devote time each to a single painting, often selected from the extensive collection of Matisse. It had been years, but today he followed the same rule. He went straight to his favorite painting and sat before it.

His thoughts wandered.

He had left the Agency several years before, to find a "normal" and "peaceful" life at StatFind. Right away he had liked the boss, Wayne Johnson. There was no duplicity in Wayne, far from it. He was competent, he knew statistical computing backwards and forwards, and he was kind.

Wayne had briefed Bill about a new hire, Jeannine, who had been forced to leave Fairland University when she lost her fellowship. Bill recalled how desirable Jeannine had been in her "grad student" attire of jeans and pullover sweatshirt.

Wayne had treated Jeannine as a daughter from the beginning. Not that hiring Jeannine was charity on his part.

234

She brought invaluable mathematical expertise to StatFind. Wayne and the whole staff knew to whom to turn if a mathematical/statistical issue arose.

For Bill, the calm life at StatFind had been welcome. The only tension, other than vying for a needed contract, had been caused by Jeannine's continual rejection of him. He winced. He hoped that if and when the present danger passed, Jeannine would return the feelings he had for her.

He found it ironic that skills he had developed as a covert CIA operative, skills purposely left behind when he went to work at StatFind, had won her recognition and gratitude. She was so damned smart. He admired that. She knew her math and numbers. If only, he …

A woman's voiced snapped him from his reverie.

"It's an interesting painting. What do you like about it?"

"Aileen! You're here early."

"Rob drives fast. He's a turnpike demon."

"Where is he?"

"He's outside. Mary Dean is on the phone. Her husband was spotted at a mall in Dillon. Rob wants to go to South Carolina to help her. I want to come with you and Jeannine."

"OK, but if Rob goes to Carolina, we'll need a car. I just returned the rental."

"I'll rent another one. Aunt Agatha loaned me her credit card. They can't track that."

"Aileen, I'm impressed. Good thinking."

It took Rob and Bill only five minutes to lay their plans. Both were anxious to get going.

***

L'Auberge Vert was a French Provincial restaurant located in Potomac, Maryland, a rich and high-toned suburb of Washington, DC. Directly across the Potomac River, was the equally high-toned, and rich, suburban town of Great Falls, Virginia. Wayne Johnson, hair carefully combed but still in work attire, turned his Buick into the tree-lined parking lot. The lot was largely full, and he located a space remote from the entrance.

As he entered the waiting area, he saw Jane. She wore a short skirt discretely tight above the knees, along with a light-colored blouse that revealed only a minimum of cleavage. Long blond hair fell loosely behind her shoulders while her face glowed with natural color, heightened by the barest touches of makeup.

The room was filled with various couples waiting for their tables. Jane saw Wayne, and headed through the crowd to greet him. Male eyes followed her steps closely. An equal number of eyes, all female, stared reproachfully at their partners.

Instantly, Wayne was conscious of the stretched elbows of his sports coat and his unpressed pants. He had come directly from StatFind. Jane, oblivious to all onlookers took his hand and smiled.

"Wayne, thanks so much for coming. They already have a table for us in that corner."

She guided him to a secluded spot, half hidden from the main dining area by potted fig trees. A wine glass, already filled, was on the table.

"I hope you don't mind. I ordered wine for you."

What Wayne needed at this moment was a good belt of scotch.

"That's fine."

Flustered, he sat down before her. Jane calmly took her seat opposite and leaned towards him. Her cleavage expanded beyond minimal.

"Are you sure the wine is all right? It's a Merlot. Do you like it?"

In answer, Wayne seized his glass and drained it. It warmed his stomach.

"Sure, it's fine."

Jane refilled his glass.

"Good, I'm glad you like it."

Wayne fumbled for words.

"Ms. Peterson, … Jane, I'm wondering why you called me."

Jane started to answer, but the waiter arrived to take their order.

***

His rib-eye steak had been marinated, but to Wayne the meat was tasteless.

He pictured his wife waiting at home, and thought of the words to Johnny Cash's song, *"Because you're mine, I walk the line. …"* It would be much easier to *"walk the line"* if Jane Peterson were not seated opposite him.

She sensed his unease and smiled.

"Don't worry. Here, have some more wine."

She reached across and filled his glass. He seized it. The contents rolled warmly down his throat.

He felt better. *It's only wine, not hard liquor.* He looked at the emptied glass. It was already refilled. This time he sipped slowly. He looked into Jane's eyes. He hadn't realized how blue they were. He shook himself.

She reached across the table and took his hand. Her touch was soft.

"Wayne, I'm truly worried about Jeannine."

"Don't worry, she's fine."

"But after what Harry and Dr. Thibault tried to do, I'm still worried."

A miscalculation, the mention of "Thibault" cleared Wayne's mind.

"Jane, you said his replacement would arrive this week."

"He will, and you will be the first person he calls. I'll make sure you are number one."

She rubbed his hand.

"You've been really good to Jeannine. She told me. You know she contributed more on that contract than Harry did. StatFind's lucky to have her."

Wayne gulped his wine anew.

She took both his hands in hers. Her blue eyes sparkled in the candle light.

"I want to help. I want to make sure she's safe. I'm afraid of Thibault, wherever he is."

"She's safe."

"But where? Thibault can reach her anyplace. He has long arms."

His brain cleared again.

"But Jane, why do you want to know?"

She leaned towards him, eyes moist.

"Because, I'm concerned. I feel responsible for what Thibault did. More importantly, I want to make sure that she's beyond his reach."

Wayne looked down. Somehow, the wineglass was full again. He downed it.

She stroked his arm.

"Wayne the two of us together can help her. Together we can do more for her than separately."

She got up and moved her chair next to his. Her head rested on his shoulder, one hand brushed his thigh.

"Please, I need to help. I need to make this right."

Whatever scent Jane was wearing worked.

Wayne put his arm around her. He wanted to squeeze and not let go.

She looked up into his eyes.

Then his wife's face flashed before him. A millisecond later, Johnny Cash's song burst into his brain. *"Because you're mine, I walk the line ..."*

Wayne jumped up.

"I'd better go. You're too damned beautiful, and I'm not used to wine. I've had way too much."

She stared.

He put three fifty dollar bills on the table.

"This will cover our meals, and the tip."

Wayne leaned over and kissed her on the cheek.

"Jane, you are most desirable. You've got it all, but you could be my daughter. And thanks for your concern for Jeannine. Don't worry. She'll be OK."

He turned and strode from the restaurant.

She stared after him in disbelief.

***

Her blue eyes flashed. Jane turned back to the table and stared at her plate. *You stupid old man. You are really stupid! Vraiment stupide!*

She had been ready to reward him for his information, and she knew how to reward a man! Her face froze in a sneer. *You don't know what you missed you ignorant unbeliever. Kafir!*

She looked about. The couple at an adjacent table were staring.

Jane straightened her blouse and left.

In the parking lot, she tapped on the window of a dark Volvo. The window rolled down. She looked at the driver. *Had he smirked at her? What had he seen?* Her eyes pierced his. He looked down.

"You searched his car?"

The driver nodded.

"Well?"

The driver reached through the window and handed her a road map of Maryland.

"Maybe nothing. Maybe something. This was on the front seat."

The map was folded, and Wayne had circled an area on the western shore of the Chesapeake Bay.

Instantly, Jane knew that this was the information she sought. It had to be. She spoke without betraying her pleasure.

"Leave. Now!"

The Volvo pulled away.

Jane looked at the location Wayne had circled. His circle enclosed a community named "Scientists' Cliffs." On the margin scribbled in pencil was a note, "Wilson Road."

Wayne Johnson, you are a fool. Quel bouffon. On the front seat!? And I got dressed up for that idiot?

She pulled out her cell phone as she walked to her car.

***

239

In southern Maryland, the road was dark. Trees crowded the right shoulder. Bill Hamm turned on his headlights. He and Aileen had talked continuously for over an hour. Now she was silent, her head leaning against the passenger side window.

It happened in a split second. The gray form burst into the headlights. With a thud, the doe's left shoulder buckled the right fender before being lifted onto the hood. The body obscured Bill's vision as the deer's flailing hind legs penetrated the windshield.

Blindly, he fought the car to a halt. The animal's body slid onto the roadway.

Aileen's head jerked awake.

"You OK, Bill?"

Bill rubbed his forehead.

"I think so, you?"

"Yes, but what was that?"

"I hit a deer, or I guess a deer hit us."

Bill went around the car and knelt down on one knee. The right wheel was jammed by the cracked fender. Windshield or no, the Accord was going nowhere.

Together Bill and Aileen pulled the carcass off the road

"Where are we Bill?"

"We're just off Route 2. There is a gas station with a mechanic's bay about a mile back. I'll walk back. We need a tow."

"I'll come with you, I'm not staying here by myself."

Bill was more worried than ever. They would not be back that night. And there was no phone at Mona's cabin, the cell Wayne had given them was in his pocket.

Jeannine was alone.

***

******

Chapter 29
Friday, November 3

The Calvert Cliffs, on the western shore of the Chesapeake Bay, extend twenty five miles southwards from Chesapeake Beach towards Drum Point. The cliffs contain rich layers of fossils from the Miocene Period, about fifteen million years ago. Teeth of various shark species are regularly found, including those of the largest predator fish ever, the shark *megalodon*. Some scientists put *megalodon* in the same genus, *Carcharodon*, as that of today's notorious Great White Shark, but the fossil *megalodon* dwarfed the modern shark. With a length of over 60 feet and a possible weight of 47 metric tons it was enormous.

Collecting shark teeth along the narrow beach at the base of the cliffs is easy, but climbing the cliffs is discouraged, and in some areas prohibited.

This policy is not simply to preserve fossil layers. The unstable cliffs are not safe. The loose sediments offer few footholds, and would-be fossil hunters have fallen to their deaths. Nor is it safe at the top of the cliffs. Continual erosion and undercutting regularly cause blocks of earth on the unstable edge to fall, crashing, onto the narrow strand below.

***

In Mona's cabin, Jeannine awoke to the sun piercing the bedroom curtains. She spread them wide, stretched, and looked out beyond the cliffs towards the bay.

"Bill, wake up!"

She stepped into the living area. The room was empty. Bill's sofa had not been slept on.

She went to the kitchen door and looked out. The yellow leaves on the Tulip Poplars held on, shaking, in the chill breeze off the bay. Weaker leaves lost their hold and fluttered wildly away. Even strongly attached leaves fell to the wind, as twigs, severed from the parent branch, dropped twirling to the ground below.

But Jeannine's attention was on the space under the Tulip Poplar where Bill kept the Accord. It was empty. Bill had not returned.

She shivered and pulled the hood of her sweatshirt tight. The waves on the bay were above normal, but not too high for the small boats that dotted the waters. It was a plain November morning on the western shore.

Like many others before her, Jeannine could not resist the allure of the Bay. Holding her arms tight to her body, she faced into the chill wind and walked to the cliff edge.

***

At MTS in Bethesda, Jane Peterson was at her desk early. On the phone was the driver of the black Mercedes.

"There's no Wilson Road in Scientists Cliffs. All the street names there are flowers or trees like 'Aster,' or 'Birch' or 'Cedar.' Hamm and Ryan couldn't get in there without someone knowing. It's a covenanted community. Hell they wouldn't even let us in. They're not there. No way."

The driver paused.

"My map has a 'Wilson Road' north of Scientists Cliffs. It runs up to Plum Point."

Jane studied Wayne's smudged map. She tried to decipher the faint letters next to "Wilson." She could barely make out the words "south" and "Plum."

"All right, look just south of Plum Point. Check roads that go towards the bay. They're likely in a vacation cabin that overlooks the bay. Call me when you find anything. Anything!"

***

Bill Hamm was nervous. The gas station was in the middle of nowhere, but the mechanic was competent, and the fixed fender, while not pretty, allowed the wheel to roll freely. But the windshield replacement hadn't arrived, and no rental car was available. There was no choice but to wait.

The station had an attached restaurant with a counter. At this early hour, Aileen was the only one seated. Bill took the stool next to her and stared bleakly into his cup of coffee.

Mona's cabin had no phone and Bill had the cell with him. Two hours more to wait, and no means of contacting Jeannine.

***

At MTS, Jane Peterson's cell phone beeped with a text message. The eight-letter text was in French.

"rstp, vite"

The meaning was simple.

"Respond please, quickly."

Jane dialed a number. Seconds later she listened as the texter spoke nervously.

"On l'a trouvé à Lac Brochet. They found him at Lac Brochet. He left a message for un nommé 'Wayne Johnson' de Rockville, Maryland! Le connais tu? Do you know him? What now?"

"Attends. Wait. I'll fix it."

She hung up. Once again that damned Thibault was a distraction.

Her plan was simplicity itself. She called the Sûreté du Québec at Saint-Agathe-des-Monts and spoke in elegant French.

"Le Capitaine Duplessis de la Municipalité de Saint-Faustin-Lac-Carré informs me that that you are investigating a death at Lac Brochet and wish to locate a 'Monsieur W. Johnson' in Rockville, Maryland. Je m'appele Jane Peterson. I'm with Mandley Test Services in Rockville. Mr. Johnson is under contract with us. I'm his personal secretary. You can fax me anything you want and I'll see that he gets it immediately."

Jane listed her fax number at MTS along with an MTS address for 'W. Johnson.'

A half hour later she held in her hands a copy of Dr. Thibault's note along with a plea from the police for help in identifying the body.

To that plea she replied that Mr. Johnson knew no one in Quebec, and had no idea why the dead person would wish to contact him. Additionally, Mr. Johnson did not know the meaning of the contents of the letter, and was sorry to be of no help.

Jane smiled. She knew damned well what Thibault's note meant.

First, printed on the paper was a "password," a sixteen element mix of numbers and letters followed by the number "P-712B". Scrawled underneath in a weak hand was the design of a star along with user names and corresponding passwords.

Even if Wayne had received Thibault's note, he could not have known the meaning of those numbers.

Jane checked a Canadian DNA data base with a name look up for Thibault. He was not there under his own name." Ditto for several USA data bases.

She knew for sure that his finger prints were not on file anywhere. Mandley security was thorough.

She texted a three letter reply to the contact "Capitaine Duplessis" in Lac Carré.

"tvb"

"Tout va bien. Everything is OK."

***

Adjoined to Thibault's former office at MTS was a dressing facility that included a spacious shower. Today it was all Jane's. She placed her overnight bag on the sink counter. She needed to freshen up.

She set the shower head to "massage," and let the water run warm while she secured her blond hair in a plastic wrap. She stepped into the steamy enclosure and arched her back as the hot water peppered her spine. Luxury!

***

Jane stepped out of the shower just as the private phone on Thibault's old desk buzzed.

She wrapped herself in a towel, and picked up. The caller spoke.

"Anan?"

"Naam, Yes."

She knew the voice, it was, Fareed Hamza. She did not speak his name, even though the phone line was secure.

"Tell me what news you have on the Ryan woman?"

Anan's soft blue eyes took on a steely glint.

"I'll get her. Don't worry. I almost have her located."

"Almost? What does that mean?"

"It means, the next time you call, I'll have her."

"All right. Make sure that you do, and never forget that you are my wife. Remember that and remember that we serve Allah."

Before Anan could reply the line went dead.

She dressed quickly in jeans and a black sweater and left the building carrying a small case and a dark jacket. It was time to take personal action.

***

If Anan acted decisively, it did not reflect the conflict within her.

The tone in Fareed's reminder, and especially his closing reminder to serve Allah, troubled her.

Over the years, Anan had accumulated doubts about the wisdom of her mentor, Moustafa. These had started with her mother's attention to Anan's studies. Some in their Muslim community had scolded her mother severely. "Anan was uppity, Anan was not devout, Anan must learn submission, etc." After all, "Islam" means submission to the will of Allah.

But her mother had persisted in spite of their talk, and Anan had relished her schooling. She knew she could think as well as any man.

She had experienced the pride in her mother's eyes as she timidly handled Anan's diploma. Christians, or was it Jesus, said that "the eyes were the mirror of the soul," and in those proud dark eyes Anan had seen her mother's soul. She could never deny that.

Anyway, Muhammed called Jesus a prophet, and Québec Catholics, though second class, were "people of the book," and at least preferable to pagans.

245

As to the Christians' blasphemous notion that Allah carnally begot a son, one of her philosophy teachers at McGill had explained that God was Spirit, and that His intellect could "beget," a concept, "a Word," and that in the infinite God, that self-knowledge could be a "Person," "The Word," the "Son" of God. There was nothing carnal in that notion, and Christians were not necessarily polytheists as Moustafa had insisted.

Anan had accepted that professor's words that day without changing any of her actions. She continued her ritual prayers the obligatory five times a day. Like many in the West, she combined times 1 and 2 in the morning before work, shut her door at lunch for time 3, and prayed 4 and 5 together after work. Allah was the master, and she owed him homage.

At MTS, Harry Roberts had influenced her too. Harry was a womanizer, with no commitment to God or man, and certainly not to a woman, but he was a considerate "lover." He taught Anan "carnal satisfaction," totally unlike Fareed, or in days past, Moustafa. Anan had liked Harry as much as she could like any man, which was little if at all.

She had used Harry as he had used her, but her experience with him taught her that she was entitled to pleasure as much as any male.

Anan enjoyed "Jane's" life style, particularly her fashionable clothes and looks.

But Anan despised Dr. Thibault. She was glad he was dead. His god was money. A coward, he had deliberately avoided knowing the use Fareed and others made of Mandley's inventions. Thibault was a fool.

Finally, she respected Jeannine Ryan. She admired how Jeannine had put Thibault in his place on that first visit. Anan liked that. And she was impressed by Jeannine's knowledge. Harry was brilliant, but Jeannine was his intellectual equal.

Moreover, Jeannine had treated Anan, or rather "Jane," with respect. Maybe "Jeanne" and Jeannine were meant to be "sisters." Maybe it was "kismet," Allah's Will.

No! One of Muhammed's hadiths said that all are "born" Muslim so that parents who do not raise their children in the true faith are apostates. Jeannine's parents, and Jeannine too, were apostates. She was not her "sister."

Fareed knew the true path. *Allahu Akbar!*

Anan resolved to end the "Jeannine Ryan" problem once and for all.

***

From the top of the cliff, Jeannine gazed out over the choppy waters of the bay. It was noon. Her sweatshirt, once worn against the morning chill, now was tied about her waist.

Far over the water, large white wings flashed brightly in the sun, Mute Swans. An introduced species, their numbers had increased dramatically since the late eighties. Some regretted their impact on the aquatic vegetation of the bay, but to Jeannine at that moment their beauty trumped all such considerations.

Closer in, boats were grouped around a circle of turbulent water. Rockfish were feeding at the surface. From the boats, fishermen repeatedly cast their lines at the rippling circle, pulling in silvery flashes of hooked fish. After only minutes, the turbulence disappeared and the boats raced towards a new feeding school farther off shore.

Jeannine was lost in these sights when she felt the earth shift under her feet. She backed away from the cliff edge and rubbed against a rope stretched between two trees. Mona had marked off an unstable section of the cliff-front.

Jeannine ducked under the rope to safe ground. But her reverie was spoiled. She was alone. *Bill , where are you?*

She headed back to the cabin.

***

******

Chapter 30
Friday, November 3

The reunion at Mona's cabin was brief.

Jeannine ran to Aileen the moment she stepped from the car.

"Aileen, I'm glad you're here. I've been waiting. I've got lots of questions about Harry's notes. You've got to tell me everything you know about Mandley's Parkinson chip."

Before Aileen could reply Bill stepped between them.

"I'm afraid you'll have to wait a little longer. The car is barely drivable, the headlight is broken and the turn signals don't work."

He pointed to the damaged fender and light and added.

"The closest rental office is in California."

"California?"

"Yes. Across the Patuxent River."

"Can't Aileen stay?"

"I wish, but the car is in her name. She has to fill out the insurance report and get a replacement. We only stopped to make sure you were OK."

Jeannine shook the auburn hair off her forehead.

"Sorry, Bill. Thanks. I got carried away. It's been quiet here. No problems."

She squeezed his hand.

"But what happened to the car? And where is Rob?"

"We hit a deer. And Rob's on his way to Dillon to see Mary Dean. Someone spotted her husband at a shopping mall there."

She looked into his eyes.

"But you weren't hurt?"

He shook his head.

Jeannine turned to Aileen.

"You guys better get going before it gets dark, and before the office in California closes."

A rueful smile.

"Hurry back."

***

Jeannine watched the car disappear down the wooded lane that was the sole access to Mona's cabin.

She was tired of decoding Harry's notes. She needed Aileen's help. She was frustrated. Moreover, she was alone.

This morning she had found a marked tree that signaled a "trail" down the cliffs. At the time, the descent appeared too steep to attempt, but loneliness altered her mood. The tree was a short distance from the cabin. She walked purposely in that direction.

Attached to the trunk was a rusted iron cable that hung over the edge of the cliff. After an initial drop, she could see a grassy ledge and easier going.

She examined the cable, grabbed it and swung over the edge.

Her feet pushed at the cliff side for footholds, slipping and dislodging loose earth that bounced off the ledge to the beach below. Moments later, Jeannine tumbled onto the ledge. She righted herself and found firm footing.

Exhilarated, she started down the narrow trail that clung to the side of the cliff.

***

Fareed Hamza, the director of security at Mandley Bionics, stared at the displays on his wall. One screen in particular had his attention. The blip on that display tracked the location of Anan's car. It showed that she was in southern Maryland, headed towards the Calvert Cliffs.

Anan was taking matters into her own capable hands. Good! He smiled. Fareed had seen what she could do with an Uzi!

Maybe his concerns about Anan were baseless. To please him, she had assumed the "decadent" western lifestyle for her assignment at MTS. She played the "liberated" woman perfectly. Maybe too perfectly? He worried that Anan might have become "Jane Peterson."

He rubbed his cigarette into the ceramic dish on his desk. Hypocrites! The society of the Great Satan condemned cigarettes while it debased women as naked animals and encouraged men to lie with men! And that condemnation of tobacco was dishonest. Because of their lucrative taxes, cigarettes would always be legal.

Fareed tapped a cigarette from his pack and clicked the silver lighter on his desk. He inhaled deeply and blew a gray cloud towards the ceiling. Since the Johnstown debacle, he had one less security team. Hazim was dead and Raakin had lost his nerve.

And Brendan, in the Mercedes, was a mercenary, a kafir, an unbeliever. He was not trustworthy.

Fareed glanced at his watch. It was time for evening prayers. He extinguished his cigarette, locked the door to his office and pulled out his prayer mat.

***

The sun was low. The sky was clear except for high thin clouds that shone as yellow streaks in the parting light. In the dusk, moving pairs of red and green lights marked the trajectories of small boats cruising the bay.

The air was cooling fast. On the shore, Jeannine shivered and held her arms to her body. She could go no further. Her feet were already wet, and ahead of her, the narrow strand disappeared under water that lapped vigorously at the base of the cliff. She stepped back to retrace her steps.

She felt something sharp. Her ankle twisted and her leg buckled, but she caught her balance. She looked down. An object protruded upwards from the marly sand. She knelt and dug it loose.

It was a shark's tooth, but from no living shark. It was far larger than any Jeannine had ever seen. Its six-inch serrated edge was still sharp after what, she guessed, must be thousands, or maybe even millions, of years. Carefully, she slid the fossil into her jean pocket.

Limping, she regained the point of ascent. Wedging herself upwards through a crevice in the cliff face, she reached a narrow ledge that wound upwards.

It was dark now, but the path was easily discernible by moon light. A stiff breeze rustled the drying leaves that still clung to the trees on the cliff edge above. Breathing heavily, Jeannine reached the starting point, the ledge with the rusty cable. She grasped and swung upwards, feet pushing for any purchase in the loose soil of the cliff face. She fell backwards.

She persisted. She took a higher grip on the cable and pushed her legs harder against the cliff. Moments later she pulled herself over the rim. Success.

Breathing heavily, she lay motionless to recoup. She rose to her feet and picked her way carefully through the dark woods towards the cabin.

She stopped. Ahead, through the trees, the kitchen windows shone brightly.

Someone was in the cabin.

***

Jeannine concealed her approach as best she could, pausing behind trees and hurrying across open spaces. Through the window, someone moved, only to disappear. Jeannine strained to see, but there was no further movement. Now there was no more cover to shield her approach.

She crept forward.

One of the kitchen windows faced inland towards the access lane. Thick bushes, Viburnums, grew alongside the house. Despite the scratching branches, she pushed through them. Slowly she raised her head and peered over the sill.

Seated at the kitchen table was a woman in jeans with a black jacket, her head covered by a dark scarf. The woman was examining Bill's laptop whose screen shone brightly as window after window appeared on the screen in response to her rapid mouse clicks.

Next to the woman, on the table, Jeannine could see a pile of papers, the notes she had made on Harry's files.

Abruptly the woman put the mouse down, stood up and shed her scarf to reveal long blond hair that tumbled about her shoulders. She turned towards the window.

Jeannine ducked and caught her breath.

The woman was Jane Peterson.

***

The rental agency in California, Maryland was small and the replacement car would not be available until morning. Bill fretted, Jeannine was alone at the cabin.

Resigned, he and Aileen crossed the river back to Solomons and found a Bed and Breakfast near the docks. With Aileen settled in her room, Bill wedged a chair against his door and slipped under the crisp clean sheets of the bed.

In only minutes he was snoring.

Awake, Aileen stared at the ceiling. In a few hours, Rob would be in South Carolina with Mary Dean. She dropped that thought for a more comforting one. Mary Catherine was safe with her mother and Aunt Agatha!

Mentally, she added up the charges on Agatha's credit card, but before she could finish, her lids drooped, and her head fell back on the soft pillow.

***

At the cabin, Jane Peterson strode to the kitchen door and called out into the shadows.

"Dr. Ryan, Jeannine, I know you're out there. Come on in. This is Jane from MTS. We need to talk."

Jeannine crouched lower in the bushes as Jane, silhouetted in the bright doorway, called again.

"Come on in Dr. Ryan. Don't worry. It's OK. I just want to talk."

Jeannine took a deep breath. She called from the darkness.

"What are you doing here, Jane? And what do you want to talk about?"

Before replying, Jane took two stealthy steps along the side of the house.

"Dr. Ryan, I see that you read Harry's notes so you know my name is 'Anan.'"

"Jane, or Anan, whoever you are, what do you want to talk about?"

253

"You can call me 'Anan.' It's my real name. It means 'clouds' in Arabic, and please let me call you 'Jeannine.' Wayne Johnson sent me. He wanted me to help you."

After this lie, Anan slipped quietly towards Jeannine's voice.

"Wayne never sent you. You work for Mandley."

Several more steps. There! Anan pointed her gun at the shadow behind the Viburnum.

"Jeannine, that's correct, but we still need to talk."

Jeannine looked up to see the deadly nozzle of an Uzi pistol aimed at her face.

Anan smiled.

"Now you will come with me, Dr. Ryan. Please. I'll tell you what I know about Mandley's computer chips in exchange for your help. Don't worry. I like strong women. We have a lot in common. We could have been sisters."

She added.

"I saw you decrypted Harry's notes. Excellent! I couldn't do that. I'm impressed."

Jeannine stood.

Anan led her through the open door. Once inside, Anan turned away and put the Uzi on the table.

"Sit down, Jeannine."

Jeannine stayed standing. Anan spoke again, still without looking.

"Jeannine, it seems I need your help."

"Who are you, Jane? I mean really?"

"We may not have much time. I want you to look at something for me."

Anan turned and extended her hand. In the palm was a small object that Jeannine recognized as computer thumb memory.

Anan frowned.

"I took this off of Harry's body. These are the last notes he made. You can decrypt them for me."

Anan lowered her voice as if speaking to herself.

"No, I didn't kill him. My husband did that. I didn't want him to."

She stood away from the laptop and pointed.

"Sit down. You decipher Harry's last words for me and I'll tell you who I am."

Jeannine sat at the laptop and inserted Harry's memory chip into the USB port.

"All right, Anan, I'll try. How much time do I have?"

"Just get started."

The Uzi lay next to the laptop, left side up, a magazine inserted into its handle. Jeannine did not know weapons, but she saw what looked like a safety switch just above the grip.

The switch was set forward of the "S." Anan had been ready to fire when she flushed Jeannine from the bushes.

She felt Anan's hand on her shoulder.

"Don't even think about touching that Uzi. Start typing."

"Don't worry. It's not my thing."

Anan laughed.

"I know."

She paused.

"You work, I'll talk. My name really is Anan. I was born in Montreal. My mother ..."

***

In Solomons, Bill awoke with a start. The pillow cover was damp with sweat.

Jeannine! She's in danger! Was it a nightmare?

He got up and paced the room.

Next door, Aileen slept no better. She tossed and rolled over. Rob was with Mary Dean, or would be soon. *I have no claim on him. I know he's attracted to her, but also to me too.*

For the first time since her divorce, she might like someone. In Johnstown, Rob had saved their lives by risking his own. *And Mary Catherine likes him.* She stared at the ceiling, forgetting Jeannine, Bill and the current danger.

Rob was with Mary Dean.

Damn it Mary, I can't help liking you! What a mess!

She rolled over and buried her face in the pillow.

***

255

In Delaware, Fareed's cigarette was too short to grip with his fingers. He tapped a new one from the pack, lit it from the glowing embers of the old, and inhaled deeply. He stared at his reflection in the dark window of his office. It was late. He had finished his evening prayers hours ago.

Fareed's inner voice told him not to trust Anan and yet he did trust her. He had seen her succeed before. She would succeed again!

The blip on his computer screen was no longer moving. He knew what that meant.

Anan had found Ryan's hiding place.

He knew he should call the black Mercedes and alert them to the location, but he also knew with certainty that Anan needed no help. She was a true soldier of Allah. He must let Anan alone to do His will.

But had Anan changed? Had his wife lost her spirit?

Fareed decided. He himself would go! The Mercedes could meet him at the airport.

He donned a black jacket, and picked up a dark carrying case.

Only thirty minutes later his helicopter crossed the Delaware line into Maryland. He flew over the eastern shore.

Fareed frowned. Anan was his wife. She was his field, his "tilth," to go to as he willed. If she was still "Anan" and not "Jane," then good. If not, he would beat her until she accepted his discipline or died for her disobedience

In either case, Ryan would die!

***

******

Chapter 31
Saturday, November 4

The sun had not yet risen when the helicopter landed at the small airstrip in Lusby, Maryland. Fareed stepped down and nodded to the man waiting by the Mercedes.

"Abed, you received my message?"

"Yes. I replaced Brendan, just as you asked."

"Good. Brendan is an infidel, a kafir. He would not understand if Anan needs correction. Who is with you?"

"I selected Mufid."

"He will be useful indeed. Where are the cliffs?"

"Just to the north of us. Solomons is just south."

"Excellent. Take those cases to the car. We must go."

A slight glow to the east gave the first sign of dawn as the Mercedes turned north. The car rolled smoothly, absorbing the bumps so that Fareed's laptop was steady. He studied the screen. The blip on the display was stationary. Anan's car had not moved. He would soon be with her.

Had she dealt with Ryan already?

***

Rob Wilson had spent most of the night cramped in his car at a rest stop in North Carolina where exhaustion (and cramps in his recovering leg) had forced him to stop last evening. Now he was on the interstate again. The glow on the eastern horizon showed that dawn was near.

Rob drove fast. He was near the South Carolina state line when he called Bill Hamm.

"Rob, do you know what time it is? It's dark outside!"

"The sun's coming up. How's Jeannine? And Aileen?"

"Jeannine's alone. Aileen's with me. We hit a deer, but we're fine. We're getting a new rental this morning. But we need to get back to Jeannine. Where are you, Rob?"

"I still have maybe an hour."

257

"I got it. Call again when you're there."

***

In Mona's cabin, the sun lit the kitchen. At the table, Jeannine, head cradled in her arms, dozed next to the keyboard. She awoke to see Anan standing over her, holding out a cup of black coffee.

Jeannine took a long swallow. She shook the hair off her forehead, hit "Enter," and spoke.

"This should be what you wanted to see."

But garbled letters appeared on the screen.

> qrz|/|nqrz|wkdw|iduhhg|kdpcd||khdgv|pdqgohb|
> vhfxulwb||kh|ehorqjv|wr|khceroodk||nloov|
> mhzv|||mdqhdqdq||zkrhyhu||lv|klv|zlih|
> dqgpdb|ehorqj|wr|khceroodk|wrr?||mdqh|
> lv|juhdw|lq|ehg||exwvkh|vsbv|rq|ph|dv|pxfk|dv|
> rq|wkledxow|||exw|vkh|olnhv|rxu|vha|vkh|
> glvwudfwv|ph|||vkh|zrqw|wdon|derxw|d100|fkls||
> iduhhg|nqrzv|mdqh|vohhsv|zlwk|ph|||kh|
> zdqwv||wr|phhw|ph|/|fdqw|ulvn|wkdw|||kh|lv|
> fudcb|mhdorxv|dqg|gdqjhurxv|

Anan reached for the Uzi.

"Jeannine, this is gibberish. Are you trying to deceive me? I've been honest with you."

"No, that's just Harry's extra trick, the Caesar cipher."

She pushed "Enter" again and Harry's message came up.

> now|i|know|that|fareed|hamza||heads|mandley|
> security||he|belongs|to|hezbollah||kills|
> jews|||janeanan||whoever||is|his|wife|
> andmay|belong|to|hezbollah|too?||jane|
> is|great|in|bed||butshe|spys|on|me|as|much|as|
> on|thibault|||but|she|likes|our|sex||she|
> distracts|me|||she|wont|talk|about||a100|chip||
> fareed|knows|jane|sleeps|with|me|||he|
> wants||to|meet|me|i|cant|risk|that|||he|is|
> crazy|jealous|and|dangerous|

"See, Anan, the actual note is mostly about you!"
Jeannine added.

"So you married again and your new husband, Fareed, is a terrorist. And you too? Just what does this chip *A100* do? What are you up to? Are you having second thoughts?"

Anan ignored Jeannine and studied Harry's message. The sound of a motor broke her concentration.

A car was coming.

***

Anan looked out the window. A Mercedes had stopped in the lane.

"It's him. Quick Jeannine, over here. Hold out your hands!"
"What?"
"Your hands, now!"

Anan slipped plastic cuffs over Jeannine's wrists and tightened the fasteners.

"Anan, what are you … ?"
"Shut up. Sit in that corner and look scared."

She shoved Jeannine to the floor and picked up the Uzi. The safety was still off.

The door burst open.

In the doorway stood Fareed Hamza.

He glared and extended his hand.

"Anan, my love, give me the Uzi."

She complied. He waved the weapon at Jeannine.

"Why is she still alive?"
"I need her to decrypt Harry Roberts' last files."

"Anan, Anan. Roberts knew nothing more of value to us. What do you expect to learn? Why do you care for his thoughts. Am I not to trust you?"

Anan lowered her eyes. Fareed stood tall.

"You are my wife. Why did you sleep with that kafir."

"Fareed, you told me to bed him. You ordered me to. You wanted to find out what he knew. I only did what you told me."

"Anan, I told you to sleep with him to get information. Allah allowed that in order that we extend his kingdom. But you took pleasure from that man, and more than once!"

"But Fareed, you told …"

"No! You dishonored me with this unbeliever. I am your husband. I must correct you for your sake. It is the will of Allah."

He signaled towards the door.

"Mufid, come in here. Watch that whore in the corner."

Mufid's Uzi was full-sized. He extended the collapsible stock and pointed the weapon down at Jeannine.

Fareed turned back to Anan and thoughtfully examined her face. He spied her scarf on the table and handed it to her.

"Wrap yourself in this."

"Yes, husband."

Fareed studied her eyes. He turned towards Mufid.

Without looking at Anan, he launched a wide swing at her head. The pistol slammed the side of her face.

She collapsed to the floor. Blood oozed through the scarf about her mouth.

Fareed grasped hair and scarf. He dragged her limp form to the door.

He turned and pointed back at Jeannine.

"Mufid, if that one moves, shoot her."

Fareed shoved Anan out the door.

Inside, Mufid glared at his charge.

From outside, a piercing scream echoed back into the kitchen.

***

At the rental office in Solomons, Bill Hamm's face flushed.

"Where's our car? We have been here an hour."

The girl at the counter smiled helplessly.

"It's here. They're cleaning it now. I'm sorry, sir, it was a late return. It will only be a few minutes more. They have to fill it with gas too."

There was no other party waiting. Bill picked up the decanter and poured himself another cup of coffee.

He turned to Aileen.

"Something is wrong. Jeannine is in danger. I know it."

Aileen did not answer.

What could she say?

They were all in danger.

***

In South Carolina, something was truly wrong. Moments before, Rob had pulled to the curve to allow a Dillon police car, siren screeching and lights blazing, to speed past. Now, the flashing red lights of an ambulance filled his rear view mirror. He pulled over again.

He continued ahead. In front of him, both vehicles turned right.

Rob shuddered. That was the road to Mary's mother's house, where Mary and the children were staying.

He stomped the accelerator. The Crown Vic lurched forward.

A police car, lights flashing, was in the driveway to the Morton home. A second, just arrived, was at the curb. A yellow police tape stretched between the pines along the drive and across the lawn, to a small dogwood with red berries. Outside the tape a small group of neighbors and bystanders stood watching as a gurney was pushed to the ambulance.

Rob stopped his car several houses away and walked towards the small group on the street. He picked an elderly woman in a bathrobe, clearly a neighbor.

"What happened?"

"He shot her. She's dead. He shot the kids too, the little girl, Annie, and Tommy. That's Tommy on the gurney. I always knew he was no good."

"Who?"

"That husband, Tom Dean. He was never any good. I knew it. He drove away in that red pickup of his. The police are looking for him."

261

Rob's face reddened. His eyes moistened involuntarily. He swallowed and clenched his fists.

"She's dead?"

The neighbor woman looked up at him.

"Dead? For sure. But who are you? Are you that new friend Mary had?"

Rob swallowed again. He started to speak, but a second ambulance, flashing red, arrived. Rob stepped back as the group of bystanders split apart to allow it to pass.

The onlookers merged together once more. The neighbor woman turned back to Rob.

He was no longer there.

Down the road she saw a blue Crown Victoria pull away.

***

Rob's vision blurred. His mind raced with disjointed thoughts that sped independently in diverse directions. He drove aimlessly.

A last a red light stopped his progress. Ahead on the right were the golden arches of McDonald's. He needed to clear his head. Maybe coffee would help.

He sipped the hot coffee and munched listlessly on his egg McMuffin.

Seated in a booth opposite was a young woman with two young children, a boy and a girl. The mother was the same age as Mary Dean had been.

With a silent groan, Rob lowered his face into his arms.

When Rob lifted his head from between his arms. The booth across from him was empty. The young mother and her children were gone.

He grimaced and stared at his hand. The Styrofoam coffee cup was squeezed into a crumpled mass. *When did I do that?* Without thinking, he grabbed a paper napkin and wiped the black ovals of coffee spatter from the table top.

If only I had gotten here yesterday, Mary would still be alive. He continued to wipe aimlessly.

"Sir, are you OK?"

Rob looked up. An attendant with a mop searched his eyes.

"I'm …, no I'm not. I just lost a friend."

"I'm sorry, sir."

The attendant moved away, pushing a wide wet swathe on the floor towards the entrance.

Rob followed the attendant with his eyes. Outside the door, a red pickup pulled into the drive-through line. Rob literally saw "red." He recalled Dean's pickup. Grief changed to anger. He muttered under his breath.

"Dean, you murdering bastard, where are you?"

In an instant, the answer flashed before his eyes. The vision was vivid and clear.

He knew!

In only seconds, Rob was at the wheel of his car.

He spun the wheels out of the McDonald's lot.

He knew where Dean was!

*****

At last Bill and Aileen were on the way. They crossed the Patuxent river and headed north towards Mona's cabin. Bill drove fast. The road was flat, but Aileen pushed tightly against the dashboard to maintain her balance as he continued to accelerate.

She glanced sideways. Bill's lips were set tight.

She did not complain about the speed. Another curve was ahead. She braced her arm against the dash once more.

*****

From outside Mona's cabin, Fareed Hamza called.

"Mufid, get out here, fast!"

Fareed's words permitted no hesitation. Mufid glanced quickly at Jeannine. She stared back, but stayed seated on the floor, back against the wall. He left the kitchen.

Jeannine's wrists were bound, but her legs were free and her mind was clear. She rose, stepped to the laptop, and pulled Harry's thumb drive from the slot. She turned in time to see a shadow outside the door. Mufid was back.

She slumped against the wall. The thumb drive slipped from her hand and skidded under the kitchen table.

Mufid entered.

"Whack."

His open hand hit her cheek, hard. Her eyes glazed.

"Why did you move, you slut? What were you doing?

Jeannine's eyes refocused. She glared at Mufid.

Fareed Hamza appeared in the doorway. He threw a roll of duct tape to Mufid.

"Tape the legs of that bitch and help me outside."

Mufid tightened the sticky tape about Jeannine's ankles. Then he balled his fist and hit her, hard. Her head slammed the wall.

She slumped to the floor, unconscious.

***

The ceiling slowly came into focus as the stabbing pain in her head subsided. Jeannine groaned, rolled away from the wall, and bumped against what felt like a body.

She opened her eyes and looked about. The kitchen was empty except for a limp form stretched out on the floor. Anan?

Jeannine focused. It was indeed Anan, barely recognizable under clotted blood, ripped scarf, and knotted hair.

"Anan, can you hear me? Blink your eyes."

Anan's eyes slowly opened and closed.

From outside, some distance away, Jeannine heard rapid repeated gunfire.

Uzi's!

Bill and Aileen had driven into an ambush!

Jeannine had to act. She pushed herself towards Anan.

Something sharp sliced her thigh. A thin stain of blood appeared on her jeans.

The megalodon tooth!

She rolled upwards to relieve the pressure on her thigh. Thankfully, her hands were secured to the front, not behind. She fumbled at the tight opening of the jean's pocket. The plastic cuffs chaffed her wrists and drew blood, but she persisted.

There, the tooth was free.

She leaned over and sawed at the duct tape about her ankles.

Millions of years ago, the giant shark, twisting its head from side to side, had torn apart hapless marine mammals using that same serrated tooth. It still worked. In only a minute she had cut through the tape. Several painful pulls and her legs were free.

She stood up, but her hands were still bound. There was no way she could apply the tooth with sufficient pressure to cut the plastic.

Jeannine stepped to the kitchen sink. She tugged the drawer open, no knives. She pushed the cutting edge of the tooth against the cuffs again, but they did not yield.

Anan reached out.

"Jeannine, give me the tooth. Let me try."

Jeannine extended her cuffed hands. Anan gripped the megalodon tooth and twisted and sawed, hard. Once more, the extinct predator's tooth sliced and tore its prey. The plastic broke apart.

Jeannine looked out the kitchen window.

"That man's coming back. Anan, can you walk?"

Anan struggled forward. Jeannine pulled her into the bedroom and pointed.

"Over there. Out that rear window. We'll head for those trees."

Jeannine pushed Anan to the sill and shoved the screen outwards. She lifted Anan up and out. Then she clambered through. Together they struggled through the brush.

Standing by the front door, Mufid heard the crunching leaves and snapping branches.

He drew a fresh clip from his pocket, jammed it into the Uzi, and raced to the back of the cabin.

***

******

Chapter 32
Saturday, November 4

Rob drove north. As he crossed into North Carolina, the cell phone vibrated. It was Bill Hamm. Rob put him on speaker.

"Rob, where are you?"

"I-95 north, where are you, Bill?"

"We're on the run. Mandley found out where Jeannine was hiding. They ambushed us when we got back to the cabin. Lucky for us, Aileen spotted them. I did a 180 and got out of there. Our new rental car has some holes in it, but Aileen and I are OK."

"And Jeannine?"

"Nothing. We don't know anything. Two Mandley terrorists chased us in that damn Mercedes, but we dumped them."

"Terrorists or thugs?"

"Both. They were yelling to each other in Arabic, and they've got some serious firepower, maybe Uzi's."

"What next?"

"We've got to help Jeannine. We need you up here."

"I'll come as soon as I can, Bill, but I've got a stop to make first. Mary Dean is dead. Her husband shot her and shot the kids too. I think I know where he is."

"Rob, I'm sorry … "

"I'll be back as soon as I can."

"Rob, don't … "

But that was all Rob heard. Bill's voice had faded into static. The connection was broken.

Rob's mood went from gray to black. He left the interstate and headed for Pembroke.

***

From Pembroke, North Carolina, Rob Wilson drove towards Carla Cooper's house. Here, only a week before, Mary Dean had stopped Rob from shooting Tom Dean.

Her words flashed on and off in his mind. *No. Rob, No. Not you. Don't shoot him. ... Not you.*

Rob sobbed. Dean had shown his wife no such mercy.

He recalled more of Mary's words. *He's my husband, at least he was. I couldn't live with you being the one to kill him. I couldn't. Not you. Somebody else has to do that.*

Mary was dead and that changed everything. He would execute a citizen's arrest. If Dean resisted, as Rob hoped, Dean would die!

Maybe even if he didn't resist!

The dirt lane to Carla Cooper's house had not changed since Rob's last visit. What was different was that Rob now knew the terrain. He parked his car out of sight of the house and walked through the pines along the road.

The woods in back of the house gave him cover. He paused behind the weathered garage. Looking across to the house, he examined the ground-level doors and windows. The windows were barred with wooden slats, and the door on the back porch had been re-nailed shut.

He studied the weeds and grass that thrived between the garage and the house. Then he scanned the bordering pines. There was no movement, no sign of life.

For the first time, Rob questioned his gut feeling.

Perhaps Tom Dean was not here.

He scanned the trees again. Through them he saw an opening in the woods. He went towards it, pushing aside the small hardwoods that grew wherever the sun penetrated the tall pines.

He emerged onto a narrow sandy "road," a firebreak that divided the pinewoods into two separate stands.

Bingo!

A short distance away, partially hidden by low brush beside the firebreak, was a red truck, an F150.

His gut had been right. Dean *was* here.

Rob quickly retraced his steps to the house.

Once more, he surveyed the old building.

All was silent.

Rob took out his Smith and Wesson. It had five shots. Rob could see all five bullets slam into Dean's chest. Tom Dean would never kill again.

An investigator would conclude it was a rage killing. True, Rob was enraged!

The windows on the second floor were not boarded. Rob easily climbed to the roof of the porch and stepped through the window. He listened through the wall. Someone was in the next room.

Rob held the revolver in both hands. He looked both ways in the hall.

Nothing.

He stepped cautiously to the door of the adjacent bedroom. He heard movement inside.

Rob pointed his gun and kicked the door open.

Bound on the floor, face down, was a woman. She turned her face sideways. Her mouth was covered with tape, but her eyes brightened.

"Mary?"

It was Mary Dean!

***

Rob removed the tape from her mouth and untied her hands. He started to remove the knot from her ankles, but could not wait. He kissed her gently.

Finally he pulled back.

"They told me you were dead! And I saw a woman's body on the gurney."

Tears filled her eyes.

"He killed my mother, not me. But he shot Tommy and Annie ..."

Her voice faltered. Rob spoke.

"I know Tommy is still alive. He's in the hospital, critical. Annie, I don't know."

He fumbled with the knot about her ankles. Finally it yielded.

"Rob, how did you find me?"

"I came here to kill Tom. I guessed he would come here."

Mary shook.

"Rob, you didn't kill him did you?"

"I would have, but I haven't seen him."

Her eyes grew large.

"You mean you didn't see him? He's downstairs!"

Her eyes opened wider. She gasped.

"No!"

Before Rob could turn, he felt a sharp pain at the base of his neck. Then all went black.

***

Tom Dean pointed his Beretta at Rob's head.

Mary threw herself in front of the gun.

"Tom, stop. Haven't you killed enough, and your own child, too!"

But her husband's eyes were blank. He stared trance-like.

He was a total stranger.

His finger blanched as it tightened on the trigger.

The sound of a motor outside broke Dean's concentration. He looked out the window. No vehicle was in sight.

He collected Rob's .38, and tossed a roll of duct tape at Mary.

"Wrap his wrists, now!"

She fumbled over Rob's wrist's, twisting the tape round and round. Satisfied, Tom tore the roll away. He tore off another strip and quickly taped Mary's wrists. Then he taped her mouth once more.

"Don't move. I'll be right back. If you're not in the same spot, I'll kill the boyfriend."

Mary shrank backwards against the wall.

Tom went to the window again and stepped out onto the roof of the porch. He dropped lightly to the ground.

Mary heard him land. She twisted her face to the wall and rubbed. The tape came off her mouth and dangled from her cheek, but her hands were still bound.

She leaned over Rob.

"Please, Rob, wake up. Hurry. Please wake up. Please."

Rob stirred.

"Hurry, Rob. He's coming back. Wake up. Please."

"Where am ... ?"

"Tom hit you with his gun. He's gone outside. He thought he heard someone. But he'll be back. We have to hurry."

Rob twisted his arms, but the repeated wrappings of tape did not yield.

"Mary, reach in my right pocket and get my knife."

Her wrists were still bound. Precious time was lost before she extricated the knife from his pocket. She gripped it with both hands, bit tenaciously on the blade, and tugged with her teeth.

The knife clicked open.

Hands still tied, she sawed the thick twisted layers as best she could. The tape separated and split apart.

Rob's hands were free.

Mary peeked out the window.

Tom stood in the yard, his pump-action shotgun held at the ready.

He looked up. She ducked back.

Had he seen her?

The answer was immediate.

"Brroom!"

Shot shattered the window, sending glass and splinters flying through the room.

She crawled to Rob. His hands and feet now were free, but his eyes were dull.

Downstairs, ripped wood rasped against shrieking nails as the boarded door was forced open.

Steps sounded on the stairs.

Mary looked to Rob. His eyes were half shut. He was dazed.

She shoved a chair under the doorknob.

The footsteps stopped outside the door.

"Brroom!"

The door handle and its attached wood flew across the room. The remainder of the door blew open under the blast as Mary threw Rob to the floor and shielded him with her body.

Tom Dean stood in the doorway. He pumped another shell into the chamber and pointed his gun downwards at her.

"No, Tom. No! Please, No!"

"Brroom!"

The noise of the shotgun blast filled the room.

Mary stared in horror as Tom pitched onto the floor, face down. His shotgun clattered to the side.

Blood appeared under his body from what was, evidently, a massive exit wound in his chest. His leg twitched once and was still. Even so, he tried to lift his head.

"Brroom!"

A second blast slammed his body. He slumped motionless, dead.

The pool of blood mingled with dirt and dust to produce an expanding dark stain that spread along the grain of the worn floorboards.

Mary gaped in horror at the torn mass that had been her husband. She looked up.

In the doorway was a man, clad in jeans and a dirty shirt, but muscular, with a black tattooed skull and cross bones visible below his shoulder. He seemed unaware of Mary or Rob.

The man looked heavenwards.

"I got him, Pops! I got the skunk! I got 'Mr. Smith' for you! The bastard's gone to hell, he's done."

After what could have been a silent "prayer" of gratitude, he spoke again, eyes still uplifted.

"And I got him with your favorite gun, Pops! The old double barreled. You can rest in peace now."

Without so much as a glance at Mary or Rob, the man turned and left. She heard his rapid steps on the stairs.

Moments later, Mary heard a motor. She went to the window in time to see a battered Ford Ranger spin dirt from its rear wheels and roar away. It was blue with North Carolina plates.

It was the same "plumber's" truck she had seen at Myrtle Beach two weeks ago.

Two weeks that, to her, seemed two years.

***

******

Chapter 33
Saturday, November 4

A thoughtful Mufid stood outside Mona's cabin. That infidel, Hamm, had escaped their trap. Hamm's abrupt maneuver that reversed his car's direction meant that he had anti-terrorist training. Mufid knew that maneuver from his own training for RPG attacks on vehicle convoys.

"Mufid" meant "useful" in Arabic, but at the moment he felt more "used" than "useful." Abed and Fareed had left him to watch two weak incapacitated women, while they pursued Hamm in the Mercedes."

And worse, he had lost them!

Mufid gripped his Uzi and studied the woods that bordered the cabin.

***

The bushes that sheltered Jeannine were mostly bare and the few yellowed leaves that remained offered scant shelter. She squinted through the twisted stems and watched Mufid as he scanned the woods.

His gaze stopped on her bush.

She ducked and crept back through the trees where Anan lay exhausted, breathing heavily.

"Anan, we have to move. Can you?"

"I'm ready to try."

Jeannine steadied her.

"Where did you leave your car? How far is it?"

Clearly in pain, Anan pointed to a large White Oak.

"I think it's over that way."

With Jeannine supporting her, she stumbled towards it.

They reached the tree. Anan gasped and leaned on the trunk.

"Anan, I don't see the car."

"Maybe it's over there. It can't be far."

A bullet hit the oak. Chips flew from the bark.

It was Mufid.

Three more shots splattered leaves and branches. They were widely spaced. Mufid had not spotted them. He was shooting in frustration, randomly, to flush his prey.

Jeannine dragged Anan ahead. The foliage was dense now. Prickly leaves of evergreen hollies and spiny stems of Smilax scratched and tugged at them as they crawled.

Hopefully Mufid could not see them through the dense tangle.

They broke into the open.

There, in the clearing was the car.

Jeannine propped Anan in the passenger seat. Anan whispered.

"Under the seat, the keys."

Jeannine's fingers fumbled until she felt the clicking pieces of metal. To her relief, the car started easily.

She guided the car on a twisted route between the trees and gained the access road.

Anan's eyes were shut. Her breathing appeared regular.

In only minutes, they reached the paved road to Solomons.

***

Second-hand smoke filled the Mercedes. Fareed pushed the butt of his cigarette into the mixture of gray ash and stubs that already filled the ashtray.

Abed, the non smoker, coughed.

Fareed lit another cigarette and glared at his driver.

"Know this, Abed. The Messenger did not prohibit tobacco."

Abed knew better than to reply. He locked his eyes straight on the road ahead and drove without speaking.

Bill Hamm had escaped their trap, and then eluded them near Lusby. Since that fiasco, Fareed's anger had sought a live target and only Abed was available.

Fareed blew smoke into Abed's face.

"You doubtless think that smoking is 'haram,' forbidden?"

"Me?"

"Yes, Abed, you. Do you see anyone else in this car?"

Abed paled. He knew Fareed's temper. Fareed kept on.

"Those who forbid tobacco are fools. They trust the science of the infidels who say smoking harms the body. Would you trust them, Abed?"

Abed risked a sideward glance towards his leader. That movement saved him. He exclaimed.

"Fareed look, the laptop. There, on the screen. She's moving!"

Fareed studied the blinking blip on the display. Abed was right. Anan's car was clearly on the move.

He motioned Abed to reverse course.

***

In the passenger seat of her car, Anan opened her eyes and stretched. The pain had subsided.

"Jeannine, pull over there, at that 7-Eleven."

"Why?"

"Just do it."

Anan pushed herself out of her car. She dropped to the ground and reached under the chassis. Seconds later, she stood holding a small object.

A pickup was at one of the gas pumps while the driver paid inside. Anan limped to the truck and reached under it. When she stood up, her hands were empty.

As Anan got back into the car, Jeannine said.

"What was that all about?"

"That was a tracking device. Fareed had it on my car so he could locate me. I just transferred it to that truck."

While she spoke, a young man exited the 7-Eleven and turned his truck north. Anan smiled.

"He's going north. Fareed will follow him. We should go south."

"Anan, why? You knew I didn't know about that tracker."

"Jeannine, you got us away from Mufid. Fareed will kill you if he catches you. I don't want that."

"But now you've tricked him. He'll kill you too."

"Maybe, but he'll think about it first. I'm still his wife."

"But can't he divorce you, just repeating the words three times?"

"But he didn't. He just 'corrected' me. He's proud, and he guards his honor. He doesn't want to lose face. And he still wants me."

"Are you willing to bet your life on him?"

"I might be."

Anan lowered her chin. She spoke in barely audible tones.

"I know one thing. I will never let him beat me again, never!"

Jeannine fixed her eyes on the road ahead.

***

Mufid sat at the kitchen table in Mona's cabin. His cell phone vibrated. He checked the caller's number. It was the call he dreaded, Fareed.

Mufid had failed. Ryan had escaped and Anan was with her.

He tried to ignore the phone, but the vibration continued.

He wiped his brow and stared at the offending instrument.

The vibration continued.

Mufid had to face him, now or later.

He picked up the phone.

***

The Mercedes was filled with smoke. Abed coughed.

Fareed ignored him. The blip showed Ryan and Anan heading north.

The phone call to Mufid had been brief. From a distance, Mufid had seen Ryan push Anan into the car. Ryan had driven away.

Mufid was forbidden to think. He was to stay at the cabin. If Hamm showed up he was to exercise his highest skill, marksmanship. He was to shoot and Hamm was to die. Thus would Allah deal justice to Hamm!

Fareed returned to the blip. There was no hurry. Anan knew her car was marked. He could trust her.

Abed coughed again.

Fareed studied his subordinate. Abed was a faithful soldier of Allah.

"Abed, stop the car."

Abed hit the brakes and pulled onto the shoulder. Fareed unlatched the overflowing ashtray and threw the gray contents out the window. Leaving the window open he motioned Abed to drive.

"There Abed, my friend, enjoy the fresh air. Allah is pleased with your service."

Fareed studied the computer screen. The blip had stopped moving. He smiled.

"They have stopped. We have them. Abed, Allah will reward your faithfulness. The Ryan woman is despised by him. You may do what you want with her before you kill her."

"And Anan?"

"She will do as I say. I am her husband. She must be a good wife."

"That is surely the will of Allah."

Fareed shut his eyes.

"Indeed it is, Salaam alaikum, Abed."

"Alaikum salaam, Fareed."

Abed exhaled. Peace was restored in the Mercedes.

***

The house was isolated and visible from afar. Open fallow fields, dry and yellow in the November sun, surrounded the modest dwelling. All was quiet.

Abed stopped the Mercedes on the shoulder of the highway.

Fareed scanned the driveway with binoculars. The only vehicle was a gray pickup truck. His eyes returned to the computer screen. There was no doubt. Truck and blip were stationary. The signal came from the pickup!

Fareed's eyes narrowed. *Anan, you are faithless. You have betrayed me!*

His forehead furrowed. He broke open a fresh pack of cigarettes. The lighter shook in his hand.

He inhaled. That calmed him.

In minutes, acrid second-hand smoke again filled the car.

Fareed stayed silent. He jammed his stub into the ashtray and lit another smoke. Still he said nothing.

Abed coughed.

Fareed glared.

"Ryan has tricked us. She found the tracker. We went north, she went south."

He paused and pointed to a town on the map.

"We will find them here. They have stopped in California."

"California?"

"It's a town, here in Maryland. Abed, don't be stupid."

"But why there?"

Fareed lifted his hand, palm outwards.

"Because Ryan, like all kafirs, is weak. She knows Anan is hurt and needs to recuperate. She will stop to let Anan rest."

"Why not Solomons? It's closer."

"Abed, Abed. Because Solomons is a dead end. They would be trapped. No, they crossed the Patuxent River. They are in California."

Fareed lit another cigarette. *Anan, you ungrateful traitor. After all I have given you!*

"Don't worry Abed. They will think we are driving north. They will relax. But we know where they are, and, Abed, we know what car they are driving. They cannot hide."

The smoke grew thicker. Abed coughed.

Fareed did not notice.

They headed south.

***

Blood-and-dirt-caked blond hair lay on the floor. Next to that was a mound of reddened gauze.

Anan lay on the bed face down. Jeannine leaned over and cleaned the wounds on her back.

"Jane, I can't call you 'Anan' while I'm doing this. I'm sorry, I just can't. I don't understand. Fareed is a monster."

She carefully swabbed caked blood and dirt from a deep lesion under the shoulder blade. Whether Jane or Anan, the shoulder's owner felt intense pain. She winced and emitted a low groan.

"Sorry, I can't help it. This wound is deep, and I'm not trained for this. I was better at cutting your hair."

Jane gripped the edge of the headboard. She squeezed, hard.

"I'm ready."

Jeannine set to work.

Slight cracks in the window blinds admitted flashes of color from the motel's neon lights. Evening was falling fast. Finally, Jeannine stood and let out a deep breath.

"We're out of Neosporin. I'm going to buy some, bandages too."

"Take the money on the dresser."

Jeannine stuffed the bills in her jeans.

"I'll be back."

***

Jeannine bought the Neosporin at Walmart where she located a payphone and called Bill Hamm.

"Jeannine, my God! It's you. Are you all right?"

"I'm fine. Really. But you, Bill, I heard all the shooting. Are you hurt? Those shots! I thought that ..."

"We're OK, me and Aileen. I saw them first. They hit the car, but they missed us. But I haven't slept for worrying about you."

"I'm OK, now."

She recounted hastily about Fareed and his henchman, and her and Anan's escape from the cabin.

Then the conversation turned personal.

***

******

Chapter 34
Sunday, November 5

The morning light that filtered through the slits of the blind illuminated Jeannine's face with alternating shades of gray. Through half-raised lids, she saw the rumpled sheets of Anan's bed. It was empty.

She sat up, wide awake.

Anan was on the floor, prostrate from the waist downwards, murmuring in Arabic. Still on her knees, she lifted her upper body while continuing to pray. Moments later she bowed once more. All the while soft syllables of Arabic filled the room.

Jeannine kept a respectful silence until the sounds stopped.

Anan stood gingerly, favoring her sore back, hands over her kidneys.

"You're awake."

"Are you done praying?"

"For now, I try to pray five times a day."

"Did you sleep well? You seem to be feeling better."

"I did and I am, thanks to you."

Jeannine shook her head and tossed auburn hair from her eyes.

"Jane, Anan, can I ask you a question?"

"I suppose so."

"You've been a Muslim since you were little, right?"

"Yes."

"And a Muslim should only marry a Muslim, right?"

"Yes."

"Then how did you marry Allen Peterson?"

"It wasn't a real marriage. He was an unbeliever. It was for the Jihad. Fareed, ordered me to 'marry' that kafir and I obeyed him. I knew I was to marry Fareed later. I obeyed Fareed."

"And Harry Roberts?"

"By then I was truly married. Fareed ordered me to find out what he knew. 'Islam' means submission to Allah. When I submit to my husband, I am submitting to Allah. You can see that."

"But you slept with Harry. I don't defend Harry, but you were not honest with him. You deceived him."

"We are at war. Deception is permissible, even desirable, to defend Islam against the aggressor."

"But you told me that Harry was good to you."

Anan swallowed. Jeannine continued.

"Anan, Fareed killed Harry, and he nearly killed you."

Jeannine lowered her voice.

"You wanted me to decrypt Harry's last notes to see what he wrote about you. That was the reason. And you didn't want Fareed to know. Am I right?"

"I suppose so. Yes."

"Anan, Fareed is dangerous. Look at you."

"So?"

"So Fareed is jealous and proud. He acts for himself. He does nothing for you, and no way does he act for Allah."

Anan fell silent.

***

The blinds were open now and the room was bright. Jeannine sat at the narrow desk and sipped coffee from a Styrofoam cup.

Anan lay on the bed face down favoring her lacerated back.

"Do you think you can you sit up. I have a Danish for you, and some coffee."

Anan took the proffered cup and balanced the paper plate on her knees.

Jeannine smiled. The scene was so "American." Jane's freshly-clipped, blonde hair and shapely shaved legs seemed the antithesis of a veiled Muslim woman, much less a dark-clad terrorist.

Reality returned when Anan turned to reveal a swollen left cheek and darkened eye.

Jeannine leaned towards her.

"Harry talked about an *A100* chip that was capable of sending a signal, maybe to detonate explosives. What do you know about it?"

"Hand me that brown envelope."

Anan took a newspaper clipping from the envelope and handed it to Jeannine.

Lebanese Leader Dies Unexpectedly

Prominent hard-line Christian Leader Kevork Abassian died suddenly yesterday during negotiations with representatives of Hezbollah in Beirut. Abassian, a staunch opponent of Hezbollah's police and administrative functions in southern Lebanon, suffered an apparent heart attack during the meeting and could not be resuscitated. According to his physician, Abassian, who had a prior heart condition, went into cardiac arrest following tachycardia and subsequent ventricular fibrillation. He was pronounced dead upon arrival at the hospital.

Jeannine lifted her eyes from the paper in a silent query. Anan responded.

"We did it. Abassian had a pacemaker, a programmable one, to regulate his heart rhythm. One of the Hezbollah staffers, our agent, had an implanted Mandley chip, the one Harry found out about."

"That chip senses specific muscle contractions in our man, say if one moves several fingers in a particular manner and flexes the wrist in a certain movement then the chip transmits a signal that impacts the pacemaker program in the target. The pacemaker produces tachycardia in chaotic bursts. The result is ventricular fibrillation and cardiac arrest."

Anan continued.

"Even if rapid resuscitation results in defibrillation, then the agent repeats the specific motions, our chip senses those and transmits again. The second time is invariably fatal."

"But surely security can detect electronic transmissions?"

Anan did not hesitate.

"They screen for transmissions before the meetings, but the chip only transmits when specific muscles contract. It takes only milliseconds."

"Jane, you mean that Mandley developed this chip for terrorists."

"Hardly. Fareed found out about it, and we use it, but Mandley developed the chip to cause failures in a competitor's pacemaker, so that Mandley's pacemaker would dominate the market."

Anan produced another document from the brown envelope. It summarized an FDA report on sudden deaths caused by pacemaker failure for Mandley's competitor.

Anan sneered.

"What do you think of your 'Western' morals now? We kill to obey Allah, you kill for mammon."

Jeannine ignored the jibe.

"So Mandley faked data on the Parkinson chip so they could modify it and use it to develop their lethal *A100* chip, and you and Fareed can export *A100* pretending it's the Parkinson chip."

"Precisely."

"What about using *A100* to detonate explosives?"

Anan finished her Danish, and wiped the stickiness from her fingers.

"Harry was off center there. It could be a backup. If a suicide warrior looses faith and fails Allah, our agent could detonate the charge. But the agent has to be close and will die too. That only happened once. We don't need backup. Once loaded with explosives, our warriors act alone and are faithful."

"Jane, why are you telling me this?"

"Because you are not like Thibault. And you are right about Fareed. He is not a true servant of Allah. He serves only himself."

Anan paused.

"Besides, I respect your knowledge and your courage. We could be sisters. Together we could serve Allah, spread his kingdom. You must agree."

Jeannine turned to face her "sister."

"Jane" was no longer there. Only Anan, blue eyes glinting like steel.

More importantly, Anan held a 9 mm Beretta.

***

Jeannine forced her eyes away from the gun.

"Jane, Anan, whoever, you know you are not going to shoot me. Put the gun down."

"Why won't you help me defend Islam?"

"I will not help you murder innocent people."

"Like Mandley Bionics did, killing innocent people so they could sell more of their pacemakers?"

"I refuse to help Mandley too."

"Jeannine, please, I am afraid for you. Join me. Allah demands obedience. You must not refuse him."

"Jane, I can't join you. Allah is your god, not mine."

"He *is* your god even if you do not know it. Accept him!"

"If I accept Allah then I have to accept that Fareed can beat you to death."

Anan's face reddened.

"Jeannine, you twist things. Kafir!"

She swung the Berretta at Jeannine's head. Jeannine tried to duck, but too late. She dropped like a stone.

Anan stepped over her and left.

***

When Bill and Aileen arrived at the motel, they found Jeannine unconscious on the floor. Bill leaned over her.

"Jeannine, it's Bill. Speak to me. Please!"

He felt her carotid artery. *Thank God, a pulse!*

Aileen handed him a wet wash cloth. He wiped the blood off Jeannine's forehead.

Her eyelids lifted.

"Bill, … What … ?"

287

"We came in. You were on the floor."

"Where's Anan?"

"She's gone. Did she do this to you?"

Jeannine fell silent. She pushed herself up to a sitting position.

"Ohhhh. My head."

"Jeannine, we have to leave. Fareed will find this motel, if he hasn't already. And Anan may come back. Can you make it?"

He helped her to stand.

"Bill, let me hang on to you. I'll be OK."

He and Aileen guided Jeannine to the car.

Bill drove slowly.

No car appeared in the rear view mirror.

***

Bill stopped in front of a frame house with a sign that read "Ruth's Bed and Breakfast."

"Aileen, we're low on gas. You help Jeannine to the room. I'll be right back."

Once inside, Aileen put ice in a plastic bag and wrapped it in a towel.

"Here, see if this helps."

Jeannine held it to her head while she recounted Anan's revelations.

"Aileen, you're the physiologist. What do you think? Could the *A100* chip disrupt a pacemaker and cause cardiac arrest?"

"I don't see why not. The latest pacemakers are externally programmable. The *A100* could send signals to change the heart rate. If *A100* tells the pacemaker to send very high rates chaotically, it would cause rapid uncoordinated contractions of the ventricle, almost no blood would be pumped and the subject would be unconsciousness in seconds."

"Uncoordinated contractions?"

"The ventricle simply quivers, rather than fill with blood and expel it. It's called ventricular fibrillation. Cardiac arrest follows."

"But could this chip emit a signal strong enough?"

"In the same room, why not? Our implanted Parkinson chip has a miniaturized Lithium cell. The basic technology is not new, but Mandley's miniaturization is. Lithium cells have been used in pacemakers since 1970. The Parkinson chip is minuscule. And as a modification, *A100* would have the same power source."

Jeannine pressed the ice closer to her forehead.

"But Aileen, why develop the Parkinson chip?"

"That chip could detect activity in specific muscle fibers, that is, in their firing. As feedback, the chip sends signals to those fibers to eliminate excessive activity. Depending on how and where the chip is implanted, different muscles are monitored."

"So?"

"So the Parkinson Chip technology affords the trigger mechanism. Implanting the *A100* chip in a would-be assassin means that simple movements, like finger flexing and wrist movements, could trigger the emission of a lethal signal. One could implant the chip in an arm, or shoulder or anywhere."

"But Aileen, Thibault faked data for the FDA about the efficacy of the Parkinson chip. You think that in spite of that, the *A100* chip can detect specific muscle activity and produce a signal in response?"

"The fake data for the Parkinson chip were to prove a 'cure.' Either chip surely can do what Anan said."

"So Anan spoke the truth."

"It looks like it."

They looked up as Bill Hamm entered the room.

"Did you hear the news?"

"What news? We've been busy talking."

"The President has arranged for the Prime Ministers of Israel and Lebanon to meet this week at Camp David to discuss, among other things, the social programs of Hezbollah in southern Lebanon."

Aileen gasped.

"Good God! Two years ago the Israeli Prime Minister had a heart attack."

Bill raised his eyebrows.

"So why does that matter?"

Aileen turned to Jeannine.

"The Prime Minister has a pacemaker!"

***

******

Chapter 35
Monday, November 6

Fareed's confidence had been atypically low. The night had passed and he and Abed had failed to find Ryan's motel thanks to idiotic American clerks and their stupid respect for privacy!

But now, thanks to his cleverness, they were at her room!

The dead bolt was not thrown. Fareed easily manipulated the spring lock on the door to the motel room. He entered, followed by Abed.

"Abed, you see the bloody gauze on the floor, and the blond hair clippings. It is as I said, Ryan stopped here to take care of Anan."

Abed did not speak. Fareed's flushed face forbade interruption.

"And this room is still booked. They left without checking out. What's this?"

Fareed examined a wash cloth splotched with blood.

"Abed, the hair on that cloth, is red. That is not Anan's. It is Ryan's."

Fareed sat on the bed.

"I must think."

Abed kept silent.

"Abed, it may be that Anan still serves Allah. That is Ryan's blood on that cloth, and that must be her blood on the floor. Now look at the bed. The blond clippings are Anan's, so the blood on the sheets is Anan's."

"I was right, Abed. Ryan is weak. She took care of Anan's wounds. But Anan was not fooled by weakness. She overpowered the unbeliever."

Fareed grimaced. *Anan, maybe you are still with us? Or against us? And where is Ryan?*

"Abed, we are done here. We must rejoin Mufid. Perhaps Anan has already returned to the cabin."

Fareed took one last look around the room.

Anan who are you, really?

***

From down the street, Anan watched the black Mercedes leave the motel.

She started her motor and pulled out.   Fareed's Mercedes turned onto Highway 4. Anan did likewise.

After a few minutes, she smiled.

There was no need to follow the Mercedes.

She knew its destination.

Fareed was headed for the cabin. She knew a quicker way.

***

The ashtray was crowded once again.   Fareed stubbed his cigarette into it.   Stale smoke hung above the dash.   The car windows were shut.

Abed's throat scratched.   He suppressed a cough.   He focused on the bridge ahead.

Fareed stared out the window, oblivious of the frothy waters of the Patuxent River below. He turned to Abed and broke the silence.

"Abed, did you notice that brown car behind us when we left the motel?"

Abed cleared his throat to respond. Fareed stopped him.

"It was Anan. She followed us. You should have spotted it."

"Fareed, there is no car behind us now."

"Exactly. Anan is not stupid. She knows we are going to pick up Mufid."

"But you said she is on our side again."

Fareed frowned.

"Perhaps she is, Abed, perhaps she is."

Fareed closed his eyes.

My dear Anan why do you sneak?

He dozed, only to awake with a start.

"Abed, you idiot, this is the turnoff to the cabin. Turn here. Quick."

Abed rotated the wheel. The Mercedes responded like the performance car it was. They rolled smoothly onto the unpaved lane.

The woods on either side of the narrow road were dry. The sandy soil was matted with dead brown oak leaves mingled with once-golden leaves of Hickory. The lane swung sharply to the right. Abed skillfully negotiated the turn, and hit the brakes hard.

A brown Toyota blocked their progress.

Fareed sputtered.

"That is Anan's car! Where is she?"

He motioned Abed to stay behind the wheel and stepped out of the car. He went to the Toyota and peered in.

"Abed, the keys are in the ignition."

He put his hand on the hood.

"That hood is warm, very warm. She is not far."

Fareed started back to the Mercedes.

He never made it.

To Abed, the next few seconds were minutes.

In the initial second he saw Fareed turn sharply towards the woods. Simultaneously, Fareed's eyes bulged and his jaw dropped.

"BrBrBrup, …, BrBrup, ..., BrBrup."

Red blotches appeared on Fareed's white sweater as he jumped backwards.

Fareed went airborne. His shoes lost contact with the soil.

Then he collapsed, a crumpled form on the sandy lane. The red blotches expanded and merged into one large stain on his chest.

Disturbed leaves settled back onto the roadway besides his body.

Abed's eyes returned to his own hands. They were frozen on the steering wheel in a death grip.

A shadow appeared on his left.

He looked up. Anan stared down at him.

She held an Uzi machine pistol. She rammed a fresh magazine into the handle and tapped the weapon on the window.

"Abed, keep those hands on that wheel. Listen to me. Fareed was a pig. He made me offend Allah. Allah will judge him."

She added.

"And I know you detested Fareed."

Abed saw the deadly nozzle of the Uzi. He could think of nothing else.

"But you have a choice. Abed, Choose! The plan is near completion. We must execute it without that pig. Choose!"

"Anan, I am with you. Fareed was indeed a pig. Allahu akbar!"

The Uzi's aim did not shift.

"Good. Good. I will believe you when I see you kill Mufid."

***

Bill Hamm drove. Aileen sat next to him. Jeannine stretched out in the back. She sat up.

"Bill, can't we go to the FBI? Or straight to the Secret Service? From what Anan told me Hezbollah could be planning to assassinate the Israeli Prime Minister here at Camp David."

"I called the FBI. They will see us, but we'll be more believable if we have your analyses. Without those we have only the rambling of a Hezbollah terrorist. You and Aileen need to show them how Mandley cheated for their chip. That adds credence to Anan's story of Hezbollah's use for it."

"But how much time do we have?"

"Not much. The Camp David meeting is five days from now. If we have Harry's CD, his last thumb drive, and my laptop with your decryption routines, the FBI and the Secret Service will have to listen. We need that laptop."

"Fine, but it's at the cabin. How will we get it back without getting killed."

Bill fell silent.

***

At the sound of automatic fire, Mufid stood and scanned the trees where he had last seen the Ryan woman. No branches stirred, and those leaves that remained hung motionless in the still air. He peered through the trees, but heard no more shooting.

A fresh breeze off the bay rustled the topmost branches of the Tulip Poplars and quivered the dry leaves.

Mufid looked up and about.

Nothing.

Action was better than waiting.

He started through the woods in the direction of the shots.

***

Anan held the Uzi loosely, but pointedly, while Abed dragged Fareed's body into the brush. The task was not easy. Fareed's body was far from lean. Abed breathed heavily as he piled dead sticks and leaves on top of the remains.

"That will do Abed. Stand still while I move my car off the road. We will take the Mercedes."

Once the way was clear, Anan waved Abed to the driver's seat.

"Abed, you drive. And be careful."

She pointed the Uzi at him.

"You and I are going to eliminate Mufid."

Abed took the wheel.

***

Mufid hid and watched the Mercedes disappear down the lane to the cabin. As soon as it was out of sight, he stumbled to the pile of brush and leaves.

Fareed!

Mufid put his hand to his mouth. He did not touch the dead body. What could he do?

His eyes moistened. Fareed had been a father to him. *What can I do? The Janazah, the funeral prayer!*

He turned his chest in what he supposed was the direction of Mecca. He knew his obligation. He said in his mind, *I firmly intend to pray the funeral prayer for this dead Muslim, for Fareed.* Then he said aloud.

"Allahu akbar."

Mufid was shaken. He knew the Fatihah by heart and had recited it all his life, but his first phrases were garbled. He started over. Without stumbling he completed it and added.

"Allahu akbar."

He started his next prayer.

"Allahumma salli …

When that was done, he added.

"Allahu akbar."

The next prayer was a supplication for Fareed. Finally he added a supplication for himself, asking Allah not to deprive him of the reward for praying for Fareed. Then he prayed peace.

"As-salamu alaikum."

Mufid's eyes were wet. He looked at his mentor's body. His muscles quivered and he shook with rage.

He jammed a magazine into his Uzi, and extended the stock so that he could use it as an assault rifle.

He pointed the gun at a tree that he pretended was Anan. He ground his teeth and spat.

"Anan, you are doubly dead, both in this world and the next."

Holding the weapon ready, he retraced his path through the woods towards the cabin.

***

It was late afternoon in southern Beirut. Through his window Waseem Hamza heard the Sunni muezzin calling the believers to prayer.

His cell phone vibrated. Waseem listened.

"It worked! Abdul Azim is to accompany the Prime Minister to America."

"Do they know he is one of us?"

"No. They think he is of the Prime Minister's party and that he is a Sunni, like him."

"And the operation for the implant?"

"That was months ago. There is barely a scar. No one will know."

"Excellent. Have him meet me this evening at the usual place."

"Of course. Salaam alaikum!"

"Alaikum salaam."

Waseem Hamza hung up. He reflected. Born in Beirut and educated in Tehran, he was a devout Shiite as was Abdul Azim.

Abdul, of necessity, had lied to hide his true faith, but Allah was not offended. Since the first persecutions of Shia Islam by the Sunni, the doctrine of taqiyya had permitted the use of deception against the persecutor.

And Abdul Azim would slay the true enemy, the Israeli leader. And no one would suspect him. It would be an unfortunate heart attack.

It was a single step, but an important one, towards the fulfillment of Hezbollah's charter; the destruction of Israel, that puppet of the Great Satan, America!

Waseem smiled.

***

In California, Maryland, Bill Hamm hung up the phone.

"Rob is still in South Carolina. He won't be back until after the funeral for Mary's mother. That's tomorrow, and we need to get Bill's laptop now."

Aileen broke in.

"What about Tommy. Is he better?"

"He's home from the hospital. He seems OK."

"What about the Secret Service?"

"Rob told me it would be better to have Bill's laptop. He said there are always threats when the Israeli Prime Minister travels. We need the laptop and we need to be specific. If only we knew who in the Lebanese delegation has the chip implant. Anan might know."

"Anan! Look what she did to Jeannine."

Jeannine looked up.

"Aileen, Anan could have killed me, but she didn't. I can't give up on her yet."

Bill broke in.

"Jeannine, Anan is a fanatic, a killer."

He continued.

"But right now we want to get my laptop back. This is what we do."

***

Mufid stood behind a Tulip Poplar and studied Mona's cabin. Anan and Abed were in there, but no one was in sight.

No matter. Mufid was patient. He aimed the Uzi at the cabin door.

***

******

Chapter 36
Monday, November 6

The shadows were longer now. The sun's rays slanted sideways through the mostly bare branches of the Tulip Poplars, Sweetgums, Oaks and Hickories. In Mona's cabin, nothing stirred.

Behind the tree, Mufid yawned and stared at the kitchen door. Where were Anan and Abed? He shifted his feet. The muscles in his thigh quivered, threatening to cramp. Mufid shifted his weight to the other leg. The trembling ceased. He refocused on the cabin.

There was movement in the kitchen. Through the window, he saw shadows pass back and forth.

Both Anan and Abed were there!

Mufid aimed at the door. Whoever appeared first would die.

***

The sun was low in the West. The outboard motor coughed twice as Bill shut the engine. He jumped into ankle deep water and pulled the boat securely onto the shore. Aileen and Jeannine stepped dryly onto a beach that was rough with the fragments of long-dead mollusks.

"How far away are we, Jeannine?"

Jeannine pointed down the shore 100 yards.

"See where the cliff projects into the water, and there's no beach. The trail up to the cabin is just by that. The boat is safe here. They can't spot it from the cliff."

Aileen rubbed her hands together against the chill. Bill turned to her.

"You're sure you can start the motor?"

She nodded.

"Good. Keep your eyes open. If we need a pick up, I'll give one long and two short flashes. Push off first, then start the motor and wait. Don't come straight to us. Stay out of range as long as you can."

"But what if one of you is hurt?"

"I'll flash three longs. You'll have to decide whether to risk it or not. It will be your call. No one will blame you if it's too risky. Someone has to warn the Israeli Minister. That may be you."

Aileen held her tongue. Prime Minister or not, there was no way she was going to abandon her friends.

Bill and Jeannine set off down the beach.

***

In the cabin, Abed sat at the kitchen table, head in his hands. He looked up. Anan stood by the door, her Uzi machine pistol casually pointed downwards. No comfort to Abed. He recalled a previous mission with Anan where a guard had misread Anan's posture as "casual."

"Anan, I am with you, but I do not understand. Why didn't you kill the unbeliever Ryan? Why did you let her live?"

She wishes to believe. I am sure of it. She will join us."

"But Fareed was a soldier of Allah. Allah does not permit Muslims to make war on Muslims. Why did you kill him?"

"Fareed believed only in himself. He abandoned Allah, and Allah allows war against the unbeliever."

Abed raised his eyebrows. Anan was different. Fareed had never bothered to answer Abed's questions. He lost his timidity.

"But you killed Fareed because he beat you! Doesn't the Qu'ran say a husband should beat his wife for disobedience. Fareed did not commit a crime."

Anan's blue eyes turned steel gray. The barrel of her Uzi tilted upwards towards Abed. He shrank back.

"You refer to sura 4:34. First, I did *not* disobey my husband. He *ordered* me to sleep with that unbeliever, Roberts. I did that for the jihad, it is permitted to deceive an unbeliever for Allah's purposes."

Her eyes remained fixed on Abed.

"Second, it is not *my* reading of that chapter that a man *must* beat his wife for correction. And it was *not* my mother's reading either."

Anan frowned. She pointed the Uzi directly at Abed.

"Fareed was a pig! He treated you like a dog!"

Abed barely heard the words. All he could see was the aperture of the Uzi's barrel, three feet from his nose.

"Abed, you said you would join me in serving Allah. Why these questions? Have you changed your mind? Speak!"

Abed swallowed, hard.

"I am with you, Anan. Allahu akbar!"

"You are wise, Abed."

She let the Uzi tilt downwards.

"Now we must find Mufid. He was always loyal to Fareed. You, Abed, must kill him!"

***

On the beach not far away, Bill Hamm spoke.

"Jeannine, you don't have to come with me. Just show me the way up the cliff. I don't want you to get hurt. You can wait with Aileen."

"Sorry Bill, I don't think you can find the way up without me. Besides, I'd be more scared without you."

She pointed.

"Look over there, where the beach disappears and the water laps the cliff. That's where we start to climb."

But Bill was not looking ahead. He was looking at her.

"Jeannine, I ..."

"Not now, Bill. We have to get up that trail while it's still light."

She walked fast down the beach.

He followed, but more slowly.

After a few minutes, Jeannine was no longer in sight. He heard a whisper.

"Bill, up here!"

He looked upwards. A narrow crevice in the cliff face offered a passage up which a body could squeeze. Bill pressed his legs against the sides and wedged himself upwards. As his feet sought footholds, they dislodged fragments of shell-filled earth that crumbled and fell below.

After several minutes he gained the top. He lay panting on a flat grassy ledge. Jeannine sat and smiled.

"The next stage is easier. The ledge we're on is stabilized by roots. Just watch out for the bare spots. We can follow it most of the way."

Jeannine headed up the narrow trail, stepping carefully until the ledge was too narrow to follow further. The cable still hung in place, just as she had left it. She grasped it and went up.

She whispered down.

"This is it Bill. Use the cable, but watch out. When you're on top, you can see the cabin, and they can see us."

Bill seized the cable and climbed.

Together, he and Jeannine crept towards the lit windows visible through the trees.

***

Anan slipped into the bedroom of the cabin.

"Abed, watch the front door, and be careful. Mufid must be watching us. He knows how to shoot."

Abed did not reply. He rose from the table and went to the door.

Mufid was tired. His long watch on the cabin door had taken its toll. Shadows obscured his view, and his left leg felt a cramp. He extended it.

Just in time, his attention turned back to the cabin. The door had opened a crack. Mufid aimed his weapon and waited.

No one appeared, only Abed's voice.

"Mufid, Mufid, Can you hear me?"

Mufid held his tongue. He lowered his weapon.

"Mufid, this is Abed. Answer me."

Mufid stayed behind the tree trunk.

"What do you want?"

"Fareed is dead."

Mufid ground his teeth. *Abed, I know. You think I'm stupid. You are the stupid one!* He drew a bead on the door and shouted.

"Abed, why did you kill him?"

Mufid squeezed off three rounds. Splinters flew from the door and frame.

At Mufid's first words, Abed had dropped to the floor. He huddled there, safe for the moment.

Mufid saw the kitchen window. He aimed his weapon. He would send glass flying throughout the room.

Cold metal pressed against the back of his neck.

"That's enough Mufid. Put it down."

Anan's voice was soft and her tone expressionless.

Mufid dropped his Uzi.

Anan waved him away from the tree. She removed the magazine from his gun and stuffed it in her waist. The stock she kicked into the brush. She called out.

"I have him Abed. We're coming in."

The lights went on in the cabin.

She pushed Mufid towards the door.

***

Bill Hamm watched until the cabin door closed. He crept toward the bush where Anan had kicked the Uzi and fumbled for it.

He turned, and whispered.

"Jeannine, I have the Uzi, but there's no magazine."

"Anan had extra ammunition in her car. If we can find where she left it, we have a chance with these guys."

"They're fighting each other. There may only be one 'guy' soon. I may not need the ammo."

"You'll need it. I'm going to look."

"Not alone, you're not!"

He followed her through the dark trees.

Behind them flames shone suddenly in the kitchen window of the cabin.

He froze.

The cabin door opened to a rectangle of light. Momentarily it framed the silhouette of someone who stepped outside and blended into the shadows.

Bill stopped to stare at the window where alternate waves of orange and yellow flames flashed brightly. Now the kitchen was ablaze!

"Jeannine, the laptop is in there."

There was no answer. The tree trunks stood silent.

"Jeannine, where are you?"

Still no answer.

Bill scanned the dark woods. Nothing moved.

Jeannine was gone.

***

At the sight of the flames, Jeannine's only thought was of the computer in the cabin. She dashed towards it.

She knew the layout. To trap Mufid, Anan must have exited through the rear bedroom window. The same window she and Anan had used in their earlier escape.

The window was open. Jeannine climbed in.

Smoke clouded her vision. She dropped to the floor and crawled under it. Fortunately the bedroom was only warm. The flames had not spread from the kitchen.

She covered her face with cloth and crawled into the fiery kitchen.

Flames blocked the window and door, but the table was untouched.

She shut her eyes against the smoke and heat. She crawled to the table and reached up. She ran her hand over the surface.

The laptop was gone.

She pushed backwards. Her leg scraped on a chair.

She felt upwards for the seat. Her hand traced a rectangular form, the laptop.

She seized it. Her fingers brushed an object that protruded from it. Harry's thumb drive! Anan must have inserted it to check Harry's notes again.

Jeannine exhaled and drew in a deep breath.

A serious mistake! Hot air and smoke seared her lungs.

She reeled. Coughing and gasping, she pushed herself back to the bedroom.

She leaned out the window to short, sweet breaths of air. Her mind cleared.

She dropped through the window with the precious computer. Harry's CD was still in its slot. And she had the thumb drive. She had it all!

***

As Jeannine lay exhausted, she heard a low moan through the bedroom window.

Someone was still in the smoke-filled room.

She tucked the laptop behind a tree, and looked inside.

Nothing was distinguishable through the dense gray smoke. She could see no one.

As she turned to leave, feeble sounds reached her ears.

"À moi, … Help."

Jeannine tore her blouse and wrapped her nose and mouth once more. Then she climbed through the window, and dropped to the floor.

She gagged. The smoke was acrid. The kitchen floor now was aflame, and fumes from layers of old varnish invaded the bedroom to make a choking mixture.

She held her breath and crawled forward. Another cry.

"Help, à moi, …"

Jeannine crawled in the direction of that sound. She paused. The cries ceased.

She reached forward. She felt a leg, an arm, then breasts. It was a woman.

Anan?

Jeannine could not hold her breath longer. She gulped. Her lungs burned and she retched. Still, she gripped the woman under the arms and tugged.

The bedroom door burst into flame. The heat stopped her progress. There was no time left. She had to breathe.

She dropped the woman and leaned out the window.

Air, not fresh, but more air than smoke, restored her.

She seized the woman again, and propped her on the sill. She pushed out and over and fell with her burden to the ground.

With the last of her strength she dragged the woman away.

Just in time! The window frame burst into yellow flame that sealed the last means of egress from the cabin.

As if to punctuate that event, a crash reverberated from the other side of the structure. The front wall of the kitchen had collapsed. A sheet of orange fire burst skyward as fresh air flooded the burning interior.

Jeannine coughed up sooty phlegm. She gulped air repeatedly only to choke once more. Finally her mind cleared. She looked at the woman she had rescued.

It was Anan.

Anan gasped through soot-colored lips. She lifted her eyes towards her rescuer.

From under singed and darkened brows, moist blue pupils scrutinized Jeannine's face.

Blackened lips mouthed a silent word.

"Thanks."

***

Bill Hamm stood concealed in the darkness. He scanned the trees across the way. Someone had left the cabin. Was it Abed? Mufid? Anan? All three?

He stepped back into the safety of the trees.

Where was Jeannine? Had she found Anan's car? And ammo for the otherwise useless Uzi?

He watched the burning cabin. A brief flash of flames revealed two men standing among the trees across the way. Instantly, one of the men pointed at Bill. The same flash had revealed his presence.

"BrBrBrup, …, BrBrBrup."

The bullets shattered twigs and branches around him.

Bill fell backwards into the shadows.

***

"What did you see Abed?"

"I thought I saw someone standing under the trees. Perhaps not."

Mufid looked at his older associate.

"Do you want me to go look?"

"Without a weapon? No, Mufid, you stay with me."

At that moment the rear wall of the cabin fell. This time there was no explosive burst of fire, only crashing sounds and crackling wood.

Abed stared into the remaining flames.

"That finishes her. The whore, Anan, has gone where she deserves. Now Allah will see that she burns forever."

He paused before turning to Mufid.

"Take note of her fate, Mufid. Allah despises traitors."

A long red welt ran across Abed's cheek. He fingered it thoughtfully. Then he raised Anan's Uzi towards Mufid.

Mufid jumped back. Abed spoke again.

"Mufid, you see where the splinter raked my cheek. That could have been my eye. You did that. You tried to kill me."

"But I thought you ..."

"You thought wrong, Mufid."

Abed ripped the barrel of the Uzi across Mufid's face.

Mufid fell. Blood poured from his nose and cheek.

"Get up, Mufid."

Mufid stood. He held his hand over a bloody nose.

"Know this Mufid. That whore killed Fareed. Why did you think I would obey a woman? I know the Messenger's teachings. I should kill you for thinking otherwise."

"Abed, forgive me. You are Allah's warrior."

Abed nodded, but he did not lower his weapon.

***

Jeannine examined Anan's head. Blood oozed from a wound behind her ear and coated her blond hair to its dark roots.

"Anan, were you shot? Who did this to you? Fareed?"

"No. Abed hit me with the Uzi. He says I'm a whore. He wanted me to burn, like in hell"

"Where is Fareed?"

"I killed him, but Abed tricked me and grabbed my gun."

"Can you walk? We have to leave. Those were shots we just heard."

"I know. My Uzi. It was Abed. Are your friends near."

"Bill Hamm is."

"Jeannine, Abed and Mufid want you dead too."

"We have to go. Can you walk?"

Anan struggled up.

"If I lean on you."

Jeannine pressed the laptop under her arm and lifted her.

"Hold on. The cliffs are this way."

But Anan's knee buckled.

"Jeannine, leave me. I can't make it."

Shots rang out in the woods ahead of them.

Jeannine pulled Anan down. She heard Mufid speak.

"Abed, what was that?"

"That was Hamm. I may have hit him."

"Then why do we go this way?"

"Because that woman Ryan is nearby. That's the bitch I really want!"

Jeannine crouched low. She put her hand over Anan's mouth, and held her breath.

***

******

Chapter 37
Tuesday, November 7

Mufid and Abed disappeared into the darkness.

Jeannine looked skyward. The vague outlines of bare branches were discernible against a graying sky. No sun was visible, but dawn was near.

She looked at the prostrate form next to her. Anan's eyes were closed, but her chest heaved and dropped rhythmically. Her breathing appeared regular. Jeannine shook her gently.

"They're gone. Do you think you can move now?"

Anan's eyes opened.

"How long have I been out?"

"At least an hour."

Anan sat up.

"But you should have left me? Abed wants you dead. You could have gotten away."

"Take my hand. The cliffs aren't far. Let's go. It will be light soon.

Anan struggled up.

They hobbled through the shadows. Arms and hands warded away the eye-level foliage. The brush thickened. They slipped under the stiff branches and crept forward.

Jeannine straightened. Coarse fibers raked her side.

The rope!

She pulled Anan back.

They were on the unstable cliff edge that Mona had cordoned off!

***

Mufid was on hands and knees, feeling through the leaves and fallen branches in the dark.

"Abed, shine the light over here. I'm sure Anan kicked the Uzi over here."

"Mufid, we already looked. It's not there."

"But that's the tree I stood behind when I shot at the cabin."
Mufid stopped. Abed had been his target! He stammered.
"I mean, … the tree where Anan surprised me."
Abed fingered the wound on his cheek.
"No matter, Mufid. The gun is gone. We don't need it."
He patted Anan's Uzi and continued.
"Let's go. Ryan is between us and the cliffs. We must eliminate her."
The sky was lighter now. To the East, a faint yellow glow signaled the coming of the sun, but at ground level all was shadows and illusion.
Abed pointed.
"That's the way to the cliffs. Mufid, you lead."
Abed brandished his weapon.
"I'll follow you."

***

Bill Hamm lay still. A rock pressed against his head. A line of blood on his forehead marked where he had fallen against it. When the bullets had cracked the branches above him, he had dropped fast and hit hard.

His head felt like a balloon ready to burst. He pushed up on his elbow. He was in the center of a dense clump of Viburnum.

A rhythmic ache pulsed back of his eyes. He closed his lids for relief. He felt something hard against his side, Mufid's useless Uzi. He groaned. An image of vivid red hair flashed before him. *Jeannine. are you all right? Where are you?*

The throbbing in his head grew and his thoughts faded. His eyes closed.

***

Some distance away, Jeannine felt the ground shift. In front of her, the earth crumbled and slid downwards. She eased back to Anan.

"We can't move. The cliff is undercut. It's ready to collapse."
"What should we do?"
"Stay still. It'll be light soon. Then we'll be able to see."

310

"Jeannine, leave me. I would if I were you."

"Maybe, but I don't think so."

"I don't understand. You saved me in the cabin. You could have died. Now you stay with me when you could get away. Why?"

"Anan, you could have killed me back in the motel, but you didn't. Why?"

"I like you. I didn't want you to die in unbelief. I wanted you to accept Allah."

"Well maybe I like you, and want a better life for you too."

Jeannine hesitated.

"Anan, 'Jane' was not a Muslim, was she?"

"What do you mean?"

"I mean you liked being free. You liked Harry Roberts. He was a rat, a womanizer and no good. Still he treated you as a woman better than Fareed ever did."

"So?"

"So Muhammed is wrong about women."

"Jeannine, be careful!"

"No. I have to say this. If I believed, my God would never condone Fareed beating me to death, and he would never say I was a 'field' to be tilled as Fareed wanted."

"Jeannine, don't you believe in God?"

"I suppose I do. But I could never be a Muslim. I'm a woman, a person."

"But Islam respects women."

"Maybe externally, but not privately. You know the power Islam gave Fareed over you. And you know you wouldn't be educated if it weren't for your mother and Quebec schools, and your Catholic neighbors!"

Anan started to respond. Jeannine raised her hand.

"Shh! Over there! Someone is coming."

***

The sun balanced on the horizon, lighting the eastern sky yellow behind scattered gray clouds over the bay. On the shore, its rays slanted through the trees, bouncing off the remaining leaves of

311

hardwoods only to be absorbed in the dark clumps of evergreen junipers scattered throughout the woods.

The increased visibility made Mufid's task easier. He picked his way along a trail interlaced with thorny green vines of Smilax.

Mufid stopped and whispered.

"Abed! Voices! A woman. Over there."

Abed listened. All was silent, except for the gentle scraping of wind-rustled branches high above him. He whispered back.

"It's Ryan. I'll follow you."

He held the Uzi ready. Through the trees he could see clear sky. They were near the cliffs.

Some distance away, Mufid spotted a rope stretched between the trees.

"Abed, look at that rope. That's the cliff edge."

Abed scanned the trees beyond the rope.

"Over there! Something moved."

He squeezed off two shots.

Gray fur flew. A squirrel, its tail shortened, chattered and scrambled high up the branches.

Abed cursed.

***

Bill Hamm shook awake. Shots! Who was shooting and at whom?

He peered out from under the Viburnums.

He spied Abed, holding an Uzi. Standing farther away, obscured in the shadows, was another man.

He heard that man speak.

"Abed, that was a squirrel. Now everyone knows where we are."

Abed fingered a welt on his face.

"Hold your tongue, imbecile. Ryan must be there. Go! Hurry!"

Those words relieved Bill. They had not found Jeannine!

Rejuvenated, he shook his head clear and, crawled away. Moments later he reached Mona's rope marking the cliff's edge. He slipped under it, and stood up on the unstable rim.

The ground quivered under his feet. He froze, rigid.

***

It was daylight. In the boat, Aileen could wait no longer. Her neck was stiff and her shoulders ached. Her only sleep had been fitful naps interrupted by worried waiting.

Bill, Jeannine, where are you?

She pushed the boat afloat and climbed in, dripping water. The craft tilted sharply. She shifted her weight to level it. Then she leaned over the motor and pulled.

"Btt, Btt."

Hardly a cough. She pulled again, hard.

"Btt, Btt, Btr, Btr, Brrrrr rrrrr rrrrr rrrrrrrrrrr."

Ignition!

She put out into the bay to a safe distance and headed towards the cliffs where her friends had disappeared.

She studied the shore. The only movement was the flapping of a lone Fish Crow. The cliffs stood gray, somber sentinels against the encroaching waters.

Aileen sat well to the rear, hand on the outboard. Her small boat yawed back and forth in the choppy waves. She brought the craft about into the wind. For that brief moment, her eyes left the shore.

As she turned back, a horrendous mixture of falling earth with twisted roots and branches slid in a roiling cloud down the cliff face and hit the bay. The impact sprayed dust, water and leaves skyward and sent a crest of water rolling toward Aileen.

She turned the boat to face the oncoming wave. The slap-slap of the bow recorded the up and down tilt of the boat. The wave raced past, away from the shore.

When the boat leveled, Aileen studied the huge deposit at the cliff base.

Something blue stood out from the gray brown debris. It appeared to be a blue jacket.

She guided the boat closer.

Her thoughts were on the night before. She remembered Bill as he followed Jeannine down the beach.

Bill's windbreaker had been blue!

Aileen drove full speed towards the shore.

She cut the motor as the bow scraped and shrieked over the fossil shells that formed the beach. She splashed into the water and raced toward the collapsed rubble.

The blue jacket moved.

Aileen scrambled up the mound. She tore at the earth to expose the branches of a fallen pine.

Wedged among those branches was Bill Hamm, his head bloodied and arm unnaturally bent.

"Bill, if you can hear me. Blink."

His lids moved. Aileen exhaled.

The blood on his head was caked with dead leaves and dirt. That wound was superficial. His left arm was bent above the wrist, both radius and ulna clearly were broken. His breathing appeared unobstructed.

His body had been protected from the crushing rubble by the framework of roots and branches.

"Bill can you move your feet?"

Bill nodded. One foot twisted free.

"Aileen, what?

"The cliff collapsed. You were on it. Was Jeannine with you?"

"I don't think so. … No."

"Never mind. I'll get you to the boat."

She wrested him free from the tangle.

He fell groaning. Angry shouting echoed from the cliffs above.

The words were Arabic.

***

Jeannine too heard the shouted Arabic.

"Anan, what are they saying? What's going on?"

"I'm not sure, but your friend went over the cliff."

314

"Bill? No! No!"

"I'm sorry."

Jeannine had no time to react. Branches crackled behind her. Someone was approaching through the vine-tangled Viburnums.

She quickly pressed Anan alongside a fallen log and spread leaves over her. Then she ducked behind an evergreen tree, a holly. Its prickly leaves tore at her cheeks and arms and drew small drops of blood.

She held her breath. Mufid appeared.

He broke free of the clinging branches and stared at the holly tree.

She froze.

***

"Mufid, where are you?"

It was Abed speaking English again. Mufid turned towards his voice.

"Over here. I thought I heard a woman talking."

Jeannine shrank lower. She shivered.

It was the slightest of movements, but enough. Mufid shouted.

"Abed, it's Ryan. She's here. I have her!"

Jeannine dove under the dense tangle behind her, and struggled to her feet. She raced along the cliff edge.

Mufid tried to follow, but the dense bramble forced him to his knees. Thorny vines tugged at his back.

He crawled clear of the tangle, only to feel the earth vibrate beneath him. He was on unstable ground.

He stood carefully and looked to his right.

No Jeannine.

He turned to the left.

An unnatural feature caught his eye, a rusty cable. It dangled from the trunk of a leafless tree at the edge of the precipice.

Mufid headed towards it.

***

With a final push, Aileen tipped Bill into the boat. He collapsed, a limp load that pressed the bow firmly onto the crushed shells that formed the beach.

She tried to push off. The boat did not budge.

"Bill, wake up. Move to the rear. I can't float the boat."

No response.

More shouts from the top of cliff. Once more in Arabic.

A reply, also in Arabic, came from halfway down the cliff. Someone had found the trail to the beach.

Aileen pushed harder. The bow still did not budge.

Footsteps sounded behind her.

Jeannine appeared.

"They're behind me. You have to go."

"The boat is stuck. I can't move it."

In answer Jeannine waded to the stern. She laid her computer in the boat. Waist deep herself, she shoved down on the rail with all her weight.

"Aileen, push out. Now!"

The bow grated out an inch and stuck.

Jeannine pushed down again. The bow lifted. Aileen shoved. The boat was afloat!

Aileen climbed in, Jeannine shoved the boat away.

"Aileen, go! Go! Don't wait."

"Jeannine, get in!"

"No, I'm going back for Anan. You take care of Bill. Now go!"

The motor caught. Aileen turned the craft and raced for the open water.

Halfway down the cliff, Mufid shouted and shook his fist.

***

******

Chapter 38
Tuesday, November 7

Mufid raced down the trail. The dirt gave way beneath his feet and he slid the last several feet to the shell-covered beach. His foot turned inwards and sent a sharp of pain up his leg. He sat on the beach and rubbed his ankle.

Abed called down from the Cliffside.

"Mufid, where is Ryan?"

"They had a boat."

"You mean she's gone?"

"I guess so."

"You guess! Mufid get back up here now."

Mufid looked at the mound of collapsed cliff that blocked the thin beach.

"Now, Mufid. Now!"

Mufid turned and limped to the crevice at the trailhead.

On the far side of the mound, chest-deep in water, Jeannine clung to the fallen rubble.

***

Mufid climbed slowly. By the time he reached the rusty cable, his ankle was an inflated mass. He grabbed the cable and pulled himself to the top. The pressure on his ankle was unbearable.

Abed was waiting.

"You had Ryan. You let her get away. Why?"

"Abed, if I had the Uzi, she would be dead."

"The Uzi? If *you* had the Uzi! You forget that you tried to kill me?"

"Abed, I only meant that ..."

Abed ran his fingers over the red welt on his cheek. He spoke softly.

"Mufid, you know that I am a soldier of Allah?"

"Yes."

Abed pointed to his cheek.

"And yet you tried to kill me."

"But I thought …"

"You thought you would kill me, a soldier of Allah. No true Muslim would do that. So you are a kafir. And you let Ryan go."

Abed fingered his cheek once more.

"What would you do if you were me?"

Mufid forgot his throbbing ankle. He fell silent.

Abed pointed the Uzi at Mufid's chest.

Mufid did not back away. He looked straight into Abed's eyes

"Abed, I am a believer. You say you are a believer. Then you know the Qur'an tells us that a believer is not to kill a believer except by mistake."

"Yes, sura 4:92. So then you admit you were mistaken when you shot at me."

"Truly, I was mistaken. Fareed was dead. I thought you had joined the whore who killed him. I would never kill another soldier of Allah. I do not make war against Muslims, even the Sunni."

Abed lowered his weapon.

"Well spoken, Mufid. We must not fight each other. We know the real enemy."

Mufid let out a deep breath as Abed patted him on the shoulder.

"We are finished here. The whore you speak of is herself dead, burned here even as she continues to burn in hell. And Ryan is gone. We will finish her later. We must take Fareed's body to Delaware. The helicopter will be waiting. We will finish the mission together."

Mufid's eyes filled with gratitude.

He felt his ankle once more. Limping, he followed Abed past the charred remains of the cabin.

At the Mercedes, they placed Fareed's remains in the trunk.

Then they headed for Lusby and a waiting helicopter.

***

Waist deep in bay water, Jeannine picked her way around the fallen debris that blocked the beach. She stopped at the trail entrance and looked up. All appeared quiet. She started up the cliff.

Up top, she hurried to the fallen tree where she had left Anan. She was not there, but a path of disturbed leaves and branches marked a trail to a large oak.

There Anan, eyes half-closed, sat with her back against the trunk. Her voice was a whisper.

"You came back."

"How are you, can you walk?"

"I hope so. I can try."

Anan struggled up, hands braced against the oak.

"What now?"

"Your Toyota is still here, but the Mercedes is gone, Mufid and Abed took it. I need to get you to a doctor."

"No! No doctor, Jeannine. All I need is a motel, a room to rest. Nothing's broken."

She stared into Jeannine's eyes.

"You know that I would not have come back for you."

"So you say."

"All right, but why did you come back?"

"Relax, Anan. Here! Put your arm around my shoulder. We've got to get out of here."

"Jeannine, you're soaked. How?"

"My friends escaped in a boat."

"Are they all right?"

"Aileen is fine. Bill wasn't conscious."

Anan fell silent.

They passed the smoldering frame of the cabin. Anan stopped and stared at what would have been her funeral pyre. Her eyes moistened.

"Jeannine, wait! ... I want to ... "

"It's OK, Anan. Don't worry. We have to keep moving."

When they reached the Toyota, Jeannine drove.

***

After nine hours of interstate driving, Rob Wilson was back in Maryland. The funeral in Dillon, South Carolina, along with his emotional farewell to Mary Dean, had drained him.

Rob's neck was stiff and his thighs were sore. He tilted his coffee mug and gulped. He shook his head clear as he turned onto the road to Mona's cottage.

He stopped the car at the end of the lane.

The cabin was gone.

He stepped out of the car and circled the smoldering charred ruins on foot. He saw no bodies. He sighed in relief.

Rob called Bill. Aileen answered.

"Aileen, this is Rob. Where is Bill? Is he all right?"

"I'm at St. Mary's Hospital, in Leonardtown, Maryland. Bill's in surgery. He fell down the cliff at the cabin."

"How is he?"

"A concussion, a broken arm, and lots of bruises. His back looks OK on X-ray."

"Where is Jeannine?"

"I wish I knew. I got Bill away in a boat. She stayed behind."

"Aileen, I'm at Mona's now. There's no cabin and no Jeannine."

"No cabin?"

"It's burned to the ground. And there's no sign of Jeannine, or terrorists either for that matter. I'm coming to see you. Give me directions to the hospital."

Moments later, Rob was on his way.

***

When Rob arrived over an hour later, the hospital waiting room was nearly empty. A young mother with a small boy and Aileen were the only occupants.

Aileen stood up.

"Rob, thank God you're here."

"What's the latest?"

"Bill's out of surgery. He's sedated, they'll check for swelling about the brain. They set his arm. He's bruised all over, but there is no internal bleeding. His back seems fine."

"Any news of Jeannine?"

"Nothing. The last I saw her she was on that beach."

Rob looked over her shoulder. The little boy was looking in the tote bag on Aileen's chair.

Before Rob could speak, the boy's mother called him.

"Billy, stop. That's not yours. It belongs to the lady."

Rob turned back to Aileen.

"What's in your bag?"

"Bill's laptop, with a CD from Harry and his thumb drive. She put them in the boat before she went back for that Peterson woman."

"Are her analyses on the laptop? We need to give them and Harry's notes to the FBI."

"They are, but I can't get at them. They're password-protected."

Aileen lowered her voice.

"Rob, forget the laptop, I just hope Jeannine's alive."

***

In Prince Frederick, Maryland, Jeannine stopped the Toyota outside a Holiday Inn Express. Anan sat collapsed in the passenger seat. Jeannine leaned near her ear.

"We need to rest. This is a motel, but I have no money. Is it safe to use your credit card?

Anan's voice was a whisper.

"It should be OK if we leave early in the morning. Mandley Security won't be as quick without Fareed."

Then her eyes closed.

Jeannine went into the motel. Moments later she was back at the passenger-side door, a magnetic key in her hand.

She helped Anan from the car.

"Put your arm around me, Anan, I'm getting you to bed."

***

Spotlights illuminated the helipad at Mandley's Delaware complex as Abed and Mufid arrived.

They bent low under the whirring rotors and ran to Mandley's Security building. At the entrance, they turned to watch Fareed's body as it was taken to the facility's morgue.

Breathless, they entered Fareed's office.

Mufid spoke first.

"Waseem will be here tomorrow. How will you tell him that his brother is dead, murdered by a whore? He will blame us. He will not understand how we could let Fareed die at the hands of a woman."

Abed shuddered.

"Waseem's temper is worse than Fareed's. I will tell him one thing at a time."

Mufid fell silent. He was happy to let Abed do the talking.

Abed moved behind the large walnut desk and sat in Fareed's chair.

The chair was most comfortable.

But would it be so when Waseem arrived?

***

In Northern Virginia, Waseem Hamza checked into the Dulles Airport Embassy Suites. His head ached. The flight from Paris had been turbulent. His sinuses were dry from the plane's re-circulated air.

He pulled off his shoes and sat on the bed. He laid back and clicked the remote, only to snort in disgust. A nearly nude woman was on the screen. *Immoral pagan unbelievers!*

He clicked quickly. A blonde news anchor appeared on the TV. She spoke in clipped tones.

"Up next, a report on the upcoming meeting at Camp David between the Prime Ministers of Israel and Lebanon."

She stopped as a yellow banner flashed across the screen.

"This just in. A five year old girl was abducted at Tyson's II Center this afternoon. Fairfax Police are requesting anyone with …"

Waseem punched the remote. The screen went blank. He shut his eyes. The tightness in his neck muscles eased.

Tomorrow, he would meet Fareed.

And in only three days the Hamzas would celebrate their triumph over the "Little Satan," that illegitimate Jewish state!

***

******

Chapter 39
Wednesday, November 8

In Herndon, Virginia, a refreshed Waseem opened his eyes. His bed in the Embassy Suites Dulles hotel had been most comfortable.

He glanced at his watch. It was shortly after noon. He had time to pray before meeting Mandley's helicopter at Manassas regional airport.

He performed his ablutions. He laid his prayer mat on the floor and started his recitation.

Allahu Akbar. *I intend to pray the obligatory Dhuhr prayer.* ...

Once finished, he sat by the phone. Fareed should have called by now, but Fareed was always busy. Perhaps he was bedding Anan. And why not? He could not blame him. Anan was beautiful.

Finally he could wait no longer. Mandley's helicopter would be waiting.

He headed towards Manassas on Route 66. A sign pointed right to the Manassas Battlefield. There Americans had slaughtered each other, unbelievers killing unbelievers. He shrugged. Too bad that war had ended.

He passed the Battlefield exit and took the Manassas bypass to the airport. The helicopter was there.

***

At the Mandley complex in Delaware, Abed arrived at Fareed's office. He took his place in Fareed's chair.

Mufid sat opposite

The phone buzzed. Abed pushed "Speaker" and talked into the receiver.

"Ryan used Anan's credit card? Last night?"

The bitch!

"Where?"

He jotted down the motel and town.

He handed the paper to Mufid.

"It's Ryan. She used Anan's card in Prince Frederick, at a Holiday Inn Express. Take Raakin with you. Help him get his nerve back. Use the gray Audi."

Mufid started for the door. Abed called to him.

"And Mufid, kill that bitch."

***

In the motel in Prince Frederick, Maryland, Anan "Peterson" opened her eyes to the aroma of coffee. Jeannine held a Styrofoam cup under her nose.

"Jeannine, thanks."

"You looked rested, but we should move. Mandley could track us through your credit card. They may already know where we are."

Anan struggled off the bed.

"You're right. We should go. We'll use my card at an ATM. We'll get cash and disappear."

Anan slipped into rumpled and dirty jeans. Jeannine laughed.

"You look terrible."

"Look in the mirror. You don't look so great yourself."

Anan pointed to the dresser.

"We need to leave now. And don't forget that mega shark tooth."

***

They left the Holiday Inn Express, and drove to a nearby ATM. There Jeannine punched the numbers with the hood of her sweatshirt hiding her hair. The watching cameras never saw her eyes. Anan stayed out of sight.

This operation was repeated at four more ATM's.

After the last stop, Jeannine handed the accumulated bills to Anan who promptly returned half of them to Jeannine.

Jeannine had never seen this much money. She gulped. *This is enough to start a small revolution!*

Of course! That was the purpose behind Anan's account.

326

Anan guessed Jeannine's thoughts.

"We have cash now. They can't track us anymore. We need new clothes and another motel to shower and change."

Jeannine looked at her mud-stained and rumpled jeans. She had to agree.

New clothes and a shower were needed!

But clothes could wait.

"I need to find Aileen and see how Bill is. And I need his laptop to warn the Secret Service."

Anan hid a frown. Then she turned to Jeannine and smiled.

"First things first, we can't stay in this town. We must go. You drive."

They left.

***

Mufid guided the gray Audi from the Eastern Shore and across the Chesapeake Bay Bridge. He turned off Route 50 onto Route 2, south.

Raakin spoke.

"Where is Fareed? Why isn't he here?"

"Fareed is dead."

"But how?"

"Anan shot him."

"Anan! Where is she?"

"She is burning in hell like all whores. Ask Abed. He is in charge now."

"In charge of Mandley security?"

"Not officially yet. But tell me, Raakin, Abed said you and Hazim had a problem in Pennsylvania. Are you over that?

Raakin nodded.

Mufid continued.

"Good. Remember, you are Allah's instrument. He will support you. The Ryan bitch must feel his wrath."

Mufid jammed the accelerator. The car jumped forward. Raakin's head jerked backwards.

Mufid muttered as if to himself.

327

"And Ryan is a thief, too. She stole Anan's debit card, money reserved for Allah's purpose."

He added.

"Now we have to cut off her hands before we kill her."

***

Jeannine's and Anan's new motel was more upscale than the Holiday Inn Express.

Jeannine showered first. She donned her new jeans and sweatshirt and descended to the lobby. Her pale blue shirt contrasted well with her freshly combed auburn hair.

Tom, the motel clerk smiled admiringly.

"May I help you?"

"Your brochure said there was an Internet station in the lobby."

"Over there, next to the potted tree. I could help you."

"I'm fine thanks."

Jeannine worked fast before Anan finished her shower. There was no time for encryption or deception. She emailed Wayne at StatFind to call immediately if he knew where Aileen and Bill were.

Done, she rushed back to the room. Anan hummed as water splashed against the shower door.

Jeannine sat by the phone to intercept Wayne's call.

More sounds of satisfaction came from the shower stall.

Minutes later the phone rang. It was Wayne.

"Jeannine, do you know Mona's email address?"

"Yes."

"Good. I've changed her password to yours. Access her email. You'll have your answer."

He hung up.

Anan, wrapped in a towel, emerged from the bathroom.

"Who was that?"

"The desk clerk. I have to go sign the registration."

Jeannine left.

Anan stared after her.

***

At the Delaware complex, Abed was still ensconced behind Fareed's desk when the phone buzzed once more.

"StatFind called Ryan. She's in a motel near Hughesville, Maryland."

Abed located the Audi's blip on his screen. Mufid and Raakin were in Prince Frederick.

"Good work. Mufid is not far from there."

He called the Audi and redirected Mufid from Prince Frederick to Hughesville.

***

An hour later, Jeannine returned to the room, Anan was waiting.

"What are you up to? I've been waiting. I called the desk. There was no problem with the registration."

"I found out where Bill Hamm is. He's in the hospital in Leonardtown."

"How?"

"I emailed StatFind, and Wayne Johnson called me."

Anan jumped up.

"He called here? When?"

"That's right. An hour ago. What's wrong?"

"Mandley monitors StatFind's phones. Now they know where we are."

Anan went to the window and looked through the blinds.

A gray Audi drove up across the street and parked.

"They're here!"

***

Mufid left the Audi and entered the motel. He approached the desk.

"My sister-in-law is here. She has red hair. Can you tell me what room she is in?"

Tom, the desk clerk, certainly knew that red head's room number!

He studied Mufid's swarthy features and rumpled sweater. It was not possible that this man's brother be married to the doll in room 203.

Besides, the red head did not have a wedding ring. Tom had made sure of that!

Mufid shook his head impatiently. Tom ignored him. This man was lying.

"Sir, if you give me your name, I'll call the room. I'm not allowed to give you the number."

Mufid's eyes darkened.

"Just tell her 'Bill' is here."

Tom dialed a vacant room. After some seconds he looked up.

"Sir, there is no answer."

"Has she checked out?"

"No, Sir."

Mufid clenched his fist. He turned and stalked out.

***

******

Chapter 40
Wednesday, November 8

At the hospital in Leonardtown a man in a white coat shook Aileen's shoulder.

"Ms. Harris, ... Ms. Harris, I'm Doctor Stevens."

Aileen opened her eyes. No one else was in the waiting room. *Rob, where are you? The cafeteria?*

"I'm sorry. I must have dozed off."

"Ms. Harris, your friend is doing fine. There is no internal bleeding, but we are watching for intracranial swelling, and we are keeping him sedated. He's very lucky, other than the arm, nothing's broken. The branches must have cushioned his fall."

"When can he talk?"

"With the sedation, it will be tomorrow morning before he's awake. Maybe a little later. By afternoon he should be fully alert. Of course if he has a setback, that could change."

Doctor Stevens touched her arm.

"You're tired. You should go rest at your motel. If anything develops I'll call you there. You don't need to stay here. I promise to call if there's any change."

Aileen was tired and she was still in her "boating" clothes.

She left to look for Rob. She found him in the cafeteria and handed him a paper with her motel and room number.

"Rob, the doctor says Bill will be asleep for a while. I've got to get cleaned up.

She grinned.

"Meet me at my room when you're done eating."

***

Aileen's motel was near the hospital. Rob found her room and knocked.

She opened the door.

Aileen had showered. Her bare feet, nails freshly polished, protruded from clean jeans. Her hair was no longer matted and twisted.

In Rob's vocabulary, Aileen was a "babe," and he knew she liked him. That did not help his resolve.

But he thought of Mary Dean.

Aileen sensed his thoughts.

"Rob, how is Mary? Is Tommy OK?"

"She's fine, but I came to see …"

She interrupted him.

"No. Don't say anything now that you'd regret later. You're all mixed up."

"But, I was only going to say that you look …"

"Never mind. We can't afford distractions. Maybe after this is all over?"

She paused to slip on her sneakers.

"This was my mistake. I'm going back to the hospital to be near Bill. Why don't you call StatFind and see if Wayne Johnson has heard from Jeannine. We need her passwords so we can show her evidence to your FBI."

She added.

"But you still should stay here tonight. You can sleep in the soft chair. I'll take the bed."

She bounced out the door.

***

The helicopter landed at Mandley's complex in Delaware. Waseem lowered his head and ran, crouching, under the spinning rotors. Away from the turbulent air, he straightened to smooth his hair.

Abed stood waiting.

"Welcome to Mandley Bionics."

"Abed, where is my brother? Why didn't he call me?"

The exact question that Abed dreaded.

"Let's go to the office. I'll brief you on everything."

Waseem's cheeks reddened. His thick neck muscles tightened.

332

"Tell me now, Abed. Where is Fareed?"

"Waseem, Fareed is dead."

"How? Who? Weren't you with him?"

"Anan killed him."

"Anan! And you couldn't stop her? Where is she now?"

"She's dead too."

Waseem frowned. His voice was low, hoarse.

"Did you kill her? How?"

Abed lowered his eyes. He dared not respond.

Waseem snorted.

"Abed, you are weak, but never mind, we have work to do. The Lebanese delegation will be in Washington tomorrow. Abdul Azim is with them."

"They do not suspect him?"

"His credentials with their party are impeccable."

"But he is a Shiite, how could he lie to them."

"Abed, you of all people must know of the taqiyya. Allah permits deception to avoid the persecution by the Sunni."

"Of course, but are you sure he has fooled them."

"Absolutely. The Americans asked the Mossad for help in the screening. They are sure that no one in the party is with Hezbollah."

"Then we will have a great victory."

"Exactly. Now tell me about Fareed and this Ryan woman."

***

At the motel near Hughesville, the gray Audi was still parked across the street. Anan turned from the window. Jeannine spoke.

"Anan, what are you thinking?"

Anan chose her words with care.

"I'm thinking that they don't know I'm alive. I know that they want you, but they think I'm dead. I could leave you here for them, and walk away free. You couldn't stop me."

She spoke with the assurance of one trained in martial arts.

Jeannine did not reply.

Anan continued as if to herself.

"But you dragged me from that cabin. You risked your life."

Anan gagged at the memory of that searing heat and choking smoke.

"And you hid me while they searched for you."

She cleared her throat.

"And you were in the boat and could have left, but you came back for me!"

Anan's eyes moistened. She was near tears.

"Why? Why me? Don't you know I wanted you dead!"

She buried her face in her hands. Her words were mere murmurs.

"What's happening to me?"

Jeannine embraced the weeping warrior.

"Anan, it's OK to be weak. My God is a God of love and forgiveness. It's OK."

Her own words surprised Jeannine. She had not "thought" those words since Sunday Bible School. Were Anan's beliefs refueling her own?

An uncertain Anan reached out. They hugged.

They stood there, each with her own thoughts.

A loud banging at the door broke the spell.

***

A long balcony fronted the rooms on the second floor of Jeannine's motel. Raakin stood before room 203 and pounded on the door. The noise brought Tom, the desk clerk, up the stairway. He shouted.

"What the hell are you doing? Get away from that door."

Raakin growled.

"This is not your affair. Leave."

Tom had played division II football in college, and though his waist now overlapped his belt, he had no fear of the smaller man.

He seized Raakin by the shoulder and spun him about.

"Go now or I'll call the police."

Raakin took a step backwards. He despised American unbelievers, especially bulky bullies.

He felt the Beretta in his jacket pocket and clutched the weapon.

Mouth dry, his finger felt for the trigger.

Tom faced him, unaware.

***

Before Raakin could draw his weapon, a voice called from behind him.

"Raakin, come with me. Now!"

Tom looked back. The speaker was the supposed brother-in-law (Mufid) who had asked for the red head's room number. Evidently, he had found it. Tom spoke to him.

"Go now, and take your friend 'Raak-whatever' with you. If I see you again, I'll call the police."

Mufid wanted no trouble. He approached Raakin and took him by the arm.

"Excuse us. My friend is impatient, that's all. We're leaving now."

They crossed the street to the car. Mufid signaled Raakin to the driver's seat.

"Drive!"

Tom stared them down the road.

Raakin drove for a block before Mufid spoke.

"Turn the corner and stop. I must call Abed."

Raakin obeyed.

Mufid leaned towards him. He whispered.

"It was her! I saw her through the cracks in the blinds."

"Who? Ryan?"

"Yes, I saw her too?"

"Her? Who else is there?"

"Anan! Raakin, Anan is alive!"

***

When Rob called StatFind, Wayne gave him the good news. Jeannine was alive! She was at a motel near Hughesville. He gave Rob the room number.

Rob hung up immediately and called Jeannine's room. He let the phone ring.

No one answered.

He drove to the hospital to tell Aileen that Jeannine was well.

After that he would go to Hughesville.

***

At Mandley's complex, Waseem lay asleep on the office couch. He was not completely immune to east-west-jet-lag. He had not removed his shoes, dull and scuffed, they contrasted with the shiny leather upholstery.

Abed sat stiffly at the desk. To him the message was clear. What had been Fareed's office was now Waseem's.

The latter's possession of the couch confirmed that.

The phone on the desk blinked repeatedly. Abed picked up and listened to the caller. When he hung up, all color was gone from his cheeks. He looked to the couch.

Waseem was sitting up, eyes wide.

"Who was that, Abed?"

"You're awake?"

"Abed, in my occupation, I am always half-awake. Now who was it?"

"Mufid."

"And what did Mufid want?"

Abed swallowed, hard. Terror seized his throat. He forced the words through his lips.

"I told you that Anan killed your brother."

"Yes?"

"And that she was dead."

"Abed, get to the point."

Abed stammered.

"Anan is not dead. Mufid just saw her. Anan is alive."

Waseem ground his teeth.

***

******

Chapter 41
Wednesday, November 8

Waseem Hamza stared at Abed a full thirty seconds. Then he sat back on the couch. This time he removed his shoes. He lay back and shut his eyes.

"Abed, instruct Mufid to bring Anan to me. Without harm! It is the Hamza honor that is offended. I will deal with her."

He turned on his side away from Abed, and continued.

"If Anan is harmed, it is you, Abed, I will deal with."

Abed backed away.

Minutes later Waseem was snoring.

***

At the motel near Hughesville, the lights were out in the room. It was dark outside. Jeannine sat on the bed.

Anan peered through a slit in the blinds.

"The Audi is back, across the street. Mufid is in the driver's seat. He's watching the room."

Jeannine stood up.

"Where is the other one?"

"His name is 'Raakin.' I can't see the passenger side. I don't think he's in the car. He could be anywhere."

"What are they waiting for?"

"I don't know. Wait, someone's leaving the office. It's that big desk clerk. His shift must be over."

The desk clerk, Tom, walked to his car. Anan kept talking.

"That clerk humiliated Raakin. They are waiting for him to leave. Mufid was always cautious."

Anan watched Tom drive away.

She looked back at the Audi. The driver's seat was empty.

Mufid was no longer in the car.

***

Mufid and Raakin climbed the stairs to the long balcony that provided access to all the rooms on the motel's second level. They stopped at room 203.

Raakin was small, but he knew martial arts. His kick was vicious. The door sprang open.

Mufid surveyed the room. Dirty jeans were unceremoniously stuffed in waste baskets. McDonald's wrappers were strewn on the dresser.

A hairbrush with reddish strands lay on the table. A damp towel lay on the carpet.

The bathroom door was shut tight. There was no other place to hide.

They faced the closed door. Mufid whispered.

"Remember, Raakin, do not touch Anan."

Mufid held his Beretta ready. He would take out the red head without hitting Anan.

He called out.

"Ryan, come out, now. We won't hurt you."

Silence.

"I said 'come out,' now!"

Mufid signaled his partner.

Raakin's kick was as vicious as before.

The bathroom door collapsed inwards. The handle and lock flew apart amid shattered splinters. The frame hung over the toilet by a lone surviving hinge

Mufid stared in disbelief at the vacant shower.

Empty!

***

In room 101, downstairs, Anan turned to Jeannine.

"They crashed the door. It's time."

They left their room and dashed for the Toyota.

Anan took the passenger seat. Jeannine jumped behind the wheel. She shoved the key into the ignition and twisted.

The motor caught.

She drove out the motel lot, fast.

They rode south in silence.

Finally, Anan spoke.

"I don't understand. Why would a stranger like Tom help us? There was nothing in it for him. He must have seen Raakin was dangerous. Why did he protect us?"

She paused.

"What did he want from us?"

"Anan, Tom didn't want anything. We were women in trouble. That's all."

"That's sexist. If I had a gun, I could have taken care of us!"

"But you didn't, and you couldn't!"

On the road a discarded plastic bag shone in the headlights. Jeannine twisted the wheel and avoided it. She straightened back and added.

"Sexist or not, he moved us to another room. He didn't have to do that. And it worked."

"He was a dumb football player. Allah gave us guns to protect ourselves from big brutes like him."

"Big yes, but dumb? I don't think so; just a generous, thoughtful guy, to me, just an American. And we'd be dead if that 'brute' hadn't helped us."

Anan fell silent.

The Toyota rolled on through the darkness.

***

At the office in Delaware, Abed put down the phone. *Damn you Mufid, How could you miss Ryan again. And Anan too!*

Waseem was snoring. The call had not aroused him. *Good!* Abed shuddered and got up from his desk. He would not wake Waseem with this news. Abed was close to despair. The brother was more dangerous than Fareed. He needed to be away from him. He slipped out of the room closing the door carefully.

Abed was a good Muslim. He did not touch alcohol, but tonight he was tempted.

He needed a drink!

***

In Leonardtown, Rob Wilson left Aileen at the hospital to wait for news from Bill's doctors.

He drove towards Hughesville to locate Jeannine's motel. The Crown Vic purred smoothly. There were few cars on the road.

The countryside featured flat open fields and dark clouds obscured the moon

Ahead on the right were the golden arches of McDonald's. On the left was Jeannine's motel, a three-tiered building. A bright orange "vacancy" shone from the office window. The lot was sparsely filled.

Rob turned in and parked.

In the McDonald's across from the motel, Mufid munched his hamburger.

He could not return to Delaware without either Ryan dead or Anan in hand. Like Fareed, only more so, Waseem abhorred failure.

Raakin jumped up.

"Did you see that?"

Mufid swallowed a bite.

"What?"

"That car! The blue Crown Victoria at the motel. That's Wilson. He's the devil that shot Hazim and me in Pennsylvania. I still have splinters in my shoulder."

"Raakin, he can lead us to Anan and Ryan!"

"No. He does not know where they are. Otherwise, he would not be here. Allah has delivered him to us. He killed Hazim. Let me kill him now."

Mufid shook his head.

"Would you face Waseem with Ryan alive, or without Anan? I will not!"

Raakin stayed silent. Mufid added.

"All right. Wilson must die. You can have him, but only after he leads us to Ryan."

Raakin ground his teeth.

***

Jeannine saw the speed limit sign and slowed. Anan felt the motion and opened her eyes.

"Where are we?"

"We're near Leonardtown. St. Mary's Hospital here services most of southern Maryland, including Calvert County and the cliffs."

"You think Bill Hamm is there?"

"It's the only place I can think of."

"And his laptop too?"

"If he's there, yes."

"You need that laptop to convince the Secret Service? Your analyses and Harry's notes are on it, right?"

"Yes."

"Why don't Aileen and Bill show them your proofs and Harry's notes?"

"The files are protected. No one can access my files without me."

Anan's eyebrows lifted.

"You mean that without you, no one can read your files, and Harry's?"

"That's right, or any other files."

"Jeannine, I won't let you go to that hospital."

"What do you mean?"

"Jeannine, you should forget Hamm and your computer. Hamm would have me arrested"

"I wouldn't let him."

"But you want to defeat our mission!"

"Mission? You mean 'Murder.'"

Anan frowned.

"Call it what you want. An unbeliever cannot understand. But I will not let you meet Hamm or recover that laptop. I will not."

"You can't stop me!"

Anan's eyes narrowed.

"You know I can. Please don't make me."

***

At the motel, Rob Wilson was discouraged. The clerk had been on duty less than an hour, and knew nothing about Jeannine and "Jane."

Rob left the motel office. There were only a dozen cars at the motel. None was a Toyota.

He was alone in the lot. He stood under the entrance lamp. *Damn. Where is Jeannine?*

Rob turned back to the Crown Vic. His back was to the light. He formed a perfect silhouette against the glow.

From the McDonald's lot across the street, Raakin watched. The target was clear. He could not miss this opportunity.

He stepped out of the car. Mufid spoke.

"Raakin, what are you doing? Stop!"

Raakin ignored him. He steadied himself on the Audi's door and aimed his weapon. Mufid, behind the wheel, reached across and pushed the door to jostle Raakin, but the trigger was squeezed.

"Crack."

Rob crumpled to the ground.

"Raakin, what have you done?"

Raakin jumped into the passenger seat. He tossed the rifle in the back

"Why did you try to spoil my aim. Wilson did not know where to find Ryan. Allah will guide us to her and I have avenged Hazim."

"I hope you are right, Raakin. At least Allah has restored your confidence. We honor Him for that."

They drove fast towards Leonardtown.

No one noticed the fallen figure in the motel lot.

***

As Jeannine drove into Leonardtown, Anan's eyes softened.

"That's a Best Western ahead. It's late. You've done all the driving. You need rest and we need to stop. We will go to the hospital tomorrow morning."

Jeannine glanced sideways. Anan's look was kindly.

"Anan, I am exhausted, but tomorrow, first thing, we must go to the hospital."

"Agreed."

Jeannine exhaled with relief.

They parked the Toyota in a rear lot and took a room on the ground floor. Its only door was onto an interior hallway.

Jeannine stood by the dresser. Anan called from the bathroom.

"You are stressed. I have something that will help you sleep."

She emerged with a glass of water.

"I think this will help you relax. We need to start early tomorrow."

Jeannine studied Anan's eyes. They were blue, moist, and caring. Why not trust her?

She emptied the glass.

Moments later, the room whirled erratically. She stumbled, and started to fall. She felt Anan's arms about her waist pulling her towards the bed.

Then all went black.

***

******

Chapter 42
Thursday, November 9

In Leonardtown, the sun's rays lit Jeannine's lids and she blinked awake. She opened her eyes to a spinning ceiling and touched her forehead. Her head felt inflated, like a dirigible striving to soar but tethered and unable to do so. At the same time her ears buzzed like engines trying to force the take off.

She pressed her face down into the foam pillow. The ringing in her ears ceased.

She gripped the headboard and sat up. The rotating stopped and chairs, dresser and window blinds came into focus.

She scanned the room. She was alone.

Anan was gone.

Jeannine struggled to the long dresser, topped by a mirror, that lined one wall. She studied her reflection as she struggled to understand Anan.

Jeannine's father, a physicist, had never mentioned "God" to her as a child. Her mother had made her attend Sunday School at a local Church, but by High School "God" had disappeared from family conversations, and subsequently none of her university professors had allowed for such a "concept."

In graduate school, Jeannine briefly had shared her apartment with Monique Laurier, a biochemist and Catholic from Montreal. Monique, now married, was Jeannine's closest friend. For Monique, God was hardly a "concept," but a "person."

Oddly, Anan, a jihadist Muslim, was also from Montreal. To her, God was an aloof "Master." And certainly not the same as Monique's personal loving God.

Jeannine had saved Anan twice and liked her, but she was horrified by what Anan was willing to do for Allah.

And Anan had spared Jeannine twice, even though Jeannine was a threat to Allah's mission. And, yes, Anan wished they were sisters, fighting for the same cause!

All these thoughts took but seconds.

Confusion. As Jeannine turned from the mirror a sharp object rubbed her thigh, the megalodon tooth.

Instinctively she felt her other jeans pocket. It bulged with a wad of bills.

Anan had had not taken her money!

She still wants to be sisters!

***

In Delaware, Waseem awoke all at once. He kicked his feet off the couch, sat up, and looked towards the desk.

Behind it Abed sat silent.

Waseem stood and glared.

"Abed, tell me that Ryan is dead."

"Ryan escaped, but Raakin shot Rob Wilson. We don't have to worry about him anymore."

"Wilson?"

"He's ex-FBI, the man who shot Hazim in Pennsylvania."

"And Anan?"

"Mufid is at St. Mary's hospital in Leonardtown looking for her. That is the hospital that serves the Calvert Cliffs."

"An interesting fact, Abed, but clearly Mufid has failed."

Abed squirmed. Waseem continued.

"Call for the helicopter. You and I must go to Leonardtown."

***

At the hospital in Leonardtown, Aileen sat alone in the waiting room. A nurse entered.

"Miss Harris?"

"That's me."

The nurse handed Aileen a slip of paper.

"A 'Miss Ryan' asked that you call her at this number."

Aileen's heart leapt. *Jeannine!*

"Thanks. Thank you very much."

346

Aileen pulled out her prepaid cell. The nurse intervened.

"No cell phones here, please. You can use the main lobby."

Aileen dashed from the waiting room. In the lobby, she punched the number.

"Jeannine, are you all right? Where are you?"

"I'm fine. I'm in the restaurant at the Best Western. But forget me. How is Bill?"

"So-so. There was some swelling in his brain, so they kept him sedated. The swelling went down yesterday. They plan to wake him this morning."

"Oh, no! My taxi is here. You're at St. Mary's Hospital, right?"

"Yes."

"I'm on the way."

***

When Jeannine's taxi arrived, Aileen was waiting by the main entrance to St. Mary's Hospital.

"Jeannine, thank God you are safe. I was afraid … "

"Me too. You were telling me about Bill."

"He's conscious, but doesn't remember anything. Rob got the local police to watch his room. But, Rob went to look for you. Where is he?"

"Rob? I haven't seen him. He didn't find us."

"Us?"

"Me and Anan."

"Anan? Oh, 'Jane Peterson.' Where is she?"

"I wish I knew."

They reached the waiting room.

Aileen stared. The wall next to her chair was blank.

"Jeannine, my tote bag, your computer, it's gone!"

Before Jeannine could react, the public address system sounded.

"Dr. Jeannine Ryan, Dr. Jeannine Ryan, please come to the main desk in the lobby. You have a call."

Aileen grabbed her.

"Don't go. It could be a trick."

"I don't think so. It's Anan. And she has the computer. I'm sure of it."

"Then I'm coming with you."

At the desk, Jeannine picked up the phone. It was Anan.

"Jeannine! It's me. I have your computer. You have no proof of anything. Stop before you are hurt. I don't want that. Give up. You can't stop us."

Anan took a breath.

"And leave the hospital, now. They know where you are. Don't worry about Hamm. It's you they want."

"Click."

Jeannine stared at the dead phone.

Aileen's eyes were all query.

"That was Anan. She stole the computer. She wants us to quit."

Aileen frowned. Jeannine kept on.

"They know we're here. We have to go."

"But Bill?"

"You said there's a policeman by his door. He has no memory. We are the real threat now. There's no time. The Camp David meeting starts in forty eight hours."

"You mean leave?"

"We have no choice. We can't help anyone if we're dead."

"All right. At the end of the corridor there's a separate exit for Surgery. My rental is near the exit, the blue Chrysler. We'll go that way."

They reached the Chrysler. Aileen took the wheel.

"All right, Jeannine, which way?"

"To Annapolis. That's the closest FBI Field Office. And hand me your pre-pay. I'll call them now."

***

The gray-haired volunteer at the hospital reception desk looked up. Mufid smiled down at her.

"I'm looking for my sister. She has red hair. She is visiting a patient named Hamm. Have you seen her?"

The volunteer adjusted her glasses.

348

"There was a young lady with red hair. She took a phone call here five minutes ago."

"Do you know where she went?"

The volunteer pointed.

"That way, Corridor B, towards the surgery waiting room."

Mufid's smile disappeared. He spun on his heels and raced down the corridor.

***

Mat Dorsey, an agent in the FBI's Field Office in Annapolis, Maryland, picked up the phone.

The paralegal, Louise, could only hear Dorsey's side of the conversation.

"Ms. Ryan, what you say sounds pretty wild. Mandley Bionics is a respected firm, and they are big supporters of the military."

Louise saw Dorsey stop to listen before continuing.

"Ms. Ryan, you should see the amputees at Navy Med. Mandley's artificial hand works like a real hand, only stronger. It's manipulated by contracting certain muscles in the stump of the arm. Bionic chips make that possible."

Another pause, after which Dorsey shouted.

"You picked a hell of a time to besmirch Mandley Bionics. Saturday is Veterans' Day."

Dorsey calmed down. Louise watched as his shoulders slumped in resignation.

"All right, Ms. Ryan. I'll call the Joint Terrorism Task Force in Baltimore and tell them what you told me. Call me back in thirty minutes."

***

In the Chrysler, Jeannine turned to Aileen.

"That stunk. That agent was more worried about Mandley's reputation and patriotism than what I had to say. I want bionic limbs for amputees too, but damn it, Mandley falsified research on the Parkinson chip, and modified it to commit murder."

She pushed the hair off her forehead.

"Probably not everyone at Mandley is a terrorist, but for sure Hezbollah has infiltrated their damn Security Department."

There were several cars in front of them. Aileen kept her eyes on the road as she spoke.

"If they don't listen, the Israeli Prime Minister will be killed. There's no time."

"We have to see this Dorsey guy face to face. If only I had my computer. No matter. I'll make him listen. Drive faster."

***

In Delaware, Waseem fumed.

"Abed, where is the helicopter? How long must I wait?"

"They had to refuel, and they said something about adjusting the rotors."

"And?

"It's ready now. We can go."

The phone on the desk sounded. The conversation was brief. Abed turned to Waseem.

"That was Mufid. They spotted Ryan and Harris at the hospital. They left Leonardtown. They are headed north on Highway 2 towards Annapolis. Mufid has them in sight. We can take the helicopter and trap them before they get there."

"And Anan?"

"She is not with them."

"Tell Mufid to keep close and not lose Ryan. We will be there soon."

Waseem strode from the room.

***

******

Chapter 43
Thursday, November 9

Rob Wilson opened his eyes. He focused on a tangle of tubing that dangled from two plastic bags hanging from separate metal posts. He followed the tangle downwards. The tubes were attached, respectively, above his left and right wrists.

He tried to move his head, but a shooting pain stopped that maneuver.

"You're awake. Good. How do you feel Mr. Wilson."

Rob saw a white coat. A face came into focus.

"Where am I?"

"You're in St. Mary's Hospital, in Leonardtown. I'm Dr. Larsen. Do you remember anything?

Rob started to move but recoiled in pain.

"No. I was standing in the parking lot, outside the motel. That's it."

"They found you bleeding in the lot. You were shot. The bullet missed your lung, and exited under your scapular. You've lost a lot of blood, but are doing well, considering."

A nurse entered the room.

"Dr. Larsen, there's someone outside who wants to speak with your patient."

The "someone" was a detective from the Leonardtown Police Department. Dr. Larsen left the room. The detective spoke.

"Mr. Wilson, do you have any idea who shot you?"

Rob answered the questions as best he could.

***

Aileen was speeding. She swung the Chrysler to the left, passed several cars, and squeezed in front of an 18-wheeler that blared its horn.

Jeannine was oblivious to the traffic. She phoned Agent Dorsey once more. His tone was conciliatory, but detached.

"Ms. Ryan, I gave your information to our Terrorism Task Force in Baltimore. They contacted the Secret Service. They assure us the situation is safe."

"But the prime minister will be killed and no one will even realize that he was assassinated."

"Ms. Ryan, the Secret Service has been protecting dignitaries for years, and the Mossad is very thorough. Both assure us they have thoroughly checked the attendees. No one at this meeting is remotely friendly to Hezbollah."

He sensed her disagreement and added.

"Only Lebanese Muslims who strongly oppose Hezbollah will be present. The purpose of the meeting is to limit Hezbollah's armed activities in Lebanon. The situation is under control."

Jeannine struggled to break his complacency. She recalled Anan's conversation.

"Agent Dorsey have you heard of the doctrine of taqiyya?"

"'Taki' … what?"

"Taqiyya. The Shiites have been persecuted by Sunni Muslims for centuries. The doctrine of taqiyya states that Allah permits Shiites to lie and deceive the Sunni in order to survive."

She continued.

"What if one of the attendees is a Shiite who has deceived the Sunni attendees?"

"Ms. Ryan, I'm not an expert on Islam, but I am sure the Mossad has considered all possibilities."

"Mr. Dorsey, if I could only meet with you."

"I'm sorry, but I have to leave the office. I'm a veteran. We're planning a ceremony for Veteran's Day, this Saturday."

He softened.

"Look Ms. Ryan, the Secret Service knows what they are doing. And the Mossad especially. They have your information. It's in their hands. You do not need to worry."

"But?"

Agent Dorsey reached for his coat.

"Ms. Ryan. Thanks very much for your information. I have your number. If we need more information, I will call you. Thanks again."

"Click."

Jeannine turned to Aileen and frowned.

"Damn it, they won't listen!"

***

On Highway 2, Mufid pointed to the speeding Chrysler as it weaved from lane to lane in the northbound traffic.

"Raakin, drive faster. You are lagging. Do not lose them."

"Harris is a reckless driver. Did you see her squeeze ahead of that truck. He could have hit her."

"Raakin, we must not lose them. Think of what Waseem will do to us. Forget the trucks."

Raakin jammed his foot on the accelerator and swerved into the fast lane.

***

In the Chrysler, Jeannine frowned.

"Aileen, I've had it with the FBI. Agent Dorsey has left the office. There is no use to go to Annapolis. We'll go to Thurmont."

"Thurmont?"

"Yes. It's near Camp David. The Cozy Inn is there. Secret Service Agents from Camp David eat there all the time. We'll take our case direct to them. I only wish I had my computer. Here, this road cuts over to Route 50. Turn left!"

Abruptly, Aileen swung sharp left off of Route 2.

Behind them, a distracted Raakin missed the sudden turn.

Oblivious, he continued straight towards Annapolis.

However, the driver of a another car, a Toyota, had sharper eyes than Raakin. She spotted Aileen's maneuver. She too turned left off of Route 2.

Anan sped to keep the racing Chrysler in her sights.

***

The Leonardtown detective finished his interview with Rob Wilson.

His brow furrowed. Rob was ex-FBI and believable. True, he carried a .38, but his Maryland permit was in order.

And it was clear that someone wanted this guy dead!

He called the FBI Field Office in Annapolis. The phone played a recorded message.

"Mr. Dorsey is not available. At the 'Beep,' please leave your name and number and he will get back to you. Thank you."

The detective did not wait for the beep. He hung up.

***

Abdul Azim was not used to flying, much less to transatlantic flights. His head ached and his sinuses were dried out from the air in the cabin. No matter. In two days he would deliver a major blow to the Jewish occupiers.

His room in the Lebanese Embassy was small, as befit his minor status. He put his carry-on on the bed and stripped to the waist. He stood before the mirror and twisted to examine his left shoulder. The scar where the chip was implanted was nearly invisible. Good.

He stretched out on the bed. He was calm and ready. His eyes closed.

Only minutes later, Abdul jerked awake at the sound of the door opening.

The Lebanese Prime Minister stood before him!

"Relax, Abdul. I've been watching you for some time now. I just want to talk with you."

Abdul swallowed hard. The Prime Minister smiled.

"Abdul, you are intelligent and a fine worker. I want you in my office as a Personal Assistant. I like your style and I need loyal Lebanese to help govern our divided country. I have seen your work for our party. You will be given more important tasks."

Abdul managed three syllables.

"But Sir, I ..."

The Prime Minister continued.

"Abdul, you know that others wish to deny us the right to live in peace. For years the Syrians were occupiers. They are gone, at least physically. Then the Israelis in the south, they too are gone. But now a nation more powerful than they threatens our sovereignty. The Iranians, and Hezbollah, are the greatest threat. We must fight to preserve our country."

Abdul finally found his voice.

"But the Christians, and the Israelis?"

"The Christians need us to fight Hezbollah, and we need them. As for the Israelis, the Americans will keep them in check."

He continued as if talking to himself.

"No, the Christians want an independent Lebanon as do the Sunnis of our party. Perhaps later we will fight them, but not now. It is Iran and the heretical Shiites we must oppose. Even now they seek to destroy us."

Abdul gulped as he thought of his nicely padded bank account courtesy of Waseem's largesse, all from Iran.

The Prime Minister's smile disappeared. He studied Abdul's eyes. Abdul felt exposed. He reached for his shirt.

"Abdul Azim, do not fail me. You and I are Lebanese. We will not turn our country over to Iran. Muhammed fought battles to secure Allah's kingdom. Allah does not want this country given to Shiite heretics! No. We must fight to preserve it."

He took a long breath. His smile returned.

"Tomorrow, the Israelis will accept our plans. They fear Hezbollah, more than ever, more than Hamas. Tomorrow will be a triumph for us. Even Israel, ignorant as they are, will help us achieve Allah's will."

His message delivered, he turned to leave. He spoke over his shoulder.

"Abdul, I need you. You will help me save our country."

Then he was gone, leaving behind a stunned Abdul, whose mind raced with hitherto unthinkable thoughts.

***

Waseem's helicopter sat motionless upon the pad. He was lost in thought. Mufid and Raakin had lost Ryan and the Harris woman somewhere before Annapolis, and Anan had disappeared completely.

This trip to Annapolis was a waste. He must concentrate on the mission.

Abdul had texted him from the airport upon arrival. Waseem looked at the message on his phone. It was one word.

"Yes."

Abdul Azim was ready. At least Waseem had one person he could count on!

***

At St. Mary's Hospital, Bill Hamm sat up and roared at the nurse.

"Where are my pants. I have to leave, now."

The nurse was not intimidated. She pushed him firmly back on the bed.

"Tomorrow, if you're good. Now take this medicine while you're sitting up."

Bill's head throbbed from his sudden exertion and the cast on his arm itched. He took the cup in his good hand and swallowed. Melissa pushed him onto the pillow.

"Good, now lie down and rest. When the doctor hears how ornery you are, he'll want to get rid of you."

She paused and smiled before adding.

"Me too."

Bill groaned.

"OK, but tomorrow, first thing, I'm out of here!"

She laughed and left the room. Moments later she reappeared.

"All right, you may as well know. The doctor just signed your discharge papers. Tomorrow morning you'll be free."

She straightened his pillow.

"Now shut up and go to sleep."

***

For Abdul Azim, jet lag had taken its toll. Even with the revisionary thoughts inspired by the Prime Minister, he dozed off.

The knocking at the door intruded into his consciousness. He could ignore it no longer.

He raised his head off the pillow.

"Come in."

A young woman stood framed in the doorway. Her ebony hair was trimmed short under a brief scarf that revealed a perfectly curved neck.

"M. Azim, le ministre, I mean the minister, says this room is too small for you. He wants you to have better accommodations. I'm here to move you to a larger room."

She pointed to his travel bag.

"Is this everything?"

Abdul nodded.

"Bon, good. I'll move them to your new room. It's the third door on the right. Do you know where the lounge is on the second floor?"

"No, why?"

"The minister is to meet you there. Take the stairs down one flight, turn right. The double doors are the lounge. You must hurry."

Abdul turned for the stairs. The young woman picked up his bag and headed for his new quarters.

Abdul's new room was much more spacious, and furnished with a large flat screen TV.

The young woman put Abdul's bag on the dresser.

She sat on the bed and texted five words on her phone to Waseem.

"He may be a problem."

***

As Aileen approached Frederick, Maryland, Jeannine's head nodded, her eyes closed and her breathing adjusted to the rhythm of the Chrysler's tires. Then she jerked awake, mind racing.

"This is Hezbollah's big chance while the Israeli delegation is in this country. But for the chip to work, don't they still have to be in the same room as the Israeli Minister."

"I think so. Mandley's micro-Lithium battery can't power a signal much beyond that."

"So the assassin-chip must be close to the target."

"Absolutely. Abassian had his heart attack during a meeting with Hezbollah."

"Aileen, Hezbollah and Mandley have chased us across three states. You see how thorough they are. They don't leave anything to chance."

"So?"

"So what if their man can't get close to the Israeli minister?

"What are you thinking?"

"They must have a backup plan!"

***

When Mufid and Abed arrived in Annapolis, Waseem greeted them. His demeanor surprised them.

Waseem was calm!

The expected rage, the swollen neck and red face, the flashing eyes were all absent.

After Ryan's escape and Anan's disappearance, they had anticipated a tirade.

Instead nothing.

Waseem appeared distracted as he consulted his cell phone. Finally he spoke.

"That was a text message from the Lebanese Embassy. There may be a problem with Azim. We must prepare in case he fails. Mufid, Allah may need your sacrifice. Are you ready?"

Mufid swallowed, hard. He thought of the seventy virgins that awaited him.

"I am ready, Waseem."

***

Anan gripped the steering wheel and yawned. She was tired, but awake. She drove carefully. She had tailed the Chrysler since the hospital. With the exception of Aileen's sudden turn-off from the Annapolis road, the task had been easy.

There was no need for speed. Ahead of her, Aileen and Jeannine apparently were unaware that they were followed.

Anan smiled at their simplicity.

But there had been nothing simple about Jeannine when she risked herself to drag Anan from that infernal blaze.

Without her I would be dead! Anan shook that thought away.

The mission must be accomplished.

At Frederick, Aileen's Chrysler turned north on Route 15. Anan groaned.

You are going to Camp David! Jeannine, don't do this. Do not force me to hurt you!

Her heart beat rapidly. Anan steeled her will. *There is one God and Muhammed is his Messenger!*

She wanted to shout "Allahu akbar," but she choked and the words were only a whisper.

She turned north on Route 15. Ahead the tail lights of the Chrysler shone dimly in the dark.

***

In Annapolis, sweat dotted Mufid's forehead. His cheeks flushed. His eyes glowed.

Waseem turned to Abed.

"Abed, it's late. You and Raakin take the chopper back to Delaware. You know what we need. Pick up my supplies and make sure the helicopter is fully serviced. Come back to the airport in Montgomery County. Mufid and I will drive there to meet you."

"But Ryan? And Anan?"

"We will stop them, but I must talk to Mufid, alone."

"And Azim?"

"Leave him to me. He will do what has to be done."

Waseem put his arm around Mufid's shoulder.

"Now go. Mufid and I must prepare. Salaam alaikum."

"Alaikum salaam."

Abed left.
Waseem turned to Mufid.
"Now we pray."

***

******

Chapter 44
Friday, November 10

Mark Baldwin, M. D., was born American and Muslim.

Like Anan, he had never known his "Anglo" father and had been raised by his mother, a Muslim, originally from Beirut. Although she insisted he speak Arabic with her, she was happily American, and it was she who chose his name "Mark."

Unlike Anan, Mark was not radicalized in early youth. He could not conceive that blowing himself into hamburger to kill others was exciting or glamorous.

In high school in Maryland, he spoke, ate, and acted pretty much like the other students. The question of religion never arose. Only his closest friends knew that on some weekends Mark frequented a nearby Islamic Center. But that was mostly for social reasons. Religious distinctions, like those between Sunni and Shia meant nothing to him.

It was at the university that Mark discovered that his country was the "Great Exploiter" of peoples and the earth. But it was Waseem Hamza, then a Teaching Fellow, who taught Mark that the "Great Exploiter" was in truth, the "Great Satan."

More importantly, Waseem convinced his protégé that Allah was real, and that He would use Mark to topple the American infidels, if only Mark were obedient to His commands.

Waseem knew firsthand what Allah's servants could accomplish through obedience. As a youth in Iran, he had participated in the ouster of the Shah and the installation of the Ayatollah Khomeini!

Mark saw the truth in Waseem's narratives.

And Waseem knew the value of his recruit. At his insistence, Mark accepted the largesse of the government and attended the Uniformed Services University of the Health Sciences (USU). He obtained his M. D. with all expenses paid by the Great Satan himself!

After his M. D., Mark finished his military obligation in domestic posts. That was fortunate. Mark could not have aided the United States in killing any fellow Muslims in the Middle East or elsewhere. Allah forbade that!

After active military service, Mark, a reserve naval officer, started his private practice in Bethesda. A confirmed bachelor, he became a successful clinician, a part-time lecturer at his Alma Mater, USU, and obtained privileges as a cardiologist at the Bethesda Naval Hospital.

Apart from Waseem, Mark was completely isolated from Hezbollah cells in the United States. Even Waseem's brother, Fareed, had not known Mark existed.

In short, Dr. Mark Baldwin was a perfect "sleeper."

***

The phone jangled in Mark Baldwin's ears. He rolled over and stuffed his head under the pillow, but the penetrating ring was not to be ignored. He fumbled bedside to locate the offensive sound and picked up. The noise ceased.

The room was dark, but the spoken words were clear.

"New Diagnosis. Check it."

The phone clicked off.

Mark jumped wide awake. He threw the covers off, stepped to the dresser and pressed the lamp switch.

The special prepaid cell was in the bottom drawer, under the cotton socks. He retrieved it and read the text message. It too was brief.

"10 am."

Mark was sweating now. Waseem's code, "New Diagnosis," was for the plan they had developed months ago.

He checked his PDA. He would have to cancel the morning appointments, but he was not due at the hospital until after 2:00 in the afternoon.

Allah be praised! He has called me at last!

He laid out his prayer mat, and started his prayer ritual.

***

At St. Mary's hospital, a fully-clothed Bill Hamm entered the room. He leaned over the bed and spoke.

"Stay still Rob. Don't try to move. Save your strength. I'll talk, you listen."

Bill lowered his voice.

"Jeannine called. I'm leaving for Thurmont right away. She and Aileen are trying to meet with the Secret Service. We still have a chance to show them about the killer chip."

The nurse's eyes signaled Bill to leave. He leaned closer to his friend.

"And Rob, Mary Dean is on the way here. She'll be here this evening."

Rob Wilson smiled, or tried too, as much as the tube in his throat would allow.

Bill nodded to the nurse and left.

***

At the Complex in Delaware, Abed looked at his watch. It was barely 8:00 am. Why had this man come here?

Abed stood up and extended his hand. It was ignored. His visitor, the Special Assistant to the CEO of Mandley Bionics, disdained pleasantries. He was a ruthless man whose power in the company was unlimited.

Abed waited in silence. The man spoke.

"Where is Fareed?"

Dissimulation was impossible.

"He is dead. Shot."

"Who?"

"Jane Peterson, a domestic quarrel."

"Witnesses?"

"Only me."

"Fareed's body?"

"It's here."

"Cremate it."

For Abed (and Fareed) cremation was forbidden. He hesitated.

The visitor stared.

"Now! Pick up the phone!"

Abed made the call.

The visitor frowned.

"Good. Now where is Jane Peterson?"

"She's on the run. She will not go to the police."

"And the Ryan woman? My man at the FDA says she has not contacted them again."

"She's on the run with the Harris woman. We think maybe Frederick, Maryland."

"Eliminate them. This has gone on too long. What the hell are you paid for? The company has a heavy investment in that chip."

Abed nodded. He could not meet the visitor's eyes. He feared this infidel as much as he feared Waseem.

The visitor turned to leave, but looked back.

"Why is the helicopter warmed up?"

Abed's reply was only partially false.

"I'm flying to Frederick to finish Ryan."

The visitor nodded.

"All right, but send it back right away. I may need it."

The door slammed and he was gone.

Abed wiped the sweat from his forehead.

He headed for the helipad.

***

Two members of the Secret Service Advance Team sat in their car at the McDonald's in Thurmont, Maryland. They munched Egg McMuffins and sipped hot coffee. In the back seat their Mossad counterpart chewed a granola bar.

To the Secret Service, security checks at Camp David and environs were a routine matter, but not to Ari Riebman. To the Mossad, no trip with the Israeli prime minister could ever be routine.

Ever serious, Ari's black hair was streaked with gray. The two American agents were younger. Their hair was short, and their shirt collars neatly crisp. The driver, Tom Autry, smiled as he spoke.

"Lighten up Ari. We've done this a dozen times. If there's going to be trouble, we'll smell it first."

Tom nudged his partner.

"Get a load of the blond driving that Chrysler. We could interview her to see if she's a terrorist."

His partner laughed and took a gulp of his coffee.

"I'll take the passenger, the redhead. You can have the blond."

Ari looked up, half amused as two attractive women (Jeannine and Aileen) entered the McDonald's by the side door. Evidently their first destination was the bathroom.

Tom finished his coffee and turned to the back.

"Need anything else, Ari?"

Ari took the final bite of his granola.

"No, I'm ready."

Their car pulled out of the lot as a Toyota turned in.

Ari looked up. The driver of the Toyota was another blond, better looking, perhaps than the redhead's friend.

Her face was familiar. *Maybe ...?* Ari shook his head clear. *No. Probably not.*

They pulled out of the lot.

***

Anan parked the Toyota in a far corner of the McDonald's lot.

The Chrysler was empty. Evidently, Jeannine and Aileen were inside.

Anan yawned. It had been a long night.

She waited.

***

Mandley's helicopter landed at a small airport in Montgomery County. Two cars, a dark Audi and a BMW were waiting. Raakin unloaded the helicopter. As Abed watched, his phone vibrated. It was Waseem.

"Abed, are the supplies there?"

"Yes."

"And the package with the blue wrapper?"

"Yes."

365

"Tell Raakin to bring it to me in Rockville. You go to the cabin. I'll meet you there tonight."

Raakin drove the BMW south towards Rockville.

Abed turned the Audi north onto I-270, towards Frederick.

***

In the MacDonald's lot, Anan was tired. She had driven all night following Jeannine and Aileen to Thurmont.

Waseem had commanded everyone to stay away from Thurmont. It was too close to Camp David. He wanted no Hezbollah presence that close. None!

And even Frederick, though permitted, was to be avoided if possible.

Anan looked at the laptop on the seat beside her. Without it, Jeannine Ryan had no proof for her assertions. Anan admired Jeannine. She was intelligent, well-trained and independent, a real woman, not like Fareed's interpretation of Allah's will for females. *Your tilth, indeed?*

And Jeannine had risked her life to save Anan! *Damn it Jeannine, go away. Don't interfere with us!*

Anan kept her eyes on the Chrysler.

***

Inside, the McDonald's was not crowded. Jeannine was on her phone. Aileen returned from the counter with two refills of steaming coffee.

"What did the Secret Service say?"

"They can't meet us until 8:00 tonight. All the advance teams are over-scheduled, and most of their checks have to be done in daylight."

"But the talks start tomorrow evening."

"They acknowledge that, but the FBI task force in Baltimore passed on our message, so they already know much of what we want to say."

"So they don't believe us. What's the use?"

Jeannine put down her coffee.

366

"We'll meet them at 8:00 pm, but look, you drove all night. You need to rest. We passed some cabins a few miles back. We need to crash before the meeting."

They left the McDonald's and took Route 15 back towards the cabins.

***

Anan waited a few seconds and followed. *They're leaving Thurmont. Good.*

But a few miles later, Jeannine turned onto a lane marked "Catoctin Park Cabins, Rentals."

Anan frowned. *Damn it Jeannine. You are one stubborn woman. Will you never give up?* She drove slowly past the entrance to the cabins.

***

The coffee shop in Rockville, Maryland featured crowded tables topped with laptops, unbought books from the adjacent bookstore, and scattered newspapers. Specialty coffee was the only thread that linked the diverse assembly.

Waseem spoke softly in Arabic. Mark hung on his every word. He had waited long and patiently for this moment. His eyes glistened with excitement as he heard what he was to do. Still if possible, he was to conceal his role in the death of the Prime Minister. He was not to waste himself needlessly.

Mark understood his instructions. He arose and left. Waseem stayed seated.

Through the window he watched Mark's car leave the parking lot. No one followed him. Waseem congratulated himself. Mark Baldwin was a perfect scimitar for Allah, a blade forged and honed by Waseem himself. A blade that would strike now and doubtless again in the future!

He listened to several youths at a nearby table. They were speaking Farsi. Typical students, they complained loudly, but were unable, or unwilling, to act on their beliefs. He sneered inwardly.

He left the coffee shop through the bookstore portal. He paused behind a shelf of travel books. No one was following him.

He walked two blocks to where Raakin waited in the BMW.

They drove north, towards Frederick.

***

Bill Hamm had driven for hours. His head throbbed, and his arm itched under the cast, but he kept driving. The traffic on the outer loop of the Capital Beltway thinned just as his phone vibrated. He pulled onto the shoulder and stopped. It was Jeannine.

"Bill, where are you?"

"I'm on 270. I just left the Beltway."

"Are you all right?"

"I'm driving with one arm, and my head hurts, but I'm out of that damned hospital."

"Sorry. Look, we're at Catoctin Park Cabins. Here's how you get there. Take highway 15 north from Frederick and ... ."

Bill memorized Jeannine's directions.

***

******

Chapter 45
Friday, November 10

Mark Baldwin, M. D., put down his coffee and answered the phone. It was a colleague from the Naval Hospital, a fellow surgeon, Hank Martino. Waseem had told Mark to expect this call.

"Mark, old friend, I need a favor, big time. Can you cover for me this weekend at Navy Med."

"Hank, I ... "

"Please, you have to, man. My dad had an accident in West Virginia. He's in intensive care and there's no one else I can ask. I'm on my way to him now."

Mark smiled. Waseem's scheme was unfolding as planned.

"All right, Hank, I'll be glad to. No problem."

"Thanks, Mark, you are a life saver."

Mark hung up and turned to Mufid. The latter was clad in a loose white lab coat with a stethoscope bulging from a side pocket.

"We're all set. Here's your badge and ID. You are Dr. Carlos Mendez. Tomorrow you will assist me at the Naval Medical Center. Try not to speak. Just stay with me and keep your mouth shut. Everyone will think you are a doctor."

Mufid nodded his assent. Mark returned to his coffee.

Waseem's plan was on track.

***

For privacy, the Catoctin cabins were widely spaced among mixed oak and Hickory woods, each reached by a long trail from a central unpaved area. Jeannine and Aileen parked the Chrysler there.

The hike to their cabin took several minutes.

The cabin was clean, but the furnishings were rustic. An old-fashioned pitcher and wash bowl stood on the dresser. At that sight, Jeannine quickly opened the bathroom door. She exhaled in relief. The fixtures were modern.

The night drive had taken its toll on Aileen. Eyes closed, she stretched on the bed, shoes and all. After only minutes, her breathing was slow and regular.

Jeannine slumped into the arm chair. She kicked off her shoes and stretched her legs.

For the first time in days, she rested. Her head tilted to one side. Her eyes closed.

In a neighboring cabin, separated from her by an acre of trees, Abed paced nervously. Where was Waseem?

The Catoctin Cabins were Waseem's meeting place!

***

Ari Riebman did not believe in chance. He could not afford to. Any time his Prime Minister traveled, the Mossad had to evaluate multiple threats to his safety.

Ari appreciated the full cooperation of the Secret Service, though he knew that this was not optional. The Mossad would not tolerate anything less. Without such assurance, the Israeli Prime Minister simply would not travel.

Ari addressed Tom, his Secret Service counterpart.

"Tom, can I look at that fax from the FBI's Baltimore task force. The one about the 'killer' computer chip?"

"Here it is. It sounds like Sci-Fi to me."

Ari scanned the paragraphs. One name stuck out. *Hamza, Fareed Hamza.*

Now I remember. The blond in the Toyota! At the McDonald's!

Her photograph was in Hamza's file.

Her name was *Anan, Anan Audet Hamza, Hezbollah!*

Ari turned to Tom Autry.

"We're to meet Dr. Ryan tonight? At 8:00 pm?"

"That's right. At the Cozy Inn."

"I have a hunch. Do you mind if I talk to her this afternoon? I'll be there at 8:00 too, when you interview her."

Tom flicked an inquisitive glance at his partner who nodded. He turned back to Ari.

"I guess not. What do you have in mind?"

"A gut feeling, that's all. Anything I find out, you'll have at 8:00 tonight."

"You're Mossad, she doesn't have to talk to you unless she wants to."

"I'll be clear it's voluntary. She'll know I'm Israeli."

"OK, Ari, go for it. We'll see you tonight at the Cozy Inn."

"I appreciate it, Tom. Shalom."

***

It was still light when Bill Hamm neared Jeannine's cabin, but the sun had dropped behind the Catoctin ridge, leaving the eastern slope shrouded in dark shadows.

He knocked on the cabin door. Aileen answered.

"Bill, thank God, look at you. The last time I saw you, you looked like hell. How's the arm?"

"It will heal. Where's Jeannine?"

Aileen handed him an envelope, addressed to Bill in Jeannine's hand.

"She left this for you. She went to meet with a Mossad agent. We'll see her later at the Cozy Inn."

Bill tore the envelope open. He blushed.

Aileen smiled.

"What does she say?"

His face stayed red.

"Never mind. She says don't wait for her to eat. She'll see us at the meeting with the Secret Service."

Aileen grabbed her coat.

"In that case, let's go now. I'm hungry."

***

Jeannine instantly liked this man with the streaks of gray in his hair.

"Dr. Ryan, I'm Ari Riebman. I'm with the Mossad. You do not have to talk with me unless you want to. Please understand that."

"Mr. Riebman, I'm glad to talk to you. It's been hard to find anyone willing to listen. And call me Jeannine."

"All right, I'm Ari. I have some questions about your call to the FBI."

In response, Jeannine talked continuously for a half hour, with only occasional prompts by Ari. When she had finished, Ari was all gratitude.

"Thank you, Jeannine, this has been very helpful."

She started to leave, but Ari touched her shoulder. He placed a photograph on the table.

"Jeannine, one more item. Is this your 'Jane Peterson?'"

It was a photograph of a woman attired in terrorist black.

It was Anan.

Jeannine swallowed and nodded.

"You know she is a terrorist, with Hezbollah."

Another silent nod.

Ari studied Jeannine's eyes.

"Do you think that she is your friend?"

Jeannine shrugged her shoulders.

"Do you know where she is?"

Jeannine found her voice.

"No."

Ari frowned.

"Jeannine, would you tell me if you did know?"

"Ari, I honestly can't say."

"Jeannine, this interview is not official. I like you. You have already been through a lot. You must be careful. This woman is dangerous."

He hesitated. Then he broke his own interview rule. He volunteered information.

"Did you know she was following you? She was at the McDonald's this morning."

Jeannine gasped.

Ari took her hand.

"Be careful. Call me the moment you see her. Don't hesitate."

Jeannine nodded and left. She headed south on highway 15 towards the Catoctin Cabins.

***

South of Thurmont Anan extinguished the lights on her Toyota and waited in the shadows on the shoulder of Route 15. Minutes passed before her patience was rewarded. A Chrysler slowed and turned onto the wooded lane leading to the Catoctin Cabins. Surely it was Jeannine.

Anan, lights still off, turned onto the lane. Ahead of her, dim pinpoints of red marked the path of the Chrysler.

Anan followed.

***

Abed paced his cabin. Where was Waseem?

The air in the cabin was chill. He put another log on the fire.

He went to the door. The shadows were dark under the trees and there was no sign of his leader. He looked at his watch, 6:00 pm. He stepped back inside.

The log crackled and blazed emitting an acrid haze that irritated Abed's nostrils. He coughed, and went back to the door. He stood on the porch and caught his breath. The fresh air revived him. Sinuses cleared, he left the smoky cabin and walked down the path towards the parking area.

He arrived just as a car drove up and parked on the far side.

A woman was inside.

Ryan!

Abed snuck through the woods.

***

Jeannine opened the door of the Chrysler.

Behind her a branch snapped.

She looked back, but too late. A hard object crashed against her forehead. She collapsed to the ground.

She regained her senses, only to realize that her hands were bound behind her back.

Who?

The answer was immediate. Abed wrenched her up by the elbows.

"Now bitch, shut up and walk in front of me. You are fortunate that Waseem wants to see you. Otherwise, you would be rotting where you fell."

Dazed and numb, Jeannine stumbled in front of him.

Abed cursed and pushed her through the brush.

***

Anan approached Jeannine's Chrysler. The car was unlocked, its door open and the keys in the ignition.

But Jeannine was gone.

Not far away, Anan heard the cracks of snapping twigs and rustling leaves. Someone was pushing through the undergrowth. She heard cursing. She knew that voice.

Abed, the devil who dealt in fire!

Quickly she retrieved the keys from the Chrysler and closed the door.

Then she followed the sounds.

After some minutes, the sharp aroma of burning wood reached her nostrils. Then she saw the shadowy outline of a cabin. She approached stealthily.

As she stepped onto the narrow porch a scream pierced the evening air.

Jeannine!

Then a man's voice.

Abed again!

Anan studied the door of the cabin and assessed her options. She knew Abed only too well. His kind were weak to the strong and strong to the weak.

And Jeannine, captive, was certainly weak!

Anan pressed her ear to the door. There was only silence.

She twisted the handle, slowly. Still no sound.

She pushed the door inward. The dim light revealed a bare room with a glowing stove and empty table. She pulled the door shut behind her. Except for the fiery embers, the room was dark. Anan froze.

A line of light shown under the door of the next room. Anan heard low murmurs and moaning.

She edged to the doorway. Abed's voice came through clearly.

"Dear Miss Ryan, you are a whore. You will die here. But I promise we will leave Mr. Hamm alone if you tell me where to find Anan. Where is she?"

"I don't know, but I would never tell you!"

Anan heard a chair crash to the floor and a dull thud. Then Abed's voice.

"Get up whore. Tell me!. Where is Anan?"

The sound of a fist against flesh.

Again Abed's voice, higher pitched.

"Speak or burn in Hell!"

***

Too much! Anan kicked the door open.

There stood Abed, gun in hand.

Jeannine's eyes were closed. Swollen lips oozed blood.

Anan pointed her nine millimeter at Abed.

"Drop it you pig!"

He hesitated, but only for a moment. He knew Anan. His voice shook.

"Anan, help me with this bitch. She knows our plans."

"Put the gun on the floor, Abed, carefully!"

Anan kicked the weapon across the room.

"Now untie her Abed."

"But?"

"Now!"

Anan's semi automatic was only a foot from Abed's nose.

He shrank back. Hands shaking, he loosed Jeannine's bonds. Her eyes opened.

Anan smiled.

"Now do you know we are sisters?"

Jeannine nodded affirmatively. She cleared her throat.

"What are you going to do to him?"

Abed flattened himself against the wall. Anan's eyes went blank.

"Leave him to me. Go, and hurry! Get away from the cabins."

Anan pressed a key ring into Jeannine's hand.

"They're yours, your car. Go!

Jeannine staggered to her feet and touched Anan's shoulder. Anan's voice wavered.

"Jeannine, please go. Hurry."

Jeannine limped away.

***

Anan turned. Abed cowered in the corner.

"Please Anan. I obey Allah, as you. We both follow the messenger's hadiths. Please, do not shoot. I was trying to help our cause."

Anan simply stared. He continued.

"I have always supported you. I will work with you, for you. Do not forget our mission."

Still no comment from Anan. Abed swallowed. Thirty seconds had elapsed and he was alive. There was hope.

"Anan, I will defend you. Waseem does not know that you killed his brother. He need never know."

He followed that lie with another.

"Your secret is safe. Mufid does not know you killed Fareed. I told him it was me. That Fareed had betrayed the mission."

Anan spoke slowly and carefully.

"Abed, you lie. You tried to kill me. You use fire, like the devil himself."

Abed's gut tightened.

"No wait. Wait. Please. No."

Anan's finger tightened on the trigger.

But a glint appeared in Abed's eyes.

Anan turned, but too late. The blow landed above her ear and she collapsed, senseless.

Abed's voice was resonant.

"Well done, Raakin. Well done. Tie the bitch to the chair. This whore needs a lesson in Allah's justice."

376

Abed went to the counter and fondled a long knife.

***

Jeannine felt her way through the dark woods to the parking area. The scraping of her shoes on gravel assured her numbed senses that she was on the path.

As she pushed forwards, she rotated her arm to test her shoulder. She felt her tooth. It moved in its socket. Abed's blows had been effective.

Ahead through the trees a light beamed and was gone. It appeared again, brighter and closer.

Someone was coming.

Jeannine crouched in the brush and waited in the darkness.

A beam of light flicked over the brambles above her. Then it flashed by. A large man, breathing heavily, strode past.

The sounds of his passage disappeared. She retook the trail as fast as stumbling legs permitted.

A few cars, including a BMW, were in the leaf-strewn parking area. At the far end, Aileen's Chrysler stood alone.

Panting, Jeannine reached the car, opened the door and thrust the key into the ignition.

She breathed deeply. There was something on the seat beside her.

The laptop! Anan had returned the laptop.

Anan had made her choice!

***

Jeannine's first thought was to go back for Anan, but she knew she would only be a hindrance to her.

Anan had left the laptop knowing Jeannine could use it to convince the Secret Service of the danger to the prime minister. She must keep that appointment.

"Lord, thanks!"

Prayer was no way typical with Jeannine, but in the last few days she had decided it couldn't hurt.

"And take care of Anan!"

She spun away as fast as the gravel surface would allow and turned north on Route 15.

She had a meeting to go to!

***

Back at his cabin, Abed pressed the blade against Anan's cheek. A thin line of blood appeared.

"Abed, what are you doing?"

Waseem Hamza filled the doorway.

"I defend Fareed's honor and yours. This is the bitch who killed your brother."

"Fareed was not *your* brother. Step aside."

Abed backed away.

Waseem turned to Anan. She stared blankly through swollen lids.

"Anan, did you kill my brother?"

"Yes."

Waseem waved Abed to silence. His eyes stayed with Anan.

"Did my brother harm you?"

Abed broke in.

"He disciplined her for adultery, but only to correct her. And he spared her life."

Waseem turned to face Abed.

"You left Anan in the flames. You wanted to burn her to death. Is that true?"

"It was to protect your brother's honor, and Allah's."

"Do not blaspheme. Do not invoke Allah. Abed, there is something you should know."

"What is that?"

"My brother was a pig!"

All life left Abed's eyes. He shrank back.

Waseem raised his weapon and fired. A hole appeared in Abed's forehead. Blood splattered the wall behind as he fell. From the back of his head, blood pooled onto the worn floor.

Waseem faced Raakin.

"Untie her."

Raakin complied, quickly.

Waseem lifted a limp Anan and pressed her head to his shoulder.

"Anan, my beauty, my brother knew nothing about women. He did not appreciate you. Forgive me for not acting sooner. I will make up for his errors."

He turned to Raakin.

"Get rid of that abomination on the floor. Bury it in the woods. There is a shovel on the porch. Go."

Raakin dragged the remains out. The floor boards stayed streaked with blood.

Waseem fondled Anan's hair.

"You have a real man, now. You are mine."

Anan shuddered.

***

******

Chapter 46
Saturday, November 11

The Lebanese Prime Minister chose Abdul Azim to ride in his party to Camp David. This was a distinct honor, to ride in the helicopter.

Less-favored staff had to travel in a van that was to leave the embassy momentarily. The helicopter would not leave for another hour.

Abdul had that hour to rehearse.

Alone in his bedroom, he rose and placed a small device on a table about eight feet from his chair.

Then he sat, tense, but focused.

He flexed his right arm at the elbow, and then, arm still flexed and rigid except for a slight rotation at the wrist, pressed his hand against his chest.

That sequence came easily to Abdul, he thought of it as a roman salute, but with an open hand not a fist.

Next, he moved his arm away from his chest, still flexed and elbow rigid, so that his lower arm projected forward, elbow close to the body. Then he flexed his head sideways, down towards his right shoulder.

The device on the table responded with a rapidly flashing green diode!

Abdul's motions, while simple, involved a large number of muscles, and a much larger number of fibers.

The chip implanted in Abdul Azim's shoulder was served by four microelectrodes that registered the firing of nearby fibers in the *biceps, anterior deltoid, posterior deltoid and levator scapulae muscles*. Fired in quick succession, this sequence caused his implant to signal the simulated pacemaker and alter its programming!

Abdul grimaced. If he could reproduce these motions near the Israeli leader, that dog would surely die.

381

He reset the device and started over.

He flexed his right arm at the elbow and pressed his hand against his chest … .

The door behind Abdul slowly opened.

The young woman peered through the crack. Her brief scarf revealed a nicely curved neck. Her eyes focused on Abdul's movements.

Moments later she shut the door quietly.

She stood in the hallway and took out her phone.

The text to Waseem was short.

"Ali has helped him."

The meaning would be clear to Waseem, as to any Shiite.

The original plan was still in effect.

***

Waseem read the text message. He prayed silently. Ali you are truly the friend of Allah, the successor to his Messenger and his first Caliph.

It was good news. He could count on Azim!

Waseem was pleased.

***

Yesterday, when Jeannine, Aileen and Bill Hamm introduced themselves to Tom Autry, the meeting had started poorly.

Initially Tom had been shocked to see the two young women that he and his partner had eyed at the McDonald's. The leap from their good looks to their evident intelligence was difficult. Besides, Tom's resistance to numbers, computers, and things mathematical made him want to reject their presentations.

But Jeannine's bruised face and Bill Hamm's broken arm had convinced him that the group had paid its dues. He had to listen. These folks had earned a hearing.

Jeannine's numerical arguments appeared logical, and her computer decryption of Harry's messages, accented by his death, was convincing.

In the end Tom had reached the same conclusion as Ari Riebman had earlier.

Jeannine, Aileen and Bill Hamm had uncovered a serious threat.

Someone in the Lebanese delegation was a Hezbollah terrorist.

The Israeli Prime Minister was in real danger!

But that was last night. This morning, Tom was frustrated.

He slammed the phone down.

The Secret Service's protestations to the State Department had been dismissed.

The Lebanese delegation had assured the Americans that the entire delegation had been thoroughly vetted.

No one could be challenged. All were from the Minister's party or strong supporters of it. None could possibly be from Hezbollah. The few that were not Sunni were Christian.

And the purpose of the Camp David meeting was for the Lebanese government to cooperate with Israel against the political arm of Hezbollah! Etc. Etc.

In brief, the State Department agreed with their Lebanese counterparts.

For the sake of diplomacy, the Secret Service must stay away from the Lebanese delegation!

Tom exploded.

"Damn it. How do they expect us to do our job?"

He turned to Ari Riebman.

"Ari, my hands are tied. But you are not bound by our State Department. Is there anything you can do?

"Tom, my Prime Minister is not easily intimidated, and he badly wants this accord with the Lebanese. I don't know what I can do."

Ari paused to think. Then he added.

"When will Ryan and the others be here?"

"They're due any minute."

"Good. Pour me some of that coffee. I need to learn more about this damnable chip."

***

383

When Jeannine and the others arrived, Ari's first words were for Jeannine.

"Where's Anan?"

"I have no idea."

She turned to Tom Autry.

"What did you and Bill find at the cabin? And where is Bill, didn't he come back with you?"

"No one was there, but there was blood on the floor."

Jeannine winced. She looked at Ari.

"I only hope Anan is alive. She saved me and the laptop."

Ari grimaced.

Jeannine turned back to Tom.

"So where is Bill now?"

"He's playing a hunch. He thinks the terrorists went to Frederick."

Ari waved Jeannine to silence.

He put down his coffee and focused on Aileen.

"Tell me everything you can about this chip implant."

***

Bill Hamm had his reasons for driving to Frederick.

He was sure the terrorists would avoid Thurmont, but stay close nonetheless. Hence the choice of Frederick.

He had seen enough of these bastards to know that they liked expensive cars, new and of foreign make, likely German. And he reasoned that they would find a cheap inconspicuous lodging on the outskirts of town.

So why not look for an expensive new car, preferably of German-make, in the parking lot of a cheap motel? Especially in a rear lot, not visible from the road!

His first two stops were uneventful. Pickup trucks, many of them F150's, dominated the lots, along with smaller cars of Japanese make.

The third motel appeared too high class for his template. He was about to pass it by when a car pulled out from behind the building.

A new BMW!

Bill looked at the driver as he passed. He was swarthy. He could be from the Middle East.

The BMW disappeared towards Frederick.

Bill turned into the lot and drove behind the building.

There were only four vehicles.

A blue Toyota, two Ford F150's and, significantly, a dark-colored Audi.

Bingo!

***

Anan was awake. She was in Waseem's suite in a motel near Frederick.

At least Waseem had not tried to bed her last night.

She was grateful for that, but it was simply a matter of time, before he would force himself on her. She shuddered. The memory of "manly" unwashed armpits and rotten coffee breath assailed her nostrils. Fareed all over again!

She arose and walked to the bathroom. This was an inner unit of the motel. There was no window, only a ceiling fan to evacuate the air.

She turned and crept to the bedroom door. Carefully she turned the handle. Locked!

She pressed her ear to the panel.

Waseem was on the phone.

Anan strained to listen. She could hear only his side of the conversation.

"Riebman? Ari Riebman? How do you know it's him?"

A short silence.

"All right. All right. So it was Riebman. What do the Israelis want?"

More silence.

"A doctor, a cardiologist, at the meeting! And a defibrillator too! How?"

Anan strained to hear more, but Waseem lowered his voice.

Anan reflected. A defibrillator! And Riebman was Mossad. Jeannine must have succeeded in alerting the Israelis of the threat against the Prime Minister.

There was no time to reflect further. The door knob turned and she jumped back.

Waseem stood frowning in the doorway.

***

Waseem slammed the door shut.

"Anan, the Mossad smells something."

He grabbed her hair and jerked her head back.

"The Israelis want to have a defibrillator and a cardiologist for their Prime Minister. Ryan met with the Mossad. How did she know what to tell them?"

He seized her throat with his free hand.

"What did you tell Ryan? What?"

He loosened his grip. Anan gasped for breath.

"Waseem, please, I tried to stop her."

"You admit you talked to her?"

"She saved my life when Abed tried to burn me alive."

"Abed was a dog, but Ryan? What of her?"

He released his grasp and stared into her eyes.

Anan opened her mouth to speak, but Waseem slammed her against the wall.

"You told Ryan!"

She struggled to free herself, but he hit her with a clubbed fist. She went sprawling across the bed.

She tried to rise, but fell backwards, eyes closed.

Blood trickled from the side of her mouth.

Waseem left the bedroom.

He stepped outside to the Audi.

***

From behind a truck, Bill Hamm watched a man (Waseem) leave unit 44, look both ways, and open the Audi's door.

The Audi roared out of the lot. Bill memorized the plate number.

He moved sideways towards the unit. The Beretta that Ari had loaned him fit Bill's hand nicely.

386

But he was awkward. His left arm was in a sling. He stuck the Beretta in his belt to free his right hand. Then he twisted the knob slowly. The latch did not yield.

He kicked and the door flew open.

Only silence. The room was empty and the door on the opposite wall was closed. Bill tried the handle. It was locked. He kicked once more.

The wood split and the door fell open. On the bed, Anan stirred.

Bill spoke.

"Jane, Jane Peterson, who did this to you?"

But Anan's eyes flashed a warning. Bill turned. A man was in the doorway.

Two guns fired simultaneously.

The man pitched forward, face down. Bill Hamm stood ready to shoot again, but it was not necessary. The man was dead. He turned back to Anan.

"Jane?"

"His name is Raakin. He missed me. I'm OK."

Bill studied the wall where Raakin's bullet had penetrated. Anan confirmed his look.

"You're right, Mr. Hamm, I was his first target. He didn't expect you to turn so quickly."

"But why you?"

"There's no time. Waseem may come back. He is a trained assassin. He will not be as easy to kill as Raakin. Help me up."

She stumbled into the bathroom.

With his good hand, Bill searched Raakin's pockets. There was no ID, only a wad of bills and keys. He put the keys and money on the dresser, while he searched the drawers. They were empty. When Anan came out the bathroom, Bill went in. The shower was clean. The bathroom was undisturbed, except for blood in the sink where Anan had washed her face.

He stepped back into the bedroom. The keys were no longer on the dresser.

He ran from the unit. He stepped outside only to see a car drive off, fast.

The Toyota and Anan were gone.

***

Bill went back into the motel. Damn it, Jane, Anan or whoever you are! You should have helped us. Who is this Waseem guy?

His eyes shifted to the floor and Raakin's body.

He phoned Tom Autry.

"Call the FBI for me. … Yes. …. The body is in Unit 44, a terrorist named Raakin. I'm leaving now. And they should watch for someone named 'Waseem.' He might come back."

As Bill turned to leave, his cell phone vibrated.

It was Anan.

"How did you get this number?"

"Never mind, Mr. Hamm, I had to thank you. Tell Jeannine too."

A pause.

"And tell her that the Lebanese assassin has the chip implanted in his right shoulder. For proof, look in his briefcase. It's how he prays."

She hesitated, then took a final breath.

"His name is 'Abdul Azim.'"

***

Abdul Azim enjoyed the ride high over the Maryland countryside.

The afternoon was bright and clear. The hardwoods had few leaves, but the sun shone on smooth branches that glistened to form intricate patterns of light and shadows. Occasional dark stands of evergreen pines stood in stark contrast to the gray hardwoods.

The helicopter passed the isolated rocky knob known as Sugarloaf Mountain, and stayed to the east of South Mountain to follow the Leesburg Valley towards Frederick.

The Prime Minister spoke.

"Do you know your American History, Abdul. This countryside is where the Southern General Lee first took the battle to the North, at Antietam on the other side of that mountain."

Abdul feigned interest. He did not care about past wars, only the present one.

The Prime Minister continued.

"We are about to pass over Frederick. That is where one of Lee's officers left his superior's battle plan wrapped about a cigar. The Northern General knew Lee's intentions before the battle of Antietam took place. Lee's invasion of the North was stopped."

"Abdul, if you know the enemies plans, you can defeat him."

He continued.

"We must ascertain Hezbollah's intentions. They must not control our country. I have no wish to learn Farsi."

For the briefest of moments Abdul felt a prick of conscience, but he recovered and affirmed the Shiite formula. *Ali is the successor to the Messenger and the first Caliph.*

Unaware, the Prime Minister turned to his protégé.

"Abdul, I am glad you are with me. Together we can save our country from the foreigners that would dominate us."

***

******

Chapter 47
Saturday, November 11

Jeannine put down her phone. She turned to Ari Riebman.

"That was Bill Hamm. Anan told him the name of the Lebanese traitor, 'Abdul Azim.' He has the chip implanted in his shoulder."

Ari was skeptical.

"And you believe her?"

"She told Bill the proof is in Azim's carry-on. Something about the way he prays."

Ari stared at Jeannine. He touched his forehead as if thinking.

Seconds later he softened.

"Perhaps you can trust her. Maybe I should believe you."

"Ari, she has been through hell. She wants no part of this. This is no lie."

His brow furrowed.

"All right, Jeannine, I might be able to do something, but if you're wrong, this will be my last day with the Mossad. I will be finished, or as you say here, 'toast.'"

***

Ari escorted Jeannine and Aileen through the gate to the Camp David Compound. He went straight to Tom Autry.

"Tom, I think we can expose the assassin. Can you help me?"

Tom locked eyes with him.

"Ari, this could be the end of my job too."

"If we don't act, my Prime Minister will die."

"All right, come with me, We'll try."

Tom led Ari to the quarters of the Lebanese delegation. He took Ari's credentials and entered.

Ari waited outside.

A few minutes later, Tom appeared.

"I told the Prime Minister it was a matter of security. He's not happy, but he agreed to see you. Azim is there now. Go in. I'll wait here."

Ari entered.

***

Ari scanned the room.

The Lebanese Prime Minister stood, flanked by two Aides each equal in size to Ari.

A smaller man stood beside them, clutching his carry-on. *That has to be Abdul Azim. Thank God, he has his briefcase. Now if only …?*

Ari swallowed hard and pointed.

"Mr. Prime Minister, this man is a traitor to your cause."

The Prime Minister glared at Ari. His aides froze, motionless.

The Minister spoke.

"You a Jew, presume to accuse one of my trusted men. How dare you!"

"Sir, I mean no disrespect to you or your nation."

"You have thirty seconds. Then you must leave."

Ari stepped to Abdul's side and took the attaché case.

Hands shaking, Abdul stared at the floor.

Ari opened the case.

He drew out a rolled-up mat and handed it to the Prime Minister.

"Mr. Riebman, that is his prayer mat. Mr. Azim is a Muslim, as am I. This is completely unforgivable. I … "

The Prime Minister stopped in mid-speech as Ari handed him a second object.

It was a round piece of flat hardened clay.

The Prime Minister turned.

"Abdul, how do you explain this?"

"What do you mean, Sir?"

"Abdul, do not insult my intelligence. You know what this is. A good Shiite does not touch his head to the mat while

392

praying as we Sunni do. Rather he puts a hard piece of Karbala clay on the mat and his forehead touches the clay."

The Prime Minister studied Abdul's forehead before continuing.

"Abdul, the skin on your forehead is slightly reddish. Is that a callus? Do you press your head on this clay tablet?"

"Abdul covered his forehead with his hands."

"Mr. Prime Minister, I can explain."

"No, Abdul, you embarrass me in front of this foreigner. Redeem yourself. Tell me honestly. Are you a Shiite?"

Abdul nodded. His voice was a murmur.

"Yes, I believe Ali is the friend of Allah and the successor of his Messenger. He is the first Caliph."

The Prime Minister frowned. His aides stiffened.

"Abdul, are you then a member of Hezbollah?"

Abdul straightened his shoulders. He raised his eyes to look into those of his interrogator.

"Mr. Prime Minister, I am Muslim as you are. This man who tries to divide us is a kafir. We must stand together against unbelievers."

The Prime Minister's brow furrowed more deeply. He spoke slowly.

"Again, are you of Hezbollah?"

Abdul glared.

The Prime Minister's eyes faded. His shoulders drooped.

"Abdul, you have deceived me. I am deeply disappointed. This kafir has shown me the truth when you would not."

He added.

"You want war, not peace. My country needs peace and the prosperity it brings. You have betrayed your people."

He signaled to one of his aides.

"Please escort Mr. Azim to my room. He is under your custody. Do not let him escape. We must question him. He has information we need."

Abdul slumped as the aide took his arm.

The Prime Minister turned back to Ari.

"Mr. Riebman, it is not easy for me to admit I was wrong. Mr. Azim has deceived me for four years. I thought of him as a … ."

The Minister sat down behind his desk.

"Mr. Riebman, Please convey to your leader that I am grateful for your perseverance in exposing Mr. Azim, and assure him that we in my Party had no knowledge that he belonged to Hezbollah."

He took a deep breath and added.

"Tell him that I pray this incident will not affect our proposed accords."

Ari nodded.

"Thank you, Mr. Prime Minister. We are grateful to you for listening. I will pass on all your comments, and your personal sorrow."

The Prime Minister sank into the chair behind his desk.

"Thank you Mr. Riebman, and thank you for your understanding. You are a tribute to your people. Now I need to be alone."

Ari left.

***

Ari watched Azim and his escort disappear down the corridor. He wanted to stay with them and assist at the terrorist's interrogation.

He called his Mossad superior who called his Lebanese counterpart. The answer was a clear and emphatic "No."

The Lebanese did not need the Mossad for an internal investigation.

All Ari could do was wait. He used the interlude to call Tom Autry.

Then he called Jeannine with warm thanks.

***

Bill Hamm's phone vibrated. It was Jeannine.

"Bill, where are you?"

"I'm in Frederick. I'm coming back to Thurmont."

"Bill, we have to celebrate. Ari convinced them. It was someone named Azim like Anan said. The Lebanese have him in custody. The threat is over. We can relax."

"And Aileen?"

"She already called her daughter. She's going back to Pennsylvania, but first we want to celebrate. How far are you from the Cozy Inn?"

"An hour, maybe less."

"We'll be finished here soon. Ari wants us to brief the Mossad on what we know about the chip. We can be at the Inn in an hour. Can you get a table for us and wait?"

"Sure, I'll sip a beer."

"Good, and Bill …"

"Yes?"

"I really want to see you!"

For the first time in days, Bill relaxed. The image of Jeannine flipping red hair off her forehead filled his mind.

"Good!"

***

Mossad agents are capable, meticulous and thorough. And they need to be. The stakes are high, the survival of their nation!

Ari was no exception. He took copious notes while Aileen and Jeannine recounted the events of the past weeks to his superior. The third time he heard the term "Mandley Bionics," he underlined it so heavily that his pen scratched through the paper.

Jeannine and Aileen were relieved to describe their mishaps, particularly after a successful outcome.

The Israeli Prime Minister was safe.

***

No matter how thorough the planning, unpredictable events can occur. Protective details dread them. Chance could mean death for their charge.

Chance now intervened at Camp David. The corridor along which Abdul Azim was escorted led past a conference room.

As Azim and his guards passed, the double doors opened wide and a group of men emerged into the passageway.

Immediately Abdul recognized the Israeli dog of a Minister, in intense conversation with his Staff. These were flanked by others whose eyes searched ahead and behind. Mossad!

The group approached.

The hallway was narrow. Abdul's escort paused to let them pass.

Abdul decided. He pushed backwards against the wall and mouthed a silent prayer. *Ali, Help me.* The image of a beautiful girl, chaste, a virgin, flashed before him.

He completed his well practiced motions in seconds.

Separate microelectrodes recorded the rapidly firing fibers from the *biceps, anterior deltoid, posterior deltoid and levator scapulae muscles,* in that order

The chip in his shoulder emitted its lethal signal.

Abdul was already exposed. Secrecy was no longer needed. The world must know of his deed!

He straightened to full height and shouted.

"Allahu Akbar!"

The Prime Minister clutched his chest and pitched forward.

Two of the Minister's aides fired in unison.

One shot struck Abdul's escort in the arm.

The other shot pierced Abdul's eye. He died instantly.

***

In the debriefing room, Ari's phone vibrated. Jeannine looked up as the Mossad agent jumped to his feet.

"The Prime Minister is down. His heart. That damned Azim!"

He started for the door and called back.

"Aileen, Jeannine follow me."

The room emptied. The debriefing was over.

***

The Cozy Inn was not crowded at this hour. Bill Hamm took a table in the corner. He checked his watch. He was early.

He downed a draft Bud and ordered a second.

He sat, sipped, and waited.

***

Ari dashed down the hall. He waved his credentials at the guard, and led Aileen and Jeannine inside the room where the Prime Minister lay on a table.

His cheeks had a blue tinge and his nose was pinched by a staff member attempting rescue breathing, but with little effect.

Aileen leaned to Jeannine and whispered.

"Cardiac arrest. No pulse and ventricular fibrillation. He'll die. Where is that defibrillator? And the doctor? He should be here!"

As if in answer to her alarm, an inner door opened and a man in a lab coat, evidently a doctor, entered. He carried a portable AED. He put the (semi-) Automatic External Defibrillator on the table next to the stricken minister.

Aileen pushed forward.

"Doctor, I'm trained. Let me help. We're out of time."

The doctor smiled at her and motioned for CPR to continue as he attached the AED leads to the chest. Then he signaled for the CPR to stop and waved the others away. Aileen watched closely, ready to assist if needed.

Ari turned to a colleague.

"That is not the Prime Minister's physician. Where is Dr. Rosen?"

"He is stuck in traffic in Germantown. This American is their backup. They say he is a first rate cardiologist."

The doctor spoke to the room.

"Clear!"

He pushed a button. The Prime Minister's chest heaved.

Nothing. He waited a moment and spoke again.

"Clear!"

He pushed the button, The chest heaved once more.

The doctor exhaled.

"We have a pulse!"

All eyes in the room followed the wobbly line of the ECG on the automatic defibrillator machine. A definite rhythmic pattern, somewhat erratic, streamed across the screen.

Ari sighed with relief.

***

A weary Aileen stood back. She noted the warm smile of the young cardiologist. She noted the ease with which he had confronted this emergency.

She had worked with many doctors. This one knew what he was doing. He was decidedly good looking, and there was no ring on his finger.

Thanks to Mary Dean, Rob Wilson was no longer on Aileen's list of possible providers for Mary Catherine.

Who knows?

Before she could feel guilt at these selfish musings, she heard Ari's voice.

"Aileen, Jeannine, I want you with me. I'm escorting the Minister to Bethesda Naval Hospital. Follow me. Particularly you, Aileen. You know these damn devices."

Aileen jumped up.

The doctor and Ari already had pushed the Minister's gurney halfway out the door. Jeannine and another Mossad agent were with them.

Ari shouted back.

"Hurry, Aileen. The helipad is this way. Come on."

Aileen rushed after the gurney.

***

His second beer was empty when Bill Hamm answered his phone.

"Jeannine, where are you guys? I've been waiting … "

He stopped and listened in stunned silence.

Finally, he spoke.

"All right. I'm on my way. It's over an hour to Bethesda. I'll be there as soon as I can.

He threw ten dollars on the table and left.

The waitress cleared his table. Behind her, the TV blared.

Breaking News. This just in.

More than 40 missiles were launched from southern Lebanon into northern Israel this morning. At least twenty people, including several children, were injured with two known dead when a bus was hit in the town of Kiryat Shimona. Most of the missiles were short range "Katyushas," but one missile that landed near Haifa was apparently a longer range Iranian Fajr-3.

Hezbollah has claimed credit for the attacks.

An Israeli spokesman told us there will be no immediate retaliation because of the talks with Lebanese government leaders scheduled today and tomorrow at Camp David, Maryland, under American auspices.

And in Local News, today three armed men robbed a 7-Eleven. ...

The waitress finished wiping the table. The tip was more than the price of the two beers. And she had given that guy poor service. She had virtually ignored him!

She shrugged and stuck the bill in her apron.

***

A helicopter, Huey-sized but more modern, stood at the helipad for the trip to Naval Medical.

Ari signaled Aileen and Jeannine to follow him and climbed into the cabin. The young doctor was attending the Prime Minister. Three additional Israelis, staff or Mossad, and two U.S. Secret Service Agents completed the group.

Aileen was impressed by the skilled hands of the young cardiologist. Apparently sensing her presence, he looked up and smiled. She lowered her eyes and strapped in.

Rotors whirring and motors roaring, the helicopter lifted from the pad.

***

******

Chapter 48
Saturday, November 11

For Waseem, there was nothing to do but return Mandley's helicopter to Delaware. He had seen the cluster of police and unmarked vehicles at the motel. Raakin, alive or dead, was on his own.

Waseem's official connection with Mandley was as a security consultant, hired by Fareed. It would be difficult to explain the decimation of their security force without revealing its ties to Hezbollah. With Hazim, Fareed, Abed, and, possibly Raakin, all dead, any explanation would necessarily attribute super powers to Bill Hamm and Rob Wilson,

His solution would be to blame Brendan, the sole non-Hezbollah "security-enforcer."

He looked out his window.

Below, was Mandley's Delaware compound.

Waseem licked his lips. Forget Mandley, the mission was a success.

Fortunately, none of Mandley's executives met him when the helicopter landed. Waseem left the Delaware Compound immediately. He would face their questions later.

He wondered if Raakin was alive. If so would he talk? Waseem laughed. No way! If caught, Raakin would be Mirandized!

***

Waseem reached the town of Salisbury, on Maryland's Eastern Shore, in under an hour. He took a motel and settled in front of the television.

The news about the rocket barrage on northern Israel tickled him. He had suggested that attack. He knew the Israeli Minister would never want to appear intimidated by Hezbollah.

The attack would strengthen the Israeli resolve to meet as planned.

Waseem kicked off his shoes and leaned back in his chair. The next news would be about his triumph.

"Allahu akbar!"

Today, the "Little Satan" would lose its leader!

***

The doctor was on the phone with the Minister's Israeli physician.

"Dr. Rosen, I'm on a helicopter with the Prime Minister now, headed for Bethesda Naval. ... Thanks. I'm glad to know the make of his pacemaker. I'm familiar with that brand, and I know it has an ICD."

Aileen translated for Jeannine.

"An 'ICD' is an 'Implanted Cardiac Defibrillator.' Mandley makes a model that is a Pacemaker-ICD combo."

"But Aileen, the doctor used an external defibrillator. He should have known there was an implanted one."

"Not really, Azim's signal corrupted the memory of whatever device is in the Minister's chest."

The doctor put the phone down.

From her seat Aileen watched the ECG roll across the AED's screen. This was not the usual 12-lead ECG, but it did not have to be. Aileen checked the second hand on her watch and counted 45 R-waves in 15 seconds.

She turned to Jeannine.

"He's at 180 beats per minute, and increasing. The doc has to do something."

As if on cue the doctor lifted a syringe and injected the patient.

Aileen blurted.

"Excuse me doctor, what was that?"

The doctor turned with a frown. When he saw it was Aileen, he smiled.

"Amiodarone, two ampules. Dr. Rosen told me his liver tolerates it well. The minister takes it regularly as tablets."

The doctor continued.

"I get the impression you're checking everything I do."

Aileen did not back off.

"Actually doctor, I am."

She looked out the window. To the west was Sugarloaf Mountain. They soon would arrive in Bethesda. Her eyes returned to the ECG. The heart beats had visibly slowed. She relaxed.

The doctor's face softened.

"You are Ms. Harris, right? You worked for Mandley Bionics, correct?"

"Yes, well actually for Mandley Test Services."

"Are you familiar with Mandley's family of pacemakers."

"We tested the P-700 series and the P-712 series at MTS. I was about to suggest that the pacemaker be recoded. The sooner the better."

"The Minister's implant is a Mandley P-712B, and it does need recoding. Ms. Harris, would you be willing to help."

Aileen unbuckled and jumped from her seat.

"It's Aileen, and the answer is 'Yes.'"

"Good. I'm Mark."

***

Bill Hamm was stuck in the same traffic jam that had stopped the Israeli Minister's physician from reaching Camp David, and now in turn prevented him from reaching Bethesda.

A chemical spill had shut down both lanes of I-270.

Wanly, Bill took Route 15 towards Point of Rocks.

***

Aileen appreciated Mark's technique. By the time the helicopter landed at Naval Medical in Bethesda, he had recoded the Minister's pacemaker.

Outside, various people including a white-coated orderly, stood at the ready. The pilot shut down the rotors.

They left the helicopter, Aileen called to Ari but he did not heed. His focus was on the Prime Minister. The Minister's party moved quickly, and both Aileen and Jeannine lagged uncertainly to the rear.

Once inside, Jeannine found the lady's room and dropped out of the race.

Aileen caught up with the party at the doors to the ICU.

One Mossad agent went to check the routes of access to the Minister's room. Ari stayed with Dr. Mark and the gurney.

Dr. Mark nodded to Ari to wait outside. Then he and the gurney disappeared into the room.

Ari hesitated. The doctor had taken good care of the Minister during the flight. Why not give him a minute alone to concentrate on his patient free of distractions?

Ari broke protocol and waited.

***

Aileen grabbed Ari's arm.

"Ari, I need to talk with you."

"About that young doc? I think he likes you."

"Forget that. I just realized he's not what he seems."

"What do you mean?"

"I mean he had the access password for the pacemaker."

"What password?"

"Each model 712 pacemaker has an access password 'hard-wired' into the chip. You can't recode or manipulate the settings without the password. The password is kept with the patient's medical records."

"Maybe Dr. Rosen told Mark the password during the phone call and he memorized it?"

"No way. It was on a piece of paper when he recoded the pacemaker. And he never wrote anything down during that phone call"

"What's your point?"

"The point is that Hezbollah got the access code from Mandley Bionics, probably from my old boss, Dr. Thibault."

"Thibault?"

"He wasn't a terrorist, but he liked money, lots of it. Hezbollah provided it. When Jeannine exposed him and Harry Roberts, Hezbollah killed them both."

Aileen handed Ari the fax from the Québec police.

"Thibault wrote this as he was dying. That's the access code next to that scribbled star. He meant the 'Star of David.' He tried to warn StatFind. He tried to make things right. Anan intercepted the fax."

"Anan? Aileen, where did you get this?"

"Anan left it with Bill's laptop."

She took a breath.

"Ari, there's only one way this doctor could know the access code."

Another breath.

"Ari, Mark is with Hezbollah!"

***

Ari was on his feet before Aileen could finish. He disappeared through the door to the Minister's room.

To Aileen the next seconds were like minutes. She jumped up to follow. She was only two steps from the door, but her legs appeared to have weights. *Why so heavy? Move, Aileen. Move!*

She watched her right foot lift and press forward. She saw her Adida hit the ground. She sensed that her other foot was in the air, swinging slowly forward. *Damn it. Hurry!*

By the time her left foot touched down, she was at the door peering inside. Her eyes scanned the room. *Where?*

To Aileen the next moments were unreal.

On the wall to the left was a colored outlet for Oxygen, unused. Next in view was the ECG monitor on wheels, unused. She flicked past the drawn curtains of the window. The nearby IV stand was empty.

She detected movement on the other side of the bed. On the floor a man in dark clothes grappled with what seemed to be a white curtain, or a lab coat? She became aware of sound, the grunts and thumps of a struggle.

All this took less than a second.

She persisted. At last she saw what she sought.

The AED was next to the bed!

It was unattended, but its pads were still attached to the minister's chest. *Good, no problem!*

The ECG on the screen was another matter.

My God!

A chaotic random pattern streamed across the display. *VFib! No time! No time!*

Each step seemed painfully slow. *Faster! Please, God!*

She arrived bedside.

She touched the Minister's carotid. *No pulse! He's shockable!*

Pure habit made her shout.

"Clear!"

She pushed the button on the defibrillator.

The Minister's chest heaved.

A detectable rhythm appeared on the screen. A pattern. *Thank God.*

She collapsed to the floor.

***

Aileen opened her eyes to a blur of red hanging over her, Jeannine's hair. The room was full of white lab coats and dark suits.

"Jeannine, is the Minister all right?"

"His heart is back in rhythm. There are three doctors with him."

"And Ari?"

"Aileen, I'm here."

"Ari, did you get him, I mean, Mark?"

"I got the bastard."

Aileen sat up on the floor.

"Jeannine, you were right. They did have a backup plan."

Aileen rose to her feet.

"And we stopped it!"

***

But Jeannine had looked away. One of the trio of doctors at the Minister's bedside was portly, even overweight.

At Aileen's voice, that doctor had turned. Now dark eyes froze Jeannine's with a baleful stare.

The doctor opened his lab coat. He was not overweight.

A bulky contraption hung above his waist. His hand reached towards it.

Jeannine's "scream" was only a hoarse whisper.

"Ari. It's Mufid!"

Ari looked up. It was not Mufid that he saw.

She was a young girl, Fatimah, slightly obese, near the bus stop across the street. No older than fourteen, her hair and neck were covered by a tight scarf. Next to her, chattering happily, was a group of Jewish children on a school outing.

The girl's eyes glazed as she opened her jacket.

Her eyes! And she's not fat! That's a vest and her hand is reaching for ... My God!

Ari stared at Mufid. *His eyes! My God! Déjà vu!*

His Beretta stuck in the holster. *No. Please God, no! Not again!*

The Beretta came free and seemed to point on its own. *The head. Ari, the head!*

No time! Mufid's hand was on the detonator. *Why does he wait?*

Then Ari knew. Mufid must proclaim Allah's triumph.

On cue, the assassin's lips moved.

"Allahu ..."

"Crack"

Ari's bullet entered just below the right eye.

Mufid's arm fell loosely to his side, no longer controlled by a pierced brain.

The lifeless body crumpled to the floor.

***

******

Chapter 49
Sunday, November 12

Waseem had not left the motel room since his arrival, not even to purchase the paper. That morning, staff had placed Sunday papers outside the doors on his corridor.

Now the pages of the Washington Post lay ripped and scattered on the floor. Waseem stomped angrily through the crumpled mass. The Camp David Meeting was postponed, but both Lebanese and Israeli governments reported that another meeting was already scheduled.

Worse, the Israeli Prime Minister was to give a televised statement this morning. All the Sunday morning networks would carry it. The minister was alive and functioning.

Waseem could not say the same for Raakin, Mufid or Dr. Mark. Where were they! Were they even alive? He had no word from any of them. Only silence.

Frustrated, Waseem sat on the bed and switched the TV from channel to channel.

He did not notice the door knob turn slowly.

The door opened.

"Crack. Crack."

Waseem slumped on the bed.

Brendan stood over him.

"Crack."

The last shot was merely insurance.

Brendan left the room. In the car outside, he texted a one-word message.

"Clear."

In Delaware, the special assistant to the CEO of Mandley Bionics saw the text. *Good. The last of those Arabs is gone.*

Never again would a Middle Easterner be hired for Mandley Security!

***

The tube had been removed from Rob's throat. He could speak, but an IV was attached above his wrist.

"Mary, you're here. ..."

Mary Dean squeezed his hand.

"Of course, and I always will be. Don't try to talk."

"But I'm a washed-up old FBI guy. You're young and pretty and..."

"Shut up and listen to me. I want you. No one else. And Tommy does too."

Rob Wilson sighed and shut his eyes. *Some guys have all the luck, and it's me.* He squeezed her hand and drifted off.

Mary did not let go.

***

Mary Catherine ran full speed to her mother.

"Mommy!"

Aileen grabbed her daughter and lifted her high. She squealed. The next moments were all hugs and kisses.

Aileen looked at her mother.

"I'm OK, Mom. Really OK! And Mom, thank you for everything."

"Aileen, where's Mr. Wilson?"

"That's over, Mom. He's in the hospital. Mary Dean is with him. But what about Aunt Agatha?"

"The insurance agreed to pay. She already has hired a contractor. But are you sure you're all right? About Mr. Wilson, I mean."

Aileen looked at her daughter, still in her arms.

"Mom, I have everything I want right here."

She squeezed Mary Catherine long and hard.

***

Bill's left arm was in a sling, but his right was securely around Jeannine. He started to speak.

"Jeannine ... "

She touched her fingers to his lips.

"No. Stop. I know what you're going to say. It's OK. Really."

She took a breath.

"We talked about this. I can see it in your eyes. It's something you have to do. I understand."

She looked down. Bill stammered.

"But I love you."

"And I think I love you, I mean I do, but you have to try this. I've seen how 'alive' you've been these past weeks. Operations are in your blood. It's who you are. You can't go back to accounting."

"We can still get married."

"No. That's not fair to you or me. You can't be worried about me or a family. And I'm not ready to be a single mother. You go back to the Agency for a year. I know you'll be overseas. I'll wait. I have plenty to occupy me here. I've talked to Aileen. I'm starting my own consulting shop. She wants to join me."

Jeannine turned her head in a familiar motion, flipping her auburn hair off her forehead. Bill looked into her moist eyes. He leaned to kiss her. She spoke quickly.

"No, Bill. It wouldn't work. One of us has to be logical. You have to try this or you'll be miserable. I wouldn't want you 'stuck' with me and tied down, always wondering what might have been."

"But …"

She kissed him hard, and drew back.

"Don't worry. Give it a year. I'll wait."

Bill's shoulders slumped. He knew she was right. She spoke once more.

"Look, I have to go. Ari Riebman's waiting. He wants me to submit a proposal for research in statistical forensics to the Israeli government. He's introducing me to an embassy staffer."

Auburn hair bounced off her shoulders as she turned and blew him a kiss.

"Remember, I'm waiting."

Then she was gone.

Bill smiled. *Damn! What a woman. Believe me, I'll be back!*

***

It was Sunday, but Wayne was at his desk. Across the hall, workmen were installing partitions for a new tenant. The collapse of StatFind's contract with Mandley Bionics had forced Wayne to relinquish that space, as well as several recent hires.

He looked out his window. A car had parked by his. *Who?*

He heard a sound. He had his answer. Bill Hamm stood in the doorway.

"Bill, are you all right. What happened to your arm?"

"Broken in a fall. It's a long story. Did you hear about Mona's cabin?"

"I did. She went there today. Is Jeannine with you?"

"She's gone to the Israeli Embassy, but she wants to thank you for sending Mona to us."

"Bill, StatFind is in trouble. We need you. The books are a mess, and with the loss of the Mandley contract, we have to cut back. It's pretty grim."

"That's the reason I'm here. I wanted to tell you personally. Tomorrow I'm interviewing with the Agency for my old position, with a promotion. I'll help you while I can, but I won't be here long."

"Back to the 'spy' business?"

"That's about it. I found out it's in my blood."

"Damn, I'm sorry, Bill."

"Me too. It was good working with you."

"And Jeannine?"

"I can't speak for her. She's grateful for all you did for her. I'm sure she'll call you. She might want to branch out on her own."

Wayne buried his head in his hands. Finally he looked up.

"This is a bad day for StatFind. Damn! But maybe you can look at the books with me for a few minutes."

Bill nodded.

"Why not?"

***

At New York's JFK Airport, Anan heard the call for her flight to Paris. Hastily she scribbled the post card. It was addressed to Jeannine Ryan. She thought for a moment. Then she wrote.

"Your Sister, Jeanne."

***

******

Chapter 50
Epilogue

Bill Hamm returned to the Central Intelligence Agency. At the end of his first overseas assignment, he was asked to stay a second year. Jeannine agreed to wait. Their plans are still uncertain.

Jeannine Ryan formed her own statistical consulting firm, aided by a sizable contract with the Israeli government. She specializes in statistical forensics and the analysis of biomedical data.

Ari Riebman returned to Israel to high, but unpublicized, honors. He was influential in obtaining the contract for Jeannine's company.

Aileen Harris works on the Israeli contract while enrolled in a Ph.D. program in Bioengineering. She holds a minority share in Jeannine's company. She lives with her mother and Mary Catherine in a spacious new home in Bethesda.

Anan disappeared.

Wayne Johnson sold StatFind and retired. Occasionally he assists Jeannine with computer analyses on a part time basis.

Rob Wilson and Mary Dean married and moved to Columbia, South Carolina. Tommy loves his new father. Periodically, they visit Dillon to place flowers on the graves of Mary's mother and little Annie.

Lise, Tom Dean's teen-aged girl friend, moved back with her mother. Her lesson learned, she attends UNC Wilmington and studies Psychology.

Jack, Pops' nephew, returned to the house near the Alligator River. Charges for kidnapping lagged. Before they were brought, he went missing in a nearby swamp and has not been found. Poaching of Red Wolves has stopped.

The Department of Justice decided there was insufficient evidence to prosecute Mandley Bionics in the deaths of several individuals who had a competitor's pacemaker.

The Food and Drug Administration withdrew its marketing approval for Mandley's Parkinson chip. Based on lies and false data in a number of applications for medical devices, the FDA imposed massive civil money penalties (CMP's) on Mandley Bionics under the FDA Amendments Act of 2007.

Subsequently, Mandley Bionics was reorganized under a Chapter 11 Bankruptcy. The Pacemaker Division was abolished. The Artificial-limb Division prospered under new leadership.

The governing party of Lebanon concluded an agreement with Israel declaring their common goal to limit the role of Hezbollah in southern Lebanon. To date, the agreement has accomplished little.

Fareed Hamza's body was cremated at Mandley's Delaware facility. Waseem Hamza's body was shipped back to Lebanon. Their Hezbollah cell, empty and unnoticed, has ceased to function.

***

******

Envoi

One year later

The sounds of East Montreal were all about her as she crossed the boulevard St-Laurent and walked onto a cross street. She strode purposely, with an air of assurance.

She was smartly dressed in a beige blouse that revealed the barest hint of cleavage. A pale silk scarf was twisted loosely about her neck while trim black hair, cut just off the shoulders, bounced slightly with each step. Fashionable sun glasses shielded her blue eyes.

There was no doubt. This stylish woman was attractive.

She stopped to verify the number on the three-story building. It checked.

It was a steep climb to the third floor apartment, but she arrived with no shortness of breath. Evidently, she was in good condition.

A small woman answered her knock. The hair that showed beneath her scarf was streaked with gray. She had a gentle face and was clearly Muslim. A reddish flush on her forehead revealed that she had been praying. On her prayer mat was a clay tablet. She was a Shiite.

The younger woman stood silent, glasses off and head down, in the doorway.

The older woman looked up into the eyes of the visitor and gasped.

"Jeanne-Anan! Ma fille! …"

Anan choked.

"Oui, Maman. C'est moi. It's me. I'm home!"

***

417

******

About the Author

James E. Mosimann is a retired biostatistician who spent many years at the Computer Division of the National Institutes of Health. He has a Ph. D. in Zoology from the University of Michigan, and a Masters in Biostatistics from the Johns Hopkins University. After NIH, he joined the Office of Research Integrity of the Public Health Service, where he was a scientist-investigator for cases of research misconduct. He has numerous publications and one text. This is his second novel.

He and his wife, Barbara Jean, live in Virginia. They have eight children, all adult.

Author's Note

This is the second book in a series following the activities of Jeannine Ryan, a specialist in numerical forensics. Like the first, it was a family project. Thanks again to my wife for her support and to my adult children for their assistance. As before, Tom's many hours of careful reading and editing significantly improved the manuscript, as did comments by Joseph, John, Theresa, Michelle, Mary and Madeleine. Finally Kateri, in addition to her comments, provided the cover graphics and design.

Thanks are due also to Kevin Harrigan, retired FBI, who read an early version of the manuscript.

The first two titles (**Misconduct's Deadly Denial** and **The Assassin Chip**) will be followed shortly by the two below:

The Prague Plot,
The Carolina Coup.

www.ingramcontent.com/pod-product-compliance
Lightning Source LLC
Chambersburg PA
CBHW060138260626
47160CB00001B/26